RAISING IT-666

The Teenage Beast

By Cordelia Malthere

Book Two

ISBN:978-0-9931450-6-3

Dedication

This book is dedicated to
My sister and my Brother.
Graziella and Pascal
With lots of love.
This book is dedicated to our childhood.

To the way we were raised together,
From fishing all afternoon in Barfleur,
To the Brioche du Vast with jam, we shared at tea time,
Passing by the 'Fraggle Rock' we watched before bedtime.
Perfect Sunday afternoons in retrospect for me.
(Wink: I love fishing, fish and shellfish, not my Bro)

To climbing in an hot air balloon,
Which had the awesome shape of a circus elephant,
In the ground of Balleroy Castle, during a festival,
For our first flight 'Baptism' with Forbes.
Very special now dated memory.

To Suzy, our sausage dog,
Which would bark upon a rock which had a crab to catch,
Just underneath it.
Which would only carry Dad's newspaper proudly,
And drop our teen mags in a puddle,
As soon as she knew they were not for Pa.

But best of all, I just love
The way she would bark angrily at the TV set,
As soon as Pa pointed to a frankly racist politician.
Clever Dog.
Undeniably the little bitch he saved from a sure drowning death,
Was totally devoted to my dad.
She was very much part of our childhood.

XXX

About the Book

Raising It-666: The Teenage Beast.
Second instalment of the Beast Saga.
The very second It started, I was just not able to stop writing her story.
She had such a compelling story I just had to write It fully from start to finish.
It was all about second chances, chances, given or not, taken or not.
It was all about a dream of an 'If'.
If a helping hand was given to you out of the blue,
Would you rise on your feet and fight your fate?
What is fate?
Is it something you let others dictate to you?
Or are you building it with your own hands, faith and efforts?
Is it a bit of both?
Or can you reclaim it all and make it yours?

One thing is sure,
You need hope either way.

Cordelia Halthere

Verse 1. Waking up.

Walter Workmaster woke up. A quick glance around him, made him realise that something definitely abnormal was going on. The room's walls were bleeding profusely, It-666 was levitating above her bed talking gibberish and the three Angels were staring at her with an extremely worried expression upon their faces. He stood up immediately and tapped on Gabriel's shoulder, calling for his attention,

-I am sorry to break the news but aren't we meant to do something? Or shall you watch her like that with your mouth opened until you swallow a fly?

As soon as he stopped talking flies poured out of It-666 body in their thousands.

Gabriel and Raphael glanced angrily back at Walter, scolding him,

-Do not open your mouth when she is like that human, you are only going to spell trouble.

He shrugged his shoulders, repeated, before disobeying and directly addressing himself to the levitating girl,

-Then do something! We can't leave her like that. I bet she is as distressed as we are right now. It, this is Ground Control to Major Town, you are freaking our arses off a bit, Darling. The flies aren't very welcome in Gabriel's clinic too. You know, they are a bit unhygienic, you never know where their insects legs have been. Now, you should calm down and stop flying for a while.

Azryel looked at the human in desperation then muttered sarcastically,

-As if it will work, when she is talking to her Daddy right now.

Walter, giving a worried glance toward the Death Angel, replied with a questioning statement,

-That would be the big bad guy in Hell, I suppose? Then I wonder why you lot, are not reacting immediately.

The man pushed Az and Raphael out of his way to stand right below the levitating It-666 before pleading to her again,

-It, you must stop right now. It, my girl, whatever he is saying, it will be just words, just words, I promise you. The only one that can do something and act upon them is you, my girl, you and no one else. You have got full control of your actions. You are free to listen to who you want, but they can't dictate to you what to do. Always remember that, It, always, you are the only one responsible for your own actions.

It-666 fell to the ground, the wall stopped bleeding and the flies disappeared from the room. Dazed, in visible shock and shivering It came to Walter, knelt by him and cried. The man kneeling as well, offered his shoulder to the distressed teenager.

Uncle Raphael looked at his Angels commenting,

-I wish one of us would have thought of that. Workmaster's way worked.

Azryel came to the girl, put his hand upon her shoulder, and demanded,

-Now It, pull yourself together, you must tell us everything.

Walter replied to the Angel instead of It-666,

-Give her a five minute break, Az. That's pretty emotional stuff that she has just been through.

The annoyed Death Angel pleaded to Raphael, and then to the teenager,

-Come, Raph tell the man that moping never helped anyone, but that sharing your problems can be the start of finding solutions for them. It, you are a Hell Baby for Christ's sake, you need to be much stronger than that. I am not going to have you crying on Walt's shoulder every time something is up. So, big deal, your very infamous father started talking to you and plaguing your mind. Like Walt said, you are free to do what you want, so why don't you talk back to him and tell him a piece of your mind. Stand up for yourself girl, and fight him off.

The effect was immediate as It-666 started wiping her blood tears away, she stood up and looking sheepishly at Azryel, apologised,

-I am sorry Az, you are right.

The Death Angel giving her a wicked smile commented,

-You will learn Soldier, that I am always right. Now, what does your evil father want of you apart from killing everybody?

It-666 could not help a rising giggle at his question as she replied,

-That pretty much sums it up.

Raphael made a sarcastic statement,

-Good old evil, some things never change especially it's lack of imagination. Did he show any subtlety on the how and when?

It-666's face became serious as she warned the Angels,

-He plans to use me. Stuck somewhere, which is not Hell, a prisoner, he needs me to free him and release him onto the world. P is his demonic servant, on a mission to render the feat possible. I was asked to bring Workmaster to be killed by P. He wants me to stay by P and start helping him to free him, as he is my father. He pledged that as I am his daughter, a Hell princess, I should be dutiful to him only. He said that the slaughtering of humanity has started, that his demons are obeying his orders doing so, killing humans, and I was to do the same on a grander scale. He said he had the powers to make me do so. Has he?

Azryel replied to her,

-If he asked for your help my dear It, this is because he lost his powers and if you listen to him then he will get them back. Now, you heard what Workmaster said, the choice is yours. Where do you want to stand? Do you want to help Daddy out, like a dutiful Hell Princess or do you want to stay with us and help the poor human sods out to prevent them from mass extinction?

It-666 seized Walter's hand within hers as she answered with emotion,

-Walt freed me and gave me back hope. I will never forget it. He gave me a purpose without realising it, I want to fight to protect him and his kind. My side is his side and I am solely following my own heart when I say this. I shall never be used for the destruction of mankind, and I will need all your help Angels to make sure it does not happen. You are all granted to kill me if my father ever manages to get to me, and turn me to a monster. From the Hell visions he provided me, well I can promise you that I won't be a dutiful Hell Daughter, Hell no!

Workmaster smiled proudly, tapping her shoulder,

-That's my girl. Well said. I knew you would come through. Trust yourself and our future, no matter how thick and thin, we will make it throughout.

Verse 2. MISS-ION: Fighting Flapping Wings.

Archangel Gabriel corrected Walter,

-Your girl, little It is our girl. She has been adopted by three Angels apart from you, human: Raphael, Azryel, and I. We are all ready to take her on and raise her. Now we need to decide where it will be safer for her to be kept.

Walter rose his eyebrows suspiciously, querying,

-Kept? She is not an animal. You, Angels are not going to keep her in a cage under a big crucifix are you?

Azryel grinned wickedly while Raphael laughed,

-That's a bloody good idea.

Gabriel coughed and scolded them loudly in the Angelic tongue,

-Right, teasing a human, a would be devil's advocate and a would be Antichrist is not a very good idea on the other hand. I cannot keep her secure in my clinic for long before having P knocking upon my door. P made the link of her disappearance with Workmaster, hence the abduction of his son Micky. We can be sure he will be relentless in his revenge especially after the destruction of his precious bunker, and his failed bargaining plans. He will want to touch all the connections Walter has in order to influence the man to give him back It-666. I cannot accept that. I need to protect Walter and my family, my sister Caro and our Micky. I need to find a safer place for It than my clinic and fast. Beside random swarms of flies, bleeding walls and tremors are fairly hard to hide if they expand to more than a room depending on how upset our little Hell Princess is.

Raphael proposed, reverting to human speech in consideration for Walter and It,

-She can be kept at mine in the AA club and I can reassure you that she will have a room with a view. All I need to keep her safely is Az. He will also look after her Angelic Army training. It will join his boot camp.

It watched as her destiny was discussed heatedly, with Walter objecting strongly to the Archangel Raphael,

-A room with a view does not mean that she will not be put within a duty-esque soldier cage, and if she is pacific how will you good Angels cope? For so far she wants to be so and her will is. How can you accommodate for that, without killing her straight off for disobedience for refusing to kill? She is a teenager who had her life pretty much crushed because of her freaking Beast label. Giving a chance to her implies the possibility of being totally pacific, ignoring her own powers and let her do so too. Can't you give her five years until she becomes a responsible adult until she is to be a soldier if she wishes to do so? Can't we give her the childhood she never had instead of showing her the efficient ways to kill more? Give her five years of nurture and care? Give her respect about her will to not be used?

Raphael was thrown aback by the plea, took a good look at the girl and the effect Walt's speech had upon her, her eyes glowing with sudden hope, he stated,

-There I have to remind you two that It is not our normal teenager. However I am prepared to make a concession. We will raise her and give her as much remaining childhood she has left, in a 'normal' way as much as we can until we all have to fight to save humanity. And for the other stark reminder, it will probably occur sooner than later, as her very Hellish father mentioned that human extinction had already started in small numbers by his demons. This I can tackle with my Army of Angels up until I will need my all crew back. It, you need a hiding place and protection. The same goes for you Walter, as you seemed to have pissed off an ancient Demon, the infamous P, so much so that you are on the top of his hit list. Not only that, he has reserved for himself the right to kill you slowly and plans to get to you by harming all around you. I assure you that this is not going to be sweet and that time to play the surrogate daddy of our 'Bambi' will be cut very short. However I am placing my best Angel for your joint protections, Azryel will babysit you. I will also leave behind Gabriel to give him a hand as I will prepare my Angels to tackle the enemy head on. I will not let them hatch any plan, any brainchild will be destroyed by my Army.

Azryel gave a most annoyed look back to Workmaster, then back to the Archangel Raphael,

-How could you let that human sway you like that? My soldiers need as much looking after, if not more with this imminent fight ahead. Fuck babysitting duty! If any of the Angels falls in the first front and I am called upon to collect their souls Raphael, rather than protecting them from death by fighting by their sides I am not going to be a pleasure to deal with, I can promise you that. I beg you to reconsider and to not split forces.

Raphael came to his Death Angel, seized his shoulders strongly and forced him to look at him, as he argued back in tongue,

-You never have been a pleasure to deal with Az. You are Death. There is nothing to reconsider. The decision has been made and I need you to consider your babysitting duties with the utmost importance. If you fuck them up, I guarantee that you will be dealt with. The girl is a broken Being, she needs to be built up, prepared for what is to come to pass. No one more than you in my entire Army can train her up to the standards required. No one more than you can protect her wanted arse which can bring destruction to the whole world, and transform her to a lethal asset in my Angelic Army against dark forces. There is a lot to do to achieve this, Angel. I am not leaving you behind at the willy nilly wishes of a mere human, Az, I am leaving you as my back up, and I need it to be stronger than ever, full of stealth. When I call you back, I will expect the girl to be fully ready, Workmaster swayed to us, protected and alive, and Gabriel up to scratch with the acquired knowledge and practice of reanimating fallen Angels, he is a Doctor who tried to play with life badly, you know better than any of us to play with it, teach him. Your mission is to fuck Fate Azryel, and nothing else.

That's a tall order. It may lead to your ultimate freedom and the one of the World.

Azryel smiled wickedly, knelt by the Archangel briefly before standing up, and took a cigar from his silver box, lit it, replying nonchalantly, back to human speech, loudly for all,

-Right, Wrath has got it all covered. Sorry to have shown any doubts, I kind of like your master plan, Raphael, as always I will be your Angel. It, you are given a growing up break but as it will be cut short very soon, I am afraid I will prepare you all the while. Expect boot camp methods from me as I babysit you, Hell Baby. I will be doing you a great favour doing so, not a disrespect like Walter is hammering. As for you Walt, a little Army training would not go amiss, if you are ever caught by a demon, knowing how to twist their arms before they torture you might become a little handy. I do not want to freak you but your arse is as demanded for as Hell Baby here, if they will keep her alive, as she is Hell Princess, as you are just mere human, they may just reap you apart slowly but surely. A little self defence can give you precious minutes where I can intervene and save your bad good for nothing human arse. You are part of my boot camp willing or not. When it comes down to you, Gab, I am going to teach you straight the mother fucker's way of life and death, and you'd better pay attention as I hate repeating myself and any bloody fucking mistakes upon those matters will render me to be very anal on you. I would be very scared and very thorough if I was you. Now didn't you mention than you lived in a cabin in the middle of some woods?

Gabriel looking at the self secure Death Angel, put a finger within his collar and released the pressure by opening it. He replied uneasily,

-I have. I am going to hide Walter there.

The Death Angel taking a puff of his cigar slowly, asked,

-Are you going to extend the invitation to the young Beast? It and Walt are best friends, both have each others best interests at heart.

So far we cannot deny that they brought out the best in each other.

Gabriel looked at the human and the teenager holding hands, replied,

-Isn't the AA a better place for It?

Azryel shook his head slowly as he cryptically answered,

-Wild beasts live peacefully in the woods...Now who made me think of that...If not her very first Tutor. He also mentioned that as soon as It entered a forest her tracks seemed to disappear from the World, and the one of every animal in that forest too... Work this one out Gabriel, for I haven't, apart that the Tutor did let me know that woods protect the young It for long periods of time. She was undiscovered for 8 years in P's woods, she lived feral for 3 in the Black forest of Germany and 5 beforehand with the nun Theresa. The AA has no wood surrounding it.

Raphael ordered immediately,

-Then Gabriel, you must welcome three guests in your cabin in the woods for the time being: It-666, Az and Walt, I am sure you will have a hell of a time with them. I hope you will grow to like It's flies and bleeding walls, Az's cigars, smoke and sarcasms, Walterisms and all his other bad human habits.

The Angel Gabriel surrendered, his wings moving slowly and awkwardly, against each other,

-Blast, great, I've got to harbour in my humble home the three great pains in the arse the world ever carried. I am overjoyed, see, Wrath, my wings are flapping with glee...

Verse 3. An' & the green Gab Hall.

The three Angels took Walter and It-666 and teletransported to the forest where Gabriel lived.

Raphael deposited the man upon his feet and stood there amazed by what he saw, he whistled with awe,

-I expected a little house in the wood, Gab, not a giant tree house covering six or seven trees. Which craftsman did you employ? I might have a job or two for him.

Gabriel grinned with pride for having impressed his Uncle for once,

-I did it all myself. It is also totally eco-friendly. Do you care for a grand tour of Gab's Hall?

Az spat on the ground,

-I always knew that Angel suffered from a strange syndrome always aloof and living on his own like a bloody hermit in the forest. He is suffering from the Swiss Family Robinson's syndrome, he can't leave a tree alone and has to dwell in them. And the palm for the weirdest Angel of them all goes to...

Raphael kicked his elbow at once and scolded him,

-To you. No one can beat you at it, Azryel, even if my nephew builds houses in trees as a hobby or what not, he will be definitely more sane than you after an eternity.

The Death Angel took a cigar, lit it as he stated,

-My bad, I deserve that kick in the teeth. Others gave me a deadly duty which takes its toll as I had the kindness to take it upon me to spare their good hearts... I wish I wasn't so kind, dutiful and stupid. I would have taken hobbies of my own, like I don't know hunting, fishing, butchery instead of killing, grabbing souls and punishing them.

Walter looked at him bewildered, asked Az then Raphael,

-How does that work exactly you being kind by killing, grabbing souls and punishing them? I grant you that it is dutifully stupid. For that part I agree with your thought process, for the rest I have gianormous doubts. Raphael, I know you are an Archangel and all that palaver, but I have very serious concerns in giving It-666 a teacher that you, yourself qualified as insane. Not only that, the most insane one of all Angels, that can't be good can it?

Azryel puffed a perfectly well rounded ring of smoke that encircled the man's face for a second before it split, replied,

-I can reassure you, human that it is picture perfect, you and the little Antichrist need someone of my calibre to be taught through the paces of the harsh world. A little dose of insanity is required dealing with your kind usually, Walter, with you I am going to need a bigger dose I think. Now do you want to shut up and visit the nice big tree house with us or shall we stare at each other doubting one another for eternity. As I said I can explain to you all later, bring everything down to your human understanding, if you only give me a chance, Walt. However I know already that I am going to have a splitting headache at the end of that overdue enlightening conversation... See, no Angel is crazy enough to attempt the feat with you human. On the other hand I think it is owed to you to understand the whys, before the day you will bite the dust and close your eyes to the world for eternity. On that dreaded day, human, I want your soul to be full of comprehension when my duty is to pick you up.

Walter Workmaster was left voiceless, the teenage It came closer to him and engaged him,

-Let's go and check our new dwellings. Like me you are a kind of refugee... I guess we will have to grow to the understanding of things of our hosts.

Taking his hand she pulled the man to follow the footsteps of Gabriel, and Raphael as Azryel closed the march.

They climbed a spiral staircase made of wood running along the large oak tree. The view from it as they slowly reached the canopy was so breathtaking that Walter found his voice back praising,

-Gabriel, you didn't warn me that you made awesome additions to your cabin. It looks sensational, purely and simply. I don't mind you having a Swiss cheese syndrome of some kind, it works for me. I can't see any funny holes yet. Did you do holly cheesy windows somewhere?

Gabriel turned around shrugging his shoulders, half with pride, half with desperation, giving a deadly look to Azryel who was grinning widely,

-Walter I do not have any syndrome of any kind, Az was just taking the piss out of me. Please, for my sake, do not take him literally and you will almost be the perfect guest.

Azryel reaching the same covered platform as everyone responded to the man,

-On the contrary human, you will do me the most favours by taking me straight and literally. It will educate you right and proper. I was referring earlier to the Swiss Family Robinson, a novel by Wyss published in 1812, about a Swiss family shipwrecked on an island. The story was turned into a Disney movie in 1960. There is no Swiss cheese involved apart from in an episode of Mighty Mouse in 1947. However I do like the design idea of Swiss cheese windows, this is something we could create in your bedroom, if we are faced by conventional windows there. A conventional man does need some sort of holy windows to be inspired like the kind we see in cathedrals, an unconventional one like you, just needs plenty of funny round holes for windows like we see in the best Emmental cheese. Just tell me how cheesy you want your bedroom, human, I am happy to punch the holes in the walls of it into shape.

Gabriel fumed out loud, pleading to Raphael,

-No redesigning in my house, no holes to be pierced and no holy cheesy windows for Christ's sake! Wrath, I do not think I will be able to cope with these three, my tranquil house will be turned into an insanity ward in no time at all. Tell me again why the AA was not a good idea to harbour them lot?

A sarcastic Raphael laughed out loud,

-Well, there is no trees around it. Within woods somehow the Beast's tracks get lost for years. It just so happens, that I am a sociable Angel living in a mighty Club, a nightclub and bar, among a crowd. It happens that you are an unsociable one, living in a tree, in the middle of nowhere among trees. You bestow the perfect home for our little Antichrist, when no one else has.

Gabriel nodded resigned, then presented the platform to them all,

-Here is the centre of the house. There is not much upon it apart from that wooden bench which stares into the deepness of the woods. If I lost a human to death in my clinic this is where I retrieve myself to ponder upon my actions of that day and analyse if any could have been a fatal mistake in my journey as a Doctor aiming to save a life. From the platform springs eight ways forward to the rest of the house. If you climb the rope, you will be at the top of that very tree, above the canopy, in an observatory room. The ladder takes you to a midway point, where my office is. If you reach for the swing you will get to the bedrooms, that part of my house is on another tree. I have only three, so we will have to fix someone in someone-else's bedroom. A slide from there gets you to the main bathroom facility which is by the river. I usually teletransport my way there and back... I need to revise this part of the house, somehow it was fun when I was a little younger. The staircase will lead you to another tree where I have my drawing room, main hall and yes the unsociable Angel that I am, did build a reception room, a rather grand one I must admit. If you take the rope bridge, it goes to the fun tree. It is still very much in project and harbours only a couple of rooms for the moment. I may develop the Swiss cheese windows there. The wooden bridge leads you to another tree, a bit further down, by the river. This is where I have my kitchen, dining room, breakfast room, conservatory, kitchen garden, storage room and the eco-room which maintains and sustains the whole tree house. Inside the tree there is a lift that takes you down underground, to a laboratory, a library and a collectors-museum maze. They are my favourite places and I'd rather be there discovering, reading or gazing at some mind boggling marvels than anywhere else at any time. And bye the bye I do happen to possess a first edition of J. D. Wyss, down there. The last elevator is invisible to any eyes but mine, it goes to the safety zone... All areas of Gab's Hall bestow that magical lift. It leads to a no-zone where your presence is hidden from time and space for minutes or more. It needs tweaking here and there. Inside the time loop hole you lose the knowledge of what is happening right now and you can't figure out when you can come out of the place safely. A massive blip, I would say but I am working on it... By the way, Uncle, expect me to plant one tree everyday that goes past by your AA Club. A little green can enhance any lives, render them more considerate about the whole damn Earth and any living upon it with their odd ways, Az and his deadly ways, It and her rat ways of eating which aim to become a very welcome veggie, and our good Walter whichever way he goes.

Raphael shaking his head in wonder, confessed,

-I think I lost touch with you for far too long, Gab. I greatly disapproved of your love for the human Wendy, maybe far too greatly for our sakes. You did outcast yourself from all Angels then. You went your way caring for her twin brother, our dear Walter, looking after his family and making sure they would stay strong and together. I admire you, for you gave your heart to them. You needed guidance all along Angel, but you went ahead with your thoughts discarding Us as unwelcoming. You slightly drifted away Gab. We always learn, constantly through our mistakes, we grow and develop. Please do plant trees by the AA Club everyday that goes past, I will know then that one Deadly Angel, one valuable human and one powerful teenager are still safe at yours. Any trees that sprout by mine will be a blessing indeed to know that you are all safe, as I leave you behind. I shall count trees everyday. A missing one will call me back from the first front to you all with my Army of Angels. It is a promise that I stand by you Gab, that I am not giving you a burden to deal with, for humanity's sake, but a treasure to hide safely in your home. The three of them are the tools to shape a non 'fated' future, Gab. They are very precious indeed. Work on your Time and Space loophole ASAP. You are a bloody clever Angel, I am proud to be your Uncle. I am going to leave you all now. My first port of call will be Ash with strict orders regarding Caroline and Micky. Azryel, I will need you to check up on them closely and to bring Caro and the kid in the tree house of Gab if any dangers are tangible to them. My second is to dig out 'P' with my Angelic Army, he deserves a staunch warning for the siege at the AA Club although he failed atrociously there.

Raphael was about to depart, when he stopped and cleared his throat slightly, addressing It-666 and Walter at the same time,

-As for you two, you may be refugees under my wings but trust the Angels you are with, for I would trust them with my own life. Az is the staunchest protector I can give you, for he is also mine. Hence, his upset for being further from me and my Army than he should. Learn fast and learn trust which is an entire education in itself. Trust me. It takes a life time but even though you will sometimes face a gaping hole facing you bare to swallow your whole faith on another plane entirely. Then you are lost to another entity altogether. Learning your own path and heart is the best way. Azryel has a heart of his own and lived through much. He can do both, help you annihilate yourselves to your troubles or raise you to challenge them and kill them at the stalks. Not very eco-friendly, but if you two stay alive at the end of the day I would say it was definitely Earth friendly.

The Archangel disappeared. The teenager looked at Azryel, Gabriel and Walter in dismay, as she shivered,

-Help me be Earth friendly, please, help me.

Gabriel smiled kindly and said, as he held the swing,

- We will. Let's show you your eco-bedroom. Trust you will have a great perspective from there, it will be inspirational.

He sat by the girl upon the swing and whisked her away to the next tree. As he arrived he sent the swing back to Walter and Azryel.

As Az caught the swing in full swing he advised,

-Right in the double bedroom scheme, I need to keep an eye on It-666 more than you do human. I intend to be there when her Hellish Daddy makes a call.

The human sat upon the swing steadily and answered,

-I hope you will cut the call shorter than what I witnessed. Her Father has a way to upset her very much. I am her adoptive father now, remember, Az. If I have to trust you, like Raphael said, then help me to show her a bit of love, rather than to let her be the recipient from her Evil Daddy. If your ways are a little hellish then the girl will not be swooped away to any Angelic nest easily, but only with great caution on her part. Tell me Azryel?

The Death Angel holding the swing smiled,

-Let's send you off to see your refugee bedroom, human. No more talking.

The man looked thoroughly disappointed, he scolded,

-I kind of knew that you were a bloody bastard unable to join your butt upon a swing by a human. Are you an extremist Angel which can't stand humans? Gab sat by It.

The Angel taking a seat beside the man upon the swing replied,

-This is because he is her Master. He has allegiance from the girl somehow. I know full well that I will never get your allegiance.

Walter gave him a disarming glance,

-Because I can't be subservient to you, does that mean I cannot fight by your side, and help you in any way possible?

Azryel sighed deeply, pushing the swing for it to reach the other platform, whispered,

-Walter, you can and always will somehow. Raphael, Gabriel and I will always have your best interests at heart somehow, too. We engaged on that journey because of you, solely you. We are swayed away by your arguments. It-666 got the fairest chance she never had. To be honest with you, we believe what you saw in her. She can be our little An' without the double n and the posh e, without the t which spell an Antichrist, the very orphan to find the 'green gables', in that instance the green Gab's Hall. We will give her our whole at our own perils. I am the only one to stop the motion if I truly find her Evil. So far the little one is an amazingly good soul and Being as you said she was. She impressed all of Us to adopt her, far away from her plight. I will be tough on her but it will be to dispel any evil, human, and I beg of you to understand it for all of us are at stake. If she truly is not she will grow to be a wholesome good being for it. She will only get a strong, good sound soul with my training.

The human asked in a secretive voice,

-Does your teachings train to listen to one's heart?

The Angel of Death nodded positively,

-It does. Hard to believe but we need to talk to each other upon the matter more thoroughly than a swing ride.

He jumped out of the swing and helped the human to reach the landing safely. Gabriel welcomed them with a proud smile,

-Welcome to Gab's Hall. Little It already chose her bedroom. Let me show yours.

Azryel looked upon the man disdainfully,

-Hell, no. I am not sleeping with him. I've got to look after the Beast. I will make myself small in the corner of her room ready to intervene if needs be. Sorry, Wrath's orders.

The man shrugging his shoulders nonchalantly stated,

-My heart orders me to sleep in the same room to make sure no one gets a cut throat during the night. My heart rules.

Gabriel nodding his agreement showed them their room, the guest bedroom of It,

-Right, I am not going to start arguing with you two by pointing out that three is a crowd. I guess you will find that out yourselves in good time. When you all want to kill each other just remember that next door is a welcoming spare bedroom.

Verse 4. Messy Missy

Azryel counter attacked the coming blow powerfully enough to floor the teenager. It-666 smiling piteously, apologised,

-I can't do it properly Az. I do not want to hurt you, so much that all my moves are implacably fully restrained all the time.

The Angel scolded the teenager,

-Stand up, and give it a good go. This time was less pitifully mediocre than last time. Imagine I am a demon attacking you if it will help.

Sitting by a tree, Walter encouraged,

-Go on It. You can do it. Kick his Angelic Arse. Think of his snoring last night. I would have given him a good kick if it was not for good Gab who gave me earplugs earlier, saying that I might find them useful.

Az grinned sarcastically to the human,

-It will soon be your turn Walter, I would do some warming up exercises if I were you rather than sitting uselessly on my backside. Gab is a clever Angel who gave me earplugs as well, saying pretty much the same, apart from that he added to me, that it would help to cut out the incessant blabber of bloody Walter. He hoped that it could prevent you from being killed by me.

Walter spat by him, rose to his feet and went to help the teenager to stand up, moaning,

-I won't be killed by you.

Azryel gave him his wickedest smile saying softly,

-Ultimately, I am afraid to say, yes you will. I have the terrible regret to remind you that I am also called Death. I would appreciate if you left my soldier to do her own standing up. She needs to learn how to fight and stand on her own two feet. If she is smothered by you, she won't have a chance of survival.

The human ignored him and asked the girl as she stood awkwardly,

-Did you hurt yourself Babe?

-I think I did, I am so sorry Azryel to be so crap at fighting.

Walter queried further, scolding her gently,

-Where? Let's have a look. And stop apologising constantly to that big bad arse of an Angel. Do you think he cares to say sorry to all the souls he has to collect? You need to toughen up a little when you deal with those Angels. You are a soldier in their Army, if you don't stand up to their bullying ways, they are all going to give you a damn rough ride. Gosh, I don't want that to happen to you.

Azryel coming closer to inspect the damage replied,

-Actually I do apologise to every soul, human. I won't let her be bullied in my Army. My Angels will respect her as an equal, I can promise you that much. It, what Walter is saying is true, you need to toughen up a little, if you are hurt, say so and do not apologise for it. Now let's repair that.

It-666 showed them her swollen ankle, as Workmaster asked the Angel,

-I guess it will not be granted and only seen as molly cuddling that teenage Being to give her a little break. I really would like to have my turn now at kicking your damn bad arse. Have you seen the state of that ankle, Az? Can you remind yourself a little that you are a supernatural Being which is much older and stronger than her? Can you show the same restraint that It is displaying constantly with you? Can you replicate the favour or is it too much to ask of you?

As Azryel apposed his hands upon the ankle, blue cooling light passing from his long fingers to the bruised skin, he could not resist a wicked smile,

-Woo ooh, we have a very p'd off human to deal with. How did that happen? Someone broke his little Baby, a big bad Angel teaching her how to fight and survive, because in his very long eternal life the very bad Angel has got one valuable thing or two to teach the young little Being in order for her to live a very very long eternal life. Look, Workmaster, all fixed up now! Your smothered Being can walk again.

It stood up smiling and warmly thanked the Death Angel.

Watching this enraged Walter further as he exploded at once, mimicking the teenage Being,

-It, you are bloody far too kind, and it is not for your own good. 'Thank you for fixing me, please break me again, I won't mind'. Well I do mind, and those Angels with great powers that can fix the damages they cause, should learn to curb doing damages instead of repairing them. The power to fix things should not be a license to hurt. Did I make myself clear Azryel? Now mocking me or her, is not taken lightly and I expect you to respond to my concerns as they are very much valid. I do not want my girl to learn that it is okay to break things because everything can be repaired five minutes later or any other super power bullshit of the kind.

The Angel gave to the man the wooden fighting shaft and enjoined him,

-My first reply is this, yes, I grant your girl to take a break for now, for her to sit and watch how a good beating is done. I believe it can be very educational for the two of you. As for you, human, I grant you your turn, it is very much needed as you badly need to learn how to calm down, but also to be more open with the ways of the super Beings that rule your unfortunate world in order to protect it. Sometimes, more often that not, those very licentious super powers are the very ones that keep your Earth a safe haven when your killing each other kind, obliterates itself for whatever reasons they see fit to massacre one another. So let's teach you a good lesson Walter. I have your concerns at heart believe me for I am Death and was born with the plights of all sown upon my breast, so tight I could hardly breath anything but the human misery out there, all wishing their way out. Didn't you wish for me one miserable day, human, did you? Who rescued you, if it was not for an Angel who watched over your shoulder. Learn and listen to Us.

Walter took the shaft meekly, looking helplessly at the Angel before him. It-666 knowing it would be almost a stand off sat by the tree, relieved it was not her on the receiving hand of the fighting shaft of Azryel. She had much to learn but the thought of seeing the man being beaten up right and proper wasn't pleasing her at all. She pleaded,

-Can I beg you, Az to reciprocate my restraint upon Walter or would it be seen as interfering with the lesson to learn?

The Death Angel replied straight away as he engaged the man,

-Interference, Babe. Watch and learn. Do not over-worry too much. I have the license to kill, but I promise you, I will fix that one up for you.

A worried sick Walter Workmaster, his anger totally abated, and rather shitting himself, took the bravest defense he could do against the blows of the Angel. He was strong and fought hard, despite his total lack of exercise. He muttered,

-I should have had the warming up session. I feel it now. One understanding point goes to you, Az. I shall not ignore your orders and watch your every move like a steady eagle ready to intervene when you hurt my girl. She has received enough pain already through torture. You need to understand that, as much as I need to understand your bloody f'ing Being thing!

Az laughed as he floored the man in a swinging blow,

-For your human understanding, I know that bloody well. I am getting her into fighting shape so she is the one to deliver blows if needs be but also getting her fit to avoid any future one coming to her. Any more concerns, human to throw at me? Beat them out of yourself.

A breathless Workmaster looked in desperation at the Angel, vented,

-Somehow, Az, although I hate you firmly, I do also like you. Explain that one to me.

The man stood up to give his first strong attack to the Angel, who replied,

-It is the 'Always Right' syndrome, my darling human. You have it as much as I do. Love, hate, cats and dogs, ultimately peace and love and a marriage made in heaven.

Walter's eyebrows cocked in a funny way, swearing out loud, while Death threw him back upon the ground in no time at all,

-Hell no!

Putting the bottom end of his shaft upon the ground, Death looked upon the man with a joyous glee,

-See, I would say just the same. Stuck together for a while, totally unappealing. Where are my bleeding headache tablets?

Workmaster lifted himself up and ran to give a head blow to the smiling Azryel,

-Let me give you a proper headache Darling Angel!

The defending kick sent the man flying fifty metres away. Walter upon the floor moaned,

-Gosh that hurts. Damn Angel, very very damn Angel. No loving you no more.

Azryel walked slowly to the man, coaxing,

-You do not mean that human, you always had begging wishes for me. Every now and then, you just f'ing gave up your soul to me so willy nilly willingly. I am not ready to forget all those calls human for they did hurt me deeply each time you made them. Are you not ready for me yet, my Darling, for I am ready to take you on and further?

Workmaster turned around to face the Angel who knelt by him, pleaded,

-Stop fucking with my mind, bloody Angel. I have a will to stay on since Gab's intervention. I am not ready to die yet.

Death offered his hand to the human to help him stand up, giving him the fighting shaft back,

-Your plea is accepted. You may live for another round.

As Walter held the wooden stick shivering with fear, he realised what the Angel was doing. It dawned to him that he was trying to teach It-666 about not giving up, that he was addressing her suicidal self throughout the lesson, taking him as a fighting example. He looked back at the Death Angel's eyes, and found himself pleading from his guts,

-Please, make my girl live for many rounds and look out for me. I love my Caro and Micky. I want to stay by them as much as I can.

Azryel patting the human shoulder commented,

-You fought very well Walter, I am impressed. Your call, do you want to fight more or take a break? I bruised you a little bit I am afraid. Although I am going to fix it, when you can't take it any more. It will always be your call and the one of It-666 upon any tuitions. I will take you as far as I can and foremost as far as you want into surviving it all. It is always your call and never mine, so be sure to make the right choice at any point in time. What do you want to do, human, learn to help yourself or learn to die fast?

Walter gave a glance at It-666, sitting with crossed legs under a tree. She looked as peaceful as a statue of Buddha. A chipmunk was upon her lap, eating nuts from her hand. He replied to the Angel earnestly,

-I want to learn and her too. You can beat the shit out of me once more if it helps her. Funny enough it kind of helped me. I know I need to train f'ing badly. I am getting out of shape somehow. I don't wanna be fair game for demons that's for sure, especially if they've got your kind of strength.

The smiling Angel accepted his answer in an apologetic manner,

-I am sorry to have been a little tough on you Walt. Lesson number one is over for you and her. Let's sort your back out, before it hurts too much and you are paralysed from head to toe. The training session will resume tomorrow. You will both learn to never be fair game to demons then. Have you got any questions? Any more of your concerns?

Walter grinned and replied straight away,

-My Baby is feeding the chipmunk with nuts that appear somehow within her hands. I find that a tiny bit disturbing although goodhearted.

The Death Angel looked disappointingly at the human,

-Suffering from short attention span, Walt. There is hardly any cure for that. Although I can lock you up somewhere to do so.

The human scolding Az replied straight away, kicking slightly his elbow,

-You are the one who focuses a little too much upon a bleeding human for Christ's sake! Watch, pay attention, and learn if you can where that bloody trick comes from. Think further: If I am good and liking you I make peanuts to make you happy, and if I am upset I can make a bomb to blow you right away. Can't say more than that, really, Az, work this one out.

Azryel shook his head in consternation, asking It-666 out loud,

-Your human adoptive Daddy is a little concerned with you handling nuts. He is asking how do they come to your hands?

The teenager releasing a fresh acorn to feed the chipmunk told genuinely,

-I grabbed them from the tree above.

The Angel smiled wickedly,

-We need to reassure your adoptive father here, your arse did not move from the ground, little one. He is only bloody human and asking. Just answer, Bambi.

It-666 replied straight away,

-It is all virtual until it reaches my hand and becomes physical. I see something that exists and call it to me. It always comes, somehow. Then I make it pass depending of its nature, plant or animal and circumstances. I am killing acorns to feed my chipmunk right now. All the ones that grew upon the tree I am sitting under. Is it bad to do so?

Walter looked lost for a good minute. A glance to the Death Angel reassured him somehow, as his mind received a ready reply from him,

-It is a little bad aiming for a lot of good for that little chipmunk. Sustained, it will deprive the chipmunk from his survival instincts, it will be spoilt to death. It will deprive it from a fair good chance.

He closed his eyes and added,

-I have to take you with me on this journey, It. It will save us both although it will be a hard journey to take. I kind of feel it already, by the gentle bruises kindly applied by Azryel. They are very much not virtual, Babe, that you just have to listen to what he says. He knows every way to know about. Watch, learn and practice, little one, best thing to do.

Walter fell upon his knees exhausted. Azryel pulled him up from the ground as he invited,

-Let's get you fixed up human. You are coming with me, now. Ask me any questions if you must to occupy your mind. It-666, session is over. I floored the poor Walter badly, I need to sort out his back before paralysis sets in.

It ran along following them, the chipmunk upon her shoulder, listening to Walter asking the Angel,

-There will be no wooden shaft by me when I am attacked by demons, I bet, so how useful was the lesson on a scale of one to ten? Please reassure me Az.

Azryel grinned wickedly as he answered,

-Sometimes the world is not picture perfect, Walter, and you do have to make things up to suit your needs. Humankind is quite good at that usually. For you, look at the first chair you can find, it would have useful legs I am sure.

The man closed his eyes in despair,

-I did not have my rating, Az, and sometimes you have designer chairs surrounding you with no legs at all. What would you do then?

The Angel laying the man upon the sofa bed in It's bedroom replied,

-Well 10 out of 10 of course as any of my teachings. You calmed down alright, human, didn't you? If I was you I would throw any designer chairs away to the assailant or any piece of furniture for that matter as you would be in deep shit if caught.

It-666 playing with her chipmunk, offered,

-I would intervene by your side, Walter, and protect you all the way.

Walter looked upon her sadly,

-Well, I just got beaten up right and proper under your eyes, Babe. You are a Being, one of the super-duper kind which sees higher means in a good fight which I will always fall short to see. For Christ's sake Az what did you do to my bloody back?

The Angel put his cooling hands upon the man's back answered honestly,

-Dreadful things, I am sorry Walter, the soreness will go within seconds. You will be back up shortly.

Down in the yard a car parked. It-666 went to the window and smiled widely,

-Gabriel is back from work.

She clapped her hands wildly, making her chipmunk jump upon her shoulder.

Walter warned her straight away,

-Right, Babe, you have a nut eating chipmunk upon your shoulder, that won't please Gab. He is not that open minded upon pets and kind of anything... I think you should tell the little thing to get lost in the forest before Gab gets a glance at it. I lived with the bloody Angel for almost four years and he has always been very particular... He has a hidden wooden baseball bat to bring you down to his ways

as well. My poor back did have a taste of it many times too. He is a
good guy, well Angel, do not get me wrong. But he is an Angel you
walk on egg shells around.

Azryel could not help smiling, confided,

-Well to be honest, you will always have to walk on egg shells
around any Angels, not just Gabriel. It is just you. You are a
demanding son of a human bitch that's all.

Suddenly they heard Gabriel shouting from afar,

-Who messed up my kitchen like that? Anyone? You'd better have a
very damn good explanation, a very very good one.

Azryel looked at Walter worried, as he stood up straight away from
the sofa, his back mended, asked him,

-Did you make a mess I should know about Walt when you went
snacking on those peanut butter sandwiches? Gab is anal even with
a tiny drop of water not wiped up inside a sink.

The man shook his head negatively and denied,

-No, I have been extra careful. I even ate all the breadcrumbs that
fell on the table.

They both turned to It-666 with anxiety as she told,

-I am afraid it's me that made a mess. It is worse than drops of
water or breadcrumbs. He is going to kill me.

Azryel enjoined her,

-Well standing there with fear is not going to help you. You'd better
come up with a good explanation and apology to Gabriel. He is
your host and his home is his castle. Let's go there and check the
damage. The more he waits the less forgiving he will be.

The three teletransported to the kitchen, where Gabriel stood, his arms crossed upon his chest and a deadly expression upon his face. He asked sternly,

-I do not have to guess who is the culprit, I know already. Why did you have to poltergeist every damn thing in this kitchen It. This is not funny nor amusing. I am certainly not laughing.

It-666 looked at him sheepishly ventured a weak,

-I can explain everything.

Gabriel pointing at a wall with knives embedded in it, the chairs all wrecked, and the floor littered with eggshells, fumed,

-I am still waiting, you'd better have a good one for me.

Azryel considered the damages with an ironic smile,

-Not bad, that kitchen is totally wrecked in a very bad way. I like the little extra touches. Those forks embedded in the ceiling and the spoons stuck in the sink vertically, it must have taken quite some power. Look the sink is pierced through, that was extreme force. Did you used speed of light, It? I am quite eager to hear what you've got to say for yourself little Antichrist.

The teenager apologised, shivering all of a sudden with shear anxiety,

-I lost control of my powers partly this afternoon when I was practising on the fighting ground with you, Azryel. I am so sorry, Gabriel, so very sorry.

Losing his patience, Gabriel retorted,

-Trust me you will be very sorry if you don't practise your tidying powers to get that room back to some sort of order. Actually, I am very much inclined to punish you by not using your powers at all to clean up your mess, It, and I will stand there in that kitchen, all night if it is necessary until I have my kitchen back the way I left it this morning. You are going to learn never to lose control, Being, especially you. Loss of control from you will never be accepted nor tolerated, not in my home nor anywhere else in the big wide world. Do I make myself very clear It, or do you want to throw your opinion at me upon the whole matter like you threw those knives on the wall?

The girl felt utterly lost for words, looking in despair at Gabriel and Azryel, she replied shakily,

-I am a faulty Being. I am not perfect. Apparently I am the worst thing ever created. I agree with you Gabriel fully. I would not tolerate myself to do any bad to anyone nor to lose control at any point in time. I was badly trying to not hurt Azryel during the fighting session. When deeply upset I could not apply my normal calming method, the one that helps me control my being. As I restrained myself not to kick Az too hard, my powers leaked out in there. I am very sorry Gabriel, very very sorry. I am so sorry Azryel, I can't fight. I am totally helpless. I hate fighting and it lashed out here. I think it's better if I am not here nor anywhere. I think dead is what I should be to prevent the worse. Maybe I should not be helped at all to survive but helped to die. I am so crap at fighting because I do not want to hurt and instead it goes badly in another place where my powers wreck everything in sight. The worst is that I know that it can happen again and again, I partly controlled myself this afternoon, I can't lose my control, I just can't like you said, Gabriel.

Sorry for the teenager, Workmaster shaking his head negatively, muttered,

-And this is Az's good work of this afternoon all undone by a tirade. Mistakes do happen. I think a growing teenage girl deserves an allowance for cocking up badly sometimes. We all learn by our mistakes. Somehow this special Being cannot have the same allowance as everyone else. I was a teenager once, full of testosterone and anger, and I made lots of mistakes, some which I am proud of and some which I deeply regret. Yet I was allowed to make them and learn from them to become an adult. So now we have that special tough rule that applies just to one Being in the whole universe, an intransigence on mistakes which is just unforgiving and plain insanely ludicrous. Great, kill me Gab, right after you are done with her.

The Death Angel came to It and his arm enclosing her shoulders told kindly,

-Don't forget one thing, little one, you can't make decisions for yourself with Us. For now you are a Being with Masters. Your death sentence lays in my hands and no one else's. As it happens, I do agree with our man Walter. Consideration for your age and your heart's aim are duly noted. Today's lesson may have upset you, rightly, as it was not an easy first one to take. Yet it will take many of those to thoroughly teach you the proper control of your Being. Let me underline that last part, we will teach you the proper control of your powers, Being. I do believe that control of one self is never inherent but acquired, and mistakes unfortunately do play a part in learning it. That overwhelming Being over there is a king of mistakes, throwing his wings about with majesty when he nearly killed Workmaster by using him as a guinea pig for a coma experiment. I forgave him for that big fat mistake, although I am punishing him for it, for he will learn to better himself with good tuition. Life is all about learning and forgiving, as Death I do know deeply the meaning of this. As your new tutor I knew full well what I was undertaking, so did Raphael and so did Gabriel. Although Gabriel is a slightly OCD Angel when it concerns the spaces he dwells in and the humans and Beings he undertakes. A mistake of just a few hours of inattention on his part cost him the loss of a human he dearly loved, he never forgave himself for it and has a problem with forgiveness to any that have made mistakes ever since. However if you listened to him carefully enough he also stated you are going to learn never to lose control. As Beings we do know the effects of those are very dear and costly hence the firm caution. I agree with his punishment, pure cleaning of that kitchen with no help of your powers, and I will let him do the night guard. Were those knives intended for me?

Shaking her head wildly, It-666 denied,

-Only walls, in frustration when you said you would play 'kill and resuscitate Walt' after thoroughly beating him. It didn't agree with me and I couldn't help absorb his human fright and anger in and letting it go somewhere else rather than on you. It came out like that. He was so cross and helpless when you mentioned it. I thought it would help him in his fight to not be blind with anger so I swallowed it. I did not digest it properly though.

Walter swore out loud,

-Yep, blimey! I did imagine myself for a second as a circus knife thrower with you, Az, attached upon a round wooden frame. Looking at the pattern of the knives on that wall, you are there in the middle pretty much safe, apart from well one knife that goes in the shape.

Gab pointed out, looking carefully at the position of the knives on the wall,

-That would be your heart if you had one, Az, if I am not mistaken.

The disappointed Death Angel turned around, ordered,

-Make sure It does her punishment Gab, as for you, human, you come with me. It, you will soon learn to not be a messy Missy with Us.

Verse 5. Tie Die Yin

Left alone with the Archangel Gabriel in the kitchen, the teenager dropped upon her knees,

-I am so very sorry, Master.

Gabriel barked,

-No, at this point in time you are not sorry enough. The sorriness just occurred by the realisation of your acts and the effects it had upon others and the room, but I can assure you that it will run much deeper at the end of the night. Now, I do not think I have received any explanations valid enough for your actions.

The Angel gave the girl a dustpan, brush and bin bags before continuing, pointing at the broken eggshells,

-It is time for you to clear the air and clean your mess. Explain those to me right now. How many potential hatchlings died on that one?

It-666 shook her head in denial,

-None, these were the eggshells of this last Spring of already born birds which still littered the whole forest.

Gabriel turned around her in an intimidating manner, arguing,

-That makes it all better, now does it? At least the last and the next generation of birds of the ecosystem of this woods are still alive and well through that damn feat. Why do their cracked eggs have to litter my kitchen? Why could their calcium not feed the ground of the forest, or help their makers's digestive systems over the Winter months when their foods are tougher to eat?

Cleaning the eggshells with the dustpan and brush, a blood tear appearing at the corner of her eyes, It replied with honesty,

-Because I did not think that far when it happened. This was triggered by sheer fear of you. I was overjoyed to see you arrive tonight, then Walt and Az cautioned me about you, then I remembered my bad blips in the kitchen, then I got so very anxious that their words became physical, it was just pure treading upon eggshells around you.

The Angel's sardonic laugh resonated in the room,

-Right, so you are telling me that sometimes, when you are anxious or scared, you are being literal with your renditions. Pure 'treading upon eggshells' around me, I will make sure you do so all night. What else did they tell you that ended up within this room? I know about the knives so you can skip that one. Gosh, can you imagine the eggshells we are treading on whenever we are saying a word that triggers you, Being?

It-666 having filled a full bag of eggshells, shed another tear,

-I understand this now, Gabriel, starting to understand it now. I am afraid of myself as much as you are, you know. I would never give me an opportunity. I never learnt to trust myself since my anger burst those nun killers into flames. Can we give back to the forest all those eggshells or are we throwing them away?

Taking the first full black bag from her, Gabriel stated,

-We ought to as Beings and we will, this is how repairing a mess works. Always think of the far reaching consequences and mend as much as you can. Some will be irretrievable and that is when the blood tears come out in your heart too, trust me. We will put the bags full of shells in the yard, ready for you to put them back in the whole woods tomorrow as evenly spread as it was before, for the whole ecosystem to not miss a vital part of it. This might keep you away from practising fighting with Azryel for a while, from upsetting yourself more and more importantly from destroying more of my home as a consequence. Now, I want to know about those wrecked chairs as I spent many nights crafting them from scratch. I am a bit of a carpenter in my spare time as you must have gathered. I love building things from my own hands the hard way, which no Angels would do. They would use humans to craft their ways. Like you I am a bit of a misfit.

The girl noticed the deeper tone of the Angel, and confessed in earnest,

-The chairs are due to another upset of Walter I dealt with today. His back was so badly hurt from his self-defence training session that he could have been paralysed without Az's intervention, repairing the far reaching consequences he inflicted. He was taught a needed lesson, to calm down and trust Azryel. Walt just asked Az how useful was the lesson if he had no fighting stick around. Rightly Death told the man to use his imagination and surrounding if he was in the worst situation, chairs were the particular mention, and Walt got cross that his lesson might have been useless, that I captured his very thoughts and released them here.

The Angel put his hands on his hips crossly asked bluntly,

-What would have happened if the man expressed his own anger? More physical damages or a more interesting point of view that may have been useful to listen to? Walter can be a very angry man sometimes. All the times he was angry, he was more often than not right. All Angels acknowledged that fact and they are more than likely ready to listen to what he has to say, also they are more than likely ready to take him into consideration if he has a forceful voice. Swallowing any human's anger to release it into any other form but their human right to plea in words or else is depriving humanity of its own say. Silencing men and women to the depth of eternity is not a solution to their pleas, any good Angel will tell you that. Who authorises you to do so, pray? If it was your good hearted thinking mind, I can tell you right now that it is only sixteen years old and very short sighted of the consequences of its own decisions.

It-666 now cried silently. She kept removing the eggshells with the dustpan brush for a long while, until she finally answered,

-I shall never swallow the anger of mankind again, I will let them fully express themselves. I did it for so long it hurts right down to my bones. I only released the hurt in small amounts before.

Gabriel grabbed her chin at once and demanded,

-You swallowed human anger since when? How did you digest it and where was it released?

The sobbing teenager replied,

-Since I heard their voices and pleas, for a long while. I cannot answer their pleas, I can extinguish the frustration to their unanswered prayers, by making their prayers die to a physical manifestation though. It makes them peaceful again for a while until they are upset again.

The Angel's wings appeared at her answer. His eyes glowed full of anger, as he asked,

-So you did mess up the world, humans and their say for a long time, destroying something now and then. An earthquake here and there, a mudslide, an avalanche, a derailed train, tell me when I can stop...

The girl stood up shouting,

-Right now, right now! I made their anger happen upon my own physical body not the world, never the outside world. One bone at a time, one cell at a time, I released their anger upon myself.

Gabriel retorted,

-I can still see you treading upon eggshells, Being. Clear them out. Down on your knees, for you have nothing to be proud of on the contrary. No wonder you are failing to speak so often. You have swallowed so much of the valid pleas, that the powers that be will eat your own words without mere consideration. You are so doomed.

It-666 fell back upon her knees and carried on cleaning the eggshells silently crying until the floor was pristine.

Gabriel ignoring her silence prepared a meal in the meantime. When the last eggshells were bagged up, the teenager proposed,

-Shall I bring the lot of them in the yard to make some space?

The Angel answered coolly,

-No. You can not escape my presence until Azryel comes back, and get my feedback upon your cleaning up your mess lesson. Now, you can focus your whole attention upon my damaged sink. How are you going to repair that one the human way?

The teenager feeling the grunt of Gabriel's displease cried again, slowly but surely,

-I do not know. I am no plumber.

Brushing the spoons off the sink in one angry stroke the Archangel commented,

-Then you should not attempt what you can not repair. This has a zero tolerance among Angels. This is pure treading upon eggshells with Us. Let me repair that one for you, put your hands underneath the sink. If you burst into a damn of human tears that would be all the ones you swallowed from them depriving them of their natural release. This is a punishment and it will hurt, for it will take into account the amount of human hearts who cried and for how long they were crying.

A deeply sorry It-666 placed her hands underneath the sink like receiving containers bravely accepting her punishment. Like the Angel told her, she felt the pain. She was in agony straight away at the amount of tears running through her hands, her arms, sinking deep into her skin like millions of tiny blades piercing her heart of the sheer sorrow. Growing paler at the realisation of what she had done, she felt the internal blood tears, that Gab did mention, crying from her own heart. When all sensations stopped she shook like a leaf, was unable to stand, feeling empty with all strength absolutely gone.

The Angel lifted her chin and forced her to look at him. She had kept her human eyes throughout her punishment, where he had seen a pure and intense sorrow. She whispered to him in tongue,

-I felt the heart tears, Gabriel. I still feel them. I don't think they will ever stop.

As the Archangel helped her up, showing her the repaired sink, he told sternly,

-You will never absorb the sorrow, anger, or words of others, have I made that clear? If you feel their pain there are things that, on the other hand, you can do. It's bringing comfort and hope, by means of words well applied, by means of acts which solve the problems that caused their initial pain, by means of bringing justice to their plights. This is what you can do as a Being. Do you understand me?

The girl nodded her ascent first, then finding her voice,

-I do Gabriel. Thank you for making me understand the errors of my ways. I feel deeply sorry to have been so wrong for so long.

Putting a couple of plates upon the table and dishing out a meal, Gab acknowledged,

-Good. Now let Us hope you will not get on the wrong end of the stick very often to prevent any other Angelic punishment. Although always necessary when they occur you will learn that they are far from pleasant. Mine and Raphael's are considered to be the most powerful, yet there are nothing in comparison of Azryel's ones, when his are not lethal, you can consider yourself lucky. The fact that he let me be in charge of your punishment tonight, is because he granted you a small leeway. Death is by nature unforgiving never forget that when you are with him. You are pretty much shattered right now, Being, I would have offered you a chair to eat your dinner but unfortunately I had a grizzly Beast's telekinetic mind in my kitchen which wrecked them beyond recognition. I can only offer you to sit on the table, however I hate that informal way of having a meal, or to sit upon the ground now that you cleared your mess up. I think with your bestial's ways you showed this afternoon, it may be the most adequate place for you.

As he handed her the dish, she sat upon the floor silently, he pursued with an ironic smile,

-I would have also offered a fork, but as they are all stuck upon the ceiling for the moment by mysterious circumstances, you get to remain uncivilised and use your fingers to eat this evening. Usually I am a marvellous and kind host, really, it takes a lot of disrespect from a guest for me to make my guest uneasy. Walter was one of those guests who needed a firm hand to help him through his major breakdown, hence his eggshells treading reference. He learnt how to walk the line with me. Do you think you can learn that without any hard feelings like him?

It-666 nodded positively,

-I think I can, Gab. I have plain good feelings for you. I am sorry for the chairs, can you show me how to make some, the hard way, from scratch? But also not forgetting those ones, can you show me how to repair all those respectfully? They looked like designers ones with no legs at all. The suggestion of Az to Walt was to use legs of chairs as fighting shafts, if they were without legs, to throw them and pretty much anything he could find as he would be in deep shit if he could not fight any demons off until Az could get to him.

Gabriel could not help smiling, partly reassured about the good and willing nature of the so called 'Beast' but also for her youthful Being blatant shortsightedness, reacting rather than acting purposefully. He flew to pick up three forks from his ceiling, then landed by the sink to wash them, commenting,

-I do not think Az and Walt would love bits of plaster, paint and wood with their food, do you? How do you like you food, Being? My food is not the best in the world, but it fills hungry empty stomachs pretty well. It is very much old bachelor stuff, pasta, rice things, and potatoes. However I know Caro is working on a special veggie menu and diet for you. I follow recipes down to a teaspoon level so I will have you properly healthy in no time at all. No rodent eating in my house. What do you plan to do with the chipmunk on your shoulder? It is a very fat one, I must say.

The teenager saw the Angel dishing out two other plates which he put upon an invisible thing where they disappeared. She felt a warm welcoming filling her up from the Angel. All the teases, the put downs, the punishments, were put back into perspective in her mind. She confided,

-That meal is delicious. Tell me what is it? I am pretty much uncultivated when it comes to food. I did not have much the past 8 years, apart from unfortunate rodents. I have no plan to eat that one apart from releasing it to the forest, but it seems to have adopted me since I fed it with nuts... Az warned me that I was damaging his natural skills and chances of survival by getting him used to the freely handed nuts. I have been interfering with nature again without knowing the far reaching consequences, Gab. What can I do?

The Angel taking his plate and finally eating his meal, standing up nonchalantly against the table, replied,

-Well, if the chipmunk adopted you for your ready food coming from your hand, then you do not have a proper pet. A proper pet loves you unconditionally. You just have a grateful chipmunk by you that is all. It is not a bad thing but if you can get the pet by teaching it the laws of nature all the while, hence helping it to survive, you get far better satisfaction from it. I would release the chipmunk myself back to the wild, and make sure it is look after by a little once in a while supply, which guarantees its survival throughout the winter. I would not mess with wildlife if I were you, until I had a proper understanding of it as well in the future. I am ready to help you gain this, if you wish me to.

-I do.

The chipmunk left It's shoulders with no further ado, and disappeared by the closest window.

Gabriel smiled wickedly,

-That was fast. What did you tell the little thing?

-That it had a hoard of nuts waiting for it for this Winter. That it will refill for its whole lifetime, for I messed up with its survival skills.

Asking in a concerned manner, the Angel asked,

-Did the animal hurt you when it left you knowing it had a granted plate elsewhere? Did you feel the grudge of disappointment?

It could not help nodding a yes. Gabriel stated,

-This is because your best help will only be respected if it is to the point perfect, perfectly adapted to the creature you are dealing with at any time. It requires a deep knowledge of the whole wide world. I can only recommend you to listen to Azryel for this. He has mastery upon all things that live. I may be able to claim Bud, Walt's dog, to live with us. It is at Caro's right now. The human swears by it instead of God, because his pet, he claims, is a steadier friend... Somehow I tend to agree. Walt went through shit and despair that took time to get sorted and fully mended. I helped him throughout although his trouble did hit me as hard as it hit him. We share a deep loss, a loved one. Walt became a soul brother, I would never give up on him, but it also meant being tough upon him. He appreciates that. In your case, I hope you will learn to do so in time, to never give up on yourself as well and to help me achieve this with you.

It-666 rose to her feet, came to the Angel and gave him a long and silent hug.

Gabriel cocked his eyebrows amused, and happily surprised, asked,

-What is that for, pray, little Being?

-It is just a thank you for taking me on, Gabriel. Thank you so
much. For me, you mean a world of good, and gosh trust me I do
appreciate that, enormously do. Thank you for letting me into your
home although I am a messed up Being. I am very deeply touched
and you have my promise that I will always obey your rules. For you,
I will try my best not to give up on myself.

The Archangel felt deep emotion rising within him. He remembered
the favourite life motto of Walter Workmaster, and tapping kindly
the teenage shoulders commented,

-Remember It, that you are a very brave Being with a good damn
heart. You deserve a chance and to live. It will be an uphill struggle
and fight to raise you but you found Us, the Angelic Soldiers of
Wrath, we do not let down, we never give up, we are survivors of
the ages. We always tidy any mess, coming from bad mistakes, from
men, from demons or from angels and if we can't, we learn from
them to build a better future. As Walter would say to his own son,
his own mantra, under any circumstances, let me remind you my
dear Bambi, that, 'We are going to do it. We are going to make it.
We are going to win it.'

Verse 6. Immersed in Eternity.

Putting the six bin bags full of eggshells in the yard with the help of It-666, Gabriel laughed,

-You could not have made more of a mess, could you?

Giving a sheepish look, she replied,

-This was my 'restrainy' kind of self slash forward mess...

The Angel putting his hands on his hips ventured,

-Why would you restrain yourself to hit Az hard? Every Angel dreams to have the opportunity to do so. But instead we have him hounding Us at our every mistakes, and his corrections are not for the faint hearted, trust me.

The teenager blinked at him, amazed,

-I respect him. I just cannot hit him properly even during training. All my strength went AWOL, in the kitchen messing it all up. I can't explain it.

Gab challenged her at once,

-Try it. Come on put words on what happened inside you. I may be able to help you if you only express yourself properly.

It came by Gabriel confessed,

-I am extremely afraid to lash out. I do not know the extent of my powers and I do not want to find out by trying them on Azryel.

-Shame, you have the most powerful Angel as a teacher, ready to let you know exactly who you are, what you can do and can't, and you just don't want to know, as you are scaring the shite out of your own self and are happier to be a messy Missy for the rest of your days. That's a great good informative choice you are on. Just tell me how many more rooms do you plan to wreck in my home, so I can manage my anger and disappointment each time I come back from a hard day's work at the clinic?

The teenager argued her point,

-I have no intention of wrecking another room. Yet I need to find a way to control myself when I am with Azryel. My way of control before was just a lullaby. Something I could repeat to my own self as I tried to forget about my surroundings. I usually cradled myself doing so performing what no other will ever do for me. Now I can't do that in front of Azryel in the middle of a fighting session, can I? I did let myself be thrown away with the big wooden stick instead of being the Beast, you all expect me to be.

Gabriel confronted her, simply asking,

-Okay, when did you plan to speak openly about it with Azryel, like you did with me? Do you think he would have branded you as a nincompoop, or help you to achieve greater control of yourself? Think about it. As long as you come out loud and clear but also clean with the Death Angel you will be fine.

As they headed their way back to the tree house, a wondering It whispered,

-I did not want to upset Az this afternoon. Yet I was more than crap I must admit, juggling with my pacific ways and trying to bring myself to fight properly. I was all over the place and nowhere. Can I really talk to Azryel like I can with you?

-You not only can, but it is a must to do so. I can only suggest you strongly to confide to him at the first opportunity. Speak your own heart and you will only find him attentively listening to you. He may as well think of solutions to your current dilemma. Now it is very late and it is high time for you to go to bed.

Opening the bedroom door, the teenager looked at Gabriel full of worry. She asked wildly,

-Where's Walter? I cannot hear him anywhere for miles around. I can read the mind of other humans living in the trendy lane at the borders of the forest, but I lost complete track of Walter. I hope he is okay, that nothing happened to him, but I would have felt it I am sure of it.

Reassuring her at once, the Angel replied, while opening the window to let a little breeze carry through the room,

-Walter is safe. He is with Azryel who is having a long talk with him addressing his trust issues with Us. They are both in the room which hides people within from space and time, my magical loophole. Remember to aerate that room regularly when you are all in there. Gosh, those two, especially Walt can get very musky at night. It stinks like hell. Can't you smell the stench in there?

The girl sat smiling away fully reassured, confided,

-How do you think I could live in my shit hole for so many years, Gab? Of course, I have a trick under my sleeve for that. I can shut my nostrils. Well to be more correct I can switch off any of my senses at any time. Smell is one that is often down to minimal level in a closed space. Switch on to its maximum level, then I will smell every human and living animal for hundreds of miles. It can be overwhelming, I must say, so I tend to be on minimal to medium level at any one time.

-Very clever, I must say, especially when facing an exhausted smelly Walter crashing on a sofa bed nearby and a very busy Death Angel in the hammock bed, who can not hide the excruciating smell of death upon him when he lies down at night. It keeps him awake most nights, remembering his every soul he had to collect during the day. In fact, that Angel stares into the darkness and hardly ever gets a proper rest. It's hard to know and see. It is Death's own plight, and conundrum that when he has the power to make others rest in peace, he will never be able to do so for himself. If you have the power to switch off your senses, he cannot do so. Death lives with the world and feels its every missing heartbeat intrinsically deep down. He hardly ever speaks about it. He shows a tough and very cynical face at all times. But sometimes he will mention the toll to Us, but when he does, it is always emotional. You must understand one thing, it is that Azryel has a very deep heart, but unlike you he is a listener and a doer. He aims to resolve human plight and Raphael backs him up all the way yet controlling him doing so. Your teacher despite Walter's concerns is the best you could ever have. He loves humans more than you can imagine. He despises them as well for their failures. He dreams away things to teach them right all day long. Raphael loves his sheer hope he keeps through his daily doom. He wants to make one of those dreams come true somehow, if not to just let Az sleep for a few hours fully and to have for the first time, a dream like anyone else. Death has only the conception of what a dream is. Do you let yourself dream, Bambi?

She shook her head negatively as she answered,

-I see visions of hell when I do so. So I put my extra vision night sky on and gaze at the stars instead. I used to do visions of nests of little animals but sometimes they got destroyed randomly by hungry bigger ones and I felt very very sad for it.

Gabriel touching her shoulder, enjoined,

-Well, you had a busy day and you must try to rest. Let me call Az out. He must be done with Walt by now, otherwise, the man can be counted as down and under...

It looked at him awfully worried. The Angel confided,

-No need to worry, Bambi. The bloody Angel loves that fucking human to bits. He and Wrath are the ones who assigned me to him to be his guardian. He dreads the day he will have to pick his soul up. That human's way of thinking gives him hope for the rest of humankind, somehow. Walter has a voice which will not be ignored, as the Angels protect it with their own lives to last longer than it was meant to be.

In no time at all, Azryel appeared within the room with Walter Workmaster. He swore out loud,

-Jeez, my head is done in for eternity.

Walter going straight to his bed and ducking under a thick duvet commented,

-Just for the night would be good... For myself I will try to switch off, too much to take in, in one evening. See you all another day. Goodnight.

Gabriel turned around and left the room almost abruptly,

-Fine. Let's give the poor man a break. Fighting and then talking with you Az is a deeply exhausting exercise.

Gab gave a little forehead kiss to It-666, saying softly,

-Sorry to have been tough on you today. You do need it though. Badly, very very badly.

Giving him a peck upon his cheek, It replied with an happy smile,

-Ninight, Gab. Looking forward to see you morrow with Bud in toes.

The Angel smiling corrected,

-It will be only with the damn dog. I haven't worked out how to make it follow me by my toes yet.

Az smiled wickedly,

-I did, I busted the training trick. You may see Gab mastering that trick by nightfall tomorrow It.

Gabriel left the room, Walter started to snore loudly, and Az mustered, before closing his eyes

-Another white and sleepless night under way.

He felt his leg touched by a kneeling It-666. Her voice whispered in the dark, pleading,

-Please, Azryel, read me fully.

The Angel put his hands upon her forehead, acknowledged,

-I smell confession is at hand. Are you sure about giving me the full picture? Don't you fear reprisal Being?

Blinking It-666 whispered conscious to not wake up Walter,

-I am sure Master, and that if there are any punishments they will be more than necessary.

Azryel read her thoroughly his wings appearing doing so and his eyes glistening with a rising anger.

The teenager trembled, fear rising in her belly, wondering if her best intentions were the best to really have at that very minute. She was already shattered by the previous punishment of Archangel Gabriel. Could she cope with some more from the most feared of all Angels?

Death answered her anxiety,

-What doesn't kill you makes you stronger, Being.

Then falling into a deadly silence, he kept gathering all the information he could get from the teenage mind of the Beast. After long unnerving minutes, It-666 offered,

-Maybe killing me would be easier than dealing with me? I am very willing to be ended. I won't fight back.

Seizing her chin, the Angel stated,

-You are also very willing to worsen your case for yourself. Can you forget so easily a promise to try to never give up made to Gabriel a couple of hours ago, or were you faking it for him, to be nice and making him hear what he wants? Can you forget your are a soldier in an Angelic Army ought to fight for human's plights in your suicidal whim that easily? How can you forget all those human cries you heard with your really good heart just to get your easy get out? Did you cancel the sound of their voices to a zero level just to cope yourself, selfishly, did you? Yes killing you would be dead easy for me, Being, but as I am the one to deal with you, as I am the one who makes the decisions regarding your life and final moment, I will make sure you have a tough hard life repaying everything you messed up in the world so far. Like Gabriel did supervise his kitchen being fixed back up, I will be watching you like an hawk as I will make you repair your mess worldwide. This is my punishment Being, the worst in your case, as you do not get an easy get away, and you will never get to rest in peace trust me until you clear your path for all your young heart's shortsightedness. Do you want me to restore your full senses or you will put them back on yourself, like a good sensible girl, and live fully as a Being?

A very distraught It-666 stared at him in the dark, as the walls surrounding them bled thoroughly. Death shook his head negatively commenting,

-Big effects will get you nowhere, It. We are not beast-ing our way in Gabriel's house. Can't you get a small lesson properly? Only words and explanations will get you somewhere. Try it, you will feel much better for it, as your energy is running on the low, the walls bleeding might not look as effective to my eyes in a minute or so. Bearing in mind, I might grow insensitive to your plea. Maybe I will switch off all my senses upon you, like you do to the rest of the world, so just try me a little more.

Trying to find her voice, the teenager pleaded desperately, as the walls stopped bleeding immediately,

-I have no wish of trying you, Azryel. Only one to comply with you. I will desperately try words and explanations with you. I did get Gabriel's lesson right through, this is why I am kneeling by you. I listened to all of his advices. I am trying to come clean, trying to get better. I am sorry I asked again to give up. I am scaring myself so much that I cannot help doing so at every opportunity. I want truly to live fully as a Being. But I cannot help to be overwhelmed by my doubts about it. I do not want to mess up, and certainly do not want to mess up the world. I need to fix the blip in my self control asap. I am a very messed up Being, and I am afraid I am going to need help to fix up and learn to cope with who or what I am. I want to help you with all my heart in your mission to help humanity. I might become one of your crappiest soldiers but at least I have good intentions and will try my best to improve and I will tidy any of my messes you pinpoint. I don't want to be blind or deaf, I will be there, fully there, and pay attention to your lessons, I promise. I accept any corrections my old ways brought upon me. I want to repair and fix up desperately.

A blood tear appearing at the corner of her eyes, she stopped talking all of a sudden her voice knotting itself by overwhelming emotions.

Azryel asked sternly,

-Have you finished your plea, Being? Are you giving up on yourself?

Shivering It-666 replied,

-This was my plea, Master. I won't give up on myself. If I die I want to die trying. If I die I want to die fighting your fight for humanity's plight.

The Death Angel smiling finally, commented,

-Then there's hope for you Being. You get to live for another day by my sides. Remember soldier that in this army you are never alone. You will always find help in your struggles. I respect greatly the fact that you chose to be fully read rather than rambling a half baked confession. It shows some strength of character and a clear willingness to come clean. As you knelt, your heart begged me for help in a silent plea. This is what you will get from me. I will help you fix up, It. If you do not let yourself down, I will never let you down. I can see through you and yes there is a lot of mess but there is also a lot of hope and promise. One thing transpires from you, it is a very good and willing heart. We just have to teach it far better ways to express itself and act. As for your self control, your inner struggles I will address them all. We will work upon your every single issue soldier, so don't let them ever stop you on your track. Now stand up, think about what I said and go to bed.

As she stood up, the teenager felt a strange sense of security grabbing her. She wiped her tears and assured,

-Thank you, Azryel. I will not let you down.

-Good. Bed now, and make sure you don't wake Walt up, I do like that human silent as well once in a while, although I respect him too much to force it upon him.

He gave her his wicked grin before closing the door and leaving the room.

Death went to the central platform where Gabriel sitting upon the bench seemed lost in his thoughts. Coughing slightly to grab the attention of the Archangel, he engaged,

-I would have thought you would be exhausted by now after sorting out the mini tornado that ravaged your kitchen.

Gab could not help shaking his head in false desperation yet smiling wildly, replied in the Angelic tongue,

-What the hell did we take on, Az? I just had to ponder about It a little. What about you, I would have thought after talking to Walter you would be desperate to rest a little?

The Death Angel laughed out, taking his cigar box from his jacket,

-In desperate need for a smoke that's all. Workmaster did give me a right earful and headache but apart from that he took in pretty well what I had to say. However, he told me he would sleep on it for tonight, a true Walter-ism as usual, filling me with slight exasperation after the bloody long talk I had with him. Jeez! That's it my hope for recovery is over. I ran out of cigars. Bloody hell, do you think I can ask Hell Baby to make some appear for me? I am pretty certain she could create fire without smoke and smoke without fire if she tried.

The Archangel giggling presented Az with a few packets of cigars from his own lab coat. Cocking his eyebrows with great surprise, Death swore,

-What the hell is happening to you Gab? You are the last Angel I would have thought to indulge in a human vice.

Gabriel corrected him straight away, faking being offended,

-I am still the last Angel that would never indulge in man's bad habits, unlike you, Az. Those are for you, I did not know which brand to get you so I bought all that were in the shop today. I know what a pain in the arse you can be when you are deprived of those five minutes of calm and peace you find in your quick smoking fix. I knew you would run out of cigars soon enough especially with the two we have to deal with at the moment. For my own peace, I did not want to chance a disgruntled Death training Walt and It, and find them obliterated to a lifeless pulp on my way back from work.

Smiling sarcastically, the Death Angel took all the packets, put them in his pockets and lit straight away one cigarillo,

-Kind and thoughtful as usual, Gabriel. I like that. Don't worry, any brand will do stuck in here with you lot, I can assure you. But I must say in your defence that you all surprised me in some way today. When I thought I had seen it all, it's an entertaining discovery to be shown the contrary. Your wrecked kitchen has to be the highlight of my day.

-Jeez, I am glad that the destruction of parts of my house has the capacity to delight you and bring some enjoyment into your dreary eternal life, Az. Just don't let that happen again when you are supposed to watch over that kid from Hell. Bye the bye, I found out that my magical loophole room away from space and time did really protect the human and yourself from the extreme hearing and mind reading of our little Beast for a while. It was a good idea to use that room to give proper privacy to that very needed conversation between you two. If it stops her powers to penetrate inside, I wonder if it has the capacity to withhold them from within too. If it does then we have our perfect training room for It-666 until she learns more control.

Azryel's eyes lit up with glee as he praised,

-Archangel Gabriel, I still have no clue to how your bloody mind works on priorities but from wanting to protect your exquisite tree house to providing me with genuinely genial clues about our well intentioned baby Antichrist is a real treat to hear. I do not know what you did to the girl, Gabriel but she holds you in great respect and more than that. I had the pleasure to read her totally tonight. All of my Angels are reluctant to submit to a full reading, it has to be demanded from them, yet It just offered it to me without being asked. I cannot take that away from her, she is an honest Being. I know that you encouraged her to open up to me, I read it in her, but the way she chose to do so indicates clear respect for Us and true will.

Gab acknowledged with a tinge of sadness within his voice,

-She is a good kid indeed. She is badly messed up though and it's going to be a lot of hard work to get her up to scratch. I am worried about her suicidal tendencies too. I hope Walter can help her deal with them as he had them himself in the past. I am afraid that my harsh talk earlier on when I discovered my kitchen sparked up her massive self doubt about her own existence. I tried to correct those when I made her tidy the kitchen, I am not sure of my success. But I feel that her Being needs a hell of a lot of reassurance. She is so deeply scared of her own self that it is pathetic to witness day in and out. We have to sort that one out, for the sake of that big heart she has. I do not want that one to go to waste. About her respect, she confessed to me this was the main reason she could not fight you properly. That's why she let you kick her arse instead.

Death throwing the ashes from the tip of his cigar and extinguishing them with his Richelieu shoe, went to the corner of the platform and leaned on its wooden railing. Looking ahead of him, staring at the dark woods surrounding them, he seemed lost in his own trail of thought for a few minutes, before he mentioned,

-Do you know what more than respect means, Gabriel?

The Archangel gave Azryel an awfully worried look, begging for more information silently. In desperation, watching the Death Angel smoking peacefully dreaming away for long minutes, he could not help asking wildly,

-It can not be?

Death turned to him with his wickedest smile, making a beautiful full ring of smoke in front of him, diving his index at the top, the ring bent to become a heart shape for a few seconds, before the Angel erased it with his cigar, replying,

-Yes, it can not be. Yet it is the case, as much as It is alive and well sleeping within one of your bedrooms. She might have a thought or two for you, maybe more, it is hard to tell, it is early but it is definitely there. I can assure you, that when I read any heart, I never do my job halfway, as I am a sucker for any traces of it, for the traces of it makes me carry on for eternity.

A dumbfounded Gabriel stood up, then sat back upon the bench, unable to express himself for a few minutes, then asked staring in front of him instead of the scrutinising eyes of Azryel,

-How? I am anal, harsh, OCD, abrupt, meticulous to a T, a f'in loner of an Angel, a pariah most of the time to my own kind, a bloody misfit.

The Death Angel came to him tapping gently the shoulder of the Angel in a falsely reassuring manner, stated,

-You have just answered your own question. Actually, your last word may have clinched the heart of our sympathetic little It. Opposites do attract each other, but also do find common ground, and that one is a big fat one staring in one's face. Now do you want me to get involved or let it runs its course? For the sport of It, this was the cherry on the top of it all.

Gabriel rose to his feet at once, angry with himself, the outside world and especially Azryel,

-Please, do not. She is quite a sensitive and very literal Being. And I freaking do mean it. She could bring chaos into my household in one heartbeat. It must be just a case of simple puppy love. I have a degree in psychology, let me solve that one. No involvement on your part. No cherry to be had at my expense.

Death laughed it right out, put his cigar in his mouth and clapped his hands together, jumping up and down with sheer joy,

-I could have nipped it in the bud for you. I am so glad your priorities lay within your freaking tree house. It will be a great pleasure to see you struggle to keep it standing tall. You are so much my Cherie at this present minute, Gab. Goodnight my Darling, sweet dreams!

Azryel disappeared from the platform to reappear in the bedroom where It-666, her eyes wide opened was tucked up in a corner of her bed. She welcomed him,

-Hi, Master.

The chilled Death Angel sat by her bed side, asked,

-You are exhausted. What can keep you awake so late?

The confiding It-666 replied,

-I am fully switched on. I can hear the pleas of all humans from miles around. It runs deep. My heart is bleeding.

Azryel stated, presenting his hand to shake,

-Join the club, so it should be.

The teenager shook his hand with a good willing smile and ventured out,

-I am also trying to find a way to make it up to Gabriel somehow for my bad blip in his kitchen. But I am stuck somehow on how to please him. Would you happen to know?

The Death Angel gave her his most beautiful grin and replied simply,

-I do. He is very OCD so just live like you do not exist and you will be just fine. No impacts on his home and you can get away with anything, I am sure.

Verse 7. Impact.

A couple of builder's vans arrived at the Mansion of P. Pressing the intercom button at the gated entrance Raphael not leaving the driver's seat asked,

-Troydes Contractors, we have a work to do in one of the bathroom suites, job number H for Hannibal, I for an eye, T for Tango, triple 6 triple 9.

The male intercom voice replied,

-BigBrother4, here, got the clearance and job reference. Remember eye for an eye, we do not want any joker in here nor cowboy builders, keep an eye on your men as I will keep an eye on you lot until you are all done.

Raphael gave a knowing glance at his incarnated Angels at the back of the van with a satisfied smile and sarcastically replied at the intercom,

-No worries, BigBro, I don't tend to hire cowboys, I can assure that those are pure Angels, they even sweep the place clean after a job well done.

-Good. We have an understanding then.

-Definitely

The black gates opened up letting the two vans enter the ground of Paul Peterson's mansion. Closing his window, Wrath finished his sentence,

-Not.

The Angels with wicked smiles upon their faces, dressed in pristine clean builders white overalls, touched each others shoulders, repeating their musketeers mantra,

-One for All, All for One.

All coming out of the vans in a regimented fashion, impressing the major d'homme who held the door of the mansion open, the Angels looked deadly serious and the part. Raphael went to the man servant, stood by him and considered his troupes as they came in with satisfaction, he ordered,

-Lets check that bathroom. Mr Peterson requires us to have a good look at the electrical circuits too. I believe he nearly had an electrical shock this morning while shaving.

The servant agreed, getting restless the more he looked at Raphael, impressed by his unusual beauty and vert de gris piercing eyes,

-That's right it was a very freaky little incident. Master Peterson did not appreciate it at all. He stormed out of that bathroom swearing that he will personally skin all electricians who worked upon the circuits.

Raphael could not help commenting,

-How very kind of him, don't you think?

The man blushed thoroughly, looked around him with anxiety and especially at a particular spot of a rococo table along the wall by them,

-I would not want to say something unkind about my Master.

Feeling his unease, Raphael stroked the beautiful carving of the console table with a wicked smile,

-Very elegant, very chic and grand, your Master knows how to surround himself nicely.

He plucked the mic out of the carved work and broke it into pieces, and told,

-Masters who give freedom of speech are infinitely better, trust me. Would you elect a tyrant at the head of a country if you could think freely?

The servant putting his fingers in his bow tie releasing a little pressure on his Adam apple, whispered,

-I guess I would not.

Raphael gave him his brightest smile, teasing the man further,

-Only guessing? You do not know for sure. Interesting. Maybe you need to be shown the way to freedom. Show us to the bathroom then, we will free your path as we go along.

The shy major d'homme looking helplessly nervous lead the march, pointing discreetly all the way to Raphael and his henchmen at the security systems in place. Swiftly moving up in a debugged Mansion, the Angels reached the suite of the politician.

Shaking awfully the servant took a bunch of keys from his pocket and opened its doors. He watched in great confusion when the henchmen stormed in. Raphael pushing him inside the room with them took the keys from his hands, softly told,

-I am sure you would like to be kept, and kept in.

As red as one could be the man hid his face as he saw Raphael locking the door behind the lot of them. He heard Raphael order his men, then turning to him,

-This is it, children, let's teach that bastard a lesson he will remember. What is your given name, human?

The trembling man managed to mumble somehow,

-Ethan.

Raphael putting his hand on his shoulder strongly, told,

-Now Ethan, you have done very well for yourself so far. Do not intervene and stay put in that armchair in the middle of the room. It will be the safest place for you to be until I say so. Your Master has a real nasty habit to skin humans, and so much more that to come with us at the end of the day is advisable.

The man sitting upon the armchair, gathered his legs up and started,

-Oh my, oh my, oh my...

One of the Angels smashing a large rococo mirror above a mantle piece turned to him barking,

-If you think you lost them human, just give them a good feel.

Raphael slapped the back of the Angel's head strongly,

-If you think you lost it, Angel, I will just give you a good feel of it.

The man witnessed the Angels breaking the place apart revealing everywhere deep symbolic markings on the walls, set in grooves full of a red substance. The more they uncover the more the place stank until he was overtaken by sickness upon the armchair. The very Angel who had accused him to have lost his balls, stood by him with a glass of water and tissues, engaging him,

-Here take, it will only get worst. Many people died under his hands.

The servant felt a knot forming in his throat and took the glass with shaky hands. He saw the floorboards being lifted up, and gazed amazed and aggravated by the collections of human bones littering the whole length of the room.

Erasing any evil markings fast and thoroughly the Angels moved to the bathroom. There Raphael stood for a few seconds assessing the room before ordering,

-We have the resident evil in here: our Beast's big bad daddy. Destroy everything.

All of them started singing in the angelic tongue at once, as they broke every single mirror panel in the bathroom. Bleeding walls stared at them, flies coming from everywhere. Raphael in a grand gesture opening his hands released swarms of bees from each of them, engaged,

-Just try me. I have a message from your dear darling sweet daughter, she is freed from evil. She is pure goodness. Disturb her again and you shall lose all powers of speech. I can guess that it is all you have left.

The most horrid voice made the walls tremble replied, as the bees rampaged the flies to annihilation,

-Wrath, do not underestimate me.

The Archangel burst out laughing, as he enjoined his Angels to rip the floor apart,

-Make no mistake, I do not estimate you at all. How can big evil you can get stuck somewhere? Very challenging, indeed. I like the bleeding walls too, very impressive, do they move or attack?

As he finished his sentence thousands of venomous snakes sprouted from the walls. Raphael looked at his Angels with a slight nod, apologising,

-My bad. Prepare the engine. This house gets to burn to the ground.

He turned back and twisting his knuckles with a big cracking noise, took one snake with his bare hand and strangled it. A powerful light rose from his holding fist which spread across the room reaching every single snake in turn and setting them on fire one by one. He grinned sarcastically, releasing the dead snake upon the ground, which turned into ashes straight away,

-I guess you will have to find another crash pad upon Earth. Difficult when stuck, enjoy the flames, they will remind you of good old hell. Am I not considerate?

The noises of two flying helicopters reached his ears despite the blaze around him. He turned around and enjoined his men,

-Let's split.

One Angel reappearing in the room announced,

-Electrically bugged up, Wrath, job done. Fireworks due in ten minutes. Ashes to ashes.

Another materialised by him, laughing, catching his breath,

-That damn BigBro was hard to lose. I managed to trick him out of the mansion somehow, he is locked outside, Wrath, ready to witness the big blast.

A last Angel teletransported back into the room,

-All safe and secure, Wrath the only human within is Ethan Butler.

Raphael opening the French windows of the bedroom heading to a large balcony ordered,

-All out, right now, in the birds. Ethan, move your arse if you fancy freedom and not being blown into pieces. I told you I will show you the way out.

The man ran with no further ado, rushing to the ladder thrown from the helicopters. Nearly all the Angels had fled the burning Mansion, apart from the Archangel who stepped on the ladder behind him, ensuring the safe climb in mid air of the human.

The flying aircrafts rose back swiftly distancing themselves from the now ardent blaze. As he took a seat by Ethan, Raphael pointing to the house as it blew spectacularly, asked him,

-What about being sure now, human, after seeing the graveyard underneath Peterson's own bedroom?

The man shedding tears, replied firmly

-I definitely would not elect a tyrant at the head of a country as a free thinking man.

The Angels replied all in chorus,

-Amen. It takes a man, a second human and another one to use their free thinking powers to get rid of monsters.

Uncle Wrath touched his Angels shoulders one by one, praising them,

-Not a bad mission. That will teach him not to siege our AA pad ever again.

Wrath cracking his knuckles loudly, added,

-I have a few more blows coming his way if he does not get the message that little It is with Us for good.

In the burning house, the brazing walls kept bleeding badly, yet upon a brick a reptile breathed its first breath. It crawled, its black scales immune to the fire, up until it reached the green lush grass of the ground, then it whistled and whispered,

-O' Wrath, you have been very considerate. Let me show you the full strength of my estimation for keeping my It-666.

Verse 8. Home Coming.

Driving back home in his jeep, Gabriel felt exhaustion setting in slowly but surely. His day at the clinic had been pretty intense and demanding. His sleepless night did not help of course, triggered by the heavy revelation of Azryel about the budding puppy love of It-666 towards him. He didn't know what to make of it at all. Lost in his thoughts, his attention was fully grabbed back when a running white rabbit crossed the road in front of his car. As he pulled the brakes hastily, his head smashed violently upon the wheel. Ignoring his commotion, and the fact that he was badly hurt, the Angel looked with a relieved smile at the side of the road where the creature stared at him with wild scared eyes, totally unscathed,

-Bloody Beast, one of us is safe at least! Lets stop the damages, I need to focus all the way, make it home and finally have a rest. Lets stay awake until then.

Putting the radio on, Gabriel was immediately caught by the news,

-'A large house blast near Boston leaves a suspected seventeen casualties. The only survivor informed that most were builders helping to repair the faulty and old electrical systems of the building. A butler working at the historical house at the time of the accident is suspected to be among the dead. Reports are that a fierce easterly wind is making it difficult for the fire department to extinguish the blaze and that the Mansion locally renowned in the wealthy neighbourhood to belong to up and coming politician, Paul Peterson, has completely burnt to the ground. Also on the news, reports of Hurricane Sandy claims that the super-storm left a further 43 casualties in her path.'

A devastated Gabriel reached the courtyard of his large tree house, worried about the fate of Raphael and its Army of Angels. Stepping outside his car, strange and scary noises came from the living room, fearing the worst for his guests he teletransported into the room at once.

There an unusual scene angered him right and proper where he witnessed a young Beast sitting on a sofa by Walter doing a 360 degrees head spin, with a goofy smile rather than an evil one. Not noticing the Angel standing crossly at the threshold of the room, she enquired eagerly,

-How was that one, Azryel?

The human by her burst out laughing, enjoining the teenager to tap her can of beer against his in a cheer,

-Not bad, it's better but you still can't do the wicked evil grin.

The Death Angel sitting nonchalantly in an armchair, drinking from his silver flask a sip of rum, commented,

-On a scale from one to ten, I would give it an 8. Good effort on technicality but I would agree with the man that it needs tweaking to make us believe that you are really scary. Let's see that scene again Walt, pass me the remote control.

Gabriel glanced enraged at just a few seconds of the film they were all watching as he stepped in the middle of the room announcing his presence by switching off the television, barking,

-'The Exorcist'! You could not show a budding Antichrist a Disney movie, could you? Whose big idea was that?

The Death Angel smiled sardonically stating,

-Great, Kill-Joy is home. No more watching scary movies, children. Gab, calm down, it was both our idea. We thought it would be educational. Walter said it could show the girl what men are really afraid of and believed in somehow, and give her maybe a faintest glimpse or idea of why she had been treated so badly since childhood. I went along with his choices of movies, 'Amityville' and 'the Exorcist', but we counterbalanced them with my choices which we were going to watch afterwards, in the aim to demonstrate to It what bad looks like and then what good looks like. Just take a look of the goody-goody 'Disney' movies she was also going to watch before your impromptu intervention.

At once, spreading the DVD's of 'Bambi' and 'Fantasia' in a single move, Gabriel gave his darkest glance upon Azryel, shouting,

-There are more important tasks at hand than training the girl to become a freak show like I just witnessed. Can she fight fit if Wrath cannot protect her anymore?

Walter contested,

-Well the scarier she gets, the less she is going to get harmed. The more chances she has to survive another day. Show him the wall walk, It.

Gabriel stood forward, his hands upon his hips, dared the young Being, who was about to do it,

-No f'in backward walk upon my wall, like if you were a freaking circus animal It ready to 'evily' impress, not in my home.

The girl stood still insecure and confused. She confessed, smiling still,

-I got 8 out of 10 on the head spin, would you prefer that?

The Archangel seizing her chin, lifting it replied sternly, smelling her breath,

-I would not. I do not like performances, I like true hearts. Your breath stinks of alcohol Being. How many beers did you have?

The teenager had to look backwards by her side of the sofa, counted upon her fingers the beer cans on the floor, and made a half hazard measurement in the air with her fingers,

-Two, and a big bit of a third one. I think.

Gabriel ruled at once,

-You think? You already lost the ability to count? Let me make it clearer for you, Being. You are sixteen and well below legal age to be allowed to drink, human or not. Those two will have to answer for it very strongly indeed. Come with me.

The Archangel teletransported It-666 away from the room dragging her with him.

A stunned girl was materialised by the natural waterfall shower in Gabriel's bathroom. Pushed, fully dressed underneath it by the stern Angel, It recovered her full senses. As her full understanding came back to her, she realised she faced a very angry Archangel. She felt helpless and whispered in haste,

-Please enlighten me Gabriel, I do not know my mistakes. We had a hard training session with Az, and he called it a day at 4pm, asking us to chill out. We watched the horror movies after a small intense debate from Az and Walt. Az was sure he could tell me the A to Z from them all afterwards, to make it all alright. However, they asked me to drink through them for me to chill at the spookiness of them. We all relaxed together. I was asked to perform some feats in the movies, which I did, not wanting to disappoint them. Some I did succeed, some I did not.

Throwing a large towel upon her shoulders, Gabriel started drying her thoroughly as he stated,

-Getting you tipsy to make sure you enjoy or agree with anything is not right Bambi. Because then, your right mind is not fully there to make the call if it is right or wrong for your own liking. Az and Walt are pretty overwhelming to deal with at any time, let alone if in agreement together. Do not let them dictate your path because you do not want to displease them. Think of your own rights and heart. Be your own self. Be your own heart. Azryel is an Angel who saw much for an eternity and did become a little blasé, so much so that his newest pupil, you, may provide him with his newest thrill. You are not there to kill his boredom. Do not let him treat you like a freakish animal that does party tricks. As for Walter, he has been through much and if he indulged his weaknesses, do not follow suit. From anyone you should discriminate what to learn from them. Copying bad habits, encouraged or not, is not clever. You have your whole life in front of you It, do not mess it up by acquiring the vices of others. Alcohol makes you lose control, annihilates your thought process after a while, and knowing who you are, you can only agree with me that you cannot let that happen to you at any point in time. I have seen the damages alcohol did to Workmaster, and I have no desire to see it happen ever again on anyone. Do I make myself clear?

He stepped away from the girl as her beautiful eyes looked upon him with deep intensity, she replied,

-You do. I feel much better, less light headed. But I can see clearly now that you are not well at all Gabriel. The vibrations around you signals hurt and pain. What happened to your head?

Turning around to check his head in the mirror of the bathroom, the Angel realised that he was not alone with the girl as Azryel was standing in the doorway, leaning nonchalantly, smoking his cigarillo, grinning back to him, he answered,

-Nothing important. See, Az, the girl is alive and well, and her head has been screwed back on properly upon her shoulders. So do not mess It up, please.

The Death Angel going to Gabriel made him turn and look at him, commenting,

-The girl is right, Bro, you stink of pain. It is no use lying to me, you have a nice wound on your eyebrow and a very visible bump on the head. Tell me where it hurts so I can fix it for you.

The Archangel tried to brush him off at once,

-It's okay, Az, it will clear on its own. I am p'd off with you right now. How can you be so uncaring when...

The voice of the Angel died all of a sudden, and he brushed away a coming blood tear from his eye.

Death extinguishing his cigar off upon the worktop of the bathroom, reacted immediately, pulling a stool and presenting it to Gabriel, ordered,

-Stop fooling me about and sit down Gabriel. You are completely worked up by something. Are you going to express you guts or shall I reap it from you?

The Archangel sat starting, a slow sob piercing through,

-Wrath and the Army did not make it.

Azriel could not help giving him his most terrible grin,

-Oh, what tragic news. Are they really? Someone must be officially tired, or be officially suffering from a brain hemorrhage. We'd better check that bump, although I am willing to let you suffer your pain and digest it on your own, knowing that you believe I would not care two fiddlesticks for my entire Army let alone for the death of Raphael and that I could have carried on as if nothing had happened.

Gabriel looked upon him totally lost and confused, asked eagerly,

-So Uncle Raphael is safe and well?

The Death Angel smiled at him reassuringly, taking control of the situation at once,

-Babe, get him a glass of water. Formidable Gab has got a big commotion that makes him talk bullshit. Yes, Gabriel, as I am Death I can assure you that nothing bad happened to Raphael and his crew, on the contrary they were very successful. Wrath nearly got rid off It-666's Evil Daddy. But he held to one square inch of his life, and I can feel him crawling somewhere. Raphael managed to dislodge him from P's and destroyed his hiding nest.

When the teenager gave the glass to the Archangel, she agreed with Death,

-I felt it too this afternoon. I had clear visions of what was going on, and shared them to Az. Right now, my father is a black mamba swallowing a rat in a gutter with nowhere to go to until P finds him.

A reassured Gabriel finally smiled back cracking a joke,

-Eating rodents, that definitely must be a family trait.

As It-666 blushed thoroughly, Azryel apposing his healing hands upon the sore head of the Archangel asked,

-What made you think that invincible good old Wrath was finally over? I would have been so devastated if that happened that I can tell you right now you would have stepped into a different scene than us three watching DVDs.

Feeling bad, Gabriel apologised,

-I am sorry for my mistake, Az. It's quite an unforgivable suggestion I made when I start to think about it. I heard the news in the car about the blaze in Boston, it mentioned only one survivor, as a group of builders all died in the house. I thought about Wrath, and got distraught.

Blue lights coming from Death's long fingers penetrated his skull, relieving a throbbing pressure, when he heard his soothing voice,

-Do not worry, Brother, Raphael is strong, well and alive, but more importantly you still have plenty of chances to have a good heart to heart with your Uncle, to clear the air and make up properly. As for suggesting to me that you are unforgivable, when you remember clearly who I am, it is not really advisable. However I will let you off this time around because what you sustained in your 'non important' road accident was actually very serious. I can still feel lots of internal brain damage, yet I am getting there to the root of it. It's amazing that you still had that power to admonish rightly and strongly all of us, like you did. Must be an Archangelic trait you share with your Uncle.

Gabriel blinking a little worryingly at the Angel queried,

-Do you happen to read me and invade my mind while fixing me up, Az?

-Of course I am. Now stopped twisting upon the stool like that, it is a very meticulous operation I am performing here. Trust me. If you put your pants the wrong way around tomorrow morning, don't start blaming me. Stop twitching, I said. I am repairing a lot of your brain cells right now. If I get you right and capture you right, I can fix it right, Bro. Do not worry I will not touch your OCD sides, I will leave them thriving for the plague of all of us.

An exasperated Gab standing as still as a statue upon his stool mustered,

-I swear you will be the death of me, Az.

The Death Angel could not resist the coming tease,

-Stating the obvious, Gabriel, see you still have neurones upside down. I need to get your Archangelic blueprint back in order, it is micro-management skill required here, so shut up for a while, I need all my concentration on that one. And whatever you say, tonight your bed time is fixed at 10 pm and I will have to knock you down to a restorative sleep.

-Bloody hell Az, trust me a little, I know I need a good night rest.

Death scolded strongly,

-Let me ask the same thing of you as I just read you fully. I will not let one of my soldiers toss and turn all night long, killing his

Archangelic self of tiredness to save a little white rabbit crossing his path. I will have to make you sleep upon than one. If you fail to obey that simple order, I will have to use my magical tricks to make the little white rabbit disappear safely into my hands.

Gabriel nodded in agreement silently, yet had blood tears starting streaming upon his face.

A worried It-666 asked him,

-What's up, Gab?

The Archangel wiped his tears up, and replied reassuringly,

-Azryel's brain surgery, little Sis. The blood in there had to leak out somehow. Thinking of you and Walt drinking maybe as well as I know the man gave up and stayed clean for longer he has ever been. As a guardian Angel it means I am facing his relapse. It always gives an angelic heart a blow. Nothing I can't deal with though.

Feeling sorry, It-666 apologised,

-It will not happen again, I promise you Gab.

Death removing his hands from the Archangel's head, pronounced,

-All clear. Ready to go ahead. Let's head to the kitchen Bro, I am starving. I need to watch your cooking skills to check you are right back where you should be. The lethal brain hemorrhage is sorted, yet I may have to get back into it and tweak some more from time to time. Watching your every move will warn me of any more intervention needed.

The Archangel grabbing the hand of It and the hand of Azryel, teletransported them to the kitchen. Gabriel stood there speechless as he saw, Workmaster pouring beer after beer into the sink.

Azryel stated looking at the amount of cans of beer upon the floor,

-That is the entire stack of beer he hid in the woods back in the days when he lived here. He dug them up this afternoon as he saw me being myself, having my regular sips and cigars. I did not address the issue with him at all, I thought I would leave that one to you Gab, as his guardian.

Both Angels turned to the girl worryingly asked,

-Did you invade his free will again?

She nodded negatively,

-No, I only sent him the message that Gab was distressed about him drinking again, after all it cost him, job, nearly life, wife, kid, and the close call to the mental institution.

Death smiled back to her, replied,

-Only? Do you want a job as a guardian Angel? I have enough power to reassign you as the tough one for my soldiers.

Gabriel was by Walter, he tapped gently his shoulder to warn him of his presence,

-Hi Walt, you look like you are on a mission right now.

The man hugged the Angel for a long minute before admitting,

-I am. I feel terrible, more than terrible, cross, very very cross with myself. I have been so good for almost two weeks now and just because I saw Az drinking, I wanted desperately that little chill feel. You know, Gab, although you are not the kind that chills. I thought about what you saw when you came in, about what you said, and I am so very sorry to have inflicted that sight upon you, Bro.

Gabriel sent a warning telepathic call to Azryel,

-My human feels different. He is really sorry Az, that's unusual. I think she is trying to influence the human from within, and it is more than thoughts.

The Archangel demanded from the human to sit down for a while and offered him a glass of water,

-It's okay Walt. Have a sit and a drink, I have been a little heavy earlier. If you are having a relapse, we will deal with it, and make it a very little one, or disappear. I promise I won't use my baseball bat this time around.

The Death Angel inviting It to sit at the table, explained to her,

-Gab has very professional Archangelic ways of keeping his humans in check. Foolproof, it usually works. It is non-invasive, in per say, as it does not mess internally with the free will of the man. Something all Angels have to respect as a golden rule. Intentions of men, bad or good, are solely theirs, not ours to decide. Unfortunately for Us, we are only allowed to influence externally. It requires skills, and patience. It is almost an art form which Gab masters in his own way very well.

Walter sipping his water seemed to gather back his normal mind at once, cynically commented,

-I can only agree with that one, like the famous artist Yves Klein, Gabriel patented a special kind of blue bruises upon my shoulders to the point perfect. I would not dare to call his technique totally non-invasive however as I do remember getting a nasty fracture, the morning after puking all over his living room. But I must admit, it influenced me enough to not do it again. You've just got to love Gab and his good old ways.

Azryel corrected looking worryingly from the corner of his eyes at It-666,

-I would not go that far. Gabriel, did you overdo your looking after of Workmaster? You know there is always consequences for misbehaving Angels.

A sheepish Archangel tried to concentrate desperately on his pots and pans to escape the sudden Death's inquisition, but ventured,

-Somehow I can't recall that episode. Like you said I must have had a worse than expected contusion.

Tapping slowly his long fingers upon the table, the Death Angel mentioned simply,

-I have leeways to make you recall every second of your Archangelic life, Gabriel, if you insist to carry on fooling me, it will only get worse for you. It is always preferable to assume your deeds with me. You know the ways with Angels, my powers of intervention over all of you lot, can be very much internal. Trust me, afterwards you will learn to never hurt that man physically ever again.

Starting to sizzle a stir fry, an unnerved Gabriel surrendered,

-Okay, it did happen a very long while ago. The bat has ever since been used appropriately to teach Micky baseball, and play the game with his dad, repairing their bonds. I felt extremely bad that day and could never end my apologies when I took Walt to the clinic to get him fixed up. Now, it's in our past and we joke about the bat constantly.

Sensing that Gabriel was in trouble somehow for what he had said, the man intervened,

-If it is not forgotten, it is totally forgiven, Az. I can vouch upon Gab to have never suffered about a bat relapse ever since, although he loves to use that threat to tease me to do things his way. He is so convincing when he does it that it does influence me in a good way. Look at the result, I am still alive. I stopped smoking. I may not be a human rights lawyer anymore but I am a good shit stirrer as a Private Investigator, and brought a few people to justice. More importantly, my ex-wife never ceased to consider me as her partner, and I have the joy to be there most of the days when my child is still growing up. I owe to Gabriel more then I can express.

With the nice enticing smell of the meal, Azryel put his decision forward,

-Right, the quality of the dinner will clinch it for you Gabriel. The words of the human gave you a truce on this occasion. However slim, it is only up to you to keep it going. But I must say, you and your food started to mean to me like those two, a proper home. Also your tree house is kind of very cool, although it kills me to admit it. You do mean home, Bro, whether you like it or not. So you must always make sure your arse comes back safe where it belongs. We would always prefer a roadkill rabbit to one jumping about causing more accident on its path. I am sure you could fix up a nice meal of it too.

Verse 9. Hit It Whole.

Within the loophole magical room of Gab's Hall, the training session had started in earnest for a few hours. It was only mid-morning but the teenager felt the full grunt of it already. She realised that Azryel was punishing her thoroughly for all her mistakes and mishaps of the previous day. She had a very hard time explaining all of them to the Angel and just knew they were not easy ones to be forgiven.

Thrown upon the ethereal ground once more with extreme force, It-666 was asked again by a deadly serious Death Angel,

-Can you explain to me again the deadly pretty little white rabbit on the road?

Her heart swelling with sorrow, she tried to stand up only to let herself fall under her own weight. This time something was broken inside her, she didn't know what bone yet, all in the excruciating pain of it. She swallowed her tears to try to give a better reply,

-I was scared of the spider walk scene in the 'Exorcist'. I thought I did not want to scare people like that so I tried to imagine being something else, than the Beast, something cute. As I performed the spider walk trick for you guys, I felt I wanted to be just a few miles away, a nice fluffy white rabbit watching impatiently for the return of Gab, by the side of the road.

Coming to her, walking ever so slowly, with a very slight swing to his stroll, Death falsely soothed,

-fluffy and cute makes it all better, does it? Focusing on being honestly the Beast and crawling backward on that wall, fully being here and there in front of us would have been less damaging to my Archangel, now would it?

It-666, blood tears pooling at her eyes, nodded in agreement,

-It would. I was tipsy and I appeared not on the side of the road but on the road. I ran from the oncoming car. It was Gab's jeep. His wheel went in the ditch as he pulled the brake badly. I watch wildly with a rabbit brain as he lifted his head up from the wheel and gave a smile of relief. I thought he would be all okay. You said I was crap at the spider walk and that recalled me fully in the living room on the wall.

The Angel kneeling by her, sternly asked,

-Where does it hurt soldier? Again expressing yourself at all times is a must. If you are displeased with something asked of you, I'd rather you say so than doing stupid escapism thoughts which materialise elsewhere with potential deadly consequences. You must concentrate on your actions and be fully there at any one time. Do you understand? If I was not there to fix up your mess, Gabriel would have slept away to his death.

The teenager saw him give her his red silk handkerchief to dry her tears as she answered him readily,

-I understand Azryel. I feel so extremely bad to have hurt Gab stupidly like that. After the cold shower, my mind cleared up and I could feel his damages. I love him so so much, he is not even the last I would want to hurt, I would never hurt him.

Recalling her severely, Death stated,

-Yet, you did and you did so very badly indeed. I may have lost one of my major Angels last night. In your defense I partly share the blame, as I should have never allowed you to touch a drop of alcohol. Gabriel's firm talking to you in the bathroom was entirely right. He also knew all along the white rabbit could only be you, when he came home and saw your state, he had his ready answer, hence your trip to the cold shower. I followed as I knew something bad was up, ready to intervene as soon as it stared in my face. Now I fixed my Archangel, but I have still to fix you, where does it hurt?

A worried It looking upon him lost, replied

-My right knee is totally screwed up. Gab knew I was the rabbit, oh my, oh my, oh my... I have to apologise to him.

Healing her knee, the Death Angel reassured,

-You do not have to. His heart has already forgiven you, but not Walter nor myself. Gab and I have good talks at night. He branded Workmaster and I as squalid babysitters during our heated chat which I had to cut short to give him a good deep rest. A worked up Gabriel can go on and on and on.

Azryel smiled to her and helped the girl up, commenting,

-Here we go again, Soldier, as good as new. Ready for another round of explanation regarding interfering with Workmaster's free will?

An annoyed It-666 smiled wickedly back at him, seizing her training shaft, swore,

-I will teach you to preach your own words, Az. Did you shut Archangel Gabriel up last night and send him to a deep sleep, when he could have had valuable words to express to you?

Moving away swiftly the Death Angel, adopting a defensive position, teased her,

-Did I raise up a little Beast by mistake? Has someone finally paid attention to her lessons? Did she finally start to listen properly to what is preached to her? Remember the strength comes from your feet positioning. Be well grounded at all time.

The teenager building upon her own anger tried to manage it to bring more power to her moves. When her shaft attacked, it was good enough to make Death shift from a couple of centimetres away. But his retaliating move made her swing away from the hit by a good metre, she tried to not lose her concentration as she lost ground, by trying to make Death lose his,

-Azryel, you did not answer my question. Express yourself, do you annihilate the voice of your own soldiers on a regular basis? Do they bestow freedom of speech or does Deadly silence rule?

Before she knew it, she was on the receiving end of a full blown attack and it took all of her focus to stay safe throughout. It was well measured, severe and if she wasn't careful, very painful. Death was cool calm and collected as he delivered the blows one by one,

-Humans get freedom, free will and free speech protected by Us. The same golden rule does not apply to Angels. We belong to a special Army with strict rules. I happen to be a general in that Army. I oversee all my soldiers with eagle eyes. My soldier Gabriel's tiredness nearly cost him his life, I was not prepared to risk him again on the road without a proper rest. Especially when a little white rabbit can startle him at will, popping from her magical tricks at anytime.

His last blow grounded her, with his shaft upright upon her neck, as Death commented,

-And one little rabbit gone and dusted. It was much much stronger I must admit. You managed somehow to give me a tiny bruise, it is by no means a feat.

To everyone's surprise, Archangel Raphael and a few of his Angels appeared within the room. Giving a good look around, and witnessing It floored with Death's shaft holding her down, he stated,

-Very disappointing, Soldier It. Death, can she stand on her own two feet sometimes? I have an important mission requiring her powers. Now, I have very grave doubts about her readiness, I may have to use my contingency plan.

Helping It-666 up, Azryel reported,

-She is only a young learning Being, Raphael. Depending on which powers you require from her, I would not myself put her in the forefront. She is getting better day after day but she is far from ready.

The teenager standing by the Death Angel gazed at the scrutinising vert de gris eyes of the Archangel only to bow hers in shame as he stated,

-She smells of trouble. Actually, a bit just like her father before her.

Azryel, putting a protective arm upon the girl's shoulders, posited,

-She is trouble all the way through but full of potential and hope. She has a heart to be respected unlike her father. It is a good damn heart Wrath. I would vouch for her to become a very good soldier one day.

Walking within the white whimsical room, the Archangel changed subject,

-A perfect training room for Beings. You do not know that their anger or upset exist from out there. We met Walter walking his dog in the forest totally oblivious that It was rightly scolded and taught right. Focus and concentration are the aim of the lesson, am I right? The be fully there at all times.

Coming back to It-666, Raphael asked her with extreme kindness,

-May I borrow your fighting shaft, my little Soldier. Because of what happened yesterday Azryel need exactly the same lesson as you do. Watch how it is done and learn by example, It, no one else but me can demonstrate to you that one.

What ensued was a right fight between the Archangel and his general. A tough call throughout, the blows kept coming faster from the Archangel towards his Angel. At the last hurdle, both faced each other with equal strength, yet Death knelt down all of a sudden, offering his all self to Wrath. Raphael smiled winningly turning around his Angel, yet asking severely,

-Did I give you a leisure cruise or a mission?

-A mission.

Uncle Wrath cleared his throat with a worrying noise,

-Pray, why do you treat It like a leisure cruise?

It-666 intervened, putting herself between the Angel and the Archangel, crying out loud,

-He does not! He is tough as hell. With him, Gab and Walt, I learnt more in a few days than the past eight years. I am messed up and do have glitches, my own actions should not be punished upon him or Gab or Walt. I cannot be expected to be dealt with or solved overnight by anyone. If you want to throw a stick, throw it at me, the weakest link.

Seizing her chin at once, Wrath asked her, enjoining Azryel to stand up,

-My dear weakest link, then you need to kneel by me and accept full punishment for all your actions since here, in Gab's Hall. You are only so young. Mature Beings could have looked after you better, that is all.

Kneeling by him, her head bowed down, the teenager replied,

-I am the only one responsible for my actions. I will assume the punishment for them all.

Spitting by her, the Archangel commented, presenting her back with her fighting shaft,

-Somehow I am fairly dubious upon your worth soldier especially when my general told me you were far from ready. I doubt you can take a good old Archangelic punishment in your stride and make something useful out of it. But if it is your will to be punished instead of Death for your erratic ethylic actions so be it, prove me wrong.

The teenager gave a good long anxious glance at Death, before nodding to him, sending him her thought,

-Come what may I should not have been so easily influenced to drink like Gabriel said. I need to think before acting and yesterday I chilled after 4 pm and did not think very much further afterwards. Without you it could have had deadly consequences. Without me it would have been a normal day, a safe ride home. I am taking this one on fully, Master.

Taking the staff she rose to the challenge, putting her feet in position, adopting a defencive posture.

Death presented his shaft to the Archangel, who nodded his appreciation upon receiving the telepathic message of his Angel letting him know word for word what the young Beast intimated to him. Azryel added with a wink to his Master, that he could only recommend her brave character to him, even if it was still very young and tender.

Raphael turning around her kicked her with his fighting shaft correcting her position, repeating some of her words sent to Azryel via telepathy,

-Come what may. Facing you It, all my Angels said it... Now, I had Death doing major repairs on my Archangelic nephew yesterday, which of course does not thrill me with joy. Somehow, your teenage fucked up little brain must understand that, now does it?

Paying full attention to the Archangel moving steadily around her, a blood tear coming from the corner of her eyes, trying to hold her stick with some strength, It-666 answered,

-I understand that fully Uncle Wrath and I am very sorry for it too, very very much so.

Overwhelmed by the strength of her sorrow, the girl knelt, presenting her back and deposited her shaft by her, saying,

-I have no excuses, I am ready to take it all in.

Raphael lifted his eyes to the sky, with slight desperation,

-I would have loved lots of fake excuses to kick your arse about, It. Honesty just kills it somehow. Pick up your shaft, stand up and show me what you have learnt so far. Az, told me you were a reluctant fighter, pacific almost to the bone. Get a grip and prove yourself as a potentially good soldier.

The teenager stood up and rose to the challenge knowing she needed to show all the good work of Az somehow. She switched two notches of her full strength back on, as she applied all her learnt moves to a T. The Archangel could feel a very restrained and respectful novice throughout. He tried to push her about and raise her to use her full power, yet all he got was a powerful Being fully controlled, swerving, swirling, paying attention to his every move and answering them strongly yet respectfully. He could hurt her yet even given the slightest or obvious chances, she would not hurt him. This was the clear respect Death and Gab warned him about.

Wrath put his shaft down and told,

-I have seen enough and in the same time not enough. You are good but not that good at all, if we think ourselves in the middle of a messy battlefield. I will have to take Azryel's word upon you, which is that you are not ready at all.

Putting her own shaft down in a resting position, It apologised to Death,

-I am sorry Master.

Azryel smiled to her knowingly, patting her shoulder, taking her shaft,

-You just proved my point, Soldier. Do not worry, I would only worry if you were sent unprepared to the front.

Uncle Raphael looking at the virgin blank space around him, turned around and sitting upon the invisible ground, announced,

-Well, if that space is not clinical, Gabriel will not be called Gabriel. Azryel, I have decided to still use It on my next mission, however I need you to supervise her throughout.

Death sat by him and enjoined all of the Angels to do so, with It-666 in a make shift circle,

-What is the brief Wrath?

The Archangel started,

-It is clear to me, visiting P's place that some human sacrifices took place there but not all of them, and the traces of the most recent ones, which allowed the Evil Daddy to communicate with his daughter, took place elsewhere. I erased his possibility to do so in that place, burning it with Archangelic divine fire yet we need to destroy the one he used recently. For we can expect that one to be used very soon in a retaliation answer to Us. I suspect that the place under the bunker has been put back into order, as it was erased by natural fast forward means rather by the Archangelic fire. We have to get back there and check the place and woods thoroughly, as it has been used for evil purposes for more than fifteen years, maybe more. We need to destroy that pentagram for eternity. This is the mission.

Having listened very attentively, Azryel commented,

-That should be a walk in the park, well woods. Why involve It when we could do the feat ourselves?

Raphael standing up, went to the middle of the circle, explained,

-Because for what I have in mind, a proper lesson to P, I need a little seismic input from It-666. It might also give her a chance to have her final answer to her Evil Father, that his ways to feed on human sacrifices doesn't agree with her. I am also giving that soldier a chance to redeem herself from having messed up one of my Archangels stupidly yesterday, by cutting all possible means of communication Evil can have with her, in front of Us.

All Angelic eyes turned to It. They did not have to wait long as the teenager stood up and came by Wrath, kneeling by him,

-I am your soldier. Giving me my own voice and the chance to stand against the terrible scheme of my Father is more than appreciated. He needs to be stopped at all costs. P needs to be stopped just as well, with all his followers. I am feeling a very active one somewhere, trying to get P reunited with my Father.

Azryel rose to his feet and coming to It, lifted her chin up and demanded,

-Let me see all his followers, Soldier, particularly that one.

The girl nodding her agreement at once was read by the Death Angel in front of all Angels who shivered for her. When he had finished, he gave the result to Archangel Raphael,

-The individual in question is a very serious threat indeed. She is a Cambion, who has been walking upon Earth for the past 400 years, escaping narrowly her execution during the affair of the Poisons in 1670's France. I am very interested to find out the secret of her longevity, even half demonic, she should not have escaped my hands. We will definitely need to hunt those followers down to the last. They did all frequent the woods of the bunker the night when Evil daddy made his call to It. So that place is definitely a hot spot for them that needs obliteration. This is the right target, Wrath.

Noticing how easy it was for It-666 to get a full reading from Death, the Archangel helped her upon his feet impressed and teasingly asked,

-Aren't you daunted by those reading, Being? They can get you torn apart, do you happen to know?

The teenager replied confidently,

-In my shoes, I rather be corrected than not, come clear and clean rather all goes big bang, if I did not mention one little mess that did happen, it could turn to be a big fat one for World's order. Death's readings are more thorough than how I can express myself. I find it the safest way to deal with me. As Walter says: you learn by your mistakes. Gabriel would add: in front of Death the safest path is coming clear and clean, and Az himself would state that what doesn't kill me makes me stronger. I kind of agree fully with all of them.

All the Angels smiled to her, standing up at once and went to tap her shoulders in a brotherly fashion, welcoming her,

-If you only learnt that with Azryel, then you have learnt something that we are all still learning.

-That is no mean feat, Kid, what you just did.

-You are a brave little one, if you do not know that.

-Impressed.com, you are one of Us.

-Looking forward to see you fight with Us on the battlefield, It.

-Bear that before being all Evil, your Father was good, extremely good. He may just have tapped into his older stronger self to create you, and that would explain the way you are, Kiddo.

-Defo, I agree with that one.

It-666 looked totally lost for a second, but her hands were grabbed by Wrath and Azryel who invited her to sit down at once, as Archangel Raphael started,

-We are very much aware that you do know absolutely nothing of your parents, Soldier. However we can enlighten you now about one side of your family until he was lost to Us. Let me tell you know that he was a very important Angel prior to his fall, and that the cause had to do with great pride on his part and the establishment of laws for humans. He was demoted to hell to rule after demons. Demons are punitive kinds which can be good and have their uses. Some, evolved to influence earthly humans to prove the point your father was making all along that humans should never have been given free will. However free will opened the future for all of Us, when closing the door upon it imposed doom and fate. Demons influenced religious human writings to create rules which originally did not exist, creating boundaries, inflexible customs, alienating one from another, and the price to pay was a human death toll, regular genocide, one believing they knew more than the other, imposing their rules, killing more heartlessly. And in order to create chaos upon Earth, he used the golden rule of free will, he created cultures with so many intricate rules that the original human heart would be purely lost into conflict with one another, not recognising the essence of any man or woman. The inherent goodness and love got lost in dictations, rules, and started stoning any who differ from their own views in good faith, diabolical indeed. They are all right and they are all so wrong because they are all so human. But we Angels know otherwise yet your father's work is a very intricate web, it goes very deep in history, so underground that a new outburst almost always caught Us by surprise. We, Angels had to start walking upon Earth undercover in incarnated human forms to start to understand the full implication of everything your father was doing. By the time we walked upon the scene the trend was set to get worse, as the Word of whoever, had spread differently for years, and kept bursting unannounced in another stronger way that decided to annihilate any other ways as they were the only way. Earth became a war zone of 'righteous from any kind' killing each other. The voice of the sole human heart was lost. But we decided to fight back like your father did with Us, we started to influence humans with our ways, teaching them to listen to their own heart once more, and the bill of human rights finally came to life. Forever evolving we are trying to deal with every single issue in it, that your

Father threw at humans with his tremendous influence. Somehow lately, I feel your Father has been channelled to a mere voice. My last encounter with him saw him diminished to stay still behind mirrors and bleeding walls. These occur when you are upset, cross or sad?

It replied straight away,

-The all tutti quanti. The walls are bleeding from deep sadness, from sheer upset and being cross but not letting it spread further. I can tell you right now that my Father is really diminished. You forced him to his last possible living form, a snake. This is not his form of choice, it was dictated by P and the Cambion, for their black masses. It is the only living form available to him. I feel him stuck in a very powerful spell. This could explain why he is still in a gutter right now and not going directly back to P. You may have unwillingly given him a getaway Wrath, from where he was stuck.

Her information took the Angels by surprise but not Azryel. The Death Angel proposed,

-If a demon and a halfling can imprison Evil for years, and get him stuck in an almost harmless form, bearing in mind we have a black mamba on the lose in Boston who happens to be a fallen Angel disliking human kind very much, why can't we do so ourselves?

A plethora of Angelic voices replied to Death with sheer fright,

-How?

-Why should we do so?

-Great, who wants to have a pet black mamba, guys? He can bite your hand as you feed him and there goes your eternal life an hour later. Any takers?

-How to keep him harmless? How to keep him away from humankind for good?

Raphael raised his hands up to silence all voices at once. The order was immediately executed. He asked Death sternly,

-Did you ever think through your suggestion, Angel?

Azryel replied strongly,

-No, Master. It is a suggestion which can be built up to a valid plan only with the input of all of Us as the task suggested demands all of our involvement. Yet Gabriel built a loophole from space and time, where the powers of the daughter of Evil can not leak out from, where all of us standing there are away from humanity's awareness. We may sit in the very room where we can keep Evil from Earth and from having an impact. Only his guardians can not be mainstream, yet it took only two thorough Evil doers to achieve the feat. I am asking for hearts well hanged for the worst. I am asking for to the bravest of Us to come forward.

Nodding in agreement the Archangel, however ruled,

-Let Azryel's ideas rest with you all. Think about them, add upon them, build upon them. Any Angel that come to me with an input will be more than welcome. Somehow in my opinion, if a Cambion witch and a Demon can keep Evil for a few punters for years, the same feat if not a better one can be achieved by Us. It will involve great risk to any who come close to the sooth sayer, so any that come forward need to be sound. For now, we have a mission to do ASAP, we need to erase from Earth the place where humans get slaughtered to feed Evil's worship. Someone else's words did not have to be a solemn truth yet again, which was followed by heartless sheep. Let's correct that once and for all and follow our own hearts.

All the Angels stood up joined hands with Wrath, It-666 and Death and teletransported to their new port of call, their new mission.

Verse 10. Sink or Swim.

Hardly any leaves were left in the forest on the deciduous trees, however the pines provided green and grey dark shadows aplenty. The Army of Angel, Archangel Raphael at its head, Azryel and It-666 by his sides materialised in its deep heart.

Wrath enjoined his troops, then the young It.

-Let's find that damned place again. It, if you can track it down for Us, it would save an enormous amount of time.

The teenager came to Raphael at once,

-Follow me, Wrath.

She went forward upon an unbeaten track, which left all the Angels following worried, apart from Death, who calmed their anxieties, with a wicked grin,

-Do not worry we will be there in no time at all, we have got the ultimate nose with Us, better than a hound she is the Beast. She usually switches off that sense especially in contact with smelly humans, like good old Walt. When it is on, she has the whole county in her nostrils, all living beings big and small up to the tiniest microscopic compound which eat dead flesh away slowly.

Raphael winked at his Angels while trying to keep track of It and Az,

-Well as long as Super nose is Super Nice Puppy, we are going to be alright, aren't we guys?

When he finished talking he bumped into a still and shivering, blood crying It. Azryel pulled him aside of her, waving to him to not talk until he did so. Looking at Death, she pointed to a large clearing, trying to find her voice,

-There. It is still fresh. It stinks of human death, blood, bones, flesh. I have visions of the last feast, it was atrocious. Most of the humans however were killed independently by the followers who brought a part of them to feed Him. Only one was slaughtered upon the site during that ceremony, I can still feel her heart beating in his mouth, she was only nineteen.

She knelt and blood tears appeared at her eyes. Death put his hand upon her shoulder, soothing,

-Please, do one thing for me, I know that scene, very well. I collected her that day. Please, help Us destroy it so I do not have to collect any souls from here to be lost. Dry your tears and fight. Express your upset and destroy his feeding ground. Clearly like Us you have enough of it and it makes you feel sick. Put a stop to it for you can, my girl, you can, like Gabriel says listen to your heart.

It-666 stood up, her eyes lit up in a strange eerie manner, she held his hand strongly before turning towards the Archangel Raphael. There she stood and simply said,

-I am at your orders Wrath.

Raphael could not help question the determination of the girl,

-Are you sure It? There will be no way back from Us.

It-666 looked at all the Angels in turn, at Wrath, at Death and then at the place where she lived for eight years, her shit hole underneath the ground beneath the pentagram, her voice rose full of anger and expressed,

-Let me express my wrath right now. I am sure of It. If the way back means being in a small cage where I am the Beast to fear, the circus freak to let out once in a while and to have human blood drooping on my shoulders, I say hell no. I say let the blood of humans run in their veins to live forever, and let me be the freed one to help achieve this, and say to my father I am not a Hell monster, that I have a freakin' heart that only listens to love and no cruelties. I will fight any cruelties done, Wrath, with you and your Angels, all the way.

Raphael embraced the girl at once, Azryel followed suit and all the Angels started singing a strange song. Their tongues drumming a beat in their palates, they invoke for Wrath's Words to bring Justice, in the Angelic language.

As soon as Wrath rose his voice the full pentagram lit up upon the ground with Archangelic fire, when he took Death's hand, souls started to rise from it and lift to the heavenly sky high above, when he seized It-666's hand, he simply asked her,

-Make it past, It. Make it disappear underground. Clean and clear this place. I am thinking giant sinkhole full of water, irretrievable for P and Evil Dad to do their deeds. If your little prison cage is still in the midst of it all, make it sink to the heart of the Earth, open it and let it sing the words of freedom for all humanity.

It, nodding, demanded to all Angels,

-Everyone is to stand behind the line of trees for I am clearing the whole area. It was consecrated and if any piece of that ground remains, sacrifices would still happen there.

Wrath ordered everyone to move behind the line, as he did so, he watched in awe as It levitated above the ground, in a lotus position. By his sides, Death whispered to him,

-I am attuned to her right now. She told me to do so to intervene if she was doing anything wrong. She is taking on the wrath of all who passed away above that pentagram to make it sink right down. So far she has gathered everyone's.

The effects started as soon as she sang a strange song. It was her usual soothing song the one which normally controlled her, but this time with some notes and words, syllables inversed. It brought the collapse of the area surrounding her. A giant sink hole swallowed

her past, the pentagram, and freed the future of any human
sacrifices in that area.

As all the Angels sang Wrath's song the sink hole started to fill with
water. It walked upon the air back to them, she knelt by Death, took
his hand within hers and confided,

-The water is made of the victims's tears, and the tears of all their
loved ones, mothers, fathers, brothers, sisters, sons, daughters,
husbands and wifes and betrothed. The Archangelic tears of
Gabriel are overwhelming. It fills a hell of a lot, and they have not
dried yet. Workmaster's ones are there also.

Azryel stroking her hand, held her tight, announced,

-That's because Wendy, Workmaster's twin sister, and fiancée of
Gabriel died here. Gab has been inconsolable ever since.

Looking back to the sink hole filled with water, It stood proudly,
and told,

-The bastards that hurt people can't use that one anymore, that is
gone right down and under. The wood stinks of hurt and pain,
Soldiers, every single tree, shall we clear them too?

A worried Death asked her,

-What do you mean, Soldier?

The teenager pointed to the nearest tree to her and a little leather
bag hanging from it near to its top,

-Those are everywhere. They are overwhelming me. They are
hanging bags of human skin containing a single part of the man or
woman they came from. The entire wood is a cemetery of human
parts not buried humanly. I smell all of them and my heart bleeds
for them Az, just bleeds, and it hurts, it is so painful what every
single one of them went through.

Suddenly her eyes turned demonic, scrutinising the trees, she turned to Wrath and Az at once, a note of sheer panic in her voice,

-We are not alone. Get everyone ready to fight, Wrath. There are Demons up in the canopy lurking at Us, waiting to attack.

The Archangel gave a single whistle which gave the alert to all Angels to be ready. As the Angels got themselves prepared immediately, Az turned to It quizzing her for more information,

-What do you see up there, Soldier? How many are there? What kind are we fighting and how are they spread in the woods? Transmit the details to all Angels via telepathy.

The eyes of It went from black to red in nanoseconds. She turned around herself scouring the forest, and sent all she could gather from the surrounding woods to the Angelic Army,

-It looks terrifying from where I stand, every single tree harbours two demons. They are everywhere in the woods, in great numbers. We just closed their portal back to Hell. They are going to be fierce upon Us and there will be no quarter given. That is all I can get from their intentions, apart from that they are sending the smaller ones in each tree to fight first, the second wave will come later with the larger demons to do the final slaughter. I didn't grow up in Hell Az, I know freakin' nothing about their kind. The smaller ones look spider like, they move fast and silently, they are lethal, each are guardians of the human remains in the trees. Do not let them sting you or bite you. The others have the shapes of gorillas, but double or triple the size for some. Do not think for one second that their bulks render them slow for as I see them moving they are swift, supple and the strength in their muscles is so much so that I am shitting myself right now.

Az tapping her shoulder enjoined her,

-You will do nothing of the kind, Soldier. You stay aware and strong at all times. You stay with me, I will look after you and protect you. Mimic my gestures, act in tandem if you can and if you are brave enough you will slaughter your very first demons today.

The Archangel made a few coded signs to all Angels for all to regroup together, as they did, they finally witnessed the first moves themselves coming from the canopy. Some took a deep breath, some looked wearily at one another, when Wrath suddenly asked the teenager,

-You are a portal yourself It, remember on your first outing you brought demons from Hell and put them right back in there afterwards. Can you concentrate on sending those back in there rather than shitting bricks, right now.

The girl nodded straight away, she dived her hands deep in the mud up to her elbows, whispering odd guttural words. As she did so the spider like demons appeared from everywhere crawling from the trees down to the ground leaving a silky sticky slime behind them.

It-666 warned immediately, carrying on her task yet keeping an eye upon all,

-Whatever you do Angels do not put a hand or a foot in their trails. It will glue you to it like a pray, and the demons will devour you alive.

Wrath shouted,

-Listen to the kid, and remember, all for one and one for all.

For a frightening moment all were engaged at once by the multiple insect like creatures, but then It stood up, her hands on fire as she called them to her in a powerful out of this world voice. They rushed to her as fast as they could. A great ball of fire engulfed them all, coming from the girl's hands. As she rose her hands, the spider demons lifted off from the ground within the fire ball, when It plunged her hands back deep within the ground, all of them disappeared swallowed with the fire inside the mud.

She rose to her feet very unstable, announcing, by the sides of the protecting Azryel,

-I hate spider thingy things of any kinds. They can't complain about not being in Hell anymore, they are deep within the hell fire, as I did not watch their landing closely... Or actually I made sure they had a heated reception. I do not know, anymore. I am drained. Keep watch on the grizzly gorilla demons...

Collapsing by Death, the teenager fainted. Wrath ordered,

-Keep the ranks. Be prepared for the next wave of demons. Az, focus on that soldier, get her into some sort of shape, before the final attack. I need her standing on her own two feet, ready to fight. I do not want them to pick her up like a dead weight easy to abduct.

Death put is healing hands straight upon the girl's heart sending blue energy in waves, his voice almost growling with annoyance,

-Come on, Soldier, where is your f'in strength and stamina? Wake up It, wake up dear girl. I need you strong right now, Soldier, right now the nasty ones are coming down from the trees. If you do not stand up now, it is going to go pretty ugly for you. If they get their hand on you, they will eat your heart out Being. Wake up.

He could feel her energy slowly reestablishing itself within her numb limbs, but it was far too slow for his own liking. He sent his biggest burst of living angelic energy to the teenager so far, unable to know if it was right for her and her strange metabolism, yet he decided to follow his own heart which was to make sure It would stay safe all the way through her first battle. He had to recall her at all costs.

When Wrath asked him hastily,

-How are we doing down there, Soldier? Any luck?

Azryel saw It's big eyes open full of angelic light within them, beaming sky high, he announced to Raphael,

-She is full to the brim with Angelic energy right now. I went a little heavy handed upon her Raphael, and I have no clue at all how it will turn out in her body.

They witnessed It glowing from every pore, as she asked them, bewildered,

-I feel more than myself, what happened?

Wrath gave her a wicked smile,

-What happened is simply Az's doing. You've been given a temporary Angelic lease of life. Now, Soldier, do not mess it up. Stand by him, do not get abducted and fight for your life, simple as A, B, C. You will learn quick, I am sure as the nasties are here, and oh gosh you were right, they are huge beasties.

It-666 could not stand up fast enough, to face the incoming danger, a quick look at Death, reassured her somehow, as he said swiftly,

-I am going to watch over you soldier, be my shadow and you will be fine on this fun outing. I will make sure it becomes a walk in the park for you, little one.

He produced a fighting shaft out of nowhere for her, while his deadly silver scythe appeared in his hand. He gave a final exhortation,

-Be focused, be there, be aware of everywhere, fight off, save your skin and the one of others if you can.

The first beastly demons arrived upon them. Death sliced two right away, while It using her wooden shaft felt slightly under-geared in face of the opposition. Anger rose within her and her shaft slowly but surely transformed itself the more she used it to fend, counter and attack. It became heavier within her hands, yet more effective at its every blow. She was amazed at the accuracy of Azryel. He was ever so deadly. She felt grateful to be by him fighting. When she missed the focus on one demon, when one would crop up behind them, when one would fall upon them from the canopy, the silver scythe of the Death Angel would be swift to respond in a deadly manner.

Suddenly she realised that Wrath was under severe attack in the middle of the field. Sending an immediate call to all Angels, she went towards him without thinking following her own heart. She saw four Angels by him in deep struggle. Her shaft became deadly within her hands, as at both tips silver blades appeared. Strong swings and silently moving forward in a deadly motion she got rid of their opponents in very few spare moves. By Wrath she used her shaft as she did in her training session with Azryel, yet her full powers were fully switched on and directed solely to the enemy.

Raphael could not help but welcome her intervention,

-It, aren't you suppose to shadow Death in your first real fight? I like your moves, they are quite welcome right now, but I am not one you can shadow easily. You just need to fight your own way by me, and you are not ready Baby, so get your arse back to Death. He is your Watcher and teacher.

She slaughtered a demon in front of him skillfully, before mentioning,

-Watch your back!

Before the Archangel could react she had thrown her fighting shaft like a javelin killing the demon behind him.

She grabbed her shaft back, and disappeared without a word within the mayhem back to Az's side. He smiled as he saw her back within his sight,

-That was quite a performance you pulled out there, Soldier. A good needed and helping hand, how was it received?

It shrugged her shoulders, as she erased another demon with her shaft's improved blades,

-I am still a baby for Wrath, and I am still f'in not ready. I am stuck with you for a while Azryel and you know what, it is an honour to fight with you, a real honour, and if I die by your side, Death Angel, my wishes would have come to pass. However I want Us to fight for a very very long while, I want to see you winning gloriously every time like you do.

Death smiling and swirling his silver scythe in a deadly stroke beheading three demons a once, replied,

-Truly, It, are you aware about making Death wishes directly? I have to take into account your very very long while now. The motion is going to pass at the next scythe strike.

As his next strike cut one demon into half, Azryel spelt out the deadly sentencing words of It's wishes, in the Angelic tongue.

Somehow, suddenly all Angels appeared to win in every corner of the woods. The sarcastic laugh of Death resonated, as he finished all the demons off by himself or almost.

When his silver scythe finally posed to a standstill, he watched his entire army alive and almost well except for five walking wounded. An exhausted Wrath enquired,

-Az, what got into you? You nearly killed them all off by yourself.

The Death Angel smiling endlessly, replied,

-I know I did because someone unwittingly triggered a Death Wish forward, somehow at the right time. It is a very hopeful one which implies the sheer longevity of Us. It came to pass within my hands. This is the outcome, and will be so for a very long while. Make the most of It's wish.

Wrath coming to the teenager, shook her hand, and acknowledged in front of all Angels,

-Soldier, in this mission, you earned your colours. You are truly part of Us. You are a wee bit too young for Us, but you are a true Hell Baby, you can, and do kick arses. Under the guardianship of Azryel, I have no doubt that you will amaze all of Us like you did today in our next battles. I will not spare you Soldier, you proved yourself to me, expect to be used by Us fully in battle. You can swim, Soldier and it was beautiful to see it happen. By the way, your sinkhole is just awesome, I think P and Evil Dad won't be very cheerful about it. Well lets see if they can sink or swim, shall we? The bets are open.

Smiling proudly It did not react when the Archangel took her fighting shaft from her hands to consider it carefully, asking,

-Where does that deadly toy come from?

Coming by him, Azryel inspected the shaft with a very pleased grin upon his face,

-It comes from me. I did not want to let my little erratic Beast of a pupil use her obliteration powers that she doesn't know how to control yet. However she has had a fair few sessions with a fighting shaft now, and she has acquired a few good moves especially defensive ones. As I needed her to protect her own small arse a little I gave her one of my favourite toys, the magical fighting shaft. It listens to its owner to become fit for his/her purposes at any time. You simply need to hold it and it will react to the purpose you need it to have at that precise moment, attack, protection, heavier, lighter, the list is endless. In the case of our little It, she started with a simple wooden shaft which slowly but surely evolved during battle, to the lethal silver implement we have here. This indicates to me that she learnt a valuable lesson today, pacifism sometimes is not applicable when your own arse is on fire. I am glad she did not turn her butt cheeks to the enemies for the slaughter, and that she finally kicked arses when needed.

Whistling a rallying call, the Archangel could not help commenting,

-I like that, Azryel, I like that very much. It's educational, it's purposeful and quite lethal in well trained hands. I could see that kind of toy being given to all my Angels for the future fights coming. I doubt very much it is going to be our last lot of demons to tackle unfortunately, especially with the little deadly Messy Missy with Us.

As he spoke, It-666's eyes turned demonic once more. Standing as still as a statue, she sent to all of them a chilling telepathic message,

-It's not over. Be on the ready.

Wrath looked at her, impressed by her strange capacities to feel her surroundings, yet he intimated to her with a tinge of amused desperation in his voice,

-Not again! Be precise, Soldier when you are doing that to Us. It helps Us to be spot on.

Her eyes turning from pure black to red, It walked to a dead demon, dipped her finger in its opened wound, licked it and lifted it to the air, scanning the woods. A disgusted Archangel could not help commenting to his troops and Az in particular,

-I wish she had not done that. We will see the result of the operation. Azryel, try to educate a little Angelic manners in that strange soldier of yours in the future. It can only help her integrate, I am sure.

Ignoring him, Death came by It, putting a reassuring hand on her shoulder. As he gave her fighting shaft back into her hands, he demanded,

-What is the score, Soldier?

-There's only four of them, the Beastly type, one small and three very large ones. They are planning to attack Us as we move along in the woods, an ambush. At the moment they are grouping East of Us waiting for Us to make a move, about fifty metres away.

Her telepathic information reaching every single Angel were welcomed by Wrath who ordered,

-Let's give them a good run for their money, Soldiers, full on attack. Watch your step and that silky slime as you proceed. No fighting, I reserve my right on the smallest one.

The Angels charged the corner at once with Wrath, while Azryel keeping It by him, and the wounded ones, told,

-You all stay put, my lot. It, adopt a defensive position Soldier, you guard them with me with your whole life, understood?

She nodded to him as she saw him positioning himself protectively of the five wounded Angels behind him. It-666 imitated his intimidating posture. She could hear Wrath slaughtering the remaining demons, but two massive ones headed their way to them. She could see from the corner of her eyes a cool, very calm and collected Death, while her heart feared for the wounded. She recalled herself as one demon tackled her full on. She had to stop him, she could not let it pass. She had to be a wall of strength to protect them at all costs. Suddenly her own fear channelled into her shaft, which the demon was holding ever so strongly in an immobile horizontal position. She swore as the demon vanished in a pile of dust and ashes, combusting as fast as the blink of an eye,

-You shall not undo me. I shall be your undoing.

Azryel holding the decapitated head of his demon stood by her with a deadly grin,

-Learning fast your lines, It. You just managed to channel your powers into that shaft, full of concentration and purpose. Very effective, child, I must get you a blue peter badge for that one. I thought it would take you another year to learn that skill. It is called controlling your own powers with one effective aim, protecting and saving. Well done, Soldier, you just helped to save five valuable Angels.

When Wrath headed back to the group, with his own troops intact, he asked,

-Death, what are the damages? Two leaked out from Us.

The Death Angel reverting to his human appearance, took a cigar out of his silver box in his smart white jacket, lit it coolly in front of a worried Wrath, taking a puff, he stated with his wickedest smile,

-When I thought your mission would be a walk in the park, Wrath, we have five wounded, but they are still with Us. Our youngest recruit can swim very well in the deep end, I must admit. Her heart is well hanged, she passed our test. Level 1 complete, Introduction to Deep Water Skills.

Verse 11. Involvement.

Within the darkening woods, Azryel was working hard mending the five Angels wounded. It, by his side and under his guidance performed some curing tasks, helping him out. Wrath had scoured the entire woods with his Angelic Army before coming back to them, announcing,

-The entire woods are clear of the demonic silky slime. We need to find a way to hide the Beasties to human eyes though. They are massive, corpulent and lying dead everywhere.

Az, turning to Raphael concerned, asked,

-You are not thinking to open up those woods to humans any time soon, are you Wrath? Or has your mind just gone walkies?

The Archangel blasted at once,

-My mind is thinking fast forward and not backward, Angel. I am working at the undoing of P on two planes: The human one and our one. Whichever way it comes, he will feel the full blow of Wrath.

Azryel focusing on repairing the shoulder of one Angel, demanded,

-How does your full blow work, Wrath? Surely you do not want your back front missing the plot, do you Archangel? I had Gabriel distraught thinking you were obliterated with your Angels only a day ago. Clear communication to Us is a must at all time. Channelling the visions of little It, will not suffice me to keep my crew up to date. It, work something upon the Beasties if you can, make them less demonic and more natural on that forest floor. Do not make it obvious, Soldier, we are not creating a theme park to deadly woods here.

It-666 went to the first dead demon she could see, and tried her hands at it, followed by a few worried Angels.

Raphael watching her from afar, replied to his general,

-You have my apologies, Az. I am forgetting you have three of the most challenging individuals under your belt. Gabriel upset at my loss that's news to my Angelic ears. I always thought he would rejoice upon my grave after I pushed him away from my Army as a miscreant.

Death shook his head sternly scolding the Archangel,

-Gabriel is the least miscreant of Us, Wrath. His heart is sound, I can tell you that much. That Archangel has got glitches, but so few and far between, that it is truly negligible. You need to allow him by your sides, and let him talk his heart to you. You would be impressed by how far he has gone, on his own, alone, with just his heart to carry him through, despite our Angelic ostracism. We did hurt him thoroughly, Wrath, so much so I regret all my deeds done to Gab at your orders. I never regret Wrath, but for the very first time, you made me do so.

Wrath sat by his wounded soldiers, changed the conversation at once,

-How are they doing, Az?

The Death Angel giving his darkest glance to the Archangel replied coolly,

-They are stuck with me for a good while and so are you Wrath until you answer me fully. Let me prevent you from digging yourself a deep ditch underneath yourself, Wrath, help yourself and come clear and clean. Talk to me.

Raphael shook his head helplessly, surrendering,

-Okay, you have got your wish Death, I will talk to my nephew, Gab and have a heart to heart with him.

Azryel smiling, lifting himself up shouted across the field,

-That's a good one, It! You've just got it. That bleeding demon turned stone cold, right down to a molecular level. Try to be bespoke to the natural geology of the site, and you will definitely rock Hell Baby.

Turning his whole attention back to Wrath, Death commented,

-Good. The timescale has changed Wrath with It upon the scene, I need you to be fully conscious of it at all times. Any heartache issues need to be dealt with ASAP. Do not let any family members unaware of your love if you do have it for them despite everything you deem wrong with them. The judgement for harsh treatment of your next of kin is going to be devastating. You will feel the full blow of it. Sort it out.

Death's threat did not go amiss with Wrath who asked worryingly,

-What's up Az?

-The giant clockwork had It's disturbing beat. It went to another mode, which is far less forgiving, it will work like a countdown unless we disable it.

Raphael looking at all his Angels answered unphased,

-I will get mathematician Gab to the task. How are our woods looking?

An Angel came to him, giving him a report,

-Young It is doing wonders, Wrath. She is thorough to the point Az made. We have giant shapeless stones forming everywhere. To human's eyes they will just look like boulders.

Azryel asked again,

-Wrath, explain to me why humans need to step in those woods?

Pointing at all the little bags hanging in every tree above them, the Archangel mentioned,

-There's a lot of loved ones involved. I am getting the states spies in for a human investigation on P. They will forensic all of those, give them back to their families, to be laid to rest in the appropriate manner depending on their background.

Death nodding his full agreement only commented,

-For once, very thoughtful of you, Wrath.

Raphael explained his full scheme, as far as it went to his general,

-P took a very cheeky stance, telling that we were dead at his home in Boston to explain all the bones to be found in his bedroom. It came from his spoke person none the less. It took an engaging twist to encourage everyone to check that their electricity circuits are up to date and safe. He still wants to run for the next presidential. I am not going to let that happen. I had one of his butlers file an anonymous tip about him, to the police. Bones at P's home are now being investigated to determine their sex. If they are all male, it was the builders crew burning to death kind of proof, as we know, it was not. Evidence will start building his case, slowly but surely. Those woods are going to be very damaging to his reputation just as well. My aim is to prevent him from running for a presidency that could impact the world.

Death gave the all clear to the Angel, he mended, who stood up and thanked him respectfully. He went to another of the wounded Angels, assessing him fully, before mentioning to the Archangel,

-Thank you for finally letting me in on your plan and scheme Wrath. Better late than never, I guess, you need to work on getting your communication skills up to scratch from now on. If I am to be your back up, make sure I do not arrive on your scene when it is too late for you and the Army. Now, I think that your human plan with P is very well thought out. Bringing him down from his politician pedestal on human terms and prevent him running for presidency will bring to my crew, Walt and Gab, utter glee. They have been working upon P's case for ages, and I can only recommend you to get from them their tedious gatherings and evidence. You might get some very good gems in there to help strengthen what you are aiming to do. It means to them, more than you can imagine. It was a way for them to bring P to justice and finally lay Wendy Workmaster to rest. They were still working hard upon it when we came upon the scene. In fact, I think it is essential that you get them involved. My next concern was upon leaving behind those human remains and their handling by the investigation team. But I am reassured by your advances, that we can leave those safely for men to deal with, with utter respect. However, for Gabriel and Walt, if Wendy is among those bags hanging in the canopy, I wish we could make her escape forensic if it was possible and give her remains to her loved one as soon as, if we could identify her.

Lifting his eyes to the now dark sky in complete desperation, Wrath surrendered,

-This is a task which will take Us all night, yet my Army needs its rest badly. Gosh Death, you are growing demanding since being in contact with Workmaster. Is he rubbing off on you somehow?

Azryel sending his mending energy through to the Angel he was looking after, crossly retorted,

-Wendy is a human in need of a proper rest for ages. She is out there, a piece of her, which could bring a much needed closure for a human and an Archangel. Day in and out, I feel their pain for her loss. They and her need closure. If your Angels who have an eternity before them to recover can show a little bit of heart, it will be more than appreciated.

Feeling better, the Angelic soldier Az dealt with butted in their conversation,

-Wrath, Az is right. I am willing to forget any rest, just for the sake of one of our brothers, Gabriel, lost and distraught since the death of the poor Wendy. Most of that sinkhole was half full by his own tears for Christ's sake. I am fit again and ready to be on the quest to bring Wendy Workmaster to rest in peace by her loved ones.

A group of Angels coming back with little It, smiling and full of cheers, reported,

-The forest is clear and full of rocks and boulders, ready to be stepped in by any lay human. That girl definitely rocks. Everything is geologically sound and so bespoke to the area, that no one would ever know a battle between Angels and demons took place in those woods.

It, looking at Azryel, sensed a sad feeling all around him. Coming to him she knelt at once, and asked,

-We did not lose any Angels, did we?

Death shook his head, still in disbelief of how good that young Being was, answered,

-We did not, It. But we lost one human, Wendy Workmaster, back in the day, which may be hanging in one of those little bags. We were thinking of spending the night to find her remains to bring them to Gabriel and Walter, for them to finally lay her to rest. It will be demanding as we will need to go through all bags and yet we might still not know it is her until I assess every single bone.

She looked at him with a very serious look, and whispered,

-I can find her for you. I have a very good nose. Let me smell how Walt was and tasted like when you saved him. She was his twin, I will find her blood print however dry it has become in no time at all. Just give me the thought of you saving him and I will grasp his blood print from you. I can then track the closest match in those woods, which will be his twin sister.

Holding her hands in one silent minute, Death sent to It-666 the information she required, then she left him, running to a tree not very far off. Levitating to its canopy, she grabbed the leather bag and held it like a treasure until she gave it to Azryel to assess.

Opening the human leather bag carefully, the Death Angel looked upon the remains, which was a hand. All the little bones scattered there did not give a clue to him that this was the hand of Wendy, yet as he shook the bag once more, he could see the unusual shine of a heavy ring which he recognised straight away. Lifting the 'Chevaliére' from the bag for all to see, making all the Angels sigh deeply doing so, he stated,

-We have the last remains of Wendy Workmaster, Soldiers, the human loved by an Archangel. He gave his Angelic Seal identifying him, to her as an engagement ring.

Seizing the ring at once, Wrath inspected it. The shine was still there and powerful, it was Gabriel's ring, definitely. Every Angel had their identifying ring worn upon their small right hand finger, which they used as a seal. Gabriel gave his seal away to Wendy as an engagement ring when Wrath disapproved of their involvement as proof of his commitment to the human.

Raphael shedding a blood tear, enclosed the ring back in the bag, and gave it back to his Death Angel to look after,

-They should have been. I would have embraced them with time.

An annoyed Death scolded,

-Believe there is no time at all and you will live better, for yourself and others. You will start using your heart fully like there is no other day to mess around, Wrath, and you will start to love fully.

Turning his attention to the last Angel to mend, Azryel was stopped to do so by Raphael,

-This can wait, Death, you will fix him later. Now that we have

Wendy's remains with Us, we can clear the woods and go back to Gab's tree house for the night. Besides you can use him to show Gabriel how it is done.

Standing up and helping the wounded Angel to do so, Az gave him a false apologetic smile,

-Well it sounds that you have just been upgraded to be the live angelic guinea pig of Gabriel. That's going to be enjoyable to watch. But do not worry, I will make sure he doesn't mess with your organs too much.

The soldier looking very afraid cried out loud,

-Why me?

Circling around him, inspecting his state from head to toe, Wrath blasted,

-Because you should not end up in such a sorry state in the first place in any of my missions or battles. The going will only get tougher, and I will not permit any of you to end up like that without punishment. You are the first to be made an example of but I can assure any of my soldiers of the same treatment if you make grave mistakes on the battlefield that could jeopardise your life. You will end up being the lab rat Angel of Archangel Gabriel. I need him to learn fast to become as good as Death to fix you up guys, and I assure you if five of you did require the help of Az at the first battle, you will welcome and appreciate the healing skills being passed down to more than one Angel. Spreading the teaching might involve practice to render it perfect and any that fall wounded will become the perfect body to exercise upon. In the grand scheme of my plans this will be the only way to be forgiven for your failure in battle, your help to others to acquire and learn the power to save life. Be thankful Soldier, that I did not ask Azryel to read you and analyse your faults on the battlefield and correct you severely for them. In this instance, I am being merciful upon you, it will not happen again. If you recidivate to get wounded in battle, you will be sourly notified by Death of the sheer disappointment and heartache you cause Us.

The soldiers looked at each other at the end of the staunch warning, very daunted to ever get wounded in the near future, when Death coldly gazing upon them, lit one of his cigars, taking a puff nonchalantly, commented,

-Wrath, this was clear mollycoddling on your part. They do need a good lesson to understand that failure is not accepted. Without the every step fault full proof analysis and correction that follows suit, I doubt it will have the clear 'you have to stay alive at all costs' message. Beside I will feel slightly under used not providing it.

Patting the shoulder of Death, Wrath corrected him out loud to good effect, as all his Angelic soldiers became extremely worried, especially the wounded one,

-Who said you would be under used, my dear Az? I do trust that your education of Gabriel will be rebarbative enough to any soldier, for it to be a pure deterrent from getting wounded ever again. It is running very late. Let Us make sure those Angels eat before going to bed. How's Gabriel's food? I heard it was very good.

Death blew a kiss in the air in front of him, taking the hand of It-666, and disappearing in front of all, answered,

-Bloody delicious, Brothers, so good I am going home sweet home right now.

A suddenly slightly worried Wrath followed suit along with his entire Army.

Verse 12. Gift of the Gab

When Azryel and It appeared on the platform of the tree-house, they saw Gabriel sitting upon the bench, his head within his hands, not looking ahead nor anywhere, but his own palms. The vibes coming from him were overwhelmingly strong and distressed. Az intimated to the teenager via telepathy,

-Stay put It, that Archangel is seeing black right now. Let me deal with him.

As he put gently his cold hand on the strong shoulder of Gabriel, Death warned him of his presence,

-Gab, what's up good old soul? Wanna talk, I am here.

Recognising the sound of his voice straight away, Gabriel gave him a lost look,

-Where have you been? I called you all again and again to no avail. Where's Bambi? Where is my Walter? Where's his bloody Bud? Where were you? I have been worried sick since I came back from my clinic. Tell me you just have done silly things in town, please, so I can call you squalid gits again. Please reassure me Az that I haven't lost anyone again.

Death's heart felt a pinch. He soothed at once,

-Gab, there is no loss. However I had to go on Wrath's mission with It. It was supposed to be a walk in the park yet it turned out to be a full on battle. Bambi did amazingly well, you should be proud of her. As for your human I hid him from all in your magical loophole away from space and time, along with his dog. I couldn't risk him being alone, in here, just in case. I know how much he means to you, he means just as much to me.

Gabriel took a breath back and just mentioned,

-Would a note from you left upon a table have hurt your fingers, Az, warning me of what was going on? What time do you call that, to come back home to tell me that all is fine? Next time if I have no warning notes about what is going on, you will face a curfew of four hours before you get to see me coming down upon you harshly.

Smiling sarcastically, Azryel could not help taking a cigar, lit it up, and taking a puff, scolded,

-Come, come, Gab, I know where you come from but giving Death a curfew is never going to happen, I come and go as I wish. However, I grant you that in the future, I will let you know what happens to your human, his pet, and also his adopted Beast, when I do something with them, as it clearly matters a great deal to you. I will send you a telepathic message to keep you well aware in the future, Brother, and I am awfully sorry for today. Wrath had a mission which could not be postponed. By the way, your Uncle is inviting himself tonight at yours with an Army of Angels desperate to eat and rest, worn out by a fierce battle with very ugly demons. Can I suggest a more welcoming stance or is it too early in the morning to ask? It is gone 1 am, blast of Us, for not killing demons faster to your liking.

The Archangel standing up tall, fully reassured, presented his hand to shake to Azryel, smiling somehow back to him,

-In the future, if I do not get a message from you Azryel, the curfew still stands, and you will not be able to present yourself at my threshold smoking peacefully I can tell you that much. Your Army is fully welcome to eat and rest at mine. I will prepare something for them. Get Walt out of that room, he must be bored to death by now, and will be blabbering non sense until dawn. I am sure I can place him by Uncle Raphael at the dinner table that will keep them both entertained. You, can sit by me and tell me all about tonight and how little It did during the battle.

Shaking the presented hand, Death promised,

-I will never get a curfew Bro, for I will always keep you updated from now on. Wrath must be in your courtyard by now. I am going to get your human, gosh, I forgot how long he spent in that totally empty room. If he didn't talk shit to his dog, he will have gone bonkers by now. It could be interesting to see him with your Uncle who's fought demons all day until near exhaustion.

A couple of hours later, all were seated in the great reception room of Gabriel eating and celebrating their victory against demons. Raphael kept fully awake by Walt was fully engaged in a heated conversation with him. It had finished her plate clean. For the first time in her life she was drifting off, and could hardly keep awake. She could hear the bustle of voices around the table like a nice and safe song where the key notes were punched by Az and Gab's conversation,

-You should have seen the silky slime coming out of them. Lethal stuff, a hand or a foot stuck in there, and that's all it takes to be food for the Spider Demons. Little It, came with such warnings from her scanning vision, smelling the woods for Us that we were at an advantage somehow all the way through. We simply could not be pounced upon unaware. This alone can make her invaluable to Us, yet after all my training which I thought could have been totally useless on a fairly pacific Being, she turned out to be a very good little fighter when needed. I am somewhat hard to please as a general, but seeing how her first battle went, I am fairly confident that we have a very good soldier in the making. The girl is a very brave soul indeed.

An happy Archangel Gabriel asked,

-So did she pass Wrath's first battle test?

-Indeed she did with flying colours. But that also means I have to work upon improving her as fast as I can for Raphael will require her to fight in any fight from now on. It makes me think the little one must be on the floor right now. It's three am, and after her first demonic battle, It needs a bloody well earned rest. Let me put that soldier to bed, arrange for Walter to follow suit, and then I can come back to talk to you some more.

Giving a glance to It-666, and seeing her dozing off upon her empty plate, Gabriel smiled kindly,

-You must all be needing a rest. Grab yours too Az. I will be busy clearing out the plates in a minute or so. All your Army has nearly finish their meals. I will prepare their beds in the loophole room. How long does Wrath intend to stay with them?

-Talk to him, and get his orders, Soldier. Stay up for me, for I have something very important for you Brother.

Azryel moved from his seat before Gab could say anything. He went to It and taking her hand teletransported her to the safety of her bedroom. There she collapsed exhausted upon her bed. Her eyes closed upon the room, and her mind drifted far away. Death put a cover upon her and going to the window, opened it wide in order to smoke a last cigar. He had to give the human remains of Wendy Workmaster to Archangel Gabriel and somehow was dreading that very moment. Seeing him so downcast earlier for not knowing what was going on with his loved ones, and how he took it at heart warned Death that he had to make sure he was all alone with him to deliver the very special packet that mattered to the Archangel most of all.

A few puffs of cigar away, Workmaster stepped in the room with his Great Dane in toe. Death couldn't help smiling at the human, asked,

-How was your day Walt?

-Very very safe, you bastard. I heard you were an amazing killing machine of Beasties on the battlefield and that you kept a very good eye upon my girl. I also heard that your training paid off. Little It fought well because of you. Somehow I am extremely grateful for this Az. In due time I will pay you respect as for now, I just need to sleep. Goodnight Az. Next time you put me in that clinical room, make sure I have a playstation in it so I can kill Beasties my own way for a while and feel much better for it. It will make me feel less useless.

Azryel stayed within the room until he was sure both were sound asleep, then he teletransported to the platform, where he saw the Archangel Gabriel doing a hundred paces waiting for him.

Gab welcomed him sternly,

-Do you know that there is still one deeply wounded Angel, Az? You should check upon him as he will have a pretty gruelling night if he stays like that.

-Good, that will teach him to not fall backwards at the first hurdle.

-I learnt that they were five wounded, yet I only saw one. Have you got a particular grievance with him? Know that I will not accept any personal vendetta under my roof.

The Death Angel could not help giving his all knowing smile to the Archangel,

-I am glad to hear it for there are issues with you and Wrath which really should be smoothed over for a long while now, and somehow both of you did let them fester away until they stank deeply for all of Us watching you both. It reassures me greatly that you will not claw each others face and eyes at yours at the very least. Sit down, Gabriel, stop turning around, your sheer restlessness is starting to make me feel dizzy, Angel. I fear that it will be a long night for you and me. I have a lot to tell you and brief you upon, as a soldier. Do you mind if I smoke?

Sitting upon the bench, Gabriel glared at him, with slight grief,

-Go ahead, I will only mind if you give that bad habit back to Walter. After his drinking relapse of the other day, I would be careful with what you do in front of the people I look after. As for Wrath and I, I put his decisions and attitudes towards me in my past, I moved on and follow my own path...

Correcting him at once, Death stated,

-Followed, Gabriel, as you are back with Us fully and cannot be left on your own any longer. You can blame it on the very odd people you are looking after, adding an Antichrist to your list made Wrath's cavalry come by for good reason. I have many points to go through with you tonight, some you may agree with, some you may argue with, some are open to discussion, some are orders. The first point is an order which I also gave to your Uncle. As Death, committed to you both, I need both of you to keep your slates clean, unfortunately, they are less than so when it concerns your very strained familial relationship with each other. Also we are coming close to a time when being unforgiving to your loved ones and family members will not pass judgement day. As Archangels, role models supposedly, you will suffer more than others the results of the contempt and disavowal you imposed on each other. Not only that as you are two imposing figures within Us, as we are about to enter the apocalypse, we need you to reestablish a strong rapport between you two. Both Archangels working fully with one another will be key to our success. Shoulder to shoulder as brothers we shall be once more all of Us. You need to recreate strong links with your Uncle, Gabriel, and only a good heart to heart with him will have the power to do so. Raphael has the same order, as I mentioned, and I want that conversation to take place no later than tomorrow. Both of you face consequences if it fails to happen by midnight. I will remain anal upon that first point until it reaches a conclusion which makes Us, the World and me happy.

His hands upon his lap, staring at the darkness before him, the Archangel replied,

-I can only promise this to you, Death, like my human said of me, I will do the same for my Uncle: If it is not forgotten, it is forgiven. It is grand time to split the blister, and I will have that heart to heart with Wrath tomorrow although I dread it. What is your second point?

A very pleased Azryel finally took a cigar from his silver box to lit up. Leaning against the wooden fence of the platform he announced,

-Gabriel, you are a very sound Archangel and I want you to know that. You should not dread to face your Archangelic Uncle, for you have in your heart valid points to put across as much as he, if not more. What you achieved on your own is remarkable. What your Uncle achieved with others is bringing justice where it is needed. Although he has very unusual ways to do so, they tend to always work for the better, a little like your effective baseball bat prop with your human, they are a tad controversial. Your skills are needed Brother to rejoin his Army fully. There is no individual path to be had but the one of the greater good which the Army of Us is working towards. Let me tell you that your plate will be full everyday of tasks and duties. Here comes my second point, I want you to reconsider your human clinic and work. I know of the tremendous input you do as a Doctor for all those humans that walk through those doors. I do not want your life's hard work to close down but to be run by your sister Caroline, while you set up an Angelic clinic, here at the tree house, in a newly created loophole room where the incarnated Angels can recover safely and be treated appropriately. You would run that Angelic clinic for Us. That type of clinic would become a necessity in the near future after every battle with demons. Wrath and I have full angelic healing powers. You learnt your way through human medicine to become a brilliant Doctor who saves lives everyday. I want you to become proficient in Angelic healing to become a saviour of Angels, and to focus upon this from now on. You noticed my wounded Angelic soldier. Your heart even made a plea for him. I want you to learn upon him, with me as your teacher to mend Angels coming back from a battlefield. The lesson is scheduled for mid morning tomorrow, as I still want him to sleep rough tonight for getting wounded in the first place. I do not want to fill your head too much in one evening, but Wrath wants us to be subtle about fixing them back up, the treatment should discourage them to be wounded ever again hence promote their full attention in battle to not slip by a mistake to another wound or a death. This second point is an order yet open to opinion and consideration.

The Archangel asked suddenly,

-Can I have a cigar, Az? A lot is to be taken in right now. My clinic to be given to my Sis, is not objectionable to me, yet I would need to keep an eye upon it to prevent it from falling apart.

Azryel puffing into the coldness of the night scolded,

-No you can not, for you are Gabriel, and I will prevent you to ever form a vice. You should give more credit to Caroline, for she has a strong character. She would rise to the challenge and not let you down nor Us. Let's talk about my third point where I need you again badly.

-Badly? Let's hear it.

-Well it concerns our little It. You spent an awful lot of time to assess her, but what are the results of your blood tests and so on? I am only asking because her Being keeps astonishing me everyday I spend with her. She does puzzle me greatly at times. Her awareness of everything surrounding her today was astounding yet sometimes a little daunting. I need you to be her confident and more than that. Living with a harsh nun, for five years, three as a feral kid in the forest and eight in a cage, does not give It the best of manners I am afraid. She is sweet as hell yet when she dipped her finger into a demon's wound, licked the blood, and lifted her stained finger up to know where the remaining of his kind are, she freaked the whole Army up including Wrath. I need your help there, Gabriel, to teach our girl some manners and think upon how she uses her powers in front of all. I mean, I know she is the born Beast, and a creature 'made in Hell' but is there any way we could refine her? She is only sixteen maybe it is not too late for her to learn some 'blend in the crowd a little more' skills. On the other hand, as she was not raised in Hell, she pinpointed to me her total lack of knowledge concerning demons. She seems to do things to them and have some control over them by instinct, yet her energy will drain to nought when she sent a whole bunch of them back to Hell, and somehow she knows the technique and correct words to do so. I know you are a bit of a demonologist, Gabriel, but also that you are worried about the girl knowing more about Evil. Your face when she was watching the 'Exorcist' with me and Walt, was a livid gem to behold. What I am getting at is that trying to keep her naive or ignorant about the dark sides who are desperate to get their hands back on her is A: Bound to future failure, B: Can harm our girl in the long term as she will have no preparation into what she is fighting. We have a duty to her to teach her who she is, where she comes from, and give her the full knowledge of her powers, and her opponents. I do not believe that she will turn bad by giving her demonic lessons, I believe on the contrary that she will then fully know her enemies and how to fight them better, to become an awesome and invaluable soldier in Wrath's Army. I can not do that on my own for you are the expert on Evil Beings of all kinds.

Standing up Gabriel paced the platform, stopped, wanting to say a word lifting his hand in the air, yet stopped short and paced again the platform. Azryel sat on the bench, blasting at once,

-Gabriel, O Gabriel, would you stop running worried each time I open my mouth? Do you know how tired I am and how tiring your incessant galloping mind is? Give me one thought, any thought even one that shows to me that you are riding your high horses again. As I said I am prepared to argue any point with you especially that one. If you care for It one notch, then you owe the girl to be fully armed for the terrible future that awaits Us. I had a moment today, recalling her from a total collapse, just after she performed the feat of sending the first wave of demons attacking Us back to Hell. I absolutely did not want her good little heart to be abducted again and falling into wrong hands. I needed to do all I could to get her back on her feet fast into full fighting form. I can not stress enough the importance of that Being to Us and the whole World. We are her protectors and should give her a full Angelic/demonic tuition that allows her to stand on her own two feet to fight to preserve her own good heart.

Sitting back upon the bench by Azryel, the Archangel finally answered,

-I am with you on that one. I have deep reservations yet I think you are all too right. I will pass my knowledge of Demons and Hell to our soldier. However, I stopped studying Demons a long while ago so I may be a little rusty. If you are tired you'd better crack on if you have any more points for me, general.

The Death Angel looking very pleased and amused, took a long deep puff of his cigar before teasing,

-I am glad to have you on board, for I know as a fact that you are not rusty at all. I sneaked into your underground laboratory where bits and bobs of demons are kept for experiment. Blood samples of our little Beast were duly compared with blood samples of a fair few demonic creatures. You went through 515 so far of your collection of a mere 10,000. One must ask, where do you find the time and most importantly where did you find the samples?

Gabriel's gab was not cut short as he gloomily confessed,

-I have been through Hell in quest of Wendy's soul. I used a secret path regularly for years, and well if I met any unwary demon in my path, they ended up here, as lab rats. It's been a way to avenge myself and her somehow. I want to put her soul to rest badly, I cannot stop until it is done.

Death put the leather bag of Wendy's only remains upon the lap of the Archangel and soothingly announced,

-We could not leave P's woods when we knew every single tree carried a bag made of human skin holding one piece of their human's now skeletal parts. We aimed to retrieve the last remains of Wendy Workmaster for you Gabriel, for you to give her a decent grave, for you to lay her to rest appropriately.

The blood tears of the Archangel streamed upon his face as he carefully opened the bag. He saw his seal shining in the middle of loose finger bones confirming he had the hand of his fiancée. He sobbed,

-What did they do to you Baby? What the hell did they do to you, my love? Where is your body, your life, your soul? I am so lost without you my love, I am so so lost.

The Death Angel standing up, enclosed the shoulders of Gabriel within his own arms. His forehead touching the Archangelic one, he comforted,

-You are not lost Gabriel. You are with Us and you are not alone anymore Brother to fight your plight and your humans' plight, the sad swan song of Wendy and the tough living call of Workmaster. Your calls are being answered. Trust that you are not alone and will never go without love. Gifted Gab found his giving answer in the depth of the night. Look forward for dawn, Archangel.

Verse 13. Bat Man Run.

Within the woods, Walter Workmaster was walking his Great Dane, Bud, with the company of the young It and Wrath. It was still early morning, just turning about eight am, which got Walter worried somehow,

-Gabriel did not go to work today. His car is still in the yard. He is usually an early bird flying from home at 6.30 am to head to his clinic. He never takes a day off. Something must be up.

Uncle Raphael sighed deeply and sent a silent plea to It-666 to not utter a word, as he announced sadly,

-It is not something that is up, Walt, it's someone very dear to you and Gab.

The man stood still for a minute staring at the Archangel dumbfounded, and at his watch in turn, shouted at once,

-You came walkies with me for the past half hour, knowing that someone I know was in danger and you stayed as cool as an iceberg throughout. Are you keeping me away from something?

Looking to the sky for help before answering the human, Raphael revealed,

-I am somehow. Gabriel has been in a distressed state since about 4 am. Azryel is dealing with him. We brought the single last remains of your twin sister Wendy that we found in P's woods, and we gave it to him to lay her to rest appropriately. Gab has been silent ever since and uttered no words. He just kept crying blood tears, holding her remains with the utmost care.

Walt asked wildly,

-Where is my big Bro, Wrath? Keep an eye on Bud, make sure he does his big business before bringing him back to Gab's Hall. He has enough on his plate right now. Little It, Gab won't be able to feed an Army for their breakfast, I leave you in charge of it. Uncle Wrath, make sure she does not burn the place down while frying some bacon and eggs for your soldiers.

The Archangel cocking his eyebrows at once to the man's orders, only replied,

-He went to the Indian Waterfall, Az said.

Workmaster nodding told,

-That is where he asked Wendy. That is where he wants her to rest. I know that place meant as much for her as for him. It meant their future together. I am going there right now, I will send you back your grieving Angel Wrath, but go easy on him for a while. Wendy meant. Although just a human she just meant. You Angels have to come to terms with humans meaning something deep.

He ran off towards the Indian Waterfall as fast as he could. When he arrived he saw Gabriel curled upon himself holding the human leather bag tightly within his strong arms and legs, like an Archangelic cocoon impossible to invade. He saw Death in full regalia, one hand upon Gab's shoulder and one hand upon his scythe.

A panicking Workmaster, harangued Death at once,

-I thought you were with him, helping him! Az, get back into some sort of shape at once, a non-if-you-give-up-I am here-to-grab-you Gab. Jeez, someone needs to teach you all, Angels, a bit of humanity somehow.

Walter went to nestle right in between the arms of Gabriel, and just hugged him right and proper. He burst into tears and let his heart out,

-Gab, O Gab, they bloody found the last remains of our Wendy.

Our little Wren is upon your laps. She was on cloud nine with you. This place meant your future together. This is what she wanted and dreamt about. Let her rest in a feathered dream, of your future life together. She has to be laid to rest. She has to, for the sake of her.

Gabriel enclosed his arms upon the human, hugging him back, before he stood up, holding the bag by the waterfall, and asked,

-Tell me how you want her laid to rest, human for I crumble at the thought of it every time?

Azryel who had returned to his incarnated human shape because of the man's harangue, was about to turn back when Walter intervened. Going straight to the Archangel, he grabbed the bag from him at once. Walter explained,

-I need to give her my brotherly sending over. My last hug is one of them and then, there's what she loved, she loved roses, red Mr Lincoln, I am going to get fifty of those to go with her in the waterfall. She also loved lavender scented candles, she lit them by her bath to chill from a hard day's work. I want all the sides of the waterfall lit with them as the last pieces of her body goes to dive into her deep rest. She just swore by granny's Epsom salt wherever she went, to restore her at anytime. I will get her lots for her sending off. Gabriel, do you want to rush it, or have you got things you learnt from my sister, you know meant for you and her, to gather for her. Azryel will happily perform the ceremony for both of us.

Death cocking his eyebrows up nonetheless agreed,

-I will. The man has needs in sending his sister to rest and I know you have Gabriel.

Moving a great stone, Azryel proposed,

-Let's lay her in the Indian cave for now, we will come back tonight for the ceremony at dusk, and do a proper sending off to her sweet soul.

Depositing her remains in the small alcove, while Death pushed the large stone in position covering them from sight, Walter stated,

-I am happy with this, are you Gab?

Gabriel came to the man and nodded affirmatively. Yet a few metres away Gab burst into a damn of tears. Walter turned to him at once giving him his shoulder to cry upon. Patting him gently, Workmaster whispered,

-Do not let go Bro. Please do not. You are the only one that can bring her justice. You set the motion and it is happening right now. Please be strong for all of Us. If you remain strong she will get her rest if you do not Wendy will not get her justice. Please Bro, stay with Us. You don't want me to scold you, do you. I remember when you told me off for being selfishly suicidal. You made me think of all my loved ones I had still living and needing me. Think about Caro, little Micky, the young It that you took on board with me, your Uncle, and myself. We love you dearly Gab.

The Archangel hugging the man, wiped away his tears, then standing tall, apologised,

-I am sorry Walter to have entertained the thought of following her rests in the fall. I love you all dearly and will fight with you. I won't give up, I promise, I won't do a selfish one on you.

A smiling Walter welcomed the apology at once, teasing,

-Good because, I was not gonna have it, you know, I was ready to get your baseball bat out.

Azryel could not help a wicked smile as he saw one finally drawing upon Gabriel's lips,

-That would have been interesting.

The man still annoyed with Death commented,

-Yes, it would have been certainly more interesting than a swing of the scythe. It would have been educational for him too, he would have learnt not to scare the shite out of me like that. I may have done some interesting swings of the bat upon your back just as well for carrying your scythe in wait by my suicidal Guardian Angel instead of talking him out of it. Sometimes Death, I wish you would get lost somewhere, honestly.

-I tried, human, all night, I could not get through to him, nor get any response. However I got his desperate soul's repeated calls for me, which triggered me to be death ready.

-I tell you what Azryel sometimes you just need a bit of love and feeling when you talk to people to get through to them. Shall I give you a crash course? I think it is badly needed don't you? As for you Gabriel, for Christ's sake don't you ever soul call him to take you away because he will bloody do it you know. He is so duty bound that he fails to make the exception for Brothers in need.

Intervening in the Death Angel's favour, the Archangel corrected,

-It is a fallacy to think that Azryel lacks love and feeling. I can assure that he does not need a crash course from anyone. Exhausted from yesterday's battle, he stayed by me trying desperately to comfort me. I wanted to join Wendy so much, I did basically a It-666's trick upon him, I switch off my hearing altogether. All I was ready to accept from him was my final pick up. I was shut to any influential words from him. He is not to blame, I am.

Walter blasted at once,

-You are definitely going to get some good swings of the bat when we get home, Bro. After telling everyone off so strongly, you do not practice what you preach. Second offence in my book, switching your hearing off when all of you guys teach my girl to stay full on. How selfish of your damn Archangelic arse, to have poor duty called Az all night and prevent him to talk you out! How brotherly was that between Angels, pray? Azryel, accept all my apologies, I did not know the part that was highlighted to me. If you want to give a few educational swings of the bat to that Archangel, I will let you do so.

Death paused the hasty walk to the tree house, pulled a cigar out and lit it. Gabriel stopped walking to stay by him while Walter carried on. Az mentioned,

-I must chill. I heard enough to get me started upon a serious one, and you definitely could do with a little break. I am going to show you my appreciation and the respect you did not have for me all night, I will let you off on that one if you just feed me upon how you managed to switch off one of your senses, and what brought you back to listen again to the world around you?

Trying to appease him, the Archangel replied,

-What woke me back to pay attention to my surroundings again was Walter's bear hug. His tears dropping on my shoulders made me switch my hearing back on. I had to know if my human was not as distressed as I was.

Calling them out, Walter ordered,

-Come on you two, stop blabbering Angelic shit, I have something interesting to watch at home. I left It-666 in charge of running the kitchen and feeding the soldiers their breakfast. Wrath is supposed to supervise her all the way yet I can see puffs of smoke from here.

This got Gabriel running straight away, very soon far ahead from Walt and Az. He tried to look for the smoke coming from the tree house but could not. He turned hastily to see Workmaster bursting into a good old laugh with Azryel grinning wickedly, advising,

-Keep running Gab, the man just told me that It is definitely running the kitchen and that Wrath who never lifted a finger to feed himself is overseeing her. There is no smoke yet, though, Bro, that part was him pulling your leg. However, myself I would not trust them with cooking appliances, and if it was my kitchen I would run.

Verse 14. Break Fast.

Coming into his kitchen Gabriel saw every soldier enjoying a good English breakfast without the beans. No havoc was to be seen, and the stoves were pristine clean as if left unused since the last time he used them. His Uncle seated at the head of the table welcomed him warmly,

-Gabriel, you must be starving, have some breakfast with Us. Please, take a seat at your table. It is a wonderful cook, an amazingly precise one, she gets the bacon and eggs done exactly to individual specification. Where are Az and Walt?

-Following.

Gab sat down and saw the teenager coming to him at once, a welcoming smile upon her face. She asked him eagerly,

-How would you like your breakfast?

-I don't feel like eating really.

Raphael looking at him intently, a little worried, told,

-Well, Gabriel on this occasion, you will ignore your feelings a tad and eat something with Us. You did not sleep all night and have a very busy day ahead of you. I need you to gather some energy. Plus, consider that you will disappoint our little cook. She did really well to take upon herself the burden of feeding an Army which would have fallen on your own shoulders otherwise. What is it going to be Gabriel, letting Us down or breakfast?

The Archangel giving a sad smile to his Uncle, replied,

-It is going to be breakfast and never letting you down, Wrath. I am sorry for the worry I may have caused. It, thank you for stepping in to help this morning, it is appreciated. It is no mean feat to feed an

Army how did you manage to keep that place so clean? I expected to see a disaster like last time in my kitchen to be honest. I will have one fried egg, two slices of bacon which I like crispy and a couple of hash browns, please Bambi.

Raphael stood up at once came to the girl, bringing a bottle of sunflower oil, and poured a little into her presented joint hands. He smiled gleefully commenting all the way about his actions,

-I just love It's skills. Watch that Gab. Now when the oil starts to sizzle, like now that's when I crack the egg, like so, and then it takes only seconds in her hands to cook to perfection. See the brown edges of the egg white, your egg is done. Here's a clean plate to dish that egg, It, now time to put the bacon rashers. You can even hear it sing as it cooks. Magical survival skills of that soldier, extremely useful to have in an Army, I can see an array of possibilities from them. Bacon is done. Last but not least your hash browns, do want them golden or well done?

-Golden. So It's powers of combustion has been used all along to rustle up the breakfast. I would wish those would be left alone, myself. I can see your forward thinking however, Wrath, but what about using my stove while you are all lodging under my roof like normal people do?

Walter stepped into the kitchen while Azryel stood in the threshold, leaning on the door frame finishing his cigarillo off. Death answered sarcastically,

-Well, we aren't very normal, Gabriel. I am sorry to state the obvious but we are shape shifting to large winged creatures every now and then. Let's not mention little It who has got pretty demonic eyes that change colours when she scans a forest with her x-ray/radar vision. Besides I doubt Wrath and It know how to use a stove.

Raphael defended his corner at once,

-True, we didn't know how to use a bloody human stove but under

the circumstances, and the orders given by Walt, I think we did very
well indeed. We fed all, we did not destroy the kitchen and everyone
enjoyed their breakfast. I prefer looking at results rather than
methods employed to achieve them. Who needs a stove when we
have got It anyway? She is much faster and more efficient. Now, It
give me your hands, let's fix them up, and you did extremely well
despite my two favourite argumentative Angels. One always knows
when they are present in the room, thinking through comments will
flow and I am so glad both are here right now. Az, I want your brief.
What is your toll, Soldier? Did you get any calls tonight?

Gabriel tried to interrupt desperately,

-Why does It need to have her hands sorted? Her combustion mojo
never affected her before.

His Uncle answered him straight away strongly,

-Gabriel, I am trying to get feedback from my general. It will be
fine, I am a very experienced healer of Being and humans, trust me
a little, beside we did this all morning. The oil affects her skin, and
our girl did feel the heat right down to her wrist bones cooking
everything for Us. Yet she is a trooper and very eager to please.
Azryel, your briefing now.

The Death Angel crushed his cigar on the door and stepped into
the room, ordering,

-Don't touch the girl Wrath, let me check her out first. That is a
result of methods. Although we can fix those glitches, up to scratch
methods can never be overlooked, never. I will brief you in private.

Raphael stepped sideways to let Azryel get a closer look at the
young Beast's burnt wrists. Checking them thoroughly, Death asked
the girl,

-When you knew the oil was burning you deep down, Soldier, why
didn't you say so and tell those guys they could not have a fry up
this morning? They could have ordered something else as equally

filling for them and for you to combust food safely without the pain you went through. This is not battle, this is trivial, you have nothing to lay in front of those Angels when at rest. Only at war all of Us lay our lives for one another. At rest we look after one another and it should come with no pain at all. If it does, you should query it. Understood, little eager beaver, we want to raise you up not burning you like a frying pan, for Christ's sake. Wrath, watch your methods before I come down heavily upon you. I am going to fix her up this time around to know how far oil and combustion can damage her when mixed together.

Wrath putting his hand upon the Death Angel's shoulder as he fixed the teenage It's damaged hands, demanded again,

-I will take what is coming to me for little It. Just tell me if you had any particular soul calls tonight. I need to know, Az, everything happening to my loved ones.

Death dealing with the blistered hands of It sternly answered him,

-Master, I am afraid I had many calls from the soul we all love. All night through they came strong, loud, and clear, far too many for my own liking, some begging and crying. I am standing before you heartbroken for them, truly shaken to my core. Embracing the soul is the answer, Raphael. It is very simple and straightforward love needed, as the human rightly highlighted to me. The grieving soul does not require punishment, it requires caring hearts surrounding it. Can you be one of them?

Bursting at once, Raphael said,

-I am one of them. I have been standing on that platform since four am, worried sick about any news of Gab. My anxieties stopped when he stepped in that kitchen alive and well, and now I will not rest until I know his problems are addressed fully.

Lighting the stove, Walter called the fixed up It by his sides, commenting,

-As Gab's problems are endless, then you will never rest at all, Wrath. It, come and learn how to use the stove, Raphael you may pay attention too. I cannot believe that an old incarnated Angel like you managed to get away from learning basic cooking skills. Azryel, fancy some breakfast to perk you up a little?

The Archangel came to watch as the man fried eggs, bacon and sliced up mushroom, while roasting tomatoes halves, and preparing some toast. Raphael teased,

-Unlike you, human, I can choose the parents suitable for my incarnated Angels, coming to my own incarnation, my families were always so well off that I never had to lift a finger. I always had many cooks and an array of servants. You and I come from totally different worlds altogether. You are breadcrumbs while I am simply upper-crust.

Shaking his head in disapproval, Workmaster gave a worried glance to Azryel who sat on a chair by the stove, deadly quiet and lost in thought. He recalled him,

-Azryel, breakfast, what do you fancy? Don't you start sleepwalking upon Us. I tell you what Wrath, humbleness certainly does not choke you. Don't you teach any lazy reliant upon others pride to my girl. Knowing humbleness of heart, hard work, good work, cooking, cleaning, your own self maintenance, is not dirty, it is essential skills. Good fortune comes and goes. You can build your own luck to a certain extent in the real world. I would have wished for an Archangel to have started from scratch and know what it feels like to be in a modest family, for they may have values that can raise a very good and sound heart.

Paying attention once more to his surroundings the Death Angel joined in the conversation,

-I fancy scrambled eggs on toast and I will have some of those mushrooms, they smell divine, Walt. Where did you get those? They don't look like tin stuff. By the way, I had a similar conversation with Wrath back in the day, although it went much deeper than that and lasted all night. The outcome was the Archangel Michael being born in your family. It is a very human environment, human in all sense of the word, humanistic too, slightly dysfunctional, yet full to the brim of good love and strong values of the heart. You are raising the next Archangel, Workmaster, and so far we are impressed.

The man felt emotion rising to his throat, he concentrated in doing the scrambled eggs for Az before he expressed himself again,

-We are not dysfunctional, definitely not Caro, maybe me, just me ever so slightly.

Uncle Raphael laughed, followed by Gab and Az, before coughing,

-Understatement. Those mushrooms were picked up as we walked the dog, Az. The last of the season before deep winter the man said. We had a crash course It and I on to recognising the good ones from the lethal and poisonous ones. I carried the lot back home and did not know what to do with them. But I would love to try some too, if my upper crust stance has been forgiven by you, Walt.

Finishing the scrambled eggs with a dash of truffle oil, and a few thyme leaves which also went in the sautéed mushrooms, Workmaster confessed,

-I knew how to cook my essential before, as a student it was a big bowl of plain pasta with ketchup and a bit of cheese on top. I mainly lived upon burgers until I met Gab. He took me to a shack by the seaside once, on my university summer holiday, one he owned in Florida. It was fishing all day long, swimming, diving, and he cooked from scratch whatever we caught. I paid attention, and watching Gab's love of good food did rub off on me. I learnt for myself what he learnt from all the humans he watched before him without knowing it. Gabriel was all about provenance, sustainable living, eco-friendly, seasonality, and gathering for your own needs respectfully, but also giving back. The fish full of eggs was given back to the sea or the river straight away, the smaller ones left to grow, a seed or tree planted after every meal. Gabriel rendered me earth conscious during that holiday of a lifetime. It has stayed with me forever. Raphael, cooking upon earth can not be overlooked. Food is a very serious human issue all over the world. It sustains a man, a woman and how many children they can love and have. Some get too much food and some do not get enough and die, day in and out. You will only have those mushrooms if you promise me to get involved deep down at once upon the matter.

Azryel taking his given breakfast plate tucked in, advised,

-Do as the man says Wrath. Serious issues are all over food, it will ease down my collections from an over fattening world to a crying out third world. Obesity and famine goes hand in hand, when one over-eats, one under-eats. Distribution needs to be rethought to its roots, not upon a matter of who can afford it and die of Diabetes or a heart attack because he can. Distribution needs to be addressed upon world populations and numbers. It goes very deep and I am ready to have a whole night's conversation with you upon the matter at hand and how to deal with it.

Cocking his eyebrows once more, Raphael asked the human,

-Walter Workmaster, how many Angels of mine are you perverting with a concern for humankind? I do promise to get on board with the World food issue, and it is as good as it gets.

Giving him a plate full, the human teased in earnest,

-All of them. I will not rest until humanity is fully heard.

Verse 15. Healing.

Deep underneath the tree house, in the laboratory, Gabriel and Azryel walked a stunned wounded Angel. As they made him sit upon a linen bunk bed, the Angel cried out loud,

-What is this place all about?

Gabriel replied undaunted,

-Experimenting.

Death grinning widely confirmed,

-Today's experiment is all about Angel's constitution. Lay at once and pray do not move. You would not like to hurt yourself by a silly move, would you?

The Angelic soldier did as he was told shivering all over. Gabriel tied him up upon the bed, securely. Azryel could not help looking around as he did so. Looking closely into a test tube, he asked the Archangel,

-What is that deep blue stuff about?

-That's It-666's blood and the way it coagulates. She has four types of blood cells, blue, red, purple and white. All four seem to be totally independent matter, doing different functions yet all-together, I have instant dynamo blowing my test tubes away within two hours. I can only separate them to analyse them as of now. However I am working on a special Being test tube glass resistant to blowing under unknown pressure, like blood that still beats a pulse without heart contact.

Death went to another experimental bench and asked,

-What is that one about?

-Dark matter. Don't ask. My papers are underneath that desk which tell all about it. The Angel is really not well, Az. Are we going to end his suffering?

Azryel came at once to the wounded soldier. His hands felt his body thoroughly and asked Gabriel,

-Feel him through Angel, and tell me what do you get about his state?

Gabriel felt the Angelic soldier through apposing his hands upon him, and gave his diagnosis,

-Broken leg, two places, deep fractures. I would immobilise him for a couple of months if he was a man. Muscle injuries upon his hips and both shoulders, the Angel was tackled to the ground by extreme force. Feeling the impacts, I would say two of the so called Beasties dealt with him.

The Death Angel smiled widely, stating,

-Bang on. Now for the healing, two months is human terms and far too long. Touch my hand and feel what is needed for his full recovery within minutes. Then feel Wrath affecting it, teaching a lesson to his soldier. We will administrate Wrath version at all times for no Angels can be complacent with their lives upon the battlefield. We do not grow martyrs here like religious human kind, we are growing true hearts and heroes, they don't die creating havoc, and manslaughter, like their shameless human religious counterparts, they do live for better days saving people rather than killing them blindly. We have a heart not a funked up and diverted religion that massacres at will or establish inhuman laws which allow a raped woman to be condemned.

The Archangel touched Death's hand, closed his eyes and felt the deep healing energy from it. He also sensed the nuances imposed by Raphael and gathered where the energy came from. He asked,

-Can I produce healing energy, the way you do, Az?

Nodding positively Death revealed,

-You do, all Archangels have that capacity however only Raphael and I had the right to use it so far. Yet you did fiddle a little with that healing power here and there. Out of want for your own clinic and patients, you experimented it, sometimes with dramatic results, sometimes with positive ones. Now that we have Raphael's all clear and authorisation, we can teach you how to use that power properly. First, you need to raise it from your inner Angelic Being towards your hands. Second, you control it throughout to the exact level needed for the wounded before you, hence always checking the patient thoroughly like we did. Third you aim with precision at the target inside the body. Fourth, this will be hard for a novice, you need to keep a full awareness on the wounded and how your healing is affecting him. This will allow you to fine tune throughout what you are doing but also will let you know when to stop. Practice makes perfect however I will not allow major cocking up on my soldiers without strong repercussion upon yourself. I will mirror your exact mistakes on your body for you to understand them and the pain they gave. Now give it a good go, and remember don't you try any experimental bullshit on Wrath's Army. Trust me, I know all of those Angels by heart and I will figure it out straight away.

A daunted Gabriel whispered,

-I respect you all too much to do such a thing.

Taking his position behind the wounded Angel, holding his shoulders down, Azryel stated,

-Your respect, Gabriel is so volatile that I do not trust it anymore. On my slate you have a lot to make up for. You exhibited even to your own human this morning that you were not an Angel of your words. Your words are hollow to me. They sink into deaf ears, ironically enough. I tell you what, actions speak louder than words, my dear Archangel, and you have a lot to prove for me to start believing you again. Clean up your act, make that do your talking.

Start by remembering never to stop caring about others and answering to your callings for they are many. One of them is right now in front of you, a healing session which is only the start of things to come. Are you going to step up to the plate, Bat Gab? Your answer is in your hands not your voice. Coming from you, I will only accept your actions as of today.

Swallowing a sorrowful breath, Gabriel tried to focus on the lesson and every word from Death. He needed to act, prove to him that he will never let the Army down. First call was curing that soldier and doing it right. He concentrated for a couple of minutes before proceeding. As he saw the blue healing energy appearing at the tips of his fingers, he smiled with reassurance yet searched for Death's confirmation in his intense gaze that he was on the right track, silently.

Az nodding confirmed,

-Good, you managed the first step. Now, think of your patient only and where he needs healing and apply. This requires your full attention and skill, Gab. That second step along with the third are crucial. Concentration is key in every way, powers as well as focus. Think of this as being similar to your operating theatre, doing an open heart surgery. Spot on precision is required at all times.

Listening to the advice, Gabriel went ahead with no rush but pure focus. Ten minutes later, the soldier was healed fully, and the Death Angel freed him from his bonds which attached him to the bunk bed. Az asked the Angel,

-How do you feel, Soldier?

-Very good, general. Much better than broken up in places that is for sure.

-Off you go. Report to Wrath at once. Do you remember what you must do next time?

-Yes, Azryel, I do not want to let you down, I will not get wounded again. I plan to train and train on the mistake I made, I did not watch my back at all times, I got tackled down, and that is not acceptable.

-Right, tell Wrath that I am grounding you for a couple of days to retrain you properly on that one. You are going to stay at Gab's Hall with me until I let you rejoin the Army.

-Yes, Sir.

As the Angel disappeared from the room, Gabriel looked anxiously at Death waiting for feedback yet it did not come. He saw Death taking his silver cigarillo box and about to teletransport as well. He rushed to him eagerly, and asked at once,

-How did I do?

A cigarillo was lit in front of him slowly, before Azryel replied,

-I do not know if I should be mad at you or not. For a first time, it was good, meticulous yet awfully slow. The worst is not applying Wrath's specific order upon healing his wounded soldiers from battle. Hence I have to make sure that soldier gets the message and keep him with me for a couple of days. You will have to answer Raphael for ignoring his specifications. Nonetheless, you did not let that Angelic soldier down at the very least. He left your lab as fit as he went into P's woods.

Disappearing from the lab, the Death Angel left the Archangel all alone. Shedding a blood tear, Gabriel felt utterly lost. He had kind of cocked up by forgetting his Uncle's orders, and therefore being extremely generous to the soldier which he had been cautioned not to do. In his attention to fix the Angel in the best way he totally forgot Raphael's fine 'don't get wounded again' tuning. What upset him more was the loss of Azryel's trust or regard. Not being able to talk to him as it will be totally disregarded at once was the most terrible blow for him, a sheer loss. He understood all too well where it came from and wished to have an opportunity to apologise to Azryel, however he knew that he would not be listened to anymore, not only that, Death was notoriously unforgiving. Half willing to make a fool of himself and pursue Azryel to make a full apology to him, yet part of him just wanting to reach an understanding shoulder, which would hug him back like the ones of Workmaster, Gabriel stood aimless for a while, in the midst of his test tubes. Suddenly taking four, he sat down by a microscope. He mixed the four contents in a little beaker reconstituting the blood of the Beast. Cutting his wrist's artery right through afterwards to collect the precious Archangelic blood in a few test tubes, before healing himself right back up, he whispered for himself,

-Thank you Death, you are an Angel.

Comparing his own blood with It-666, and having had a snapshot of two Angelic constitutions, Azryel and the soldier, Gabriel worked upon determining the nature of the Beast. His discoveries made him smile thoroughly and forget about his heartache. Two parts of the blood matched the Angelic blueprint, and one part was matching an Archangelic one. He could not believe how far from getting It as a Being he had been in the past investigating all demons to get a match when her nature was 3/4 Angelic. Thinking that her father was a fallen Angel, he really should have sussed it out much earlier, Gabriel kicked himself. He separated the non Angelic compound from the rest of the blood at once, feeling he was finally getting somewhere. He also expected that this was the part exploding his test tubes when mixed with the others. He trialled this at once, and left that experiment to do its timely work, while he investigated the fourth part carefully.

A couple of hours later, his hands wrote at a fast pace the results of his observations. A couple of blowing test tubes, called him to check on his side experiment. As he checked, a blowing reaction only occurred with the mysterious fourth part mixing with the Archangelic one. It remained innocuous with only Angelic blood.

Gabriel finally had an explanation why It-666 could perform such deep down healing and damages, she was partly Archangelic, and could understand bodies like Raphael and Death did. For him he still had to understand the fourth part and he needed Death to help him figure that one out faster, for he felt he had just isolated the part that made It so special.

He had to reveal his discovery to someone, and as Azryel would be deaf to his voice, his Uncle had to be his first port of call. He also remembered that he had to have an in depth overdue heart to heart with him and disappeared from the room at once.

Verse 16. Which is which.

When Gabriel reappeared by his Uncle Raphael's sides, he was surprised to find himself in sunny California, in a magnificent garden full of flowers of all sorts. He could not help mentioning,

-When I wished to be by you Wrath, I was far from imagining you would be in such a place. You are definitely not a flowery type.

The Archangel grinning to him argued,

-And you would be surprised Gabriel by who I am, what I like and dislike. Having lost contact with me for so long, you just lost touch with my Being and concerns. Making assumptions regarding me, will only put you in the troubled waters of insults. Either you know something, either you do not. If you do, talk, if you don't remain silent. Are you acquainted with the expression about assuming? So do not be an ass with me, Gab for it will not pass. Now, what brings you to wish being by my side? You who prefers avoiding me, and that is a proven fact.

Taken aback his nephew fell upon his knees. Remaining silent for a few minutes Gabriel spiralled in his deep sense of being totally lost, before apologising,

-Uncle Raphael, I am utterly sorry for everything, past and present. I can't express enough my regrets. I have been drifting away for far too long, so much so that I feel completely lost. As an Angel I am drowning every day that passes a little more, grieving the love I will never have and never receive, which makes me want to finish it all. I am so sorry to drown like that in front of you all. Pulling the curtain call upon myself is unforgivable and I do understand that. I will not do so Wrath, never, for the sake of you all. Being back with Us, I intend to curb those feelings of utter loneliness with no one to turn to for comprehension. I am by your side to apologise to you fully, to make up, to beg for your forgiveness and understanding, to obey Azryel's orders for he is so right, to repair the rift between us, to tell you that you can count on me to stand by you in your fight and missions, and that I will provide you with all the help I can give. I am here by you Wrath to offer you my eternal life back as your soldier, if you will have me back after my ostracism from your Army.

A knot formed in Wrath's throat, a blood tear appearing at his eyes ran across his cheek, as he held the hands of his pleading Archangelic nephew. Noticing the deep red cut on his right wrist, he asked,

-How can you promise me to be my soldier? This morning you promise me that you would never give up at the breakfast table. However a few hours later you have a fresh wound telling a different tale altogether. What am I to believe, you or your acts?

Gabriel shook his head at once negatively, desperately and tried to explain,

-Please do not cry Wrath, please not on my account. It is not what you think. I needed to draw some Archangelic blood for my experiments. I would have never asked you nor taken some from little Micky. The only one readily available for my test tubes was mine. I tried to heal myself back but I could not get the scar to disappear. I made an amazing discovery somehow comparing it to Bambi's one. I am trying to assess her Being, her true nature since Walter brought her in my clinic, for she is a utter puzzle to solve. Focusing on solving her, keeps me away from my darkest thoughts for minutes if not hours. Read me if you must to reassure yourself about my explanations, Uncle. However I wish for you not to go further than when you saw me this morning. This is my wish, but if your wish is to read all my thoughts and actions since our last fracas of years ago, I will respect that wish and submit to it fully.

Stroking the forehead of his nephew and his wrist, healing his scar doing so, Wrath simply told,

-Since you are so lost, Gabriel, I need to bridge all the gaps. It is my wish to be the one to open my arms to you, to offer you all my understanding and comprehension. So I will read you fully.

After few long minutes of reading his Archangelic nephew, Wrath's tears streamed upon his face,

-For Christ's sake Gab, why did you shut your voice to Us for so long? We would have listened. We would have been here. I sensed your great pride being a major factor in your silent struggle. You did more than well alone, yet you took a major toll which needed to be addressed sooner rather than later. Stand up, for you are completely forgiven, and I offer you all my apologies too for it is pride and stubbornness which kept me away from you, just like you. I must warn you that Azryel has been fully deceived by you. He is not taking that lightly and is set to work on your case slowly but surely taking in consideration your deeply grieving suicidal Being. He has not given up on you whatsoever, Death will teach you lesson after lesson, to bring you fully back from your drowning and loss feelings. If he will not listen to you, you must listen to him. If he does not believe in your respect, you must believe he still holds you in great respect. He cares for you more than he will ever show right now, for he wrecked his brain out to work out a bespoke rescue plan for you all night and all morning. He is my right hand and my left. He knows how much you mean to me. He will embrace you and stay by you until you are fully recovered. He is fiercely loyal, and I can not bestow upon you a better guardian Angel to watch over you, Gabriel. His tough love will pull you through and forward, trust me. My gift to you, my answer to your plea is Death, but not as you wished it, far from it, for Az will keep you alive, sound and fighting everyday in my Army, soldier.

Both Archangels embraced each other in a long and silent forgiving hug. Both wiped their tears in synchrony when a beautiful woman walked straight to them her arms holding a bunch of red roses. She addressed Raphael ignoring the presence of Gabriel,

-Raphael, I gathered all my 'Mr Lincoln' roses yet I am short of two to make the fifty required. You can check their quality, as I revived some of them to full bloom. You are welcome to pick two flowers among all of mine to make up for the missing two. Which other flowers did poor human Wendy love or have meaning to her?

Gab paying attention straight away understood why his Uncle was to be found among a garden of flowers. It touched him deeply. He answered for him noticing Wrath's silence,

-She liked red poppies. They always reminded her of her grand father and granny. Her British grand dad past away during World War one. Her American Nan, a nurse during the war, flowered her home and garden with poppies religiously in remembrance of her short lived husband. She always used to say that her granny wanted to sleep forever like her husband under a poppy field in Flanders yet remembered to fight it off proudly, in order to fight everyday for her only child and to show her true colours, red like a poppy, remembering soldiers, for she was now the lone soldier to protect her kid through thick and thin. Wendy planted poppies to remember her Nan, her Grand Dad and that life was worth fighting for.

The deep ocean blue eyes of the woman gazed at Gabriel from head to toes, and after assessing him, stated,

-You did not walk through my doors invited. You did not even knock. Your will and wants shall be disregarded in my house until propriety is restored. Do justice to all the dead you are speaking of, think before you act.

A dumbfounded Gabriel disappeared at once to reappeared by the door of the Californian villa. The place was enclosed by extremely large white wash walls. As he rang the doorbell, humbly, he could not help noticing the single row of Californian poppies lining neatly all walls. He waited for a quarter of an hour before a young beautifully dressed maid showed him in back to the garden. There he stayed put gazing at the awesome beauty of it and not daring crossing it uninvited anymore to rejoin his Uncle. Seeing his Uncle walking towards him, holding two red poppies, by the demanding beautiful Being, Gabriel asked humbly,

-I am ever so sorry for my intrusion. I wished to be by my Uncle's sides not knowing where he was. May I be let in? May I be welcomed? I want to pay for the roses.

The beautiful blond haired woman held her alabaster hand out to him and invited him in,

-You may be let in, Gabriel. As for your money, you may keep it. Raphael, I will not put any of those items collected today on to your account due to the circumstances, it is a gift from me to our old friendship.

Raphael taking her delicate hand deposited a kiss upon it,

-Demeter, thank you. To receive us on so short noticed is greatly appreciated. If you need any help from Us, it will be granted.

Smiling the Lady welcomed,

-I am delighted to know that for I may need your help in the future Wrath. Let's check on the candle making, and Mr Workmaster. My maid seemed to like him a lot, she was all smiles, rosy cheeks and fluttering eyelashes. Is the human single?

Butting in Gabriel replied straight away,

-No, he is not.

Raphael corrected,

-Technically he is. It is complicated Demeter. His heart still belongs to his ex-wife, my lovely niece Caroline. Forgive my nephew Gabriel, he is very touchy when it regards his human. He is an overprotective Guardian Angel who has set his heart to re-unite the couple somehow. He knows my Caro still loves her blondie-bear and that Walter still adores her. That man is part of my family and will always be kept jealously by Us.

A nodding Demeter understood, her eyes lighting up with a strange joy,

-Then he is a chosen one that passed your grades to carry your Archangelic line, I guess.

-You did guess right, the man is a chosen one. I made him be the father of incarnated Archangel Michael who is now eight. In due time, Walt will become my grandfather, for his daughter still to be born will become my carrier to bring me back in my next incarnated human shell.

Arriving in a large atelier, they saw Workmaster helping to make candles putting dried lavender flowers inside the liquid beeswax conscientiously while the maid was boxing up all that were ready. Demeter asked Walter,

-Special man, how many candles have you got so far?

Cocking his eyebrows full of circumspection, Walter replied,

-We have 24 candles so far and 12 under way. I am far from special, Ma'am, I am just plain human with tendencies which gave me the nickname of Wreck-man. I prefer that to any superlative that don't suit me.

Smiling kindly to him, Demeter stated to Raphael,

-A humble man was missing from all your previous choices, Wrath. Louisa, how long for the last 12?

-Another hour, Mistress.

-Wrath, you have my apologies to not have had the stock to reply adequately to your full order.

The Archangel seizing her hand at once and kissing the tip of her immaculate fingers, commented,

-Demi, between old friends, you do not have to apologise for that, beside my unusual demands were very short notice. However, I still have a demand to make which is of the usual serious kind.

The beautiful Being pushing her blond hair from her shoulder, smiled wickedly,

-Does Wrath seek a Witch? I am at your service, what do you want from me?

Raphael couldn't help his coming laugh, yet became deadly serious the more he spoke,

-Actually I do seek the services of my favourite white Witch to track an evil witch. It's an important job, which is going to lead to others. Consider this as a mission and you will be rewarded handsomely. Let's use that hour of wait briefing you on and starting you on the quest I have for you. Shall we go to the special room? Gabriel and my human have to be there too for the mission was started by them almost six years ago when Walter's twin sister Wendy, betrothed to my nephew Gab, was the victim of a human sacrifice.

Demeter bowed to the Archangel. She left the room swiftly saying in the Angelic tongue,

-Follow me Wrath. Your two grieving family members are welcome in my space.

Turning hastily, Raphael ordered,

-Gab, Wreck-man, come, remember one thing, disruption is not accepted in Demeter's sanctuary. She is a goddess so watch your language at all time. I don't want to bring back to Azryel two toads, he will have to kiss better. Comprendo?

The man gave a long look to Raphael and Gabriel yet said nothing but nodded his head in agreement to the leading Archangel. As they followed the goddess, he noticed that the crystal staircase was going up and up and endlessly up, spiralling against an alabaster wall. Small alcoves and niches containing gods and goddesses representations from all over the world attracted his attention at every step of the way up. His own mind was spiralling out of control, as if he understood well they were following the ancient Greek goddess Demeter, a Being which he always thought was the figment of the imagination of some creative human scholar with an agenda, political or religious. Yet, she was alive, well and a white Witch in Beverly Hills. He wondered how many gods and goddesses were alive and walking the Earth like the incarnated Angels and Demons. The thought was dizzying, yet it meant that if it was the case no religion was right or wrong, that their gods coexisted with each other, and were even friends. Like the Archangelic Raphael was with Demeter, they accepted each other's fundamental existence. He had not seen Wrath pulling the sword and annihilating her for being a lesser goddess or a lesser Being following a lesser God than his. He only saw deep friendship and respect between one another. The man entered the sanctuary room with a wide and confused smile with sudden hope reaching his heart.

The goddess closing the door behind him, seeing his peaceful smiling face, asked Workmaster,

-Dear man, your twin sister passed away six years ago, and we are about to track the criminals down. How can you smile?

-Because you, Demeter coexists. It means possible peace to my heart, rings the bell of possible peace for all humans, all over the world. How many gods and goddesses past and present, are walking upon Earth?

-Far too many to be a safe world for humans. For humans have a tendency to kill each other over us, trying to promote one of us at any one time to be the premium god to be worshipped over all gods and goddesses. If they only knew we do get along just fine with one another, pay each other due respect, and live along one another peacefully as we are all working for the common good, I guess they would be surprised, as unfortunately, our starkest followers preach words we never uttered, make laws up we never ordered, asked the unthinkable, the unforgivable, to our genuine followers. Some won't be swayed by the preachers of hate coming from all religions, yet some will be swayed by their clever explanations, orders and vindictiveness, will grab a gun, or whatever their barbaric will tells them to do and kill their human brothers with great pride, speaking of war, that has only been spurred in their own hearts. Unfortunately for us, we receive daily misguided invocations and prayers, set by lay human for us. Take one of us, Odin is being worshipped by human sacrifices which he never ordered and dislikes. Likewise religious genocide will never be forgiven, as it was only preached out by the haters. The intelligent kind that read the religious books for you and give you their own political agendas as the truth to be followed, promised heaven and earth. If human starts to read from front to cover their religious books they will find that many transmitted laws and saying taking for granted are totally inexistent. Only humans like sheep-ing their way through life unfortunately. They like listening to another they think knows better, and extinguish their own say and heart doing so. The result of a heart stopping listening to its own beat, to listen only to the beat of haters is deadly. That heart gets lost to hell, thinking that whatever heroic bullshit would have brought him heaven, fame, and maybe lots of virgins, depending on the religion. They only discover fallacy on the other side, that they were lied to, and a sentence for straight murder of a human or many. Peace for all humans is a dream for all of us we are still working upon, day in and out.

Workmaster blinked wildly, as if all his thoughts had been condensed in Demeter's voice, and could only swear,

-Blimey. This is big shit.

Wrath laughing, called upon Demeter,

-Let's not reveal too much to Walter, he can talk for the world and takes everything at heart. Get him started and we will be here all night besides I am looking for a four hundred year old Cambion which originated from France. She escaped the 'Poison Affair' and execution in the 1670's. She is a witch involved in human sacrifices and this is all I know, I am afraid.

Walking to the middle of the room to a huge crystal ball, Demeter stated as she placed her hands upon it,

-Do not worry Wrath, I can work upon that information.

Soon the room fell into complete darkness apart from the glowing huge crystal ball, the goddess whispered,

-I think we did make an observatory contact. She does not know of us spying upon her via her crystal ball. This could be interesting, it's like having a web cam in a culprit's house.

Raphael, Gabriel and Walter, paid attention to the crystal ball. They could see blurry images becoming clearer and clearer. Demeter sang a few words in tongue, and a green translucent mist appeared floating above the ball emitting sounds, voices and words, becoming comprehensible rapidly,

'You have to help finding him, Bitch!'

Gabriel recognised the voice of Paul Peterson straight away, and whispered his name in his uncle's ear.

The goddess, her eyes transformed into pure gold, turning to him at once, told,

-Talk Gabriel, you may all talk and share any information you gather from what you see and hear.

-It's Paul Peterson, the up and coming politician, an incarnated demon. He is the one that killed my Wendy.

Concentrating on the images they saw infamous and handsome P seizing the woman's beautiful grey-blond hair into his fist, while his other hand was at her neck. The Cambion witch did not look intimidated at all by his strangling move, she laughed. It was a chilling and sinister laugh which sent shivers down the spine of Walter, who asked,

-Are they fighting?

Raphael scolded him,

-Shut up and listen. I don't know yet.

'You know my price, P. You pay and you will get.'

They saw the demon tackling the Cambion, pushing her forcefully against a table. Turning her violently, so he faced her back, he laughed back.

'Bitch, I will f'in pay you. You will be so sore when I am over. What will you do with another demonic kid? You're not even capable of raising them properly.'

Gabriel stopped watching feeling utterly sick, while Walter commented,

-Great, he is fucking her rough. That's like watching hard core porn with a demon in it and a half demon, and they are planning to make another little demon.

The goddess turned to Raphael and asked him to follow her by a table full of opened magical books,

-I know your Cambion, Wrath. She is an extremely powerful witch called Cato. She was a maid of the Montespan, mistress of the Sun king of France. It is a blood pact, which allows her to be hidden from Azryel which kept her alive for so long. To get to her, you will need all my help and magical expertise. I will keep an eye upon her and work at her demise.

Coming to Raphael and pulling his sleeve with excitement, Workmaster shared,

-I knew it was worth watching until the end. P just fucked her hard in order to get her to work her magic in Boston to find the father of It. Her Evil dad is still on the run. P has no clue about his whereabouts that's why he is prostituting himself to the witch to enlist her. Gosh he was a rough bastard with her, but she did not mind at all, she looked like she craved it.

Gabriel and Wrath scolded sternly the man at once,

-Too much information, Workmaster.

Looking at the man attentively the goddess enquired,

-Who is It, Wrath?

The Archangel gave a very dark look upon Walter, before answering,

-Someone that came upon the scene, that you must not know about. It is a secret which must never be revealed to anyone, nor Beings, nor gods, nor humans and especially not demons. You are sworn to our staunched secrecy and warned that my wrath will fall upon you if you fail to keep It secret. Keep It secret with your whole life.

The goddess knelt by him and promised,

-You have my word, Wrath. I shall never mention It again. I will keep It secret.

-Good, rise. I trusted you Demeter for an eternity, and I will keep on trusting you, for I know how sound is your heart. The day you will hear me blow the trumpet, is the only day I will be prepared to speak about It, not before. I am doing everything in my power for that day to never come. Keeping It secret with our lives will save the World. Now, let me brief you upon your new mission. I need Boston and all its surrounding area witchcraft proof for a few days, until I find a fallen one from getting back into the wrong hands. Can you do that?

Smiling wickedly, Demeter turned a few pages in one of her huge leather bound books replied,

-I can and more, I can stop that witch for you. Archangel Raphael, your visits have never been boring, I can tell you that much. You can't stop from keeping me on my toes. I just love that. You should come more often.

-I will. I have to come back to tell you how well your Boston mojo worked for me. If I am disappointed I will be such a bore that you will never want me near your back ever again. I have to love you and leave you, Demi, duty calls. Thank you for your help. My Army will be protecting your endeavour with Cato. I am assigning a couple of Angels to you that are versed into white magic. You may find them useful in any stand off, they are both highly trained soldiers. Expect them at your doors before the sun goes down.

The goddess clapped her hands. Before the Archangel Raphael's feet appeared the 48 roses, the two poppies, the 36 lavender candles in a wooden crate, and a little muslin bag tied neatly by a red bow full of Epsom salt.

-Your order Wrath. I am going to work straight away on the other one. I will not let any witches double cross me. You will get there before P.

Taking the hands of Gabriel and Walter, Raphael teletransported all of them back to the tree house.

Verse 17. Mind the Gap.

When Walter reappeared to the platform with both Archangels, he could not help swearing,

-Jeez. That was educational. Why keep that you lot, demons, angels, gods, goddesses, cambions are walking upon Earth from humans?

Raphael answered him,

-Because it would jeopardise humans everywhere. Knowing that, we would have World War Three on our hands. That is why. Anymore questions?

A smiling Workmaster answered,

-No more questions.

-Good, because, I am going to strangle you right and proper the next time you forget to watch your tongue opposite a powerful Being like that goddess. You can not open your mouth and blabber away your incontinent chattering which reveals far too much in front of anyone but Us and only Us. You badly jeopardised the safety of little It-666. If I did not have a strong relationship with Demeter, human, we would have all the powerful Beings walking upon Earth at our doors right now asking for It. However, the goddess will have two of my strongest Watchers at all times making sure she doesn't break her secrecy vows. If I have to remove that Being from the World because of your stupidity human, you will also get a feel of my wrath. Do you understand your mistake Workmaster? Or are you foolish enough to carry on like you always did, ignore it, and repeat it in the near future? For uncontrollable stupid talking I have a straight remedy, I can cut your tongue right now, and spare the whole world doing so. Talking about It is never allowed in company which is not from Us. This is the last time I have to swear a Being and spare two of my valuable soldiers to have him or her watch, do I make myself clear?

A sheepish Walter nodding in agreement, replied,

-I am so sorry, Raphael, I did not think one bit, I forgot myself with the excitement of knowing that P did not get the big Evil daddy back. It will certainly not happen again. Thank you for sorting my bad cock up, I would be so upset if anything happened to It because of me. I will think twice, thrice before saying anything in front of anyone that is not part of Us.

Wrath tapping the shoulder of the man whispered wickedly,

-Twice or thrice thinking before talking to Us would be a good thing too, a much appreciated thing. As for your silence it may give you my straight forgiveness, Walt, I will let you think about it.

-My straight answer is this don't push it too hard on my guilt trip, Wrath, it will get you nowhere, I will think about what I am saying in the future when I am not in the company of the trusted ones, my family and Us and that is all.

As soon as Walter stopped talking he saw his little son running on the footbridge to him. Opening his arms to Micky, his face lit up with sheer joy,

-My dear boy! Who brought you here?

An excited Micky answered his father, while jumping into his arms,

-Azryel, he took mummy, Asha and I to uncle Gab's house because he said it was safer that way. We are going to live here from now on. I stopped school a week ago and Asha has been teaching me lots, that I am an Archangel and all that cool stuff where I can disappear from the kitchen and reappear where I wish to. Az said uncle Gab is the best teacher for me as he is an Archangel like I am, he also said Gab needed a love your own family incentive too in order to keep going. I did not understand what he meant. What does that big word 'incentive' mean, dad? Az is full of big words. When I listen to him, I just get lost somewhere usually I start thinking of football. I wish I could learn the trick to look like I am here and present to not be rude but then to teletransport in the garden and just kick the ball about. Yet I don't think that is possible to be here and there at the same time. Let me show you, Pa, how I disappear. I will be standing on that bench in two ticks.

Walter gave a quick look at Gabriel who just held his uncle Raphael's hand, silently. He could see a blood tear piercing at the corner of the eyes of both Archangelic Beings. All of them saw Micky do the teletransportation trick perfectly. The man applauded his son, grabbed him from the bench, and praised,

-Wow, that was impressive, my little Archangel. I am very happy for you and mum to live here from now on. Like Az, I won't be as worried as I am now knowing you are just a few miles away, but too many miles for my liking and his. Azryel does speak big words but you need to listen to him for he knows what he is talking about. When Az is there with you and addressing you my lil' one, you must pay attention, always, no escaping to the garden, no football dreaming, it would be rude, but also it would be stupid. Azryel is a very important Angel that will keep mummy, daddy and you alive, you must respect him at all times, listen and do as he says. Understood, my lil' bit?

-Understood Daddy.

-Good, now give a hug to uncle Gab because he needs one, and thank him for allowing you in his house with mummy and to teach you to be a good Archangel.

The kid ran to Gabriel, encircled his neck with his little arms, and gave him a big fat peck on his Angelic cheek,

-Thank you uncle Gab. I promise I will be good and orderly. Azryel said I must tidy after all my games to keep you happy. I will put all my toys back in the toy chest, I swear. Mum and I got your spare bedroom and we will make ourselves as small as we can.

Gabriel hugging his nephew back told him at once,

-Little Micky, you and your mum are family, do not make yourselves small in my house. Toy tidying is a must, but play about my dear child, play. You have got only one short childhood at a time as an incarnated Angel, I want you to enjoy yours as long as you can.

Suddenly all saw the Death Angel appearing upon the bench and lighting a cigarillo calmly, he considered the scene before saying nonchalantly,

-Have I interrupted a moving scene? My sincere apologies. As you can see I decided to bring everyone under a single roof. It's a safety call when we do not know where the big Evil is. I do not want him lurking in the garden where lil' Micky kicks about his ball. Walter's family by my sides at all times is best. It will also do good to Gabriel. How did your day go at Demi's, Wrath? Mine went well. It-666 has been bonding and training with the Army nicely this afternoon. All the soldiers worried about her, gave her a chance within their hearts, good or bad. I think they will not give her up at the first hurdle on the contrary. The subject of the lesson was all about being tackled by many adversaries at once. I needed to fine tune my five that got wounded at the last battle but also it was the perfect opportunity for It to experience multiple opponents training. She had only one to one with me and the battle in P's wood had been a crash course for her. She did really well this afternoon, so well that she won almost every tackle done upon her to start off. I had to reestablish the balance for the soldiers not to get scared that they won't be able to win against her ever in the future, bearing in mind she is the Beast and only sixteen. I joined in some tackles to ground her right and proper a few times so she doesn't get any big ideas. Asha although lacking training with the Army for a few days now, being the appointed bodyguard of Caroline, impressed me by being the only Angel apart from me managing to floor our girl almost single handedly. His technique was fast, strong and deceptive. He didn't let It-666 to think of her next move, nor his. He had a clear edge upon her throughout. I am going to make him teach the other Angelic soldiers his technique most probably tonight when our little Antichrist is sleeping. The sooner the better, to reestablish the confidence in the guys. The Angelic

Army will keep training until dinner time when it is called out, giving us peace for the funeral ceremony of Wendy Workmaster.

Archangel Raphael stroking his chin worryingly, answered,

-My day at Demeter's was mitigated. First I had Gabriel coming unannounced in the house of a living goddess, which took me nearly ten minutes to convince her to forgive him, and not to curse him to be intruded by everyone in his own house. You can imagine the dilemma when you know as well as I do that Demi is a Being of her words. Bless, he was only doing what you ordered so strongly, and we did make up, Az. Second and last, I had my man Workmaster not holding his tongue again. A very bad blip which means the goddess is aware of the existence of It-666, and I had to swear her in to secrecy. I had to put two Watchers upon her at all times to make sure she does so. I think it is a precaution but very necessary under the circumstances. It is my Army being punctured by two strong soldiers. I have to send the white witchcraft twins before the sun goes down. They are the only ones that can deal with Demi as a witch and control her. Now, for the positives, Evil dad of It is still on the loose. P did not reestablish his connection with him. He is seeking the help of the powerful witch Cambion in order to get his hands upon him. For the gritty part of the transaction and terms, I will let the human to fill you in as he was the only one to watch it all. This has to be done kids free, no little It or Micky and in the loophole room. I am going to retrieve Evil dad before anyone else does. I have Demeter on duty to make Boston and the whole area witchcraft proof giving Us time to do so. When my hands are upon him, I need you to have all your suggestions fully working Az, to jail him. I am going to quest for him with my Army as soon as I have the mind signal from Demeter. At my feet is all we have for tonight's ceremony. However short noticed it was, the goddess did not even bill me for it. She was ever so kind and respondent to what happened to Wendy. I am just wowed by her, so much as to consider her my later years Archangelic sweet heart. The only thing with eternal goddesses, they do not recycle with time as we do and renew their shapes. They had only one infancy in their eternal life which happen so far away that playfulness is simply not going to happen. Yet, there is something about Demi that can make me eat my own words. Getting back to serious matter, Az get the Indian fall ready. I need to send my twins off and I need to do a fresh assessment on It. What you said about only two of my Angels, you and Asha being able to tackle her at sixteen worries me greatly. This will not be an easy thing to hide from her and needs to be reestablished at once. Training is definitely called for after Dinner time and without It-666, general. Any other orders Azryel, apart mine to extinguish your cigarillo and never smoke in front of Micky?

Death put his cigarillo down at once without arguing, replied,

-You making up with Gabriel makes my heart sing with joy. Well if it ever could do so anyway. My only order is for Gabriel to talk to Caroline about the clinic. It remains his decision. The work/baby of his life is to be given to her. Having her under his roof, allows him to have an influential say about his clinic at all times. I want you all in one hour for the ceremony. Walter, who do you want to assist? Little Micky, you come with me to give a hand preparing the waterfall for the funeral.

Gabriel nodded his agreement while Walter replied,

-I want it private, only our family members, Raphael, Gab, Caro, Micky and It. Although It never knew Wendy, including her will give her the feeling that she is adopted by us and that she is now family.

The Death Angel asked Gabriel,

-How do you feel about that Gab? Do you agree with Walter? In my opinion the man just let his good heart speak and his concept of raising It as his own child has to be commanding.

The Archangel remained silent for a few minutes before he spoke finally,

-She is family. It needs that sense of security, warmth and belonging. I feel bad that her first family gathering with us is a very sad occasion however. But I agree with Walt that we need to have her, there with us.

Death smiled kindly and taking the wooden crate upon the ground, asked little Micky,

-Now little Angel, pick up those flowers and follow me. Gab, Walt, Wrath, see you all later, and don't be late. We have a busy evening before us.

The child did as he was told and followed the Death Angel eagerly, and blabbering,

-Az, why is it called an Indian waterfall? Were there Indians living in that cave by it? Do you think a brown bear is sleeping inside it during the winter? Do you think it is going to snow this year, for it's pretty cold already?

Azryel shrugged his shoulders in half desperation, yet could not help smiling irresistibly,

-Now, little Workmaster, you must learn not to talk as much as your daddy does. One question at a time, my boy, that gives people time to think and reply, is always recommended.

-But then I would not think of the other questions anymore. I would forget them.

-Good, all the better.

Archangel Raphael watching them go commented,

-Walter, having that child here, will not only do Gab lots of good, but to you as well. If you want to reunite with Caro, your chance of a lifetime is right here. This time do not cock up with my niece. Seeing the smile upon Azryel, I know your kid will do that Death Angel a world of good. He could have let Micky stay with you yet he made him tag along with him. Who would have guessed that Death had a soft spot for children. Mind you who would have guessed that he knows all the Disney movies too by heart. Although he would not let it show, he is the ultimate softie.

Looking at his child striding along beside the Death Angel, trying to keep up with his fast steady pace, chatting happily to him, Workmaster could not help smiling as he answered,

-I would not call Azryel that. But gosh do I respect that Angel, he cares definitely more than he lets it show. I know that him and Gab will teach my son to be a good Archangel. I have faith in them both. I would not mind you Raphael getting involved with Micky's education too, for I am certain you have much to teach him as well as an Archangel. As I never had a father in law, I always treated you a little bit like one, would you treat yourself as Micky's appointed grandad, Uncle Raphael?

Wrath cocking his eyebrows to the human grinned wickedly and queried,

-Since invited I will do so, Walter. Thank you, it does touch me coming from you as I thought I kind of held the part of an evil mother in law with you all along. So have you got some sudden faith in me, like you do with Az and Gab? Let's move on, I need to check our little It out, and brief my two Angelic Watchers before sending them to keep an eye on Demeter. Come with me and witness what I do as the leader of the Angelic Army. Gabriel, stop being aimless. Go and make sure your sister is comfortable in her living quarters. Have that necessary clinic talk, it's essential, as I need your whole focus on creating a clinic for my Angelic Soldiers ASAP.

Gabriel disappeared from the platform at once, leaving Workmaster alone with Wrath, who replied,

-The mother in law part was true in my heart until you came into the scene for It-666. Yet I know Caroline although fearing you, respected you, that you raised Gab and her up since their parents' accidental deaths. The way they both turned out speaks for itself, Raphael. Both are saving lives in their clinic day in and out. I have faith in you Wrath to be the best grandad to my child.

A truly smiling Archangel took the man with him to the loophole room truly satisfied.

Verse 18. Let It Be.

The sun was about to set upon the horizon. The little Archangel called out from the other side of the waterfall,

-Azryel, I think I am all done. What do you think? Would it look good for Auntie Wendy? Sorry it was two questions... I forgot the one at a time thing.

The Death Angel looking and smiling answered,

-Very good, Micky. I think you did a great job, and that your Auntie Wendy would have been very proud of you. As for questions, down to two is pretty good for a little Workmaster, I will accept that for now. Shall I teach you a new Angelic trick?

The child clapped his hands with glee,

-Oh, yes, please. What is it this time?

-To light candles the easy way. The funeral party is going to arrive any time soon, candle lights will just welcome them to the right mood to have under the circumstances.

-Big word Az, big word warning, 'circumstances'. What does that mean?

-Mmm, it means that something or an action done in the past has to do with what you are doing right now for example. The meaning is slightly broader Micky but I will go through it with you another day, however your father as a former lawyer would tell you it is a very important word to know. At the present, it simply means we light candles in the memory of Auntie Wendy. Trick time?

-Trick time! I got it I think, Az, the circumthing-thing out.

-Circumstances, Michael, or no trick time.

-Cir-cum-stances.

The child gave the Angel a winning smile as he appeared by him.

-Good. Getting your words right is important. The power of understanding is within them. Your father fights with words for better laws and human rights, something you should be proud of and aim to replicate. The trick with the candles is simple, just rub the tip with your fingers and think of a soul you love, mum, dad, Gab, and it will light, let's try it. Who do you think of first?

-Dad!

-Good, that's shining for sure. Let's go to the next candle.

By the time Micky had lighted all the candles, they saw Raphael walking with Walter and Gabriel, It-666 following them with Caroline.

Caroline tried to make small talk with no real success, as sadness was grabbing her heart the more she walked,

-Your hair is growing, It. Very short still but you are a curly blond, my love. Give it one more inch an you will look very Angelic. I wanted to buy you dresses today but Az said you needing clothes did not call for dresses as you were a soldier. So I only could get a couple of black and blue jeans, and the track suit Az was swearing by for your training sessions. I could not go past his watchful eyes for any bits of clothing. If I did not get a pink top for you, he agreed on a red long sleeves number that's got a neck line that is cool yet safe. You and me, need to go shopping one day, free from those dreary Angels. Uncle Raphael did to me what Az is doing to you, back in the day. They think of what is best for you, neglecting to ask you if it would hurt your feelings. Make sure you do not go wild like I did on Wrath, talk to Az and confide in him. Death is the one you can call at any time and will help you to survive, strangely enough.

When they reached the Indian Waterfall, all fell silent. Michael appeared by his dad and his uncle like the Death Angel had ordered him. He held their hands tight. Azryel started the ceremony. Caroline held It's hand all the way through. She whispered a few secretive words about how Wendy was to explain what was happening to the teenager, yet she cried when the bag made of the human skin of Wendy containing her bony hand fell in the waterfall. It-666 grasped her pain and hugged the woman tightly.

The roses and salt were fed into the waterfall, with Raphael, Azryel and Gabriel singing strange Angelic words. When the red roses sank, Wrath called the ceremony off. Walt, Caro, him and Micky went slowly back to the tree house. While Gabriel stood still, demanding to stay there for a few more silent minutes. Azryel and It stayed by him quietly. All of a sudden, they saw the grieving Angel rushing in the Indian cave, crying blood tears. They followed him at once, worried.

When he stood still by a rock with strange designs carved upon it, Gabriel barked angrily,

-Wendy is not resting in peace. She is out there, somewhere. I have to lay her soul to rest. She is a lost soul in hell, I have to find her. I have to make her rest, Azryel, properly, not the human way with candles and roses. Her soul that deserved heaven got hell because she got caught by a demon. I need to go and find her and make it right.

Pushing himself in front of Gabriel, the Death Angel ordered,

-You are not going to wander for her soul in hell anymore, Gabriel, you are far too valuable as an Archangel to do so. You mean so much to Us that we can not loose you to hell. You need to focus on the living and make sure that the same death does not happen to them. Walter, Caroline and Michael are all at great risk. We need to protect them. For that we need you here Archangel and nowhere else, certainly not hell. Is that clear?

A distraught Gabriel resigned himself, breaking down into tears, as he sobbed,

-It's clear. She is lost, so lost. I will fight for her through her family, keeping them safe.

Calmly Azryel gave a strong hug to the Archangel, his shoulder to cry upon and soothed,

-There, Gab, there, let it go. Shall we all go back to the tree house? It is late and we have got a little boy and an Angelic Army to feed.

When Gabriel broke the hug, he saw the young It teary eyes, and scolded her at once,

-You didn't swallow my pain, did you, Bambi? You must dry those tears my girl, like I do. Let's go home, you must be starving too after your day of training.

Wiping her eyes, It replied, as they left the Indian Cave,

-It's sympathy, Gab, just sympathy, I can't help feeling your sorrow.

verse 19. Saving Souls.

Although 1 am, It kept staring silently at the ceilings. She could hear the peaceful snore of Workmaster, but there was no signs of Azryel yet. Wondering when Death will finally get his rest, as counting the hours, she realised that it was more than 48 hours since he did have one. The young Beast could not help being impressed by the stamina and sheer strength of that Angel but also how devoted to the others, his soldiers, he was, putting their needs before his. Thinking of it she felt she could not have found better hands to fall under. She was also very happy that he had been appointed the Guardian Angel of Gabriel.

The announcement was made at the dinner table by Raphael. The teenager understood why it was needed. She could feel deep within herself the grief of the Archangel. Her own heart bled when Gab stood by the secret path to Hell, crying out loud for the lost soul of Wendy. She wished she could do something to help, something which could solve things, just something. She could only admit to herself that she was very fond of Archangel Gabriel, very fond indeed, and she could not grasp what it was. Twisting and tossing upon her bed, she thought hard and strong, why did she like Gabriel so much? Was it the way he did not give a toss about her wishes? When she asked to be called simply It, he carried on regardless to nickname her Bambi unlike the others. She loved that pet name deep down, it reminded her of her first meeting with Gabriel, the night of her arrival at the clinic, and the way he dealt with her all the way through. Closing her eyes for a few minutes, reminiscing, a blood tear appeared rolling upon her cheek.

She had to do something to quench the pain he felt. Like Azryel, she did not want him to go and get slaughtered in Hell for his quest for Wendy's soul for Gabriel was a multitasking key part Archangel badly needed for the times to come. The Angelic Army could not afford to lose him in one of his erratic full of sheer pain moments. Thinking deeply she resolved that the fact that Wendy Workmaster lost her soul to Demons as they sacrificed her, and that despite being solely a good human she had to dwell in Hell because of it, and that this was the main cause of the pain of Gabriel. He needed her to rest in peace and he knew she simply was not. He went to Hell to find her many times yet did not manage to do so and always came back empty handed or with a demon to experiment upon.

Having a light bulb moment, It stood up and went to the sleeping man. She could feel soul as well as bodies, maybe she could track his twin sister's soul by its similarity to Walter. Maybe being the Antichrist she could go to Hell and come back unscathed. Yet she would have to become her ugly self, the demonic Beast, and then she would scare any souls away from her. How could she make Wendy's soul follow her willingly? Dilemma. However, if she took someone that knew her, just like Walt to convince her to follow them out of Hell; but then she needed to make sure the man would stay safe throughout the Hell journey. How could she work that one out, she wondered. Making Walt look like a demon himself could be worked out and having only his face and voice revealed to his sister when they found her, she gathered.

Smiling endlessly she imagined Gabriel knowing that Wendy was not a lost soul anymore, that she could go where she was supposed to go in Paradise. It was worth a try. It would be a surprise for him for tomorrow, seeing Wendy's soul in his house ready to be laid to rest. It had to be his own special surprise. Things had to be put right somehow. She was ready to do it, and woke up Workmaster,

-Walt, wakey, wakey, please. Walt, no more snoring I have an idea. Walt?

-What's up, lil' one?

-I can't sleep.

The man raising himself to a sitting position commented while yawning,

-I gathered that one. Tell me what is the big idea that keeps you awake.

-Well I thought about Wendy being a lost soul and Gabriel being so distraught about it. I know that I can track her down there in Hell faster than any one as the Beast smelling and all knowing about my surroundings. But in Hell with a scary monster like I would look like would poor Wendy follow me willingly? I guess she would rather stay put. If you come with me you could convince her that I am safe and working for the Angelic Army as a soldier, and we would swiftly get out of there with her. I would need to disguise you a bit like a demon so you would remain safe throughout. It is a wild gamble, but I am willing to take it for mourning Gab and the poor Wendy and reestablish some sort of right order. Gabriel and all the others are too important to be lost in Hell, I can call them if needs be, only if we get into some trouble. Wendy's soul safe in paradise will end Gabriel's grieving. What do you think, Walt?

Scrubbing his chin, pondering, the human replied,

-I think it is scary shit yet worth doing to be honest. I want Wendy in Paradise not Hell. Transform me and let's be off before Az notices our absence. We need to be back before he goes to bed, before he goes off on one. Let me write a note for him to put in his hammock.

'Az, don't be mad at us, It and I went to Hell to find Wendy's soul. It's a downright favour to Gab, we do not want to lose him out there. Peace to Wendy will mean a peaceful Gabriel. We are working on it, if it works.'

The scrambled note done, Walter asked It-666,

-Can demons be nice looking? I do not want to scare the shit out of my own sister.

It smiling wildly replied,

-They can. It doesn't make them safer though. Incarnated P chose a handsome human shape to gather prey endlessly and he is not short of takers. Looking like a demon will not make you one, it will be

just a suit, a costume, that wears off as soon as I say so. Give me
your hand, it is a neat trick.

Workmaster gave it with no hesitation, and was transformed into a
large and muscular blue skin demon. He looked at his large hands in
amazement, swore,

-Holy shit! Look at the size of those! they are gianormous. I feel
taller and stronger. Are sure it will wear off? Did I have to be so
massive?

-Positive, I made you like that to give you a fair chance if we ever
have to fight any demons down there. Now we'd better move fast
so no Angels seeing us like this, slaughter us by mistake.

She transformed her own self into the Beast in front of a gob
smacked Walter. From head to toes she had skin the colour of the
night, large bat wings, terrifying red eyes, retractable claws, and teeth
like a vampire. She was taller yet lean. The shivering man asked her
at once,

-Just tell me that you still got your heart in there? Is it your true
shape?

-It is Walter, and my heart is still there beating, liking humanity and
not wanting to hurt anyone.

-Let me tell that you look frighteningly awesome, a right picture of
the devil like in Fantasia, but in feminine form. I am pretty sure
even those demons will be scared to cross your path tonight. Let's
go. Take your fighting stick with you just in case.

A nodding It-666 took the magical stick from under her bed, and
unwrapped it carefully from the red satin wrap enveloping it,
another gift from the Death Angel, for doing so well at her first
battle. She stroked impulsively the embroidered black letters, A A's
It. This was what she would be fighting for tonight, the Angelic
Army, and for one of their soldiers in particular to protect him
from risking his Archangelic life by strolling Hell grief stricken in a

endless quest for a lost soul. She had enough power to find that soul fast, hopefully bring it back to Gabriel, so the soul could be taken to rest in peace in Paradise, by the Death Angel.

Workmaster recalled her from her reverie by a tap upon her shoulder,

-We got to move on fast, It. If we are caught out in our demonic state there will be no possible rescue of my sister. We will be kaput before we would have a chance to explain that we are you and me. Come.

The Beast grabbed the hand of Walter and teletransported with him to the entrance of the Indian cave. She ordered, as they walked in,

-Follow me very closely, if I have to start fighting, you must do so too, for then we will be in danger. I gave you powerful demonic strength so you will be able to protect yourself adequately down there but I will keep an eye on you and your sister at all times. If we face too much pressure I will call upon Azryel to rescue us. He slaughters demons like no other. He is our plan B. I will move fast, like a hunting dog so you can't pay attention to your surroundings, only upon my tracks. One other point, some demons if like me, can read minds, so I blanked ours from them, the spell will last for a couple of hours. So we want to be back before then as we would be in great danger otherwise. Understood?

The large blue demonic Walter could only say, shitting himself a little, as he stood by the rock with the strange marking, where It stopped walking,

-Understood Soldier, I won't lose your sight, trust me. That's for sure.

-Good. Gabriel did a very good job on that secret path to Hell. It's invisible to demonic eyes. Which means this is the way in and out for us. Somehow I can't understand why I can see it. I am going to reinforce that spell. Which means I am going to make it invisible even to myself.

Tapping her shoulders as she started spelling the secret path to Hell, he enquired anxiously,

-Is it a good idea It? Because we are suppose to come back that way. What if inside and in great danger you can not see the door anymore. It would be a big blooper.

A smiling Beast reassuring him responded, as she carried on steadily with her stronger spell,

-There is not only one sense out there. I have 12. Do not worry Walt I will not drag you in with me if I did not work out your swift rescue in case of trouble.

-Great, I have only 5 or maybe 6 senses. I feel a little like a deflated human right now. Thanks kiddo, I needed that moral boost before going to Hell. Have you got a tail I can hold not to get lost out there?

Done with her spell, It-666 turned to the transformed human, and hugged him tightly,

-You are a man, Walter Workmaster I would not lose for the whole world. I can arrange the tail thing for you, it is no problem at all. I am going to create one, right now, and it is not a bad idea at all under our circumstances. By the way Walt, you have 5 senses, you are a typical human and the one that made me love humanity, brought me hope and the ability to see further than my own nose with your words that touch the heart and the spirit. You are meant to be, very precious to the Angels, and to my own heart. If I had an ability to choose my own dad like the incarnated Angels before I was born, the Beast would have begged by your feet to be accepted as your child. What you have done for me since we first met has touched my heart very deeply, I am standing by you fighting for humanity's cause instead of dying of a stupid self abort because of you. I have been shown how I could do good, I have joined an Army of Angels, who your words convinced to give me a chance. Walter, you will come out of there alive or I will die defending you till my last breath but this won't happen because of our plan B. Be confident, dad. I want no other dad than you, human rights lawyer Workmaster, Private Investigator who brings people to justice. Do you think I am ready to lose you in Hell? Hell no.

To demonstrate it, she made a very long and sturdy demonic tail appeared with a deadly pointy end, she explained,

-This will be thrown into the first demon that dares to touch you. I will make sure you are always with me and safe.

-You go girl, It, we need to find you a proper name when we come back, one you love, with Caro, Micky and me. We will then have a naming ceremony with all the Angelic Army. So far my It, you have made me proud, very proud. Let's keep your fighting spirit on and go to our own little 'big fat' mission. I am looking forward to saving Wendy's soul.

Going through the path together at once, Walter and It arrived in Hell. As soon as they reached the exit, the Beast poked her wrist with her clawing nail, taking a drop of her own blood carefully she levitated it to the emplacement of the entrance, made it disappeared from sight. She smiled proud of herself and using telepathy told Walter,

-There, I can smell my own blood from afar, it was drawn so many times under torture. Let's go and find Wendy. I can already get her soul substance. It is so faint, so weak, so battered. We have to get her out of here fast. With me dad?

-With you all the way through.

Speeding like no other, the young Beast reached a deeper underground level where the human sacrifices to gods, deities of all sorts, demons and the devil were all kept. All were lost souls, being lied to, tempted or simply taken by criminals of all sorts. All were kept in a somewhat distressing physical state of what they were upon earth at their time of death. It wondered how she would find Wendy's. She had to think fast for it was clear that the souls were

injured beyond belief and could not walk out of Hell unaided. Her
nose fine tuning to a particular cell, she pointed it to Walter, and
sent to his mind,

-This is Wendy's cell. She is in an appalling state, I can restore her to
a running state in minutes if she is not scared of me, and a gliding
one which is even faster. I can also make her invisible to demons
which could be safer, but it would be temporary, two hours at most.
You have to go in first and talk to her, dad. Let me restore your
human face for as long as you talk to her. It will be very emotional.
Be prepared. Mention Paradise, and she will listen to you, for she
knows Hell does exist for good having been there for six long years.
Be her hope, Walter, work your human magic, convince her with
your words to follow us.

She broke the lock with her fighting shaft swiftly and opened the
door for him. The frightened soul of Wendy backed right towards
the end of her cell in a little dark corner at the sight of the demonic
shape coming in yet wondered why she had not heard the dreaded
rattle of the jailers' keys. Her jailers and torturers were not due until
a good 6 hours at least. She just had her torture session with the
other souls about half an hour ago. That demon broke in to her cell
and something was not right, this was not how the place worked
with the impeccable clockwork that runs you to a thread of a soul.
Then she heard him talk, softly, tenderly and she recognised the
voice from her happy past. At first she could not make out if she
was victim of a demonic joke but the more he spoke, she realised
that her twin brother was really here, and here for her,

-Don't be afraid, Sis. I am no real demon, it's me, Walt. Wreck-Man,
you know...no you don't know I was called Wreck Man after your
death, because I was so distraught, I had a bad break down. I came
to fetch you, my lil' Wren, my lil' Half, remember? I have friends in
Heaven and on Earth now which deal with souls and humans and
know stuff which you may believe now that you have been down
here for a while, for me it was a discovery. Gabriel is an Archangel,
would you believe that? He is still grieving you badly, and has been
searching for your soul in Hell to get you to Paradise since
since...Oh Wren, I have so much to tell you but no time to do so.

My life is at risk as I stand before you in demonic shape that will disappear in a couple of hours. I am helping you with someone looking worse than I right now, born to be looking like a devil, the power of one, yet with the heart of an Angel. She will get us out of Hell, Wendy, trust me and follow. My nickname at home was Peanut Butter and that you know for you teased me endlessly with it.

Workmaster's extended his large demonic blue hand to his twin sister's soul with great anxiety and care to not distress her any more. To his surprise she seized it at once, went to hug him,

-Peanut, I still can't believe you're down here, you're my big Bro big time. I will follow though I am in a bit of a bad shape. I will try to run as fast as I can behind you.

As he looked upon her away from the shadowy corner, Walter acknowledged the state of his sister as she passed away, and before he knew it blood tears appeared at his eyes. He wondered if It-666 had done just a cosmetic costume job upon him or a greater one. He felt also great anger against demons and especially P who had slaughtered poor Wendy, who appeared before him with a missing right hand and a hole where her heart should have been. She must have died painfully fast. He took her to It and told reassuringly,

-She will allow you to glide out of Hell fast and swift, in her trail. She will also render you invisible to demonic eyes for a while. Trust her, Wren, she is your path to Paradise, despite the way she looks. I trust her with my own life, Sis.

Wendy took a long worried look at the devil looking like creature before her and saw her kneel by her presenting her clawed hands to her in a disarming way, pleading,

-Wendy Workmaster, my name is It, a soldier of the Angelic Army of Archangel Raphael. I am here to help you get out of Hell. I am here to bring you to Archangel Gabriel.

The soul put her shivering left hand in the palm of the Beast, forcing her own self to trust her despite her frightening appearance.

She never saw demons kneel before humans beforehand, but rather torturing them and ripping them apart. That devil creature definitely sounded different. Wendy answered,

-Take me to my Gabriel, It.

She felt great warmth invading her by her hand coming from the creature, injection of strength replacing all the weakness of her present state. She started levitating and disappearing from sight. She tried to look at her hand lifting it but saw zilch, she had been rendered invisible there and then. That impressed Wendy right and proper, she swore, yet she could not hear her own voice,

-Blimey, you got some powers about you It. I am talking but I can't hear myself. What's happening? It is so freaky.

It voice reassured her,

-I rendered you invisible and silent to all but me and Walter, we can see and hear you. This way you will remain safe throughout. Do not be afraid Wendy, my powers will only help you escape Hell and will never harm you.

Wendy nodded to her, her understanding and was ready to follow them, yet she saw her brother looking at all the other cells, blood tears in his eyes, telling the Beast,

-Those souls are in atrocious conditions, all are missing a limb, sometimes the head, and all had their heart removed.

-They are all Paul Peterson victims, Bro, in this section, we are 76 down here but the number stopped rising for some reason.

-That's because It, and the Army of Angelic soldiers of Raphael, destroyed the consecrated places he was doing his human sacrifices. It, do you think we could save those lost souls too and bring them to Azryel?

The Beast feeling the tremendous pain deep down of all the victims told,

-We can't let them down here, save one and leave the rest behind is unthinkable, I would not forgive myself. Walt, go to them, warn them of my appearance, tell them about the invisibility and silence trick I will perform upon them, and we will round them all up and go.

A smiling Workmaster could not help hugging It-666, before doing what he was ordered,

-That's my girl! Soldier, you have a sound heart. I'll go and tell them about the great escape from Hell that they are all about to do.

Within minutes they had rounded up the lost souls. All invisible and silent, happy to be given the chance of their eternal after-life to seize their freedom from Hell, they followed It and Walter in an orderly fashion as asked by It. Although all were frightened of her, they were obeying her as they would obey any demon in Hell to avoid punishment, yet the difference, was that the Devil creature was talking to them about hope and Paradise, no harm to be done to them any more, and the ability for them to rest in peace. They would rather follow that type of Devil anywhere she was heading for she sounded far better than all the rest. For them the She-Devil was a commanding and commending soldier, that they would obey to the letter and hope for the best of her endeavour to get them out of here.

Very soon they reached the upper levels of Hell, all unnoticed and It lead them through a large door to a sort of great hall, but there they saw a group of large soldier demons, two of them holding on a leash two massive Hell hounds with six heads. That did not look very promising whatsoever. The Beast assessed the situation straight away scanning her position and throwing telepathic orders at once in their minds,

-Stay together and stand your ground, do not back down in front of the enemy you will forever regret it. The way out is right behind them, they do not know it. They are just aware of the blood scent I left there, it was found by the Hell Hound, so they sent a patrol there for me, only me. They are not aware of your presences my lost souls, not aware at all, you will be safe. The only entrance to that Hall is behind us, they are only a dozen with two massive Hellish dogs, I am going to close those doors to prevent any further patrol and take them on. Walter it is fighting time and stay clear of the hounds, I will deal with those. I am sending a message to Azryel right now as I speak, the rescue will come soon.

The large heavy metal doors shut themselves closed in a loud bang, which made all jump apart from the Beast who stood still.

One of the Demonic soldiers rose his voice, trying to bring courage to his patrol,

-Coming home, at long last, Beast, we were wondering when you would accept your fate.

All the surrounding walls started bleeding heavily, as It-666 answered,

-This is not my home. There is no fate to be accepted. I am free and on the loose, be prepared to say your last prayers.

-You won't be free any longer now that you stepped in here, you will be prisoner before you know it and you will accept your fate, Hell Princess. Unleash the Hell Hounds upon her. Kill her blue Demonic servant, obviously a traitor to his own kind.

Verse 20. S-O-S

The Death Angel smoking a cigar peacefully upon the platform at the tree house received the telepathic distress call of It-666. He teletransported straight away, back to the loophole room where all his Angelic soldiers were training still and Raphael welcomed him back,

-This was the shortest fag break you have ever taken, Az. I know you are a workaholic but we can spare you for 5 good minutes when I am here to supervise the soldiers.

Azryel warned him immediately,

-We left one soldier unattended tonight, a crucial one, It, who went on a freaking rescue mission with Walter in Hell to get Wendy's lost soul back and bring it to Gabriel. She is stuck there with him fighting for their lives, having found Wendy's soul and all the lost sacrificed souls killed by P. She needs our help ASAP to get out of there. She sent me all the stats. I need you, Asha and Gab. I already called out Gab by telepathy, he should be at the secret path of Hell, he knows about, and waiting for us.

Wrath vented,

-Damn f'in good hearted teenager, putting herself in the worst of situations just like that! I will have to teach her rough to be open with Us and tell Us all at all times. Don't get involved in the punishment that call will cost her, Az. I will deal with It this time around, what's the stats?

Asha having received his call came by them at once, as Death spelt out,

-We are dealing with 12 soldier Demons. The patrol kind she said, big, tall and frightening, plus two Hell Hounds, nasty beasts with six heads. She is in a hall and she secured it for no other demons to step in. They have no idea of the secret path, so we will come right behind them and slaughter them straight off from behind whilst she deals with the front. She is worried about Walter. She transformed him as a blue Demon to have strength to fight off before she went there. So be aware to the only big blue one on the scene for it's our man Workmaster. But she told me she cocked up, by marking the entrance with her own blood, Demons know she is down there and will do anything to keep her in. The human lost Souls, she tried to free are safe for another 45 more minutes. Big fat mission, let's go.

Teletransporting to the Indian cave by the entrance of Hell, Wrath, Azryel and Asha found an anxious Gabriel, saying to them,

-Let's go, poor Wendy is in there.

Death barked,

-Wendy is kept safe by the Beast, Soldier, you don't do battle, you are going to do the rescuing of all the lost souls It is trying to save from Hell. They are invisible to demons, and the secret path has been kept secure and is invisible to them too. Touch my hand and be invisible to Demons at once and get to those souls, bring them out of Hell and keep far away from the fight. It is saving 76 lost souls including Wendy, so do trips, 10 at a time, order them to stay put by the waterfall until I can deal with them, as we do not want tortured ghosts roaming in your nice fancy tree-house to keep us awake all night, do we? Understood? Focus? There is not one soul to save, there's 76 desperate victims. Now bring Us down there to save the young Beast that put her life on the line to do so.

Gabriel opened the path to Hell to them and obeyed Az at once. What they saw was a fierce battle. The two Hell Hounds were lying dead on the floor, the blue Demonic Walter was kept safe by a foaming Beast standing in front of him. He was bleeding badly from a main artery. She threw off three assailants strongly against a wall, and they acknowledged that she was badly hurt herself yet still keeping strong. There was only 6 demonic soldiers left, as the door was being rammed.

With a click of his fingers, Death reinforced the door at once, then went to kill the three thrown Demons of It as they were knocked down. Wrath dealt with two, while Asha tackled one. Death came to Ash first and beheaded the Demon he was fighting in a swift stroke. The Angel crossly muttered,

-I had the upper hand, Az. What's up?

-We do not play fight, we kill straight. They saw the teenage Beast in action, they can't survive.

Before the Death Angel reached Raphael, he saw the two demons who tackled him dead on the floor. He smiled,

-I can guess you are fairly angry right now, go easy on the girl, she meant well. She dared more than we would have for humans souls. Bear that in mind when you deal with her. She is wounded, I need to look after that soldier, as soon as you allow me to. She will pass away in 4 and be alive in 2.

-Let's get out of here, we are done. Gosh she is strong, Az, she killed 6 Demonic soldiers and 2 Hell Hounds by herself. She has a mind of her own as well. We can't leave her unattended, never.

Gabriel came to his uncle and said,

-All the lost souls are safe and outside waiting. I can see all demons are dead yet the door is being rammed, let's get out of here.

Azryel ordered,

-Mission is over. Successful. Let's keep it that way. Off we go back to the human World and close that path. Walter and It are fit to walk out yet damaged.

A big blue Demonic Walt leaned on Azryel's shoulders as he went through the secret path while Gab lead the way out and Wrath closed the march with the wounded It.

The Archangel Raphael coming out of Hell ordered,

-Gabriel, this secret path to Hell has to be locked at all times. It made it secure but we do not want her to put her life at risk like she did. Make the path unavailable to her unless permitted by Us. Azryel look after those lost souls take them where they should go respectively and come back to me as soon as.

Clapping her hands It made all the souls visible and gave them their voices back. Wendy went to her at once and hugged her Being impulsively,

-Thank you, thank you so much from all of us stuck down there. I am so sorry you are so wounded. I wish you to get better soon Soldier. You did fight awesomely well down there. The way you killed those Hell Hounds was so swift, it blew us all away. Scared us too, but the result is we are free, thank you for making the call to your rescue guys at the right time. It, I don't know what you are but you are definitely smashing. Just thank you for fetching all of us and freeing us.

It hugged the soul back tenderly, for a long silent minute, and big blood tears came running fast and steady upon her face.

-Thank you Wendy, this means a lot to me, but you mean a lot to someone who has not a lot of time to be with you, for you will be sent to Paradise, go to him at once, Gabriel has been trying to find you for so long.

The soul ran to Gabriel who was spelling the secret path to Hell to be lock at all times to the young Beast. Jumping at his strong neck she stayed there silent and crying, while he hugged her firmly.

Wrath could not stop the souls coming to It and thanking her humbly for their escape, one after the other. He went to the bleeding Walter, shook his head to him in a disapproving fashion,

-You could have both been killed, how helpful was that?

The large demonic Walter holding his bleeding arm close to his chest answered,

-My sister is going to Paradise, Wrath, that's all that counts to me. Gabriel is safe and well and will never get lost in Hell to quest for her. This was the mission: protect your Archangelic nephew. I can bleed any day for Gab, he has done so much for me. We helped in our own bleeding way, we will get better at it, I hope in the future, although I do need to pay more attention to Azryel's training. I was the weakest link down there. My girl made me proud, Wrath, she is a true fighter. She was laying her life for me and all those souls, it was clear as water.

Raphael grabbing his arm, scolded,

-What is clear to me is that you are both stupid. Look at your arm, the injuries there are lethal, Walt. Your girl put you in grave danger all the way through. What use it would have been for her to die in front of you to protect you, tell me? Never go alone, in the future, never, you and her are part of Us. Any mission involves all of Us at all times to ensure they are safe. Understood human? Well big blue thing at the moment.

The Archangel sent his healing energy to him and Workmaster could feel his blood replenishing itself within him. He saw the wounds on his arm disappearing. He whispered sheepishly,

-Thank you Wrath. I understand where you are coming from. But please understand where I come from. You disapproved of Wendy and Gab's relationship. Would you have done a mission to Hell to make sure she could rest in peace? Would you have considered one? She is my twin, kind of a part of me. She means to me enormously like Gabriel does. I would move Heaven and Earth for them or in this instance go to Hell.

Raphael checking the other scars of the demonic Workmaster, replied,

-Didn't you see me going to Hell as soon as I knew you were there and in trouble, human? Grow some faith in me Workmaster, it will be useful for your safety. Be open, do not hide anything, and do not assume I would not have done such a mission if the idea was presented to me first of all. You would have been surprised. The mission may have ended with no scratches upon yourself too. Now, lets get you back in human form and off to bed, you have done enough to annoy me for the rest of the night. It, get your ass over here Soldier, and sort this mess of a demon out. I healed him thoroughly, he just needs a little human makeover.

It hugged the blue Workmaster before apologising,

-I am sorry Walt we had to fight our way out. So sorry.

-It's okay, Babe I never expected a trip to Hell to turn out rosy and hunky dory. Result is we had Plan B, and the great escape of the lost souls did happen. We screwed up a little along the way but for novices, I would pat your back and mine myself. Being a big blue thing was entertaining, I think I will sleep better for it tonight, I am exhausted. My Sis finally going to Paradise made my night It, so you have nothing to be sorry for.

Transforming Workmaster back into a human under the watchful eyes of Raphael, the young Beast could not help feeling sorry for him, for getting badly injured down there. She felt entirely responsible and knew that Wrath was thinking exactly the same thing.

She saw Azryel disappear with the lost souls. Asha enjoined Workmaster to walk with him to the tree house. Gabriel and Wendy sat by the waterfall, hugging each other and whispering, having being given some precious minutes. The Death Angel would return for Wendy later. It felt her hand being grabbed by Wrath as he ordered,

-You come with me Soldier to the loophole room.

Teletransporting to the white and empty ethereal room, It felt her heart sinking low, as she heard the first sentence of Wrath,

-Do you know what is coming to you, Beast?

Simply falling upon her knees, she apologised to the Archangel,

-I am sorry Wrath, I screwed up badly.

Raphael shouted,

-Apologies not accepted Being. Yes, you screwed up badly, look at your state, for Christ's sake. My man Workmaster who does not know how to fight properly, demonised and taken to Hell where he got badly wounded. You are part of an Army, Soldier, you do not work on your own, especially when you are sixteen and cannot put A plus B together. Do you happen to know where is the worst place for you to be at all times, do you, Beast?

It whispered,

-Hell. I gathered that a little late. I felt the heat down there, Wrath.

-Good for you, you haven't felt the heat up here yet, Being, trust me. How on Earth did you think that putting a speck of your own blood could be a good marker and a clever idea for that exit? Pray. Enlighten me with your sheer stupidity, Soldier.

A blood tear rolling upon her cheek, the teenager admitted,

-I did not think that one through. I wanted that exit purely invisible so no demons could invade the woods and the tree-house of Gabriel. This is how far my scheme went. I forgot myself, I thought of others throughout. I forgot that my blood would cause a stir down in Hell.

The slap that hit her strongly, sent her to the ground, as the Archangel stood over her,

-Never forget who you are, Being, never. You can not afford it, and I can not afford an amnesic Beast which put herself and my human in danger. You went to the worst place you could ever go to. If you didn't have the bright idea to call Az to the rescue, what would have been the consequences? Did you think about them or you just ignored them?

Bursting into tears It-666 gathered herself together and remained seated upon the floor, she sobbed,

-I have to be honest with you, Wrath, I did not think about them. I had my plan B only and I put all my trust in it if things turned sour like they did. The first demon I killed told me that I would be a prisoner and that they would make me accept my fate as the Beast. That's when I realised the consequences Wrath and fought hard and strong for them not to happen.

Raphael turning around her annoyed, sternly told,

-I have a remedy for your forgetfulness, soldier, and your clear lack of perspective, I condemn you to remain in your true appearance, in this room, isolated from all, to think about your actions and what the consequences could have been. When I come back to get you, I wish to see a soldier willing to talk to their peers and Army to propose missions but no loner which screws things up badly and gets others hurt in her trail. I will decide then if you can rejoin my Army or stay a stupid Beast.

The Archangel disappeared from the room leaving a completely distraught Being.

Verse 21. Be a part.

As the Death Angel appeared into the loophole room, he could see It still in her demonic form, enveloped in her wings, sitting upon the ground within a puddle of her blood. She had respected Wrath's punishment to the letter. He sighed sadly. Raphael had asked him to check upon her, saying that she had nasty battle wounds to be dealt with. He also told him how heartbreakingly honest the teenager had been with him, not trying one moment to escape his wrath.

Putting his hand upon the wings, he stroked them gently announcing his presence to the creature,

-It, it's me Az. How are you doing, Soldier?

Sorrowful demonic red eyes looked at him, and he could see that the young Beast had not ceased crying since the departure of Wrath. Opening his arms at once, he hugged her,

-Come here, you big girl. Tears aren't useful, Soldier.

-I am so sorry Azryel, so very sorry. I should have said where I was going, what I was doing. I have been so so stupid, it kills me. You can't imagine.

-I can. I saw the Hell Hounds, Walt's injuries and yours. I also saw Workmaster's note in the hammock. He shared the same stupidity. Having him as your adopted Dad promises to be fun for me and Raphael.

-I am solely responsible, Az, I devised it all, please read me and know all.

The Death Angel smiled at It's offer. Her straight honesty was just plain to see. He accepted and placed his hands upon her head, soothing,

-Dry your tears It. Everyone makes mistakes. Your are not the first one and you will not be the last one to do so. What's important is to learn from them. What did you learn tonight?

As Death read her, It opened her heart to him, wiping her tears away,

-Involving you from the start in any big plan, to know if they are okay, possible, or need to be worked at. I learnt to never go to Hell. Big fat mistake, I scared myself down there. I thought I would get stuck and abused and could only hope to see you coming fast. I learnt I was part of an Army and not a lone soldier, that I could not manage the whole thing on my own. I learnt how to kick myself over and over again for my sheer stupidity, as Wrath put it simply, flashing my blood down there, was being a total nincompoop and had dire consequences. I am so sorry for Walter and dragging him unready thinking that he would be safe simply disguised as a demon.

Azryel stopped his reading satisfied, more than satisfied with the young Being he had to deal with, and stated,

-Good. Learning to never do a loner upon Us is essential, especially being you, It. Now, let's look at your wounds soldier. Some nasty nachos went into that leathery skin of yours and I am afraid to say they were poisoned. You are dying away slowly like Wrath warned me. Let's give you a lease of life, like he ordered. My stupid soldier who goes into a mission to follow her own heart, Wendy blessed your soul and has not been talking all her way to Paradise about Gabriel but only you and how awesome you have been fighting those Hell Hounds single handedly. She said something that is true, you are an Angel despite appearances. I want you to learn that tonight. What you did for those lost souls was no mean feat. You did the best you could think of. You are part of an Army and involving Us would have rendered your plan perfect. Learn to trust Wrath. Although he is going to answer to me for your tumefied cheek bone, It.

-No, it's okay, I deserved the slap, it was like a wake up call, Az.

Death starting healing her, kept smiling widely, commented,

-It's not okay, Soldier, you are a teenage Being and there are other ways to make you understand. Beside Wrath can be heavy handed sometimes and he needs to comprehend that himself. And for that sort of enlightenment, there's only me. So, why Gabriel? Did you find out?

A puzzled It confided straight off,

-No. But I feel I can do something stupid again just to see the smile on his face when Wendy went to him.

-Something like what?

-Going to Hell and back again, and get bitten by poisonous Hell Hounds.

Azryel putting his energy into healing the nasty bite, laughed out,

-Do not count on me to fix you up the next time if you are that stupid, Soldier. The answer you are looking for It is simply that you are in love. Love makes you do things you would never do for anyone else and you fail to understand them yourself, you just want those individuals happy at all cost, including your own self. Love is a long story which never ends and affects everyone at any point in time. You are in love with Gabriel, It. I can feel it in you. You would lay your entire life for him, am I not right?

It nodded positively and silently, as the Angel continued,

-The question is my dear Soldier, is your love acceptable? A, you are far too young, yet love can not be helped. B, Gabriel's heart is taken by Wendy and will be blind to your exertions which qualify your love as unrequited. C, this is a painful kind of love to have It, which will leave you hurting all over. I can only recommend this to your young Being, don't rush, you have your whole life ahead of you. For all you know tomorrow is another day and you may fall in love again with someone else who may return your love and then you will feel transported by blessed wings. As your general, I do not want to see any of my soldiers hurt in any shape or form. I do not want to pick up the pieces of your broken heart It, and mend it back together. Think about it, my dear girl. Gabriel has given his own heart to a human, he can not give it again. I do not want you to be at a loss, for you deserve to be loved back It.

Blood tears pearling at her eyes the Beast whispered,

-I cannot be loved Azryel. Look at me. I am the Devil's daughter, a monster. I will never be in a position where I will receive any kind of love.

Scolding her strongly, Death lifted her chin up,

-I am looking at you and I see your sound heart that rescued 76 souls from hell Soldier, I do not see a monster at all. I see Walter Workmaster's adopted daughter. You can be loved Being, and you are already by a man which gives you his filial affection and you have mine. Your appearance does not make your Being, only your heart does so. I see a beautiful Being before me and nothing else. I see a young distraught Being that has got lots of growing up to do in order to love and be loved. On a lighter note you could have done worse than falling for Gab. You have good taste. I hope your future love would be of equal standing but maybe less anal.

He wiped with his thumbs her tears when Raphael stepped into the room, asking,

-How is my soldier Azryel?

-Getting there, Wrath. I would appreciate that you do not touch that young Being in the future. The power of your words are enough for her understanding. If you cannot keep your cool, I will make you do so.

Raphael approached and looking at the Beast's sorry eyes, replied,

-I know you will. I just overreacted. It will not happen again. How is she?

The Death Angel keeping his healing hands upon the back of It-666,

-Almost fixed. The poison is all gone. I repaired her fractured ribs, and she will be ready to have a rest in fifteen minutes. I had the pleasure to read my soldier and I cannot recommend enough her good heart and intentions to your consideration. She has learnt her lesson Wrath.

-Is she part of my Army?

-More than ever, she went there to protect Us from going there, especially to prevent Gab to do so.

Raphael kneeling by It took her hand within his,

-If you want to fight for Us, Soldier, include Us in your fights and we will be right by you helping to put things right. Be a part, never apart. Be an arm, not at harm. Is it clear?

It hugged the Archangel at once,

-It's clear Wrath. I am ever so sorry. I will be a part and a arm.

-Good, then when Az has finished fixing you up, you can transform back into your human shape. If you had done so earlier, you would not have survived the night, Being. I need you, Soldier for a very important mission tomorrow make sure you and Az get a good rest.

Verse 22. Breaking News.

Arriving in the kitchen, following Azryel, It saw all the soldiers becoming silent at the table. Raphael stood up and pulled a chair by his right, inviting It to take a seat,

-Here is the Hell Hounds killer. Finally awake. I hope you feel rested, Soldier. I have a mission for you. I am taking you to Boston to track your Evil Father. We need to get to him before P. Have you got an idea of his whereabouts?

The teenager sitting down by him replied,

-More than an idea, Wrath, I think I know exactly where he is. He is stuck in his snake shape, the black mamba and has taken refuge in a sewer.

-Good, the only thing we need to work out is how to take him and transport him here safely as he didn't choose to be the nicest snake in the world and to find something that contains his Evil powers within. Gabriel you will be in charge of finding out the perfect container and I want that new loophole jail room for It's father ready for my return.

The Archangel nodded his agreement when It mentioned,

-The cage, I was kept in for 8 years partly contained my powers. There was something in the metal which kept me weak and diminished.

Wrath commented wryly,

-That's very helpful now that the very cage lie at the bottom of a sink hole full of water.

Her eyes becoming demonic and a vibrant red, the young It glowed powerfully remaining totally silent.

A worried Gabriel scolded Raphael,

-I hope you didn't start her on a Beast kind of tantrum, as the last time she poltergeisted that kitchen the knives went stabbing the walls.

The door of the kitchen smashed open by itself and something came crashing upon the table with great force. Broken plates and warm breakfast flew upon the laps of everyone around the table. It ceased glowing and looking very pleased with herself told, as she pointed to the very cage stating with a giggle,

-Look Wrath, I did it, I got you the cage for Gab to study.

Azryel could not help laughing, soon joined by all of his soldiers, only Gabriel remained staunchly serious as he scolded the teenager at once,

-Great, crash landing your cage upon my kitchen table if impressive is a tad messy. Now, was it necessary to send all the breakfasts flying and breaking all my crockery, messy Missy. In my home, I do not want to see you use your bestial powers, Bambi. Don't let me tell you off again, it's your last call before I make you sleep rough outside in the woods with all the other animals and refuse to have you in my home at all times. You will be restricted to my yard. Did I make myself clear?

The smile disappearing from her face, blushing tremendously under the scrutiny of the Archangel, It apologised,

-I am sorry. I can fix it in an instant.

-Obviously I was not clear enough, you are not allowed to use your powers in my home until further notice, Bambi. The day you will learn self control and the correct measure of powers then we will discuss the matter, not beforehand. Now Azryel stop laughing and give me a hand to clear her mess.

A nose diving It-666 gave the most sheepish look at Raphael saying,

-I hope it may help.

Wrath responded with confidence,

-I am sure it will, It. We will not contest that, however what we are contesting here, and it is a problem unfortunately not dissimilar to yesterday, Soldier, is that intentions are not everything. The proper delivery of good intentions is crucial. You need to work upon your delivery very badly, to stop being a walking disaster. First of all, instead of going straight ahead from intentions to actions, you are missing the vital part of communication of what you intend to do and how. You will be surprised to find yourself among lots of Beings who have a multitude of powers, ready to listen but also advise you on how to achieve a better delivery than the one intended. In my Army we always have consultation meetings before going into action, we share our intentions with each other. It helps having our efforts perfectly coordinated to a common goal and makes it easier to achieve it. So instead of going on a wanting to please all glowy poltergeist mode, speak to us. We may have advised you that getting the cage was a great idea, that crash landing it in the kitchen was not so great and could have been seen as very offensive by your host, which could have told you where it would have been appropriate to put it in his house. The way for you to develop in the future is straightforward, Soldier, share and speak up before doing anything half stupid and half decent. By starting doing that we will have less of your sorry ass apologising, less cross Angels and an altogether better understanding. Pray, when do you think you will be grown up enough to start our sharing and speaking scheme that we have in my Army? When do you think you can stop messing about in your odd ways, Soldier?

Taking her lecture attentively, she noticed that the Archangel was less cross than Gabriel and had made valid and serious points to her. She replied to him,

-I will share and speak from now. I will try my hardest to stop messing about.

-Good. Due to your young age, It, we kept away from you a correction done by Azryel. Gabriel and I will be in charge of your corrections until the time you will become old enough to take them. I can assure you that they are very far from pleasant and keep my soldiers on their toes at all times. You have a great deal of growing up to do until then, as leniency, patience, and tolerance will not be part of our deal anymore, like it is with any of my soldiers facing Azryel explaining their actions. Patch up fast It before it is too late.

She saw the intensity of the gaze of the Death Angel upon her across the table. She could only say that she respected him greatly and trusted him with her life. The teenager bravely promised,

-I will patch up. I don't want to disappoint Azryel in the future, nor Gabriel nor you, Wrath.

The Archangel Gabriel putting a breakfast in front of her and another one by Raphael, welcomed,

-Bambi, you are always full of good intentions. It cannot be denied. But like Uncle Wrath said think carefully of your delivery in the future. I have to thank you for yesterday and your heroic endeavour but like you who did not want me to go to Hell and get into some troubles, if you have shared that thought with me, I would have told you likewise, I did not relish seeing you in your appalling state in trouble and in Hell. Now although Walter told us all about how you got rid of the Hell Hounds, before you came into the kitchen, I want to hear it straight from the horse's mouth and I am sure the entire Army do too, as they were all impatient for you to wake up, like I was. So be my guest, tell Us.

A blushing It-666, smiled back to him with a sorrowful glance,

-I am sorry for the cage, the crockery and all Gab, I will do delivery check in the future, I promise. Did you see the size of those dead Hell Hounds when you came to fetch the souls? Proper beasties, you can't go in front of them and say 'hello, what a nice pretty doggy', you would get your hand torn off in a single bite. I am not into swearing but they had six bloody heads each, all as ugly as one another, so when those are unleashed to rip you apart, you kind of think straight away, shitting bricks, 'What the hell am I doing down here?', and then knowing you have 76 souls relying on you behind you to free them, you get a grip on yourself. The only way out of there in my head was fighting to the death. I used my wings to lift myself away from the path of the nasty charge of those Hounds, jump on the back of one of them, used my fighting shaft like a lance and pushed it all in with all my strength before the animal realised what was happening. Its death was swift and it was properly terraced in one go. Yet I had the other one to deal with quickly, for the demons were set on killing Walter as they took him as a traitorous demon at my service. Little do they know that it is me that is at humanity's service. Checking upon Workmaster, he was being badly tackled by one strong demonic soldier, only one. The demonic patrol relied on that one to do the job at minimal cost. I threw my lethal stick into that large demon which pierced him through and through and got him off my adopted dad at once. But as I paid attention to save Walt, I was grabbed from the ground without my fighting shaft by the remaining Hell Hound, one of his lethal jaws crushing my right shoulder, luckily I am ambidextrous and threw a stunning punch with my left at the head of the Hound that got me. My Walt was thinking on his feet and threw my fighting shaft back to me. Right on time, as the heads started lifting themselves up again, chewing bits of me, I aimed for the heart and did not miss it. Then I ran to Workmaster fighting his second demon, to protect him with all my strength left until Azryel came to our rescue. I was counting and dreading every second that went past. After killing my sixth demon, seeing Az, Wrath and Asha together, I knew the heavy cavalry had arrived, that my man Walter would be mended from his arterial badly bleeding wound, that my souls would have their great escape and way to Paradise. All I wanted to do at that moment was to collapse and cry by someone understanding like my Tutor. I shook the feeling off to stay put by Workmaster until the last of the demons was killed. Wrath helped walking me out of Hell in a state which did only scream to me that I had bitten off more than I could chew on this occasion, that I was stupid not to share with him and Az what I wanted to do to save the soul of Wendy, to prevent Gab from going to Hell for good. In front of all the souls down there killed by P, I could not justify saving one over all the rest of them. If they did not know about Workmaster's and my dilemma, I knew my heart would bleed for them day in and out. We could not do one measure, given the chance we had to do the full monty, or at least try. Dad and myself were ready to die trying to save all those lost souls and we nearly did, but for my plan B which was if things turned sour, I would called immediately Master Azryel to the rescue and when I saw those Hell Hounds in that hall, trust me, the alarm bell was sounded loud and clear with all the stats in front of my eyes, I could give him.

When It stopped talking, she realised all had been paying attention to her with their mouths slightly gaping. Shyly she started eating her breakfast silently, when Wrath by her stated,

-One thing is for sure, It, you have a courageous and sound heart about you. You also got a mind of your own, not unlike your adopted father Workmaster, a very caring one too. Far too many mistakes for my liking yet after Azryel who's unbeaten and at sixteen, you have the best potential as a soldier, I ever saw in my entire eternal life. Eat up your breakfast. We need to hunt your Evil Father down this afternoon after our Angelic consultation, and hopefully my clever Gab would have worked out the specific metal that could numb Evil a little by then.

His nephew told him,

-I am going to melt that cage into a box to contain the Evil black mamba for transportation purposes. I will strengthen it for your safety. If the little one could work out her coma-mojo upon her own father, without her getting a poisonous bite, you would all make a safe trip back home, knowing that this one is impossible to teletransport.

Turning to It, Wrath asked,

-Could you do that without touching the snake? For knowing your Father, its poison at the moment is near enough his only protection against others. Which means his home made Evil brand could be particularly lethal for humans or Beings, within minutes, if not seconds. I do not know if Azryel could even fix you up from his particular bite. If not would you be willing to take the risk for Us?

Some Angels stopped eating, interested, waiting for the answer of the teenager, who replied immediately,

-I would and have to take that risk Raphael. I have to have contact with his skin in order to affect him. I can paralyse him, stun him, send him into a coma or hibernation whichever way you prefer. Strangely enough I can stop or reverse the process remotely and even from very far away. I do not know why and how it works, I am clueless on that matter. I just know I can stun or even kill like that by fiddling with the internal electricity of any creature. I can even relaunch a heart that stopped beating for long, even years, I can do the same with brains and organs. If you want a bunch of living dead or an army of them, ask me anytime, yet without their souls, they are scarily like automatons.

Wrath wiped his mouth slowly, calmly, as he had to collect himself to prevent his anger before asking the girl,

-Did you play with the dead, It?

Intervening at once the Death Angel answered for her,

-The young Beast did, Raphael, with only one human and it was far from playing. We are talking about a five year old little girl in the Black Forest which had lost in dramatic circumstances the nun who had been looking after her for all those years. She wanted her back, not understanding that a single shotgun took her away from the living. She loved her like a mother, one who told her not to make zombies out of the little birds that past away in the forest, one that taught her that the creatures needed also their little souls as well as their pulses. The little girl soon found a way to make animals return to life with their souls if it was close enough to their death. Unfortunately that way did not work upon the nun as by the time she came back to her after her grief stricken run away from the crime scene, her soul had been carried away by my Soul Takers and lead to Paradise. The child realised that she was not getting back the human she knew of. She remembered the nun teachings about zombies and soulless animals, and reverted her attempts. Little five years old It buried her with her own hands, flowering her grave daily for as long as she lived in those woods like a feral creature. I would not dare to lift a finger at those fruitless attempts and at that lost traumatised little Being she was back in those days. I would only pinpoint that our soldier is ready to sacrifice herself for Us, before knowing if I can sort her out or not.

Archangel Raphael told It before asking Azryel,

-Sounds like you have a staunch protector in your training teacher, Soldier. Like Workmaster would see mitigated circumstances in that case, I will as well. Learn that we consider it a sacrilege to play with the dead yet as Az informed Us, your only experience was far from making sport of a dead human. Grief makes us do stupid things at five or even at thirty-six like Gabriel, who did put himself at risk regularly for the past six years, making trips to Hell. I am happy and somehow thankful that you resolved that one for Us by your intervention of yesterday yet remember that you are not a lost Beast in the forest anymore. You are not alone. You are with Us, you can talk to Us, even big bad scolding me or big bad scary Az would have loved doing and taking part in the Wendy's soul delivered upon a tray surprise to Gabriel from the start. We would have kept it secret from him and 'gift like' and we would have also kept you and my Walt out of harm's way during that trip to Hell. For we do care about your own life, health and safety, as you do for Us. So Az, tell me if you can get my soldier back if her nasty Daddy bites her?

A smiling Death Angel strongly replied confidently,

-I can. I saved her Father many times before when he was still part of Us. I worked him out back then, and I worked his daughter out by mending her twice. My soldier can trust that I will be able to counter poison her in good time, if she ever passed away, I will throw her soul right back in her body and refuse her passage. It is a little unheard of but I did it a few times when I could not accept the passage of an essential human who had a mission to achieve which would make the World a better place. If we teach that Being right all of Us, we could potentially fix the place right up fundamentally. I can fix her up and you can all fix her in your own way. Never let her on the loose like you did with her father, never ostracised, thinking that far away from the eyes will solve the problem, for it will remain. Tackle and solve is the answer and it does not mean that death is the only answer at all. I read that Being more than I did any of you. I know a sound heart when I hear one, if it was not in her father full of pride, it is in her, ready to die for you or humanity at a moment's notice. My trainee will make sure you will all get back from Boston to the tree house safely. Understood kiddo?

-Yes, Master. I will make very sure of it.

-Good, I will never expect any less of you, Soldier, at any point in time young or old.

A nodding in agreement It-666, sent all the Angelic soldiers shivering. They all understood that Death was the true Master of the Beast. They did not know yet if the future would mean dread for it or blissful salvage. They knew Azryel but they did not know It that well. However, if the Death Angel knew her by heart as she let herself to be read thoroughly by him regularly, keeping no secret from him and ready to lay her life for his Army, they realised that a powerful alliance had been unworldly and silently struck.

Wrath pushing his plate away casually commented,

-Right, breakfast is over. Gab, I may relocate here if you cook that well. Az told me how good it was but after a few samples my boy that's heavenly food you are on about. Azryel always tells the blunt truth. The truth is little It has a Master and Death has one as well. Someone to answer to is essential at all times to keep everyone safe and in check. I answer to the very Tutor of little It. He never warned me of her coming because he had faith in her. When my Master tells me to sound the apocalypse I will. Let's have our Angelic consultation in the loophole room. Archangel Gabriel, I would have involved you in that Angelic meeting, if a proper jail and containment box wasn't needed for It's Father. I need your chemical expertise on that one and you have only a few hours to do so, don't let Us down Gab. We rely heavily upon you on this mission and on the little one.

Verse 23. HOPE.

The loophole room was filled with the Angelic Army, yet a circle of twelve Angels formed at its centre. Wrath stood in the middle of the circle in his full Archangelic form. Death kneeling by him bowing, offered his shoulder as a support. Standing outside the ring, uneasy, not knowing what she had to do, It looked totally lost. Until Asha broke the ring to show her the way, revealing,

-When you have a Master, within Angels, your place is right by him. You belong to Death therefore you must kneel by his sides at all times in consultations. Your Master belonging to Wrath will always kneel by him and be in the middle of the circle. Therefore you belong here too. Freedom of speech is the rule among Us and is the point of all consultation. Although you will kneel by Death all the way, you can express an opposite view to his during a consultation, it will be listened and dealt with if need be as a group. In consultations, we put things to motions. The following hours we fight and act upon them. The hand of your Master upon your own shoulder as you are by him means your total endorsement, that your Master will lay his own life for you, if it lay any lower, it means that for him to do so you have to prove yourself. Azryel has fully been endorsed by Archangel Raphael since Roman times, ages ago. Az has been kneeling by him since the time of the fallen ones before that, which is speaking of thousands of years. So if your hand is held by your Master, be proud for it starts there. It means more than you think. It means he is your dedicated guide at all times. Take your place in the circle It, welcome to Wrath's Army. Your first battle and yesterday's feat earned you the place in the consulting circle. Kneel, listen, learn and share your heart out.

The teenager ready to kneel by the black winged Angel and the four winged Archangel, was stopped by them to do so, Azryel and Raphael ordered in one voice,

-In your true Being's form, It. Not your incarnated one, look at Us. Truth rules. We wear our true face humbly at all times among

Beings. We wear our heart upon our own sleeves. What you see is what you get, a true Being without cover.

Az pursued,

-Black winged, a scythe laying by my side, I can not hide that I am Death, Azryel, the Angel who has the deadly duty to collect souls day in and out.

Raphael patting the Death Angel's shoulder, added,

-Face up to what you are, in our circles It to be accepted, be your true self. To be welcomed in my consulting circle, I do not want to see the incarnated Being, the covered Beast walking upon Earth, I want to see her true face, like she did yesterday freeing souls from Hell and reestablishing some order.

Transforming herself into her true Devil shape before all Angelic eyes, the young Beast felt utterly naked and apologised,

-Please do not be alarmed nor frightened by my appearance, I mean no harm. I am sorry to have been born this way.

The Archangel smiling full of kindness, ordered,

-We know that child, take place by your Master. Gabriel has not shared with you yet his discoveries upon your true nature. You are two parts Angelic, one part Archangelic and the last is something else altogether, close to demonic but it is not. He is still working upon it. That makes you three quarters of an Angel, little one, so the best part of you. Appearances are just that. As Angels we work beyond those. Now let the session begin. Asha please resume for Us the situation.

As all Angels sat in lotus position, Asha left the circle to stand by Wrath, and explained,

-Although the destruction of P's place in Boston could be seen as a success, it did not annihilate the Father of the Beast but released him into the wild. When we would have all presumed that he would return to his demonic servant P and resume his Evil deeds and dealings with him, he did not. Our fallen Angel hides in the sewers of Boston imprisoned in the shape of a black mamba. It raises many questions from why to how he has been reduced to such a state. Incarnated demon P, unable to find him has enlisted a witch Cambion to help him. It is believed that the named Cato and him have a very old partnership maybe as old as her four hundred years. Boston and its surrounding area has been rendered witchcraft proof as we speak to prevent them from finding our nasty snake. Young It, can you tell us if they are close to finding him or not?

The Angel made a map of Boston appear in front of them waiting for his answer. Gently tapping the hand of It-666 he was holding all along, Az encouraged,

-Speak my child.

Remaining knelt the teenager revealed,

-They are far from finding him. They are looking above ground in parks and trees. He feels where they are and has displaced himself constantly putting miles between him and them.

Lighting a red little floating fire ball upon the virtual map, the girl explained,

-My father is exactly there moving slowly but surely.

Lighting a green light in another area of the map, she pursued,

-That's where P and the witch are. Somehow I can feel my father having a very strong intrinsic fear of that Cambion. I think she is entirely responsible for his present state for he is fleeing her like the plague.

Wrath commented,

-It could explain the situation, when we have our hands upon your slippery Evil dad, we can ask him. Thank you for your contribution It. Asha you may take your seat. As we have all seen where we have to go, is everyone confident upon this mission or not? Please come, speak up and not all at once.

A fiery Angel came pointing at the floating fireballs, fired out,

-I am fiercely opposed that after babysitting his Evil daughter in our Army, we are now going to cater for his diminished self. Let him rot in the gutter swallowing rats with great pride.

Wryly, Raphael argued at once,

-Yes, for it would be a very intelligent thing to do. Take a seat behind everyone, imbecile. May someone enlighten this one why are we not doing that?

Standing up Azryel rose his voice, giving an unfathomable look at the shamed Angel,

-How dare you speak of babysitting It, when you were part of the five wounded in P's woods, protected by her and I at the charge of the last two demons. Speaking of rats next time you are injured you will be the lab one of Archangel Gabriel. I am pretty sure he will enjoy dissecting an Angelic tongue that fails to bring something constructive to the table. Why do you think P is so set to find our 'so labelled' diminished fallen Angel? Because however diminished, that freaking Being has the power to control the entire World. In which hands do you want the World to be controlled, Pray? Enlighten Us?

Shying off the Angel whispered, as red as a poppy,

-Ours.

Opening his black wings in an impressive fashion, Death ordered,

-Speak up.

The trembling Angel knowing, he had woken up the anger of Azryel obeyed,

-Ours.

His reply was welcomed by the four wings of Wrath opening up with great majesty and anger. The Archangel ask coolly,

-Come here, and get your punishment.

Reluctantly stepping forward, the Angel looked helplessly around failing to recognise his mistake. Asked to kneel opposite Death, he shivered uncontrollably, when Azryel, crossing his arms upon his chest, sarcastically demanded,

-This promises to be educational. Children, today, we are having a 'leçon de chose' and the object is 'how Angels fall'. I can play it fast forward and have this one laying flat upon his proud little nose on the ground in two seconds, but you will miss the important point. I need everyone's attention as Wrath and I will not hold anyone prisoners here. I will need prompt answers from all of you when asked. First question, the World belongs to who? Raise your hand in order to speak.

Everyone understood that the Death Angel was far from joking, that he had the full backing of an upset Wrath, and that wings could be lost during the session. All were being assessed by Azryel and the Archangel and would face demotion from the Army if they failed to pass their test. Asha was the first to raise his hand. Az smiled to him encouragingly,

-We have one taker. An Angel that respectably earned four wings during his eternal life. Speak Ash, and may your answer please Wrath about your own heart.

With a voice half trembling and half secured, he advanced,

-The World belongs to humanity, and we are here to protect it, and ensure it stays that way.

Wrath smiling irresistibly announced,

-One Angel is keeping his wings, who's next. Thank you for playing the game Asha, you are still part of Us. Next question, Az.

The Death Angel turned around the shamed Angel, lifting his chin right up in front of his peers, he ordered,

-This one is just for you Yahoel. How does it feel to be put on the spot and to shame? Tell Us, we are all ears, all here. How fast do you want to fall?

Death lifted his silver scythe from the ground and everyone braced themselves for the worse.

Blood tears appearing at Yahoel's eyes, he sobbed, asking,

-I failed to answer correctly, did I, Azryel?

Coming back to him with the scythe, nodding positively, Az sternly replied with a tinge of mockery in his voice,

-I am afraid, you did. You are also failing to answer my last two questions. Do you even realise those answers are your only chance I gave you to stay with Us and to make Us a solemn plea?

The kneeling Angel turned, offering his wings to Death confided with honesty,

-The World has to stay controlled by humanity, and we have to protect it to keep it that way from all Beings. I can see the answer now clearly in my mind. I failed to recognised the call for plea, Az. Please take my shame away.

Little It could not bear it anymore and threw herself between the Angel's wings and the silver scythe which had remained still in the hand of Death. She pleaded, desperately,

-No. No harm, no cutting, no falling. Catch him before he falls. Teach him, help him. Correct his failing like you do for me. I beg you, Master.

Yahoel turned at once, seized It's hand, applying a reassuring pressure upon it, told,

-Little one, calm down, I did not lose anything. Death is swift, my wings would be gone by now, trust me. I got my sorrowful all clear.

Bursting all of a sudden into a damn of tears, he hugged the teenager, and carried on,

-Your Master taught me all the way through, helped me and corrected me. I have been made an example, It, which spread his tuition to all Angels present. Trust Azryel, never to let a soldier down, he catches Us before we fall. If we let him down, our last breath is taken by him, not from his own will, from our own failure to listen to him, learn and do as he says. I have him to thank for my eternal life not to be cut short, as he has been so many times to my rescue that my two hands will not suffice to count it. The last time, you stood by him. Please accept my apologies It, you are far from Evil, and trust your Master, Sweet heart to guide you all the way.

A slightly confused It turned to the Death Angel, blushing under his scrutiny. His eyebrows cocked and with an irresistible smile, Az told her off,

-The next time, you put your little Being between my scythe and my take, you will be taken instead Child. Trust and respect my calls. I am a judge and a punisher since, kind of much much before you were born. Sixteen times Eternity if you can figure that one out. A little tip, before letting your heart do the all saving talk, if the tip of the scythe remains upon the ground for 8 seconds after an Angelic plea, an Angel keeps his wings. He remains to be eternal. How long can you keep my scythe grounded upon you, Sweet Heart, this is the question? Care to answer that one for me to get a brownie point or a blue peter badge.

Returning by Death's side, It just fell upon her knees, grabbed one of his hands, replying,

-I am sorry Azryel. I did not mean disrespect. I honestly don't know how long your scythe will remain grounded upon me Master, you are the judge upon that one.

Squeezing her hand full of self assurance he wished to pass to the teenage Beast, Death praised,

-And that is the good answer, It. Do you want to know what my soldiers get after their full induction training? Angelic wings. Do you fancy a make over my little Sweet Heart? I have the power to make it pass, as long as you pass Wrath and I's test. Calling out to you my soldiers, who wants to see the Beast earning her Angelic wings among Us?

One soldier stood up and spoke,

-I must say that little It breaks my heart through and through. I fought a few metres from her at P's woods. I was constantly being looked after by her fighting shaft. From nowhere her help came, terracing a demon, I did not see coming behind my back. The girl means good truly, sincerely with all her heart, and I am ready to give her the chance of a lifetime. I want to fight by her again and again, as I felt safe knowing she had my left and back fully covered. I want her to get the chance Az is offering her. I am ready to help her throughout that intensive journey. Who else has a good word to say about the little Beast?

Archangel Raphael spoke out, decisively,

-I have. When she thought I had too much of a hurdle upon the very same battle field, she came by me, slaughtering as many demons as she could. She kind of allowed me to gather pace, catch a breath, and fight on. None of you, respecting me, will dare to do that. Yet I never felt disrespect when she fought by me, on the contrary. Like that soldier, I felt safe, looked after for a few minutes, until I sent her back to Az as he can keep an eye on that strong

soldier safer than I ever could. I want her to earn her wings and be
your watching Angel during battles. Eremiel's daughter proved
herself to me, many times. In Hell, she did not take the easy option
of getting one human soul out. She would not forgive herself if she
did not show the way out to the 76 victims of P. Human souls she
was ready to die for if her Master who received her call did not
come. We found her as we stepped in, with a crushed shoulder,
poisoned to a slow death, yet standing fiercely strong and protecting
Walter Workmaster with her own life. When I walked her out of
Hell her own heart was kicking itself that she had not done enough.
Which one of you would have undertaken a trip to Hell to save a
human soul, end up with 76 to put them at rest and right things up?
Which one? I am not witnessing the teenage years of the Beast, I
am witnessing the one of an unknown Being with a true heart. Like
Metatron, I am ready to help little It through that intensive journey
that Azryel had for any one of Us to become full Angels. Who else
has got the heart to plea like she did for one of Us just now, not
knowing our ways?

All the Angels' hands lifted themselves up. A very pleased Wrath,
pursued,

-Now that we achieved the true acceptance among Us of her Being,
I hope not to listen anymore to almost insulting comments like we
heard from Yahoel about It. Besides her Army training, being done
by Azryel is far from being babysat. Having all done it at one point
in your Angelic Soldier careers, you know what I am talking about.
What a sinecure, training with Azryel is! I should really make you all
be retrained by him, just for my pure enjoyment and unsure that I
have humble hearts in my Army and no Angels with undue pride.
Wouldn't it be so swell?

Looking at each other in slight disarray the soldiers dreaded Death
with all their guts, and feared that Wrath was not just being cynical
but in earnest. Azryel coming to their rescue, replied with a sarcastic
smirk,

-It would be very swell. I would push them so much we would end
up with a plethora of Archangels in no time at all. But I am afraid I

have to decline that very tempting motion, for the young Beast is keeping me very busy with her good heart that stands in front of big bad killing scythe, runs in Hell to fetch souls, fights Hell Hounds, causes some havoc without knowing it. Gosh the list is endless with that teenage Being. I am fully entertained, I must admit, I get to kill plenty of demons with that walking straight into trouble soldier. We are living in exciting times my dear Angels. Presently, we need to imprison Eremiel, and hide him from Earth so we don't end up with an Apocalypse. We don't want nasty P and his nasty Witch getting their crafty hands on him and use him to find the powerful daughter, abduct her and Big Bang, no more World to set a foot on, with everyone gone to live happily ever after in Hell. Now, do we?

Smiling irresistibly Wrath stated,

-Any more spooky scenarios to press Us into action, Death? Solely based upon that one, I will pass the motion that it is a necessity for Us to keep Eremiel in prison and that I am afraid that we are going to be his jailers and guardians in order to protect Earth. We can not afford to leave him alone and rot in a sewer, for we have a duty to protect Earth, for old Evil will never go away and be actively at play. Who is with Us and agrees to the motion?

Lifting all their hands the Angelic soldiers passed the motion, as Wrath carried on explaining,

-Thanks to It's tips, we have the exact location of the Father, and Gabriel is working on a containment box for his transport which should keep Us all safe on this mission. Moreover this soldier will put herself at harms way of the black mamba in order to send him into a straight coma. So throughout our journey the security should be maximal.

A soldier raised his hand anxiously. The Archangel stopped talking immediately, and invited him to talk,

-Speak, Angel.

-Pardon me for the interruption Wrath and also maybe exhibiting my stupidity. I have a question or two. Maybe the others share the same questions as I do or maybe I am the only second imbecile here.

-Stop turning around the pot, and feel free to ask, Soldier. Don't demean yourself beforehand, I will decide if you are moronic or not.

-Well, I keep wondering if the little one has such extreme powers, why not let her kill her Father in that sewer instead of Us going into all that trouble? Why do we have to wake him up whilst he is in our prison for he isn't very pleasant to deal with? Couldn't It send him on a sleeping beauty sleep for an eternity?

-Very interesting questions, they are not totally stupid Soldier, and worth answering. Let's open the debate with Azryel.

The Death Angel made It stand up with him holding her hand throughout,

-It's very easy to discard someone, I speak from experience, however taking the trouble to let them live may teach you a great deal more. In this instance we have a ring of demons which P is a leader of, and humans involved in crime and sacrifices. As a punisher I need to unravel all of them and stop their deadly toll upon Earth. They make me lose precious souls to Hell. Their actions grieved one of our most valued Archangels so much that I had to stand by him with my ready scythe, a couple of nights ago, my heart bleeding for him not to give up the fight. When I see that amount of distress from any one of Us, I am spurred to act and dig out all the culprits that caused it. Eremiel is the only who knows all of them. Waking up from his coma is essential as we have to make him talk. Asking It to do a parricide is out of the question. First of all, as a teacher, I know that let's kill all, it will make everything better is not an appropriate answer. That's what demons do, not Angels. We deal and find appropriate solutions to any problems. As for the eternal beauty comatose sleep of that Being after I got all my information, it might be a good idea. Wrath, care to share your thoughts?

As Az sat back by the Archangel offering his shoulders, It sat back, thinking she agreed totally with her Master. She heard the voice of the commanding Archangel stating,

-One day, a very long time ago, Eremiel was one of Us and we tend to ignore that fact all too often. Very proudly we are willing to get rid of him swiftly. Yet, Azryel is right, what can we learn from him? What happened to him ever since his fall? Why is he fearing a Cambion Witch? Do we have to fear ourselves a half demon of only four hundreds years, who managed to escape unnoticed from the scythe of Death? Her association with P is bringing demonic children to this World. This is the price the demon has to pay for her services. Why? Is she bringing up an army of dangerous creatures? A lot of questions can be raised to him. Not only that, if our little Evil snaky does not go back straight and willingly to his demonic servant, something is seriously up. We have to make him spill the beans at all costs. We can make him have a very long beauty sleep afterwards. One thing that would be good is if we could render that sleep a proper makeover one, sending him appropriate dreams and nightmares where Eremiel would be properly and virtually re-educated and retrained all the way through. If his soul ever responds in a sudden back from his no-man's land Evil ways to Angelic ways then we could have a future meeting to discuss his wake up call.

The Death Angel tapping the hand of the Archangel smiling widely commented,

-Lots of wishful thinking on that one, Wrath. I would let Eremiel have a big fat long undisturbed sleep myself with no wake up call at all. Giving him your kind of torturing nightmares and waking him up thinking he would have learnt his lesson will sent you straight to the emergencies. Although he was part of Us, I doubt his appreciation of Us would have remained. He is a self-made Evil now. Impossible task, if you try, please soldiers just be wise enough to pass the motion to let Eremiel sleep forever.

Little It shivering by Death asked him extremely worried, blood
tears showing in her eyes

-Is my Father that bad? Is he that far gone not to respect Wrath or
Us, ever? If I have some of his blood in me, if it's bad, shall I make
myself sleep deeply too, paralysed for eternity? Am I beyond hope
as well?

Immediately, kneeling by It the Archangel Raphael hugged the
young crying It-666 tightly, soothing her,

-Shh, little Soldier, learn that nothing nor no one is beyond hope.
Your Father was extremely good before he turned extremely bad. If
a change can happen one way, it can happen the other way just as
well. Your blood will never decide of your own heart or actions. It
may affect your Being, giving you extreme powers in your case, but
you can learn to be at their helm and direct them to your own very
special heart's will. No big deep sleep needed for you, Being, you
have been given a chance by Us all. Just make sure those Angels do
not retract it ever from you, for getting it back from Us may never
happen. Sometimes troubling ourselves to catch up someone falling
is too much to ask, especially when that someone looks beyond
repair from so many falls and suffers from a failing Us all heart, like
Eremiel. Chin up and cheer up, kiddo, you can not be sleepy in my
Army. Remember, be a part, be a fighting arm. Dry your tears and
behave.

Taken a little aback the Death Angel stood up and strongly told to
the whole Army,

-Right, Raphael is not backing down on the motion concerning
Eremiel's fate in our hands. He is prepared to make his prison
sentence a time to recover that fallen Angel and give him a chance.
If you fell would you want Wrath picking you up or not? Wrath is
not sweet when on your case. He is far from patient too and
Eremiel will be put in a torturing soul course he will remember
forever. If old Evil play the switch back and forth the consequences
could be devastating and I am not willing to lose Wrath over
Eremiel. A matter of big chances is at stake, if no one else wants to

speak vote ahead.

As Death finished his sentence Gabriel appeared in the midst of them, a very glowing smile on his face holding a simple looking like engraved square box within his hands like the most precious item upon Earth. Jubilant, he boasted,

-Meet the newest version of Pandora's box!

Wrath standing up welcomed him wryly,

-You could not have chosen a greater time to speak of hopelessness than now, Gab.

Not understanding his Uncle one bit, the younger Archangel defended his creation at once,

-Well, let me correct you on that one, I have Elpis protecting the very box lining the outside. So there is plenty of hope in there. Strengthened and working like an alloy to the particular metal, she is going to make sure Evil stays within. She impregnated that box so much that even from within our black mamba might turn to a grass snake before you Angels come back home. Goddess Demeter lent a hand from afar upon the box creation, not only allowing it to pass her witchcraft free zone but adding elements which protect Us from it's content power. You will all come back home safe from that mission soldiers, I am happy to announce. I even got a specific grant for the two members of Us who will be keeping an eye on the box. It goes beyond measure and will last until our ongoing dealings with the goddess. Wrath and Azryel, you will be protected by Demeter whenever in close contact with the box. Once in the box, Evil will be secure and properly contained. What do you say, Wrath?

Taking the box from his nephew's hands, Raphael inspected it carefully, before asking,

-Very trendily pretty. All the codes that were on the previous Pandora's amphora could have been scraped on this one but I can let you have one Archangelic license or two, I guess, especially if you took care that Hope was lining the outside of it and not the inside. As long as it stays that blessed way this time around, I think we can give that container of Evil a shot. Any handling precaution we should be aware of, Az and I?

-Simple. Do not open it. If you want Evil released then do. I will then relocate to a crater in Pluto and give up my tree-house to you upon Earth. I know you aren't going to miss me that much. Your Army maybe for their breakfast.

Gabriel taking a quick glance at the young Beast, asked all of a sudden,

-I can feel that young Being has been crying. In an environment of Angels I would have thought she would have been safe. Never forget I am her first original Master.

The teenager stood up coming to the Archangel and appeased him, kneeling,

-Read me if you must to settle your mind. If an emotional session, this consultation is fully educational, Master Gabriel, I assure you.

Laying a hand upon the shoulder of It, Azryel stepped by her sides, and explained,

-We looked after her Gabriel, Bambi got the full approval of the Army. They only had to take into consideration her good heart which speaks for itself. You know that as well as Wrath and I. Her blood tears were raised upon a prickly issue we are discussing right now. A matter of hope. Can we give a chance to her Father or not? I aim to the definitely no direction while Wrath aims to a may be yes and taking the consequences of it if it turns bad. Join our circle Gabriel and debate. It has been a long while since you joined Us in a debate, and we all miss your thinking outside of the box voice. Please, kneel by my sides, Gab and your Uncle's. Join Us.

Independent, free thinking, Gabriel, knelt as he was told to do so. He felt his shoulders straight away being held by Death and his own

Uncle. He was fully endorsed by Azryel and Wrath. They would lay their lives for him. Bowing his head, the Archangel expressed himself,

-When I saw It in my clinic with the sign marking her as the Beast, a few days ago, I would never for all Earth's sake given her a chance or a single window of hope. Yet upon the compelling plea of our human Workmaster, I held my Archangelic fire at once. His point was not guilty until proven so. I decided to check her out fully. Given a night to do so, it gave me dread, much, much, dread but also hope, much, much, hope. I knew I had under my care a very lost little Being which cried out loud constantly for her own death. Assessing that soul, I knew It was worth being helped. This is what giving a window and a chance is. Knowing how good the daughter is, I would ask for that very dangerous reassessment of the Father. I would lab rat his soul but not consider release. Little one passed the Archangelic standards so much so that I looked after her recovery from her last suicidal stunt, as I knew her heart was a benefit for the World rather than a deficit. I doubt the Father would pass the same test with flying colours. For he has been proven guilty. With extreme caution, and particularly not telling Eremiel during his time in our prison that he has a shadow of a chance with Us, I would analyse if it is possible to even consider the matter by observing the subject himself fully. His ignorance of all hope is crucial as he would behave like he usually does. Prison is a perfect environment to condition the subject and to perform a great deal of behavioural experiments. Yet knowing how fake, he can be at any point in time, and how he can fool anyone like no other, the risk of misplaced trust I am afraid may always be there. Reassessment of Eremiel, yes, correctly and thoroughly done. Trust to be rehabilitated, never to be given to that soul. This one has done too much to ever be let out. Beside it is grand time he gets punished. If I were you finally having your hands upon him I would make sure his prison time is punitive, that he understands the consequences of his crimes at some point and never re-offence between the four walls containing him forever. The only chance I would give him, which is protective of Earth and Us, which is caring for the sensitivity of his daughter as well, is to let him clean his soul fully in his eternal prison. This is as far as my generosity would go if he is ever capable of grabbing the opportunity of clearing his soul.

When he finished talking he felt both of his shoulders being pressed by Azryel and Wrath, all Angels started whispering, before a couple of them told,

-Speaking for all of Us, we agree with the Archangelic opinion of Gabriel. Although it is the hardest, Eremiel paying finally for his sins, awake and aware of them is sound. The logistic of it and the security has to be there to be implemented.

A grinning with desperation Azryel stood up and turning within the circle, took a cigar out and lit it. Taking a puff before bursting out,

-Hold your fire, Children. Let's not pass that motion that easily because big Gab has spoken. Two important words you mention there, soldiers, logistics and security. Those have to be implemented even before we wake up big Evil from short comatose sleep trip. As talking to him to get any information from him will not be a piece of cake, I can assure you. Gab's got an insane thing with lab rats. He is keeping bits of demons that are still alive in his basement. Let's get him the biggest Evil on Earth and let him play with it for an Eternity. Heavens forbid. I don't think that idea is as bright as Einstein's ones. I think a comatose Evil is far better to deal with to be bluntly honest after we get what we want from him. As, who is going to have to be generous and try to make Eremiel repay his crimes for an eternity? That won't be you guys, that would be my ass on the line, everyday, for I will not get impatient Wrath close to the guy neither clever Gab with his poncey experimental shit on, and watch him explode as soon as he touches one hair of that freaking Being. By the way, Gab, explain to me why would you experiment and analyse him when you know from the start you are not going to let him out in the future? Do you love wasting time? Or are you such an incurable geek?

The Archangel making a stand, smiled with great assurance, replying with utter self confidence,

-I am an incurable geek that I can not deny. Studying the Father of the Beast will allow me to understand her better and give Us the help we need to ensure she never turns like he did. While Eremiel has no chances left with Us apart from being asleep for eternity or paying for his crimes, I will make sure that It keeps her chances securely at all times. I will not be wasting my time, I will be investing it for that soldier, It, to fight with Us for an eternity, to never let her fall, to catch her back at every small trip, to never ever let her reach her own Father's stage. I am not selfishly indulging my test tubes, like you are implying Azryel, I am into getting to the bottom of things and yes you can expect me to be very precise and anal about it.

Strolling by him, Azryel smoking his cigar and pointing it at him asked nonchalantly,

-Good, you took a Being on and try to be thorough about It. Hats off to you, Soldier. Did you think about the logistics of what you are asking?

Gabriel seized the cigar out of Az's hands, took a long and slow puff, before returning it to a dazed Death and a room full of stunned Angels, then answered coolly,

-I did, very much so indeed. Why do you always have to take World's burden upon your own shoulders, Az? Do you love wasting your own time, or are you such an incurable caring general? For a start, I can make the session to get the information from Eremiel go easily, truthfully and painlessly. It involves simple hypnosis and a snaky state of paralysis carried on by myself and the young It. I need her to make him reach the stage of pure unabated confession. She is able to do that. To follow I do not want you exhausted at any point in time, especially since you are my appointed Guardian Angel.

Stopping his speech and fluttering his eyelids to Death, Gabriel made the Angels laugh out loud, before he carried on with all their attention,

-To follow I have made a smaller loophole room ready for him. It is not a palace, it is a jail. When this room looks ethereal, his will display the pain he caused in the surrounding walls, grabbing his heart painfully at all times. Constant torture not involving you, nor Wrath, if he even dare to feel joy at his surrounding, goddess Demeter imposed that his body will endure the suffering he sees. Now, I am not a true punisher like you or Wrath. I worked out the logistics, and It can give Us a bit of security if she manages her own Father's body throughout. Can you do that for Us, Soldier?

The teenager grabbing her own body confessed to Gabriel at once,

-I think, I can. I am not completely sure, yet I am not diminished as he is right now. It is a spell, he is under, however. It can fade as soon as we deal with the Cambion Witch. Then security will go. We need to work a similar spell, I am afraid as fast as we can.

Turning to Azryel, Gabriel acknowledged,

-Security is still to be worked out on the long term, Az. I will be right on it, and make it flawless. I want to keep your hand upon my shoulder for eternity. I will not see you go for the entire World. Geeky me will work something out before you know it.

Death stroking Gabriel's cheek commented,

-Like asked, you worked your Archangelic ass off in the past few days. It is pleasing to see, Soldier. I will keep Us all secure for the time being, then. Let's box up big old Evil and knock him down for a while. Nothing will please me more. Let's hope for the best. Brothers in arms, all for one and one for all.

Verse 24. Sewers, Snake and Rats.

In Boston's sewers, a group of Angels followed It as she tracked her own father. Azryel right behind her smiling at how fast she was moving, commented to Wrath following behind him,

-We will be there in no time at all, so make sure they are ready for the encounter. It is like having our own Blood Hound Beast sniffing the Devil out.

One soldier whispered behind him, holding the box,

-As long as she can knock him down as fast, I swear I will be happy.

Giving him a little elbow kick, Wrath scolded him right away,

-You stink of fear Angel, come, you will stay safe behind the firing line throughout. Get a grip.

Their minds were invaded by the telepathic warning of the Beast, as she stopped abruptly,

-Fifty metres, he is there, coiled and dangerously ready. Wrath I need your Archangelic fire now, before he can slide away. There is only one nook he can go to a little further up, if he has an inkling about reaching it, he will be more lethal than staying here.

Standing still and silent the young It was scanning the darkness of the sewer in front of her with her demonic red eyes. She did not pay attention to the Angels behind her bumping into each other, into a panicked halt from their previous fast run, as she concentrated fully on the heart beat of the black mamba.

As Raphael came by It-666's sides, Azryel turned around and barked into the mind of his soldiers,

-For Christ's sake, stop shitting bricks like that. It's just freaking

Eremiel in a bleeding snake form. Take position, and be aware of your surroundings. Even a human dangerous snake handler could do it.

Assessing the situation, Wrath ordered by telepathy,

-It, give me a circle clear of that putrid water. Soldiers, you stay behind the line of fire. Azryel, there is going to be a fierce stand off involving It, myself and her Father. You must trust us to deal with it and stay behind my protective fire. As I need you to pick that girl up and save her as soon as she falls and take her behind the line. Hopefully she will have done her mission by then.

Touching the water at their feet, the young Beast made it disappear at once from the entire sewage system.

Immediately Wrath encircled the snake by a ring of fire, three metres wide. The Angelic fire walls reaching a couple of metres high, licked the ceilings of the sewer.

Azryel noticing their one metre thickness swore at once in all his Army's mind,

-Jeez Wrath, do you want to set my ass on fire, I have to cross those walls, remember. You, lot were scared of Eremiel, I am scared of Wrath overreacting badly on that one mission. I am sure Gab will be able to cook something with a carbonised snake, and my grilled balls, somehow. Enjoy your dinner tonight guys, remember to pick up my ashes from the sewer. Gosh your asses are really looked after by that Archangel. I wish he could care a little more for my own bum cheeks.

Straight away, it made his soldiers smile, a little reassured, when Death turned to Wrath, he gave the Archangel an all knowing cheeky wink, and a personal telepathic thought,

-Get on with It, big boy. I got those guys under watch, and pepped up.

Raphael taking the hand of It made her cross his fire safely and stood by her within the circle for the confrontation. The black mamba's eyes turned from green to red before their eyes. Eremiel hissed,

-Wrath, coming back for me. I wouldn't have expected any less from an old pal, from one of Us. You brought my daughter along, how sweet of you. She is very sweet isn't it? A good little thing made by I and Lilith in a night of very passionate love when we desired the end of the Earth.

Warning the teenager straight away by telepathy, the Archangel told,

-Do not let him mess up your mind, Child. This is what Eremiel is good at. Sweet talking anyone swiftly to their own doom. You do not want that and I do not, Soldier. Think of who has never let you down, pleaded and preached for you, our human Walter. Your heart choses your own parents, not the ones inflicted upon you by a soulless fate. For you are not a thing It, an object to cause an Apocalypse, you are your very own person. Set your heart free, silence this Evil shitness. With me Soldier.

-All the way, Wrath. He is so dangerous right now. Stay back. He has no intentions to let you or me to live this one out. I made an emergency call. Let it happen. There's no way I am going to be unscathed, but I worked a solution out. Tell Gab, Az and Walt that I love them, they mean everything to me.

Before he could react the Archangel saw rats falling from the sewer's ceilings down to the heart of his circle by dozens. As they reached the ground a swift Beast, touched them one by one with mind blowing speed, transforming them into a 82 centimetres giant rat species. All rodents attacked the black mamba at once, keeping him away from the Archangel at all times. It then touched the tail of the snake as fast as she could. But she could not escape his bite in time, as he revolved upon her hand and sank his teeth into her. Forgetting about herself, she concentrated all her powers to stun the black mamba into a coma. When she collapsed by the collapsing snake, she knew the Angelic Army of Wrath would be safe as long as they kept her Father in the box.

Making his own SOS call to Azryel to get the box in, Raphael knelt by the young Beast checking her out.

When the Death Angel was by him, boxing the back mamba up, he did not pay attention to him, blood tears slowly drooping upon his cheeks, holding the young Beast tightly.

Azryel soothed him straight away, taking the unconscious girl from his Archangelic arms,

-Get your shit together, Bro. She has a pulse. The Father is boxed up, we are ready to go. Let's get our asses out of these sewers swiftly. Archangelic fire off, Wrath. We just gave a good hundred gigantic rats to Boston. We definitely made very happy humans today. Evil is out for a while and we just have big fat rodents to show for it. I got to teach that soldier less creepy ideas, if she makes it through.

Taking It-666 away, within his strong arms, engaging everyone to run with him, and with Wrath following with the box, the Death Angel remembered the exact way out in the maze of sewers.

Soon in their van, the Angels were heading back to the tree house. A very concerned Archangel kept staring at the collapsed It upon Death's knees, and asked worryingly,

-Did her Father get the best of her? She has not moved an inch since we left those sewers, Az.

-Shut up, Wrath. That soldier is thoroughly damaged and I am working upon our sweet little It. Let me concentrate on her recovery and not her toll bell. Please. Keep quiet, all of you keep quiet, so I can deal with her faint heart rather then her strong toll bell ringing.

All of them witnessed the Death Angel fighting to save the life of the young Beast, with great concern. Seeing him trying in desperation the human way to deal with snake bites, they fell into utter disbelief. Azryel sucked out and spat out poison until all was removed as fast as he could. His every single spit burst into sulfuric scented flames. When he was done, It coughed upon his shoulder, her first sign of proper life since they left Boston and he swore,

-Fucking son of a bitch! That mother fucker gave you a proper nasty bite. How are you feeling, Soldier?

Collapsing back upon his chest, the teenager closed her eyes and whispered,

-I am dying, Az, I feel like I am.

Touching her heart at once, Death injected all his healing energy through her heart. Before he knew it, Wrath was helping him, with his Archangelic healing energy, kneeling by him, trying to save the young Beast in his arms. He could feel that Raphael had put a plea to High Above for It who had put her neck on the line for him and everyone. The toll bell ringing in his head stopped at once. The teenager coughed again and again within his arms and complained, finally opening her eyes,

-My body is burning like Hell. Az, take me there swiftly.

Death replied with a wicked smile, giving her a bear hug,

-You are not going anywhere, my little Soldier, we are keeping you. I am not going to take you to Hell any time soon, you protected an Archangel with your own life, who just made a plea for you in return. For the burning, I can not help. Why don't you use the sewage water, you just swallowed out of Boston. Although, it is a tiny bit filthy. Repair Boston's sewers, and bring those damned rats to a normal freaking size and maybe I can deal with your burning internal organs. Never forget to clear up your mess Soldier, especially since your one is pretty special. Get the strength from me, and clear out at once, It. Don't forget to thank Wrath for your lease of life.

Turning around she saw the Archangel kneeling by Azryel and her, holding her damaged hand tightly. Hugging him at once, she commented,

-Thank you, Wrath, thank you so much. I could not have done it without you. His voice kept hissing within my mind trying to mess it up, trying to make me lose my focus in order for me to not use my powers. Your warning against his words triggered my idea for the rats. I had to do exactly the same tactic, and try to make Eremiel lose his focus so he could not attack, go to you or anywhere. Calling out all the rats of Boston to our rescue, making them monster rats as they reached the ground to keep him busy. That made him stop talking shit in my head too.

Laughing and crying at the same time, Raphael confided,

-I tell you what, that was emotional. Eremiel was hissing his shit in my mind as well, nothing nice, nothing good to repeat, until he was too stunned to carry on and fell into his coma. However hard it is, you must never pay attention to his words. He causes chaos with them, incites murders and crimes, brings people against one another. The only people you should listen to and believe are the ones that have your best interests at heart. You did well, Soldier. I am proud of you. Now, as Az asked we need to fix that monster rodent issue in the sewers of Boston as soon as possible. Help yourself with my Archangelic energy, if you have to, little one.

Sitting by Azryel, It's demonic eyes turned red, she kept holding the hands of the Death Angel and the Archangel. Concentrating until she saw inside the sewers, until she felt every single rat within them, speaking strange words, she glowed green powerfully.

For a few seconds the van lifted from the ground, when its four wheels touched back on the tarmac, the Angel who was driving scolded,

-For Christ's sake, tell her not to levitate the van. That's going to blow our cover.

It's eyes became normal again. She smiled to them with satisfaction, stating as she released the Angelic hands,

-The sewers are back the way they were. I put the water back too. To thank the rats for responding to my call for help, I cleaned it too. All the rats are back to their normal size.

Taking a cigar out of his jacket and lighting it, Azryel commented with an amused smirk drawing to his lips,

-I must say, I can't help liking that Being, she cracks me up. I hope you enjoyed using my energy to talk shit to rodents and clean sewers up. While you were at it, you could have cleaned up our clothes and tumble dried them, for I am starting enjoying the smell in this van. Running behind you to collect your Evil Father, my guys did collect lots of stools too. Don't do it if involves levitating the van again, we don't want to startle unwary drivers like that.

Wrath could not help smiling irresistibly to the girl, yet warned,

-Az, don't encourage her. It, don't clean Us, that Angel will have to bear the smell with Us.

Death replied cockily, making a perfect round puff towards the Archangel,

-Great, one must love your missions Wrath to follow you in miles of shit. I tell you what the look on the face of Gab when we are going to step in and soil his pretty tree-house is going to be priceless. I am all for clearing that mess up before his Archangelic ass refuses Us entry. What do you say my soldiers, motion to clean that shit up? We might as well, it won't hurt Us. Come on Wrath that stench is vile. How about thanking Us for getting your Evil snaky?

Rallying behind Azryel, the soldiers lifted their hands up. Giving a cheeky winning smile to Wrath, speaking with his cigar at the corner of his mouth,

-Right, motion passed. Babe, hold my hand, and work your mojo for my guys. Warning, Met' the van is going to fly again.

The giggling Angelic driver, looked at Az completely bemused,

-Cool, do it fast, there's not a cat in the street.

A little consternated Wrath held the other hand of It and gave her the go ahead. It took only a few seconds for her to do what Azryel had demanded. When it was over, a very pleased Death Angel looked at his Doc Martins with glee, saying,

-Now, that's better. That girl is definitely worth calling back from any deadly toll bell.

Scolding him at once, the Archangel warned him,

-Don't play with that Being's powers in a willy-nilly fashion, Az. That would only enrage Archangel Gabriel more than pieces of cac' on his floor. Beside I saw the box lifting itself up, I hope we didn't wake up Evil snaky in there.

Looking at each others, then worryingly at the box the soldiers gave a killer glance to Azryel, who asked It immediately,

-Is it a possibility, Soldier?

Reassuring them at once, the teenager replied with assurance,

-No chance at all. I went very heavy on his nasty guts. As he bit me he was sending me lots of his Evil crap through my hand as well as the poison, something my body would not have coped with, so I sent that stuff right back to him. It's a mirror shielding technique and it almost worked like a treat. That was powerful shit which would have hurt him very badly, his own body would not have been able to cope with it just as well, which means that Eremiel kind of welcomed the coma I gave him for he knew it was his only chance of surviving in my hand. He will not be able to ever wake up until I say so. To be honest I don't fancy meeting his nasty guts again. Az proposed that in our prison, he should be put back to sleep and not fiddled with. I totally agree with him. He is extremely dangerous. Well, he nearly killed me. My body still feels the effects. My organs are in pain.

Straight away the Death Angel praised her, putting his healing hands back upon her,

-Let's sort out those organs, Soldier, I must say I am very impressed with the way you dealt with him. You think on your feet, and in this Army it's an excellent quality, I can assure you. You done really well on this mission. I can tell you that we are all very proud of you.

Verse 25. Coming Clean.

As soon as the white van arrived at the tree-house, they saw Walter Workmaster and Archangel Gabriel, running from the platform to welcome them. Metatron parked in the yard and went to open the back door. Wrath was the first to jump out, holding the box with great care, followed by his three soldiers, and Azryel helping the young It out.

The human looking at his watch addressed Wrath straight away,

-What time do you call this, Archangel? It's nearly four am. We were worried sick Gab and I. Next time you take my girl on a mission, it has to be outside of her bedtime hours.

-Look who's talking, the very man that went strolling with her in Hell at two freaking am. Next time missions will be during daytime just to please your paternal instinct.

Looking worryingly at how It could not walk apart from being helped by Azryel, Gabriel demanded,

-How did it go? Feedback. Why is the Death Angel badly burnt and my girl in such a weak state?

As soon as he said that Walter went to It, and asked kindly,

-How are you doing, kiddo?

Leaving the support of Az, she stumbled to the man, and just hugged him. Blood tears came rolling slowly upon her face, as she told him,

-It's gonna be okay, Pa. Wrath gave me a lease of life and Az is sorting me out. I can tell you, Walt, you are the only dad I want, the only father I will ever accept.

Hugging the emotional girl tightly, a very worried Workmaster looked at Raphael for explanations. The Archangel enjoined,

-Lets all go inside, the little one is exhausted. I can brief you both to what happened in the safety of the loophole room. Let me put Eremiel in his prison first of all. He can stay in his box for the night. I am not ready to make him talk anytime soon. I have heard enough of him for one night. Although we will have to pry information out of him sometime tomorrow. Gabriel show me the way. Az carry on fixing my soldier up in the loophole room and take Workmaster with you. I will come over with Gab. For the others, well done and be at rest.

A curious Wrath followed eagerly the Archangel Gabriel to inspect the prison he had created. As he deposited the box within the cell, he was gob smacked, and expressed his wonder,

-I knew you were a wiz kid when you were little, dissecting insects. When you started mapping some genome up at twelve, I realised I had a genius in my hands. But this is something else creating invisible rooms outside space and time in barely any time at all, visible only from the inside, a space totally protected. Gab, sometimes how your mind works utterly baffles me.

Shying a little, Gab changed the subject readily,

-It's nothing really, pure mathematics and physics, just formulas which I learnt how to use to an adequate level. I want to know what happened to little It, Uncle, I was worried sick every minute that went on with no signs of you lot coming back.

-Worried for Us all or just for It, Gab?

Nose diving the Archangel turning around the room, looking at the movie pictures of Eremiel's crimes around him asked,

-Do you think I went a little too far with the room decoration?

Cocking his eyebrows, glancing around, a sarcastic and all knowing smile rising upon his lips Uncle Raphael, said,

-No, I think it would be perfect for Eremiel. Would you consider him as an appropriate father in law, or would Workmaster be the perfect one for you? After being almost your double brother in law, I think Walter's complicated family would be better for you. You would complete the dysfunction to the perfection. I do glean information wherever I go, Gabriel, and as the Master of Azryel I tend to be kept in the know. You will not be able to avoid that conversation with me my dear nephew. Now, know that I learnt my own lesson and that I will never ostracise you from the rest of Us because of a relationship you decide to form or not. You are the original Master of the Beast, like you said and you care for her tremendously. I can see It like the nose in the middle of your face. Be honest with me, is it a feeling similar to the one I share with the Death Angel, an Angelic feeling which will make us lay our life for one another or is it a feeling similar to love and the one you shared with Wendy?

Put upon the spot, Archangel Gabriel faced his Uncle and confessed,

-A bit of both. It is very early stages, Wrath, but I can't help thinking of her young Being, dealing with the blow and the bad luck to be born at wrong date and to the worst father one can ever bestow. It's a compassionate love more than anything else. She does touch my heart and I want to help her. Since Az told me that she has her very first crush on me, I have been worried not to encourage her in any way. You can trust me to do so until that Being becomes an adult. Then I doubt her love for a nerd like I am would have remained or grown. If she is still so in love with me to run to Hell and back for my sake like she is at sixteen, then dear Uncle I will let myself cherish her.

To his great surprise Raphael gave him a bear hug, patting his back as he welcomed his confession,

-Dear Gab, if you ever wed our little Trouble, I will stand by you, as our man Workmaster gives her a way. I will not discourage you nor her. She is such a self sacrificing Being, and sweet as Hell that I can only want an Archangel to look after her and be constantly at her sides. You should have seen her in Boston's sewers, you would have been proud of her. Unlike her real father, she has a sound soul about her. I have a piece of information for you, a nugget that may help you in your quest to resolve her puzzling nature revealed by our very Eremiel. As I always said Evil talks too much, the mother of It is none but the infamous Lilith. They planned her to be the end of the Earth. Knowing little It is working with Us, and a traitor in his own eyes, he tried to kill her and nearly did. I can't hide the fact that as Azryel was saving her, he kept hearing her toll bell ringing. I intervened and made the Archangelic plea for her life. I am so grateful I was listened to. When you go into that room, you must understand that her young soul is fully shaken from seeing Eremiel. She made it clear to Us that she rejects him as her father. Now, lets go in your loophole room to check upon her and see if she is ready to go to bed. Not a word about her mother please, the teenager has had enough to handle for one evening. My Az needs some tending too as well, I will need you to help me fix him, for your education. He is an atypical Angel, which you might find interesting for your study of our young It. He told me himself he was not dissimilar to her. Let's go for if I let that Angel patiently suffer for too long, my ears are going to pay for it for thrice the time, if he decides to ever let go of the matter that is.

Teletransporting into the loophole room, Gab and Wrath, saw the Death Angel still sending his healing energy to the young Beast as Walter stood by worried. When he realised the Archangels had arrived, the man warned them,

-There's a chance that It is going to lose her hand. Az is fighting it but his own energy is nearly depleted. Take a look at that Angel and you can work out he is very injured himself. Wrath, Death has been whispering your name every five minutes. Can you do something? Was he calling you?

Both Archangels came to assess the situation. Wrath replied to the human at once,

-It was Angelic distress calls, Walt. Az rarely has them. Something is up within her body he can not deal with in his current state. Gosh, Gab how did you make those rooms? Even an Angelic call can not reach the outside. This is the first time ever I missed a call from Azryel. Keep an eye on Death as I look after It, do not intervene upon him until I say so. Just make him comfortable.

Gabriel taking charge of the Death Angel just saw him collapse by his feet. Kneeling and nestling him upon his knees, he could feel him nearly exhausted of all his energies. Stroking his burnt shoulders, he realised he had been made to cross Archangelic fire. Azryel would carry on burning away slowly but surely until Wrath intervened and reversed the effect of his own fire. It made him understand how dedicated Death was but also so over looked. Holding one of his hands tightly, he proposed,

-Az, swallow some of my Archangelic energy, go ahead. I need you there, mate, so swallow away until Wrath can sort you out.

He could feel a weak swallow of energy going on within his hand, the Archangel could swear he never had seen that Angel as drained as he was right now. A blood tear came to his eyes at the thought of it, and he scolded his Uncle out loud,

-Don't you ever leave that Angel unattended for that long, Wrath. For you will hear me pestering you for thrice as long as it took you to react, mark my word, Archangel.

 Raphael paying attention to the damaged young It, barked to him,

-He will get sorted. Death can wait, he the toughest of Us all. Beside I am teaching him not to be so mouthy with me, because each time he has to cross the fire. And I can tell you right now, that I will make him cross the fire again and make him wait again until I decide for him to be fixed up.

An upset Gabriel put his other healing hand at once upon the Death Angel, whispered,

-If you are awake, Bro, you do not need to endure that amount of pain. I do not know how to heal you but if you know how to, just use the inflow.

Feeling his hand just squeezed a little, Gab witnessed a kind smile upon Death who managed to utter,

-Only Wrath can cure me from his fire. Thanks for the concern, Bro, for I am feeling like a very disposable item right now. Keep talking, make me stay conscious. Wrath will be a while with the little one, I can tell you that much.

A worried sick Gabriel demanded,

-Tell me what is going on, Az? Please, I beg you tell me.

A weakened Azryel stated simply,

-Aftermath of engagement, battle wounds. Two casualties only, It and I. She suffers from the nasty snake bite given by her Evil Father who tried to kill her, and I only suffer from crossing the Archangelic fire to retrieve her at my Master's orders, and also a big fat depletion of energy trying to cure little It. Eremiel has been mutated somehow. His genetic makeup has been changed, it happened after the birth of It. I will need you to investigate that for me, Geeky one.

Seeing the swollen blue hand of It turning back to a pink human one within his Archangelic ones, Wrath gleefully announced to a relieved Workmaster,

-One little Beast sorted, no lost hand, she can keep her one, yet I am afraid the scar of the bite will always remain there as a reminder of her own Father disowning her. It's so powerful I can not touch it.

Walter went to hug the teenager, and commented,

-We can live with that reminder, for we disown him too, don't we, my It? Guess what, Caro, I and even Gab worked upon finding you a name all night. We came up with one that pleases all of us. We just need Az to be up and running before we deliver the news to you. Gab said as Az was your Angelic teacher, he had a little say upon the matter. But my own say is if you don't like that name, we are going to wrack our brain for another one of your own liking our little Sweet Heart.

Finally going to his Death Angel, Raphael stated with a winning yet kind smile,

-Have we got one big Angel down or not? Have we been patient for proper mending? Who is going to be a teaching lab rat for my Gab?

Suffering from all his Archangelic burns, Death managed to smile back to Wrath, accusing,

-Freaking wicked Bastard. I would have loved being informed of the intended exercise. Have I been that bad lately? Usually I do not slack. Forgive me if I ever did, Wrath.

Raphael putting one healing hand upon Azryel and holding one of Gabriel to teach him healing the Archangelic way, replied in a soothing manner,

-I can not fault you Azryel, at any point in time, even when you express yourself with slight rudeness to your peers or myself. You never slack, general, you are thorough. Today I need to give our back up healer the ability to heal my best Angel, my general. I need you to keep on going, Az and another pair of Archangelic healing hands as well as mine will become very necessary in the future. For a very few minutes tonight, I am afraid you will have to be one of Gab's lab rats. I am there so you will remain safe throughout. Close your eyes, Death, I will make sure the lesson is thorough but as short as I can. Knowing you, I am giving you a license to swear throughout.

-Bloody f'in Hell, Wrath. For crying out loud, overreaction, Wrath, overreaction, Jeez, who's going to find a cure for that? Gab, if you mess up with one single blood vessel of mine you are in deep trouble, very, very deep trouble.

The wicked Wrath starting the healing of the Death Angel scolded him,

-You are in no position at all to do such warnings, my Az. Besides I won't tolerate them at this precise moment given with liberality to either me or my nephew. Do not worry Gabriel, you are here to learn, so please do mess away with one of his blood vessels or even two. I will show you how to fix the damages. We do learn by our mistakes so it's almost an imperative to make some.

The kneeling Gabriel couldn't believe his Archangelic Uncle's cruelty, while the Death Angel closed his eyes in deep desperation, yet he whispered,

-What on Earth took me to choose a renown torturing punishing Archangel as a Master... I must have been so desperately down and under the weather. Come Wrath, you must have a grudge or two with me to talk like that? What's my punishing lesson all about?

-Shh, it's alright, you are going to be fine and learn some manners, not to smoke in front of our two kids, Micky and the young It, less cockiness when talking to me and never to ask the Beast to use her powers for willy-nilly reasons for I have the power to deplete you totally of your own.

Trying to lift himself up but not succeeding, Death fell back upon the ground, by the two kneeling Archangels, accepting his fate, by his state of great weakness only, he stated,

-I wish you didn't mention that last part to Gabriel, Wrath. Now, I am in for proper torture. Walter, put my soldier to bed, she doesn't need to see how Angels deal with each other to teach them harsh lessons after her long night.

The Archangel Raphael lifting the chin of Azryel, simply asked,

-Who makes the calls, general?

A gulping Az replied,

-You, Wrath.

Looking at the tired girl, already asleep upon her adopted father's lap, Wrath told the human,

-Take her to bed. Keep an eye on her bitten hand, if it turns blue again even just slightly, come to get me straight away, Walt. Do not worry about, Az, he will be as good as new tomorrow if slightly less mouthy.

Lifting It in his arms, Workmaster nodded but commented, before leaving the loophole room,

-If you want the simple advice of a mere human, I would not touch the mouthiness of Azryel for one bit, I love just the way he is. If I understood the whole situation, I saw an Angel that devoted himself entirely to the recovery of my child, ignored his own state all along, and did not beg once for his own recovery. When shown such great patience, stealth and dedication by one of my soldiers, if I were you Wrath, I would give that Angel, patience and kindness. For all the care that your Death Angel is showing day in and out, forgetting about his own self, I would just give him as much care and respect I can and never forget all he does for Us. I hope I will not see that Angel downcast one bit tomorrow, for I want to keep seeing his sarcastic smirks and having meaningful exchanges with him. I will keep an eye on little It, Wrath, you can count on me. Can I count on you, for Azryel? Don't tell me, I will see the result from my own eyes tomorrow.

When the man had left the room Raphael looked at Gabriel feeling remorse, and proposed to him,

-Let's sort Azryel out. No messing about with him, do try to get it right first time around Gab. Mimic just as I do and we will have Death upon his feet in minutes. No torture session for you, my Az, just plain healing. I hope that the length of time it took me to come to fix you up, was lesson enough for you. Forgive me if it made you feel like a disposable item, for you are not one, I can assure you. That man made a right plea for you, I thought you were like cat and dog, what have you done to him?

Wiping a single blood tear pricking the eyes of the Death Angel, Gabriel answered for him,

-He does his usual, he teases us to death all day long while protecting us. Myself, I appreciate greatly his presence in my house, ironically enough, he is the life of the party. With him, Workmaster and the teenage Beast that we are raising, I never have a single boring moment. Coming home and seeing all of them watching 'the Exorcist', chilling and them two encouraging the young It to do a 360 head spin like in the movie, for example, if I was in the right set of mind at that moment in time, I would have seen the black humour of it. But they all had a big Gab Archangelic telling off. Now, what made Az believe that I would torture him? What did he make her do this time around?

Azryel begged the Archangel Raphael desperately at once,

-Don't tell him, Wrath!

-Don't move like a fidgeting little girl, Angel, do you want me to mess you up? Stay still, do not move one inch, my Az. Hope he didn't disturb your healing move on his cheekbones, Gab? How are you doing with those burns? There are pretty superficial so it should be child's play for you Archangel. What Death's unrest is about, is that during that specific time you took as an example, you told him not to use the Beast's powers like party tricks...

Interrupting him Gabriel asked wildly fearing the worse,

-What did he make her do this time around? I never ever want to let that poor thing think she is a circus freak.

-Oi! Watch my cheek, you Muppet! I am going to be the circus freak, if you don't have steady hands, Gab. I just must made the little one clean up her mess, with a little extension to our own. She was great, she did it all. For we had hundreds of big fat rats, shy of a metre long in the sewers of Boston, no more water down there, and having run in miles of shit we smelt like one, Bro. I thought that you would appreciate Us turning up a little cleaner than what we were, that's all, so your nice poncey tree-house doesn't reek as our van did nor like the bleeding sewers of Boston.

A brightly smiling Gab tidying up the mess he did upon the cheek commented,

-Wrath, you definitely overreacted on that one, if you think that your Army can crash at mine with all the filth of Boston upon them, you are mistaken. I would drag all your smelly asses to the river for a good clean up before being allowed to enter my home. It sounds like you had fun, Azryel. What was all the giant rats all about? Why not clearing the water of the sewage system before paddling in miles of shit? I would have ordered the young one to do that, myself. A. It would have improved the moves of all the soldiers, which means you would have been faster on the job. B. A snake in water is much faster than a snake upon ground, which implies much less exertion for all to track him and follow. C. Pure hygiene, cleanliness and less risks of spreading nasty microscopic bugs and viruses upon your clothing whilst out. You'd better clean that van inside out tomorrow before I let my humans Walt and my Caro step in it.

Lifting his hands from Azryel, Wrath stated with a wicked grinning smirk,

-All done Death, get your sorry ass off the ground. You are entirely mended. I am afraid to say you were right about Archangel Gabriel.

Standing up Azryel shrugged his shoulders, made a few kicking moves in the air with his legs and fists, before acknowledging, taking a cigar from his jacket,

-Well done, Gab, you did well for your first time mending me, although I might strangle you tomorrow if I find a scar while shaving my beautiful face. Make sure you concentrate upon the healing job at all times with my soldiers. I usually have a silence rule in place when healing, I think it will benefit you as well. Now, for the mission we had fun, trust me, but I think Wrath and I would benefit from your ideas on how to use the young Beast effectively on our future endeavours. What you just said, shows some planning skills and I want you to use them in our next consultation. I need you to be present at the start of them and ask Us, how we are going to go about our mission. Then think about it and if you can offer any improvements just share them. You bragged about being the Beast's original Master, and let me tell you that your kid is good, brilliant even yet scarily so. Even protected behind the Archangelic fire line of Wrath, my soldiers were shitting bricks as they saw all the rats of Boston running upon the sewers's ceilings. All of them switch on to an aggression mode unbelievable to witness without a slight panicky heart. We are talking big Angels there, seasoned and all. Then you see the rats falling from the ceilings like rain, some burning in the fire, some making it to the centre of the circle, where It touched them, changing their genetic make up in an instant and having an army of monster rats at her fingertips to attack her father and prevent him from killing Wrath. She did not want Raphael's help in the ring of fire because her father was set on killing both. So she worked a solution as fast as she could involving the rodents of Boston, yet she knew she was unlikely to make it herself. Wrath had her last words. Tell him, Raphael.

The Archangel told his nephew, while lighting the cigar of his general,

-She is a fully self sacrificing Being, Gabriel. Azryel and I realised that upon this mission. We will never be able to guarantee that this soldier will come back from the front lines. She will lay her own life for Us, in front of Us, protecting Us and then we can only watch aimlessly and provide her after care. The amount of energy spent by Az and I to make sure she is staying with Us, frustrates me greatly. Her own toll bell rang tonight. We need to devise a safety net, before she goes all 'I am laying my life for you', telling me to tell my Gab, my Az and my Walt that you meant everything to her. To my eyes, she has clearly devoted herself to Us, and especially to you three. We have to put into that soldier's head that she is so valued that she simply has to let Us get involved in helping her out. I need you three on the ball to make sure she understands that I need living soldiers and not one offs. Do whatever it takes. But if she uses her Solomon skills next time around, advise her to call something nicer and keep them less monster like, yet with what she was dealing with, I would have called out for Frankenstein like porcupines myself.

A kindly smiling Gabriel went all thoughtful, before advancing,

-I will get upon it and get Walt on board. Her and her rodents... Letting her have her own pet, might teach her the responsibility over the life of that little animal and the importance of staying alive during it. Shall we get her a hamster or a guinea pig? Hopefully, she will not roast on them at some point, I am feeding her enough. She is back to a normal sixteen year old weight for her size.

Puffing his cigar, Azryel could not help mentioning,

-That's very outside the box thinking from what we were saying, Gab, but I like it. As long as we keep the wheel spinning cute hamster where I am not sleeping, I am fine with that scheme. When are we going to head for the pet shop, letting our girl speak to all the little beasties, animal talk talk? I will definitely prefer that mission, to running in a sewer. I would leave the guinea pig out of the question, just in case she thinks you are her role model, my dear Gabriel.

Verse 26. Gab's Ark.

Azryel smiling wildly, holding plenty of shopping bags stood in front of a shop window full of watches. Gabriel coming by him, informed,

-We are moving on, Bro. Caro, I think, finished to clothe our teenager up. We are going to head for the pet shop now. I should have rethought involving our humans in a shopping trip. You are fully loaded like a donkey and my own hands are getting full. We have a 'guilt trip' Wrath switched on. He is going the full lavish Monty. Someone has got to tell him where to stop, I do not want him to teach my It that money grows on trees.

The incarnated Death Angel looking at Gab, scolded him at once,

-Do you think you are going to use your wealth when you are buried? Please do not tell Wrath to live less or your self sacrificing girl to do so, let them be. They are both born eternal but as both are extreme fighters, both can lose their lives without a warning but the toll bell. Raphael has been lavishing upon his Army since I have known him. Best suits, best shoes, best watches, it's his way to reward them. He is not the lavish type with kind words, he never has been. He shows his appreciation by paying in human material kind.

-Don't you think it would be better the other way? For my young Beast's sake, I would prefer if he boost her self esteem up a bit with meaningful words every time she does well, for any goods he gives her she does not take to her grave but every single true hearted word she will.

-You are right but a freaking killjoy, Gabriel, do you know that?

Raphael coming to them put his hands upon their shoulders, and confessed,

-That was fun, I had my Caro who wore killer heels at Uni, telling the kid to never try them on. Those are supposed to give bad ankles syndrome... We have got It a few pairs of sensible shoes. Looking at Rolex, Az, do you fancy one of them?

Looking back at the watches in front of him, the incarnated Angel told,

-Well, yes one of them, but if you told me how well I did on my last mission, I would prefer it.

-What's stinging you all of a sudden?

-Big Gab and his reasonable arguments, but if you insist I'll have that one, there in the corner.

-That's better. In all honesty, It nearly did it all on this outing, you only had to cross my Archangelic fire, put the snake in the box and save my girl's life.

Getting involved Gabriel laughed,

-Just, that was a tall order, especially knowing your kind of fire. Come, Wrath praise him a little.

Shrugging his shoulders, Raphael left their sides to enter the shop and buy the watch.

With a pleased grin Azryel enjoined Gab to follow him to the pet shop nearby. Caro and Walter were already there with It and Micky. Seeing the pleased smile on the face of the teenager being asked to do like the little boy and pick her own pet hamster, Gabriel couldn't help confiding to Az,

-Thank you for letting her go out. I know that you and Wrath are protecting us, but this is the first time in her young life that she has been allowed to live one day like a normal kid on a family shopping trip. Yet, we are willingly letting her out to fight with our Angelic Army. I think we should offer her the ability to enjoy that type of day more often.

Watching all the little hamsters climbing all at once on the arms of the young girl as soon as the cage was open, Azryel gave all his shopping bags to Gabriel, and whispered to him,

-We will see, I am still waiting for something to cock up to be honest like her talking hamster lingo right now, let me intervene before all the animals in the shop go and say hello to her.

Azryel putting his hand upon the shoulder of It, intimated to her kindly by telepathy,

-We said one pet not a thousand and no chatting to rodents in the pet shop. Tell them to go back in the cage at once.

Sheepishly giggling, the teenager did as she was told with all the little hamsters returning to their cage, and confessed,

-Sorry Az, I forgot myself.

Walter, by her turning around confided to the Angel who was closing the cage,

-It's okay, no one paid attention, the shopkeeper has not noticed.

Azryel shaking his head in desperation yet smiling irresistibly and kindly,

-Okay, I haven't seen what I just saw and we will say zilch to Wrath otherwise there won't be any outings for you in the future, It. So, which hamster do you want? I am going to pick it for you so you keep your hands off that cage. Walt did you chose a cage for the little thing?

Workmaster presented him with a large one with a clear pink plastic bottom already furnished with all the hamster accessories paraphernalia. Pointing at one hamster among the dozen, the excited teenager asked,

-I want that one. Thank you, Az.

Looking inside the cage, the Angel failed to recognise the hamster, and swore,

-Bloody hell, I would find a needle in a haystack more easily. They are all look alike. I will pick one and if it is not your one, it will still do, one freaking hamster is as good as another.

When he glanced at the disappointed eyes of It, he immediately tried to make her cheer up again,

-Okay, how about you chat to your specific one and make him do something that the others don't do, like cleaning his little nose so I can distinguish it from the rest.

Throwing her arms around his neck, Az received an unexpected peck upon his cheek from the pleased girl. He turned to Gab with a big smile on his face, and told the teenager,

-It's not me you got to thank little one for getting a hamster, it's Gab, it's his idea, go and give him a kiss.

It ran to the Archangel and throwing herself at his neck kissed his cheek before he had time to put any bags down or react. When she returned by the cage Azryel had the proper hamster she wanted within his strong hands. He asked her teasingly with a wink,

-Is it that one? What did that fur ball have in particular that the rest didn't have? An extra whisker? A longer tail? Ratty attributes? Or is it because it looks as cute as Gab?

-I don't look like a rodent, thank you very much Azryel.

A widely grinning Death putting the hamster in his cage, teased further,

-Here, in you go, lil' Gab, in your fanciful lil' home.

When Wrath entered the pet shop, he saw his nephew complaining straight to him,

-Azryel is absolutely not sortable. We can't take him out like that, he is worse than the child. He is calling her hamster Gab.

A smiling Raphael admitted,

-Yes I don't take Azryel into town as often as I should. As long as he is having fun on this shopping trip, with the little one that's what matters. Did Micky choose his hamster? When you are all done I will be at the till.

Caroline holding a similar cage to the one of It's hamster but with a clear blue bottom announced,

-All sorted, Micky's hamster is in there.

But Raphael was not paying attention as he headed to a part of the shop far from the till. Azryel and It went to follow him, while Workmaster told his son and ex-wife,

-Stay by uncle Gab.

Wrath standing still by a snake's vivarium, lost in his thoughts, had a worried Az touching his shoulder trying to recall him,

-Raph, what's up? Our Evil snake is properly boxed up and all is safe.

Tapping the hand upon his shoulder in a reassuring fashion, Wrath said,

-They have got snakes in there.

Walter behind them commented,

-Yes, this is why it is called a pet shop, Raphael.

It stood by him, held his hand and shook her head disapprovingly
to him,

-Shh, Dad, that was scary shit in those sewers.

A begging and anxious Azryel asked Wrath,

-Raphael, please share your thoughts with us. Are you suffering
from flash backs?

Turning to him with eyes glowing wickedly, and an evil smile Wrath
revealed,

-I have a very vicious idea which could get rid of P and his witch,
and provide Us with time to give a proper childhood to our young
It. Let's buy a nasty snake.

The Death Angel sternly warned the Archangel,

-Now, I am definitely worried. Let's not rush things through and
Let's discuss it beforehand with the Army. Besides I am not sure
Gabriel would appreciate his home being turned into a zoo with
another dangerous snake.

But there was no stopping Wrath as he looked at all the snakes
available in the shop,

-Tough, he will have to. We will discuss everything in the loophole
room. What I have to propose is a tad controversial as customary. I
will need you all to refine it to make sure it will work to a T. It, help
me find a good decoy Evil father, which one looks the closest to
him and if not can you make it look more like him?

Half understanding Wrath's idea, Azryel encouraged the teenager,

-Soldier, are you able to help Raphael for the moment? It does not
mean that we will automatically go through with everything he says,
we will discuss them thoroughly later with the whole Army. Walter

keep a stand by that door and don't let any shopper check that area, tell them it is closed for the moment as it is snake feeding time.

Coming by Wrath, It-666 gave him a hand to find an appropriate snake,

-Let me help, Raphael. We can't find a black mamba in here, I know it but I can pinpoint to one with a near enough genetic make up. I can tweak the snake to become one at home.

A smiling Archangel welcomed her help, saying,

-Soldier, I am doing this for you and it will involve you all the way through. You protected my life yesterday, and I am trying to work out a solution to protect yours.

Taking his hand, she lead him to a particular vivarium, pointing to the snake inside,

-We need that one. It's a water cobra, it's the most closely related to the black mamba in the entire shop.

A winning grin drawing upon his lips, Wrath told Azryel who was by him reading the label telling all about the snake and how to look after it,

-Meet my very own pet, Az. My pet project is called Deadly.

-If you don't mind me saying that looks less cute and attractive to me than the five or eight Great Dane puppies we were suppose to have. I guess you are going to dump the looking after of that deadly pet upon me as usual.

Cracking his own knuckles with delight, Wrath stated with great satisfaction,

-Of course I will, you are so good at it. Go and fetch what that particular one needs. As I see you haven't forgotten about your puppies, I might let you have them if you do exceedingly well with that one.

Azryel turning to It with a childish ironical smirk on his face, told her,

-I am so excited I am going to get puppies, as I named your pet, I will let you name mine. Come and help me find the proper gear for Deadly. As you know all about your beasties, it will help Us go away from that shop before any one else gets another uncontrollable pet fancy. Bet upon Gab's face Soldier, smile or no smile?

The teenager followed the Death Angel eagerly and handed him the necessary snake keeping kit. She replied,

-I bet on no smile with a look of desperation. I love the name Gab for my hamster by the way. You know I couldn't help blushing when I kissed Gabriel thank you. I hope he didn't notice.

-Wishful thinking kiddo, Gab notices everything. When you gave me your thankful peck I felt his look burning behind my back. I could swear I did feel a pinch of jealousy too. Be careful of who you hug even innocently by Gabriel in the future. I know him to be fiercely protective. You don't want to be locked away in a little cupboard, do you? Eight years of caging must have rendered you sick of it. Now, I have the losing bet, thanks It, he will smile and be all comprehensive from the start.

-We've got everything, let's go and check his face. I am eager to win my bet. What's the stakes?

Azryel with his hands completely full told the teenager in a confiding tone, and a wicked smile,

-If I win you have to name one of my puppies, Raphy. If I lose you can rename your hamster how you want.

A pouting It scolded the Angel,

-That means that you will not lose anything at all.

-I never do, Soldier. Walt get the shop assistant to handle the snake for Wrath, and give that cage to him, for it is the one we want.

Going by Wrath who was lost in the fascination of the Boulengerina before him, Azryel recalled him,

-Raphael, wakey wakey. It and I have a little bet going on. Care to join in?

-What's the bet?

-The reaction of Gabriel seeing us coming back with a cobra to take home. Just a plain smiling or no smiling Archangel. What's your bet?

-Definitely not a smiling Gab.

The shop assistant came to them with Walt and the vivarium to be purchased and queried,

-Which snake do you desire?

Wrath pointing eagerly to the water cobra, answered,

-That very one.

Putting a pair of glasses on, the assistant took a worried glance at the vivarium and stated,

-We can only sell this one to an expert handler, I am afraid. Which one of you would it be?

Azryel putting the teenager forward, replied,

-She is. We bought her pet snakes since she was almost in the cradle.

Looking suspiciously at the five foot tall short haired blond teenager before him, the man asked,

-Do you all know what to do in case of emergency?

Workmaster getting involved as Azryel and Raphael gave a common positive answer to the shop assistant with sarcastic smiles drawing on their faces, added,

-My adopted daughter and I reside at my brother in law's house, who is Doctor Purallee. I can tell you that it is truly the safest place on Earth to keep any deadly snake. He is the tall guy with all the shopping bags by my son and wife, also a Doctor, if you need a signature of safe sale.

-It won't be needed, Sir. Doctor Purallee did my mother's hip replacement and she was overwhelmed with the amount of care and standards in his clinic. Our whole family is now registered at Purallee's. Would you like a discount, Sir? I can give you a good price for that snake. Does your daughter want to put the cobra in his vivarium herself?

Walter pushing his blond hair from his forehead proudly, presented his hand to the sale assistant,

-A discount would be welcomed. What is your family name? I will make sure the Purallee's give your family percentages off the medicine whenever you need treatment there. My girl would be tremendously pleased to put her new pet snake in it's new home.

The young man after shaking Walter's hand, went to diligently open the shop vivarium for It, and stood there to make sure the teenager knew what she was doing. The water cobra came forward and coiled itself to the teenager's presented arm. Putting him to his new vivarium was seamless as the snake left her arm at her telepathic command. She closed the lid giving a bright smile to Wrath, Az and Walt. It stated,

-I am ready to go home when you are.

Azryel gave the vivarium for Walt to hold as he took himself, all the snake gear he had put by him,

-Let's go.

As Wrath went to the till. The human carried the vivarium with the cobra, It and Az by him as he smiled coming to Gabriel and explained,

-Wrath wants his own pet and it is called 'Deadly'. Don't ask me, ask him. By the way we got a discount on that one, providing a family, the 'Walton's' registered to your clinic, pay a little less for their treatments. I talked about percentages, you can do the math to your own good will from there, Bro. We are ready to go home, apart from if you want us to get you a pet?

Dropping all his shopping bags at once, a sulking Gab shouted,

-Raphael...

Workmaster turning to Caroline, It, Micky and Azryel, enjoined,

-That's when we run children. Pick up your hamsters, I've got great Uncle's snaky in hand.

As they reached the parked car, putting all the animals cages in the boot, Walter and the Death Angel burst out laughing. Patting each other's back, the Death Angel whispered to the man,

-Thank you for your plea yesterday, human. It worked. Wrath mended me with no pain at all. He taught Gab properly too without messing me up. Workmaster, you are a man that truly makes my days.

-Good, if I didn't teach you as much as you teach me Angel, I would feel unworthy of your care. Now let's get in that car and enjoy the faces of Gab and Wrath when they arrive.

Taking the driving seat Az asked,

-Is everyone belted?

Caro replied sitting by It and Micky,

-We are.

-As daddy said, children, Uncle Gab may be a bit edgy and maybe Great Uncle Raphael now, so minimal talking is best on the way home. I will play some music, what do you fancy, Caroline?

-Whatever my Walt wants, I love his taste.

-That would be Santana for me, Az. Brace yourself, the fiery Archangels are coming.

Raphael sat by the driver's seat fully silent.

While Gabriel taking his place by Walter in the back seat of the car, vented out, belting himself up,

-Right, so tell me Workmaster, how many more pets will I have to welcome in my house until it becomes a proper zoo?

Azryel starting the car, replied for the man with the wickedest grin,

-Eight.

Bursting out loud, Gab could not help swearing,

-What? Are you fu...

He could not finish his sentence as Workmaster slapped his thigh straight away, telling him right off,

-Swearing in front of my kids, not allowed, Archangel.

Gab gave him a furious glance before asking in a falsely contained manner,

-Pray, why eight my dear, Az? As I happened to home an Army of Angels, the Devil, the Beast, Death, Walter Workmaster and his Great Dane, my very Archangelic Uncle, two hamsters and a water cobra called 'Deadly', I simply wish to know the reason and the nature of the eight I am supposed to welcome.

Wrath could not help laughing any more and poking the Death Angel as he drove, begged,

-Come, tell him.

A very serious Azryel answered,

-Your Uncle promised me eight Great Dane puppies if I do well in our next mission. As I live with you for the time being, and as I am very rarely unsuccessful, I would love you to accept those into your home. If not to let me live in a tent with them by your tree-house, so I can still keep an eye on you all at all times.

Thinking and nose diving Gabriel asked,

-Are you looking forward to those puppies, Az?

A straightforward answer came by a positively nodding Death Angel,

-I am. I will teach them to guard your tree-house day and night.

Leaning back and listening to 'Jingoloba' of Santana, Gabriel stated,

-Green light for the eight pups, Az. Wrath, no more snakes in my house, 'Deadly' is the very last deadly snake I can cope with. Kids, I have no problems with your hamsters as long as you make sure you keep them clean. Caro, please help me there and don't get a pet yearning at any point in time. Workmaster, when a family has got seven children registered in my clinic that is when I start earning money. Please do not do any bargains you are not allowed to do.

Walter replied straight away,

-Archangel, when you have a big human family that care so much for their kin, their entire family, that they are willing to pay your fees for good care, that is when you need to show a less business like attitude and a more human one. Use your heart a little and your business will be thriving without you paying attention to it, Bro. Be that all welcoming and humanistic Archangel, I know of.

Gabriel just closed his eyes and held Workmaster's hand until they reached his home without another word to say.

Verse 27. FEAR...

Within the jail room, Gabriel holding the shoulders of It-666 with reassurance, asked her once more,

-You are fully briefed and you know which stage we desire, as I trained you all afternoon about hypnosis, Bambi. We will be safe as we are using your invisibility powers upon Us. Eremiel will not have the ability to feel Us, but he will hear Us and respond to Us. He will also remain partly paralysed all throughout preserving our security. He will not be able to concentrate on his surroundings and react to them. If you keep up as I told you during that whole session you will be fine and all of Us too. Now, are you ready to perform?

Shivering and extremely worried the teenager looked helplessly at Wrath and Azryel. She simply did not know if she was ready whatsoever. So much relied upon her during that hypnosis session that she did not want to mess things up. Her long silence made both Archangel and Angel walk to her, both grabbed one of her hands. Azryel proposed to her kindly, feeling her deep insecurity,

-Would you rather postpone the session, Soldier, until a moment when you feel ready? As your general, I have no desire to see it rushed either. You are a very important soldier, It and paramount to the success and security of this hypno-thing we are going to perform. Tell me what concerns you the most? What is troubling you?

The young girl confided to the Death Angel at once,

-Fear, Az. I have that fear paralysing me, the fear that I will fail everyone as soon as I hear him talk things that I refuse to listen to, that I am scared of, that will unsettle me and make me lose control. I wish not to hear him ever again. I think I will never be ready to hear him talk. I wish I could curl somewhere far away from his presence.

Responding to her, Azryel opened his arms to her warmly and
kindly,

-Come and grab a big reassuring hug It. Where is my brave soldier
gone to? Where is my little Beast that killed Hell Hounds on her
own? Where is my courageous It that stood strongly in front of
Eremiel kicking his ass so much that he is at your mercy, all boxed
up and in his eternal jail? I know about bouts of fear, all my soldiers
have them at any point in time. When they do appear, Wrath and I
work on them, so that our soldiers can fight again without their
crippling effects. I understand where yours come from after your
experience in the sewer. But do not go, curl somewhere and hide,
letting fear rule your life, for then it gives an easy ultimate win to
Eremiel. You are a fighter It, you fight for the value of your own
heart and Us. At this present moment you achieved the total control
over this fallen Angel, while he failed miserably to just influence
you. Would you let the fear of him reverse the situation now that he
is completely paralysed, comatose and basically within your power
to make him do exactly what you want him to do? I believe in you
Soldier, to not let fear rule you, or undermine you at any point in
time. So stop trembling like a leaf and stand tall for Us.

Pepped up, It left the arms of Death trying to stand tall for him,
Wrath and Gabriel. The Archangel Raphael taking her hand with
the snake bite, and showing it to the teenager demanded,

-I want you to take a good long look at that scarred hand, It. What
do you see?

A slightly wondering It, considered her hand which reminded her
of every moment of the battle in the sewer between her and her
real father. She replied insecure,

-I see the hurdle, the battle between Eremiel and I in Boston's
sewers, every second of It.

Scolding her Wrath stated,

-That's being very shortsighted Soldier, surely with your powers you can do better than that. Who is standing by me, with a mere battle wound? That would be you, who is standing by you holding the very hand that won the fight between Eremiel and you? That would be a powerful Archangel. Who is in a box, in jail until we say so, and for as far as I remember, we said it would be for eternity? Just tell me who has not won the battle with Us Soldier? It is grand time that you learn that our motto is one for all and all for one. We will stand by you in fight as you do for Us. We will get you back from the brink, like we have a couple of times now. You are not alone anymore but part of Us and we will look after you as you will do for Us. We all get scratches in battle, yet we get up and carry on the fight so that our spirited hearts live on to protect humanity. I have one upon my left flank thirty centimetres long that reminds me not of my enemy, but my victory upon him as he gave way and fell below me. It reminds me of Azryel who fought to protect me until the end of the battle over me. It reminds me of him mending me when everything was over and my Army had won the fight. It reminds me of Us but not my enemies, for I would never give them the chance to have a slight hold over me with remains of fear. I extinguish those with two fingers right off as I am with Us, safe and well ultimately. Now, tell me who is standing before Us, alive and well and who is not? Who should fear Us, my soldier?

A fully understanding It-666, held the Archangelic hand very tight trying to convey the importance of what Wrath had said to her. She replied confidently,

-I am standing before you, I am alive and well because of Us. I won because I am part of Us. Eremiel did not win, and he should fear Us. I will see that snake bite, those two little blue points as you and Az, pulling me through from death's doors, keeping me with your Army, with Us.

A very pleased Raphael hugged the teenager, patting her back, commenting,

-That's my soldier. If you want to wait for another day, I can cater for that, until you feel fully ready. But I want you to consider that we need to bring a ring of individuals down, demons, cambions, men and women which are involved in human sacrifices and that we have a duty to stop. Eremiel has all the information we require to act quickly upon them. The sooner we get to know everything and everyone, the sooner we can stop losing human souls to Hell. Time is essential and crucial, and you will acknowledge that full well, having experienced your very own toll bell Soldier, which I silenced as soon as Az told me he was hearing it to allow Us to call you back within my Army. I can not hide that what we will hear from Eremiel will probably be disturbing to most of Us but we must not lose sight of our mission for it, our own aim. You can ignore what that fallen Angel says and let Us deal with it in order to keep your focus on your tasks, to keep that mission secure.

Having a light bulb moment the Archangel Gabriel interrupted his Uncle,

-I have the solution. We can impose a Parental Guidance upon It, protecting her young sensitive mind throughout.

Azryel and Raphael cocking their eyebrows, looked baffled at Gabriel, as his Uncle scolded,

-Try to make sense, Gab. Unfortunately, Az and I do not bestow weird 'Frankestein-esque' brains like yours full of experimental ideas.

Taking the hand of the teenager, and holding it tightly, Gabriel revealed,

-Since what Eremiel has to say can be highly disturbing, and since it could have a serious impact on It, I say it is our duty to protect and prevent her from listening to his words like parents would do. Since our young one has that incredible capacity to switch on or off any of her senses at any one time, and although I told her off in the past demanding of her to always be switched on, I can only strongly advise and recommend that It uses that skill. By switching off totally her capacity to hear temporarily, It will be preserved from any distress. Azryel could stay by her reading her all the while, ensuring that she does not listen to Eremiel but also to make sure the little one stays emotionally sound throughout the session. When it is safe for her to hear again, Az will signal her. This will allow that young soldier to totally concentrate and focus on bringing that fallen Angel to the state of hypnosis I demanded of her and to maintain it until we have finished with him, and then to put him into a comatose state once more.

The Death Angel, his eyes glowing with respect and admiration, admitted,

-It has to be said that Archangel has got a genial mind about him. Considering the potential security jeopardy that an emotional Beast could cause to the operation, the implementation of Gab's idea is a necessity. I think we should extend the PG idea to those walls. For Christ's sake Gab, when you said you were not a born torturer who were you kidding? I am freaking Death, the Grim Reaper and five minutes into that room is already giving me nausea. I rather you did not go all 'Clockwork Orange' upon that fallen Angel for, if Eremiel ever goes free, your guts are going to be all over the place Gab. It, I hope you did not pay attention to those walls?

Covering her eyes with his hands, Azryel repeated anxiously by her ear,

-Did you pay attention to them my young Beast? If you did, do not get any bad ideas from them for that was the shit that Eremiel was on about when he turned Evil. Pretty nasty stuff, and I am not talking about 360 degree head spinning gizmo party tricks. Any of them reproduced at any point in time, and I am afraid I will have to put you to sleep. This is an extremely well meaning warning It.

With a small voice almost like a whisper, yet feeling the security and safety net that the Death Angel provided her at all times, the teenage Beast answered,

-I did not, Az. I was concentrating on how to do the task at hand without cocking it up, rehearsing it in my head. I can assure you that I have no intention to turn Evil like Eremiel. I have more wishes to turn like a fluffy creature like my hamster and join my Gab in his pink cage. The only footsteps and example I will follow Azryel, are yours.

Shaking his head with slight desperation, annoyance but resignation, Gabriel clapped his hands and the walls of the room became depressingly grey as he commented,

-Why not stay true to your own self It? Why not create your own path? I am not totally convinced that following the footsteps of the Grim Reaper or becoming a fluffy rodent are great things to do. Especially the last time you turned into a cute little white rabbit, you cocked it up so badly that I suffered from a head injury and I had to endure Az brain surgery, and his all knowing fingers fiddling with my neurones and brain cells. Azryel, the room is safe now, you can remove your hands from her face.

Grinning wickedly, Death had not expected the little turn in the conversation. He truly enjoyed the little nuggets, he was picking from it. His suspicion that the Archangel Gabriel had started to become jealous over the young Being were confirmed. Deciding to stir things a little, he argued with false pride,

-Pray, what's wrong with my footsteps and my fingers, Archangel?

Looking at him in a way which intimated Death not to go there, Gabriel stated,

-You are hardly an example I would like my girl to follow.

Following the exchange attentively and warned via telepathy by Azryel that he was about to demonstrate to him, that Gabriel's supposedly compassionate love was turning fast into a passionate one, the Archangel Raphael intervened,

-Our girl, at only sixteen has a lifetime before her to chose which footsteps she aims to follow. As responsible adults here, we will only teach, train and guide her. Isn't that right It?

She nodded positively yet defended her initial words strongly,

-It is right Wrath, but I would like to mention that Azryel is my very best of friends. He is an example for me and yes I would like to follow his footsteps. Like me he was born with a bad deal on his plate, yet for an eternity he managed to keep a very sound heart through it all. He cares so much and would lay his own life for any one of you, yet he knows how to keep going to ensure his looking after is eternal for his soldiers. I sincerely admire that in my general, teacher, trainer and confident. Having a dilemma similar to mine, I found an understanding confident and a helping hand to show me how to grow up and stay sound. He did the very best with his bad hand which qualified him as the Grim Reaper, I intend to do the best of my bad hand which qualified me as The Beast from the start. I would never willingly disrespect my friend who saved me from Hell, from my injuries, and who saved you Gabriel from my silly rabbit run, but also who stayed by you all night when you were lost in grief. He is an example of steadfast friendship which could be stern at times to warn you to stay in the right direction and stay alive doing so, but also the one always there to tend you back to life despite his own needs and plights. He is an example of devoted friendship, loyalty that all Angels should follow.

When she stopped talking, she realised by the deep silence of the Angels that she had created a stir. She saw Gab and Wrath going to Azryel and embracing him, patting his back. She finally heard Gabriel,

-Accept my apologies, old Bro.

Then one thing was kept away from her, their telepathic exchange, as Gab asked Az,

-Has the young Beast befriended you, Azryel? I thought you never bestowed, had or allowed yourself to truly befriend anyone because of the way you hurt when you have to take them to the Afterworld.

-Wrath can tell you that I do bestow friends ever since a conversation with your sister Caroline.

-Yes, Gab, Azryel struck friendship with Asha, Walt, Caro, I and the
teenage Beast. With It, he is her confident, she hides nothing from
him, tells him all the secrets of her little heart in love with you. He
knows all and advises her accordingly without judging or repressing.
As for him, the Beast and him got battle bounds, recovery bounds,
but also he just found his best little mate. He can chill with her
unlike he does with any other. The fact that his duties and her fate
are making them true friends, must not shadow the fact that she has
a strong puppy love for you and that you, Gabriel are developing a
more intense love for her. I warn you that, to be allowed to flourish,
your love must wait five whole years and hers must develop or
remain. Az and I will be your watchers at all times from now on.

When the Angels broke their shoulder to shoulder brotherly ring,
they saw the teenager by the box reading the codes engraved upon
it. She told them,

-The new Pandora's Box is very secure, can one of Us stay by it
during the session with the lid in hand and go bye bye Evil snaky
nice talking to you but enough is enough at a second's warning.

Smiling wickedly to her Wrath reassured her,

-I can do that, with great pleasure. I will lead the session asking the
questions with Gabriel. You will stay by Azryel who will ensure you
are keeping strong with your hypnosis mojo. Az will give you the
signal to send Eremiel back to a deep sleep and when it will be safe
for you to hear again. Your focus in this mission soldier is
paramount so Gabriel and I by Evil snaky, stay alive and well. Go to
your post, and no mess up allowed.

Running by Death, It felt his strong hands upon both her shoulders,
asking,

-Kneel It. I don't want you to get a case of wobbly knees or weak
legs on this one. You've got Gab next to Eremiel, and I've got
Wrath next to him. Focus and precision, Soldier. I will use telepathy
to send my orders to you. I will read your mind constantly to make
sure you are okay throughout the session. Now switch off the

senses that could disturb your control and let me be your remote control.

-Can I switch off more than one sense?

-Yes, for your sake and ours, I said so Soldier, just make sure we remain all invisible if the Big Bad Mamba wakes up, the same mojo you did for the 76 lost souls in Hell.

Disturbingly, the teenager's eyes disappeared from her face, and her ears were swallowed in. Smooth skin replacing all those apertures. The Death Angel stated,

-Our girl doesn't like her former daddy very much. We have a full peek a boo down here. She also swallowed her tongue to prevent herself from shouting to Eremiel and ruin our session by expressing the anger her guts feel from her last encounter. Bless, kiddo is giving me the remote control to her powers right now I can feel it through my fingers. She won't be able to switch any back on by herself. She surrendered herself to my control. Wrath, that's what a true friend is all about, complete trust in one another. Ready when you are, call the shot, Raphael. It is performing right now the hypnosis. I will tell you when you can open that box safely.

Watching the teenager without eyes, kneeling by the Death Angel, a worried Gabriel could not help commenting,

-Is she curling in her corner, frightened, Azryel?

-No, she is gathering strength right now. She wants your particular ass to be so safe that she wants her mojo to be to the point perfect, she is tuning to Eremiel. Wrath and I do not have to get disheartened because if she feels in her body she will ever fail, she just created a trigger in her former father's heart which will induce him to sleep forever. The girl is being thorough in ensuring our safety. She is not curling Gab, she is fighting our corner and gathering pace.

Lifting one of his hands, Death warned,

-The session can start. It is safe to lift the lid of the box, yet It just told me for you to watch the eyes of the snake. If they ever turn from green to red, do not ask any more questions, just close the lid and keep well away from the box. Do not be tempted to ask and gather more from Eremiel, because it will spell your doom.

Wrath with no further ado lifted the box lid and kept it well in hand to thrust it back to a close if needed. An inquisitive Gabriel went right ahead to inspect the limp black mamba with his own hands throughout the length of his slippery body. When he had finished his assessment he stated,

-He is ripe. Let's get all the juicy bits he can offer Us. Ask away Wrath.

His Archangelic Uncle did not wait to be told twice, as he ventured his first question,

-What a poorly state you are in, Eremiel... You crawl in sewers, why?

The whistle of the snake came through loud and clear,

-I am wounded. I hide.

-Who wounded you? Who are you hiding from?

-I am a pariah, I am hiding from all. The shit that I stirred is my bedstead. Yet, I am one not allowed to rest, not allowed to hide. My daughter was the last to wound me. She is dead by now. A useless cursed weakling she was.

-Cursed? Can you explain how was she cursed?

-Someone Catholical-y evil played a game on me. He died for it. He did get more than one congregation together to curse my child to be plagued with a heart. She was cursed while in the belly of Lilith. She was born with a heart, she was no good to me, I killed her.

-Who cursed the child?

-RIP, Father Arthur Williamson, a very caring and humanistic soul if ever there was one. Even though we tortured him to get him to reveal the hiding place of It, he had abducted from us and it could mean humanity's downfall. I rewarded his tortured and deadly revelation, by granting him a passage to Paradise. He rests in peace in Hell, believing he is in Paradise. His cell is top of the grade, knowing that under torture he was weak enough to give humanity the future fated full apocalypse.

Withholding his anger, Wrath pursued,

-Who else wounded you?

-Archangel Raphael. Although he freed me doing so. He burnt down the mirror walls that kept me in for years. A remnant of my Archangelic skin preserved me while I crossed his fire to reach the safety of the green grass. He made me reach out for the only shape I am allowed to have apart from the Evil mirror shadow.

-Who is giving you allowance?

-Cato.

-Does she hold your soul?

-Hell, no. She is a Swallower. She is making an army of Swallowers.

-Who has your soul?

-I have always been my own Master.

-What is a Swallower?

All around them the walls started bleeding profusely, as they listened to the answer,

-The worst kind. They swallow up powers of Beings they managed to imprisoned. P is helping to build that Army because he believes in Cato more than he does in me. I treated him rough for so long that he has become a traitor. Hence shitty sewers were a happy place with plenty of fat rats to munch on.

-Name the Swallowers, their servants and the Beings imprisoned by them, Eremiel.

The black mamba's eyes became red. Wrath put the lid back upon the box. Yet, he saw the walls turning grey again with blood letters through all of them. Gabriel pointed to a few names, and stated surprised,

-It is the list of all we need, Wrath, all of them.

When he saw the list was covering all the walls, and saw names they both knew, he became worried. When all the names covered the ceiling and the ground, he told,

-We have to make sure we have all the names, and I am not sure there is enough space in there. Young It has to be a recipient for the list.

The older Archangel disagreed,

-We have enough to work on Gabriel for a long while. Let me touch the walls and absorb the names of individuals to deal with. Let's keep It out of Swallowers's way for as long as we can. Az, make her send her father back into a coma.

As the Death Angel gave his order to the teenager, he saw her hands lifting in the air twisting and turning before resting back upon her lap, he giggled sarcastically,

-Let me just check she has not strangled her dad right now. All safe. She knocked him out right and proper. He is in his eternal beauty sleep. Wrath, tell me when you want that soldier to be able to see and hear Us.

The Archangel flying about the room, concentrating on gathering the names of the Swallowers, ordered,

-Keep her in her state, Az. Eremiel was very thorough. A big S marks a swallower while a small S marks a swallowed one, a lot of gods and goddesses and powerful Beings have already been swallowed. The powers they have gathered altogether put Earth at tremendous risk to become Hell at any point in time. We are at war, Children. There is no other way about it. When do they plan to use all those gathered powers is still in question. We will have to come up with a world wide battle plan as soon as possible, Azryel.

When all the walls were back to grey, Wrath enjoined,

-Death, get that soldier fully back with Us, she has done her duty. We have the names of the perpetrators and their victims. More than we bargained for. Yet the stakes have been upped tenfold, if Evil lived in a sewer in fear for a few days. Gosh, I can even recall myself making that very wish, believing it would be blessed days. Brace yourself for the worst. Prepare yourself for an Apocalypse.

Verse 28. AIM-E

Turning around the lab of Gabriel, Wrath was doing the hundred paces, frenetically thinking as far ahead as he could. Until his nephew interrupted his thoughts,

-Uncle Raph, if Az was here, he would tell you that you are making him feel dizzy. Stop turning like a caged tiger, take a seat and just think, in a less swirly motion. Please, I am trying to concentrate down here. I am getting closer although I wish I had a goddess blood sample right now, to be precise Lilith's one and Eremiel's blood sample as he had been mutated. That mutation is most intriguing. Imagine if Cato can transform the structure of an Angel to a Demonic one like child's play. That's a tad frightening, you can't leave any soldiers behind on a battlefield, Raphael, as if you will, you are going to find them in her army in no time at all, a shadow of themselves, fighting Us.

The Archangel sat by him and putting his head within his hands upon the desk, confided,

-Stop with the tad frightening, Gab, we may have a bloody Apocalypse upon our hands. You and I will have to sound it, somehow at some point. Az and I will have to postpone it with the Angelic Army, before it all explodes. I wished somehow it could have been averted, that our human Walt had time to rewrite it all, that our It-666 would have had a proper end to her childhood, that Archangel Michael was fully grown up as he was the one meant to take charge of ending the Apocalypse. I do not want to leave any of my soldiers on a battlefield to be transformed or swallowed into a demonic army. Where is Az when I need him? He always disappears for hours.

Seizing his Archangelic hand without request, and grabbing a blood sample from it as fast he could, before emptying it into a test tube, Gabriel replied,

-The Death Angel disappears less in my home than he used to do at your AA club. When he takes a break here, he is always careful that Bambi is looked after. She is with Caro and Micky, which implies Asha will be with them at the moment. If Az's disappearance is longer than ten minutes, that means he is not having his regular fag breaks but that he is catching up with his Soul Takers. When he takes Walt's dog on a walk on his own in the wood, this is what he does, almost regularly at dawn and dusk. He is very secretive about it because he hates talking about his duties.

Returning to his microscope casually, like if he had done nothing out the ordinary, Gab added,

-I think you are being very pessimistic my dear Wrath since the session with Eremiel, and I saw the same amount of names upon the walls as you did. We need to find a solution for those Swallowers walking upon the Earth, and certainly not go into a panic attack with big Apocalyptic calls. I am going to work upon the genetic make up of those Swallowers. If only P and Cato have been making them, it will be easy. If the witch fucked about with many demons and Beings, it will be much harder.

Ripping his plaster and cotton ball sealing his needle's puncture, and throwing them in a nearby bin, Wrath put two of his fingers upon it and made the small bleeding hole disappear. Shaking his head in desperation, the Archangel asked,

-What would be the aim of the game, my dear nephew, when you just mended me like a human would do? Pray? You have the capacity of healing me faster with your Archangelic powers. Are you still not able to use them properly? Or is it reluctance? By the way, I thought you already had your Archangelic sample of blood. Why take mine now? I think Azryel prefers your home to mine, I am worried about him not returning to the AA.

The Archangel Gabriel got up and brought a flask containing a very strangely colourful liquid in with a divine smell, pouring a small glass to his Uncle, he invited,

-Drink that. The cordial of the Gods, Ambrosia, I reconstituted the recipe. It will do you a world of good especially when I can confirm that Death feels at home here. To be honest, I do like having him here, it's like having one very powerful Angel as a guard dog, one bestowed with clever repartees. If he decides to stay, he will remain as welcome as he is now in my home. Wrath, you heard how Eremiel said how he treated his servant, and how his servant treated him in return. You have a most dutiful and devoted Angel in Azryel, yet I can tell you right now having witnessed it, that what that Angel is craving for is simply being hugged, thanked, liked, and respected for what he does for Us all. He does not get that from you. After what he endured in the last mission, a human had to plea to you to not torture him. Wrath, how could you do that to him? The most loyal soul attached to you, how could you treat him like that? I understand the lesson to learn how to treat that most special Angel had to take place, but a simple word of warning to him, a caring word telling him the aim, that he was not left in pain to be tortured but to teach me to look after him because you care for him at the end of the day would have made a world of difference. You admit to miss his presence when he is absent and you dread him making his nest in this house and failing to come back to yours, when are you planning to tell him, at the end of the World? Buying him grandiloquent present fuelled by your own guilt will not replace respect and appreciation. If you do not want to lose him, make sure you work on keeping Az better than you do right now. The young It is correct, as Angels and Archangels, we have grown an habit to take Azryel so much for granted, that the way we treat him is simply not right. He has been the general of your Angelic Army for an eternity, and that without proper recognition, and even friendships up until a few days. We have to put things right.

Before him his Uncle stood up, finishing his Ambrosia in one go as he confessed,

-We will. I am not proud of how I treated Az the other night nor him for so long. Close to an Apocalypse I need him secure to me and can not afford to lose that general. I will rectify this, leave it to me. I feel secure being under a roof he is under and my extended stay at yours with my all Army has a lot to do with it. That beverage is nice, what does it do? By the way, I am still waiting for you to answer me about my blood being taken like that, and my other queries. Don't you think that a little guilt trip will ever make me lose the plot, Gab.

Refilling the glass of his Archangelic Uncle, and pouring himself one, Gabriel returned to his slabs as he replied, smiling,

-Far from me, is the idea that I can make you lose the plot. I have taken your blood sample and want to take the ones of the whole entire Angelic Army. I can make sure the individual genetic makeup of your soldiers is preserved and safe. I can work upon a solution to get them back from being in the hand of a Swallower, to bring them back to their former selves. Not only that, I can work on a grand scale virus which could infect every Swallower who tried to snatch their supernatural powers from them, a powerful virus which annihilates all the powers they had absorbed so far, recognising them as not belonging to their initial make up. The virus would be safe for non-swallowers, and could be easily ingested, secretly, regularly as a celebratory Ambrosia glass. Only you, Azryel and me should know of it to protect the plan throughout. So no one could say it existed under torture.

Looking at all the colourful flasks and test tubes within the laboratory of his nephew, Wrath welcomed the ideas,

-If you can work those out, I would be very impressed and grateful for my entire Army. As then my soldiers could concentrate on disabling every Swallower and free their prey. This, if properly done would undermine Cato and her schemes. We could also pay visits to all the other super Beings walking the Earth which are still free and cleverly make them ingest the virus which would protect their powers against any Swallower they could encounter in their future. I definitely like your ideas they are brilliant. I will get you a couple of Cato's creatures to assess and dissect if that could help you out?

-Indeed it would. You seem to have a plan as well, Azryel said, with that snake of yours. What is it, Wrath?

-To be honest a decoy Eremiel in his evil snaky shape to put in the sewers of Boston for P and the Witch to find. Invested with some of the mojo of our young Beast, it would occupy them and convince that they have the real deal for a while but also we could use it as a lethal weapon against them. Let's say they organise another human sacrifices ceremony, our decoy could teach them a nasty lesson giving them a bite which they could not recover from. That poisonous bite with no remedy could be created by you or our young Beast. After the elimination of P and maybe the Witch, our snake would return to its original self, a simple water cobra. What do you say?

A thoughtful Gabriel tried to picture the plan in his head, before he replied,

-It's crafty. I wish to know the plan's every detail, for it seems to rely heavily on my girl yet again.

-Correction, Gab, 'Our' girl, the only one allowed to call her 'my' is her adoptive father Walter from now on. For I am not going to have you consumed by jealousy over It. I know you far too well Gabriel, and how devastating your passion can be when you have one. Remember your own mistakes. Although you loved Wendy and she loved you, you did so in a choking way. Deep down I know that part of your tremendous grief is that you blame yourself for her death. Free spirited Wendy was not unlike her brother, and should have been allowed to breath a little more. When she was your medical secretary, she found herself in the hands of a control freak who was heard by Walt many times. She was even being told off for smiling to customers if they were men. The truth is she could not be with you 24/7. She made the fatal mistake to find another job and became the secretary of Paul Peterson, an ambitious and young politician at the time who happened to also be devastatingly handsome. I know you had a row with her over it, and that at the end of it, she was so shaken that she wanted to rethink your relationship and engagement. That is why she took the opportunity to travel with P for his political campaign, it was supposed to be a month of reflection and when she came back she would have told you if you were still an item or not. As we know, she never returned, having been sacrificed by the incarnated demon P. Now I am not telling you not to have or develop love or passion, I am warning you to control and watch yourself to keep it sane this time around. Yourself, as the Workmasters, Azryel and I know full well how sensitive, and emotional the teenage It is. I will not hesitate for one minute to move the Workmaster family under another roof if you display again one ounce of jealousy when the young Beast hugs anyone, for whatever reason thankfulness, to get reassurance, to cry upon one's shoulder. I will not tolerate insane jealousy towards that Being, and I will protect her from you if necessary. I won't let you mess that one up. I won't let you drive that one away from you. You deserve to be loved just like anyone else, and I will be here to help you all the way.

Opening his arms to his Archangelic nephew, who shaken by the home truth he had just received, had blood tears prickling his eyes, Wrath pursued,

-I won't let you go adrift, Gabriel, not anymore. If you need a confident and if Death is a little daunting to be yours, I am more than willing to be the one that you pour your heart into. I will help you deal with your growing passion for our Sweet Heart. Like Azryel is helping her understand her growing sentiment for you. She had no words to describe how she felt, bless her.

After hugging his uncle, the doctor sat back at his lab table, prepared a slab with his Archangelic blood, before finally expressing himself,

-Wrath, I welcome your concern and involvement. I only hope you will be a very patient listener with me. I thank you to protect It in such a way and your strong will to respect the desire of our human Walt to give her five years of childhood if possible. Taking her shopping with her family instead of taking her on a mission made her day. It was the first time I saw her smile so often and so brightly. I must admit that she is blossoming with Us. I remember her Bud-Caro sleep trick back at the clinic to make sure you would get involved with her, to warn the Army of Angels of her own existence. I did not want to tell you who I had before me fearing that you would come, not give her a single chance and annihilate her. As it happened I was so wrong, and she was so right. She feels my pain and sorrow constantly and deals with it. She probably knew then that I needed you to help me, and to help me dealing with her. She brought you back to my path to reunite me with Us. We have an incredibly understanding Being in our hands. Eremiel said she was plagued with a heart, cursed to have one by Father Williamson. We need to do a trip to Hell, Wrath for we need to understand if the curse Williamson did is eternal or clocked. That soul who abducted the Beast at her birth has information which are vital for keeping our young Being as good as she is right now. A trip to Paradise to speak to nun Tess who looked after It for the first five years of her life would not go amiss either. You and I know that catholics do not let their women perform exorcisms since Apostle Paul violated the teachings of Jesus and transformed them to his own liking and understanding which rule their church now, and push women away by pure unabated sexism from religious leading roles. So we have a very special Sister here in Tess taking upon herself a very challenging role to protect humanity. If it was not for Williamson speaking under torture, she would not have been killed, she would have remained a foster mother for the young Beast. Seeing how It turned out at 16, I believe that human taught that Being very well indeed in her formative years. The Tutor who got involved in checking the feral little It, teaching her all sorts of things like controlling her powers better, for three years needs to be in touch and help Us. The young Beast still yearns for being at his feet. Anytime she thinks of haven, she thinks of curling by him. Why?

Raphael putting his hand upon the shoulder of his nephew, replied securely,

-For the Tutor has all the answers you seek all along. He is a gift not a given. He comes and goes at his own will. He can leave you at a moment's notice to never return. You can seek him and never find him. I can bring you and Az to Paradise to meet Tess, with no problem. I will need It to find Williamson in Hell and to bring him here for interrogation. Azryel and I will be with her all along to make sure the mission runs smoothly. Like you, I think the curse of It needs most definitely a thorough investigation. Well I believe your plate and mine are going to be full for a while. When we are overwhelmed the last Apocalyptic call has to be made by us Archangels.

Verse 29. Of Death and Life.

Walking deep into the woods surrounding Gab's tree house, Walter Workmaster was determined to find his dog, Bud. Holding a linen bag full of nuts of all kinds, he wished the young It was by him, and not by Caroline enjoying a girly-girl session he could not stand. He would have taught the teenager to recognise an hazelnut from a chestnut and not to paint her eyelashes in the latest 'Manga' fashion. Yet he had been warned by Caro that the teenager had to connect with her feminine side, or whatever that meant. He knew he had adopted a Being out of this world with It-666. Gosh, didn't she turn his mind around in a full spin since he discovered her, he thought, smiling wildly. The Atheist Walter was by now a dumbfounded man, who went to Hell to recover lost souls, was protected by two Archangels and a Death Angel, knew that demons and incarnated ones where walking the Earth, and that Wrath's job was to protect the World as much as he could. He spat on the ground,

-Where did that freaking Death Angel go with my Bud?

Stepping deeper into the forest as dusk settled in the man finally found Azryel and Bud. The Death Angel was in full regalia sitting upon a dead trunk and the Great Dane was by him in a stately sitting position. Around them was a circle of Beings with no faces at all, just covered by a red cape, dressed in black tunics. The man swallowed his breath at once when his dog came by him wagging his tail wildly revealing his presence in that little wood clearance. He lifted his hand shakily and went to sit by Death with a small worried explanation,

-Do not mind me. I am Walter Workmaster. I wanted to escape my own home for five minutes but pretending to walk the dog was not working when the dog was not to be found. So I went on a find the dog quest instead. As I can not see anyone smiling, I can make my pop around to check where my Bud was, very short indeed if you prefer?

Azryel putting a hand upon his shoulder asked,

-Why were you escaping home Workmaster?

A nose diving man confessed straight away.

-I want to give her childhood back to It-666, but Caro is preparing her to be an adult.

-Parenthood takes two, human. To give and to prepare goes hand in hand for a blessed child. Unfortunately children do grow up, Workmaster. You have five years at most with adopted It and twelve to thirteen with Michael. You need to make sure you give the most to your children, but also prepare them to be sound adults in that short time. Can you do that?

A thinking Walt replied,

-If my children are not taken away from me I can. I am worried sick with It being a soldier. I saw her fighting in Hell, Azryel. She was awesome, yet would have died without you. When she came back from Boston, you and her were in such a state, I was bracing myself for the worse.

Presenting an almost translucent skeletal hand for the man to hold, Death stated,

-Such is life, unfortunately, a bed of colourfully scented roses full of thorns. What is Caroline doing to your girl which is having you running away from the house?

The human taking the hand shivered uncontrollably doing so and swore,

-Gosh, Az, you are freezing cold! Have you got Arctic blood in your freaking veins? It is having a pampering and make-up session with

Caro. She looked like a vamped teen when I left and there was no stopping my Caro. She always wanted a baby girl, and now that It is our girl, she is over the moon. With her aquamarine eyes and short blond crop, It is cute as she is, 'au naturel' but Caro didn't want to listen for one minute and called me an old fashioned grandpa.

Grinning irresistibly Death stated,

-It has not a big ego, and no confidence at all about her appearance. That Caroline is making a fuss about her can only do her a world of good. Her incarnated self is indeed pretty, she needs to know it, and cherish that shell. A bit of self love and self esteem are badly needed by that teenager, Walter. We have to make her understand that she is no monster at all like she believes she is. My soldiers have started calling her the Sweet Heart. You need to prepare yourself that as she grows up, she will start dating whom she likes. At the moment she has a puppy crush on Gabriel. Hence that is partly why she dragged you to Hell to get your sister's soul back. As it is her first love, human, you can expect it to be powerful.

Paling as white as sheet, Workmaster, repeated, numb by the revelation,

-No, not Gabriel.

Cracking his bony knuckles in deep amusement Azryel could not help stating sarcastically,

-Oh, yes, none but Archangel Gabriel, your very own Guardian Angel. Your adoptive daughter has got taste. But do not worry too much Walter, Wrath and I are monitoring the situation. For to make matters a little more complicated, our good old grieving Gab has started to fall for It.

Blocking his ears with his hands the livid man, shook his head in a negative fashion, pleading desperately,

-Stop, I heard enough Az. I can't cope with more. A first love crush was a bombshell on its own, with control freak Gab, it was massive attack, with him falling in love with her, it's apocalypse now. You don't understand.

Laughing his heart out, the Death Angel tapped gently the shoulder of the man reassuringly,

-It's not that bad. If he does not scare her a way, we could have wedding bells in five years time. You giving her a way, and I would beg him to let me be his best man. It would make you the father in law of that Archangel and you could swing your own baseball bat at him if he starts being a control freak with It. I do understand. I know Gabriel very well indeed. I have him under my belt, like It. Trust me, human I will keep a very close eye upon them and their relationship.

Death felt his hand being grab strongly by the man, as he asked,

-Will you make sure my little It doesn't get burnt by his Archangelic fire? Gab is a passionate one when he loves.

Pressing his hand back Azryel vowed,

-I will. Any bows or boyfriend It will ever have or be allowed to have would have to prove themselves to me first. Gabriel has been given by Wrath and I, a five year wait to court your daughter.

All of a sudden the man smiled again widely,

-Good. I feel better. I will bat Gab's wings off if he ever upset my It one bit until then.

-And I will let you do so, Workmaster. Now, you can take Bud and return home as I have to complete my meeting with my Soul Takers.

The man looking at the intimidating Beings, pleaded,

-May I stay with you Azryel? I will be good, and just sit and watch. I will not talk nor intervene, I promise.

A slightly surprised Death Angel considering his plea commented,

-I rather have you heading home to be fully honest, human. The sessions are unpleasant and more often than not upsetting. We will talk about the dead and their respective souls.

Not backing down Workmaster's blue eyes full of sadness looking back at Death begged him,

-I rather stay by your feet Azryel and learn about your duties. I want to know how, as a man and a friend, I can help you and support you. It would be a lesson of respect also for me, so in the future I would abstain to address you as I did in the past. Please, let me be present. I would not insist if you give me the order to leave your sides for I will obey you.

Astonished and touched by the man's will, Azryel enjoined him, before addressing his Soul Takers,

-You may stay, Walter. If it becomes too unbearable for you, touch my hand upon your shoulder to warn me, then you may leave us. I rather you not getting involved in the proceeding of our session but if you must interrupt and talk or ask something, I will tolerate it. I present to you my dear Soul Takers, Walter Workmaster, a human which has caught the interest of Angels since his primary school days when he saved another pupil from drowning in a swimming pool. Presently looking after the safety of that man, I initiated him about Us. Him and his family are fully aware of our existence and you may consider them as peers. You may be truthful with them as they are now part of the secrecy. Now, let us resume where we left. Semi, proceed with your report.

The Soul Taker glided to the centre of the circle, where he knelt before his eerie voice replied sounding like a long spooky sobbing whisper,

-The soul of little Barry Barlow has been welcomed to Paradise by his grandmother. He could not stop blabbering along the way. A happy child, he was until human Roger Long came along. Simply a careless hit and run, Master, the man was texting to his wife if he needed to get her something for dinner. He panicked when he saw the child flying above his bonnet, and ran far away from the scene. Roger's soul is distraught beyond belief and he has not returned home yet, he is by a cliff as we speak and we may have to pick his soul up tonight.

Sighing deeply Death asked,

-How is Barry's father's soul copping? After losing his wife to breast cancer two years ago, only his son kept him going.

-I fear another suicide, Master. After burying his little son properly by his mum, he wants to join them. His Guardian Angel thinks it will happen, he will try his utmost to change the will of the human, but he says the timescale he is working on is very slim. As for the soul of Roger, his own Guardian Angel is very pessimistic. If he managed to get the man back home tonight, he knows that if Roger reads the news tomorrow and he believes he will, if he learns the child didn't make it, he will not allow himself to live another day. One death, many more to come, as the wife of Roger loves him to bits and relies upon him for everything. She is an insecure soul, Master. Without him, she will give up herself in a matter of months. What do you want me to do, Master?

-Work with Zine upon the situation by the cliff. Roger Long has to redeem himself before he passes away. Bother him all night to prepare him for the shock of the result of the accident. For Ben Barlow leave it to me. That soul has to live, his breaking ground discovery towards a cure for breast cancer can give a better chance to many women.

Bowing his head to the ground, the Soul Taker disappeared with another one from within the circle.

Azryel called out,

-Kabe, come forward. Father Williamson's death, brief me again about it.

As the Soul Taker knelt in the middle of the circle, he humbly asked,

-This was so many years ago. Eleven to be exact, Master. His soul is still in Hell. Why enquiring about him now?

Sternly Death replied,

-Because he was very important.

Sighing the Soul Taker recalled,

-His soul was so distraught that he just followed me without a word. Eremiel tortured him then killed him, like a cat plays with a mouse. The only fault of the man was to have been caught being a priest. Like all the victims of Evil, I was unable to read or assess that soul.

-This is where we made a mistake, we assumed he was a simple kill for the sport of it by Eremiel, because of Williamson's religious profession. Yet he was more than that, Eremiel avenged himself by torturing and murdering that priest for he was the very one who abducted his daughter at birth, not only that Arthur Williamson had cursed the Beast before her birth. The powerful curse gave the Beast a heart. She was born a sensitive Being, full of good sentiment and intention, with a moral soul. This deactivated totally the destroyer she was meant to originally be. This was an insult to his conception of his ultimate Beast that Eremiel was not ready to forgive and forget. Under torture the priest did reveal where he had hidden his daughter. The mission to retrieve the Beast failed miserably at first yet caused the death of the nun Tess who was working with Williamson closely. Hood, you were the one that picked up that soul eleven years ago, talk to me about it.

Another Soul Taker glided to the middle of the circle and knelt by Kabe, his slow voice filling the air,

-When I took her, a ferocious fire was burning four men alive which Zine came to collect. Her soul said to respect her vows of secrecy. I did and did not read her soul, so I begged for guidance, and a voice answered my call, ordering me to take her to Paradise. I thought she lived a solitary life in the wood, and did not see any child. She was a murder case for me. But I remember Zine saying that the murderers had self combusted, that he believed it was some sort of miracle from High Above, an immediate punishment for the death of the nun. As I heard the voice calling for her to be in Paradise, we assumed that it was the case.

The Death Angel shaking his head in desperation, coolly observed,

-Assumptions, it seems my dear Soul Takers that we have been plagued with them for far too long. We failed to investigate matters of the highest order. Firstly I need to speak to the soul of Arthur Williamson and then to the soul of the nun. They behold important information which will be necessary to Archangel Raphael's quest to prevent an Apocalypse. Do you both remember specifically where those souls are in Hell and in Paradise?

-We do, Master Azryel. For Arthur Williamson, his cell is in the middle of the infernal fire, as for Tess, her soul is known to be in the higher level of Paradise with some saints.

Raising himself up, Azryel called out the end of the session. When all the Soul Takers disappeared, he turned to Walter Workmaster, transforming himself back to his incarnated self. Pulling a cigarillo from his silver box, he asked the man with sarcasm,

-I am surprised you did not butt in the conversation every five minutes. I believe you lost your tongue. Shall we try to find it together? Come on, Bud, walkie time again.

The Great Dane wagged his tail and followed Death and Walter as they started to walk slowly back towards the tree house. When finally Walter expressed himself, a tear slowly rolling upon his cheek,

-What happened to that little boy is utterly sad and has far reaching consequences. It's heartbreaking.

Tapping his shoulder gently, the Death Angel took a long thoughtful puff, before confessing,

-It gets to you. The father of that child is a wonderful doctor, who worked very hard to advance breast cancer research since his wife was taken away by the disease. His suicide before completing his work would be a true loss for medicine and humanity. Life is very precious Workmaster. I can't stress it enough.

A nose diving man apologised all of a sudden,

-I am deeply sorry, Azryel to have made that call to you when I tried to kill myself six years ago. I hope you will forgive me one day. But I can't forgive my own self.

-The only positive, from your stunt, was that Gabriel realised that your breaking down needed him. He would have probably attempted to kill himself over Wendy too otherwise. It made him look after you instead, and take charge of your family, Caroline and Micky. You are a good man Walter. You need to forgive your own self. A lot of water has gone under the bridge since. You stopped smoking, drinking and you are a wonderful father. Now, do you think that Caroline has forgiven you?

Tears rolling upon his cheeks Walter almost whispered his answer,

-I sincerely do not know, Az.

Stopping walking the Death Angel considered the blond man. He gave him his red silk handkerchief, feeling that after all this time, Workmaster was still beating himself up for his break down. He asked wanting to see how deep Walt's loss of confidence was,

-Dry your tears. Tell me if you have not considered to propose to Caroline again?

Taking a little red box from his black jeans' pocket, the man showed him a very elegant diamond engagement ring, as he announced,

-I have been dreaming about it since the day I was told I was divorced from her. Trying to patch up under the guidance of Gabriel, saving money for three years to get her the best looking diamond, I have been waiting for a small sign that I had not lost her love totally.

A happily grinning Death Angel asked him full of sarcasms,

-Pray, what type of signs do you want, Blondie Bear? That woman loves you, and that is staring at you like a nose in the middle of your face. She is worried sick that P wants your guts. If she has not forgotten what happened 6 years ago, she understood you were grief stricken and she truly forgave you a long time ago. Caroline has never looked for another man either because in her heart you are still the very one she wants to be with. What do you think happened to your original wedding rings? Do you remember the day she was so irate that she asked you to give your ring back to her, telling you, you were a free arsehole?

-I remember that day, I knelt by her and begged her not to do so. Yet she grabbed my hand and removed it herself. I begged her again and again, but she closed her door. I was heartbroken, I stayed kneeling by her door, crying until Gab took me away. I could not speak to anyone for days. I felt that all what was best in my life was absolutely gone for good. I remained totally lost in my own pain, in the corner of Gab's living room. He coaxed me to eat and drink yet I had lost all my appetite until in desperation he force fed me. I would have crammed in that corner for an eternity, but three weeks later Caroline came with Micky. My little boy's arms around my neck reminded me that I needed to carry on despite my pain, I finally started talking again to him. But also I understood that Caroline would not deprive me of seeing him. I kept apologising to her and thanking her. She did not respond to me, but she had tears, which kept running during the two hours of her visit. I have no ideas of what she did with the wedding rings. I never dared to ask her.

Taking the hands of the man, the Angel could feel the heartache still vivid and raw within him, as he soothed him,

-The harsh Caroline is long gone. She is full of remorse about that day. She honestly thinks that knowing of your break down, she did just push you over the edge. She was behind that door crying just as you did, holding those two rings like the most precious things she ever had. When she realised you were still there completely distraught, she called Gabriel telling him everything. She was sorry then but even more sorry when Gab reported to her concerned self everyday how you were doing. Gabriel thought you had lost your mind, and did not want her and Micky to see you in your sorry state. However she insisted that she had to do something, anything to help you out, that giving you up to a mental institution was not a solution especially when she was greatly responsible for your state. Until then she never realised how deeply you loved her, as you were already divorced. During that visit, she saw a broken man, loving her still, begging to be forgiven. That image of your distraught heartbroken self will stay with her forever. She went home that day having forgotten to replace your ring back upon your finger. She put it instead with hers upon that thin velvet black ribbon she wears constantly upon her neck. She vowed that day and made Gabriel do so too, that they would never give up on you. She has been patiently waiting for you to make a full recovery. Her deep shyness towards you is not due to your mental break down at the death of your twin sister, but has more to do with the guilt she harbours day in and out about wanting a divorce and that fatal day when she caused you so much distress. Caroline is a sorry arse, I am afraid just like yours. I think it is grand time to reunite those.

Hugging Azryel strongly, an incredulous Walter Workmaster still asked,

-My Caro always loved me?

-That is pushing it a tad, human. But you know, even when she calls you, Arsehole, which his her favourite nickname for you when she is a little p' off, she still loves you deeply. She was very shaken by your break down, taken aback and she did not know how to react. She only thought for the safety of Micky all along. When she had Micky secured, she devoted herself with Gab to your recovery. Did you know she bought herself a fake wedding ring to wear anytime she is not with you?

-No. What is that ring all about?

-If you read what is engraved on the inside you will see the word 'forever' while on the outside it is almost a plain band apart for your initials, 'W W' entwined. Gabriel can tell you how long she wore that ring, himself. It is since the day after he removed you from her door.

Leaving the Angelic arms of the Death Angel, Walter called his dog and ran to the tree house, smiling like the happiest man,

-Come on Bud, let's go and kneel by Mummy.

Verse 30. Pink Glasses.

Walter rushed into the guest room and saw a grown up looking like It-666 with her hamster in her hand teaching Micky how to talk to his own hamster by telepathy. He did not care about the oddity of his children, he only cared about Caroline who was reading a book about vegetarian diet for children upon her guest bed quietly. Kneeling by the bed, Bud sitting by him in a stately fashion, he opened the little red box containing the diamond ring, breathless. Workmaster apologised at once,

-Forgive me Caroline for not waiting for a perfect moment. I have been with Azryel walking the dog and he believes every minute counts. I do not want to count another minute without you fully in my life. May I humbly ask for your forgiveness and your hand? Caroline Purallee, would you be my beloved wife?

Dazzled by the ring, her heart overjoyed with happiness, Caroline jumped out of the bed and hugged Walter at once. After a long deep kiss, she asked cocking her eyebrows, yet with tearful eyes,

-I thought you would never ask me again, Blondie Bear. You have my hand my Walt and I forgave you ages ago, could you not tell? I would love to be your beloved wife, Workmaster, the one I never ceased to be in your heart. That is a smashing ring. I did not know you could afford something like a nice rock.

-I was a pauper for this, Caroline, I saved all I could to get this ring for you. I am afraid I am not the wealthiest husband on the planet but I can work on that. I was a good lawyer in my day. If Gab allows me, under my fake identity I may return to be one.

Kissing wildly his cheeks, his mouth and forehead, a gleeful Caroline jubilated,

-My Walt is back, fully, fully back.

Hugging her tenderly, Workmaster whispered,

-I am back, Caroline, and I promise I will not let you down this time around. I will always be here for you and the children. I am sorted, trust, I have none than Az looking after my own arse. You can't go wrong.

After another kissing sprint, the Death Angel walked in the room and smiled wickedly. He looked around and told without apology,

-I am afraid Walter, I have to take It with me to the loophole room for our Angelic Army meeting upon the expected Apocalypse. It would be an honour to be your best man, if you would have me? For the way you were kissed just now, I doubt very much you faced a refusal.

Grabbing the hand of Caroline, the man ran to Azryel with her, both knelt by him. Each human took one hand of the Angel, as Walter spoke,

-Azryel, the honour to have you as a best man is all ours. You are right like always, my Caro said yes.

-Right, Children, I do know I am always right. Now, let's get on to proper business. Put that shiny ring upon Caro's finger with no further ado, for she is desperate to have the glittery diamond upon it. Let's get on with it. At long last, your two hearts are back together. There is one star in that sky shining brighter for it. Would you hand me your wedding rings, Caroline? You will get them back on your wedding day, a day of your own choosing.

-Can it be on my birthday, in two days time?

-Yes, it could but do you not want more preparation for your wedding? Do you not want the full monty?

Shaking her head desperately, Caroline confessed, as she handed her wedding rings to Azryel, removing them from around her neck,

-All I need is my Walt by me, and my day would be a blessed day. He would be my best birthday present ever.

A voiceless Workmaster hugged her, tears prickling his eyes. The long silent hug of the couple touched the heart of the Death Angel, who called their children out,

-Little It, Micky, come here to congratulate your parents. At long last they are getting married again. The happy event is set for the day after tomorrow. We are going to need your help. Mum will need a bridesmaid, and Dad requires a little ring bearer, are you ready to step up to the plate?

Micky put his hamster back in to it's cage and ran to his parents, grabbing the hand of the adopted teenager with him, dragging her along. He enjoined her as he threw his little arms around the couple,

-Come, Bambi, come, group hug.

Smiling happily It joined in, shyly at first but the reassuring hands of Walter and Caroline went over her back, securing her within their embrace.

Caroline stroking the cheek of the young Being tenderly, then the one of her son, said,

-Your family is getting tightly reformed, Bambi. Dad and I are tying the knot. Fancy being my bridesmaid? What should we have, heavenly blue and white theme or I see life in pink colour glasses, bright pink and glittery silver theme? Micky, carrying those rings is a big job. No losing of one allowed. Can you do it my little man, and bring it to mummy and daddy by the Indian Waterfall on a velvet cushion? Az, could keep an eye on you so you don't trip to make sure the precious rings get to their destination.

Winking at the Death Angel, the future bride to be asked him,

-If you don't mind it, Azryel, I would love you to perform the ceremony. It would mean a great deal to me and also for Walter, I am sure of it?

Workmaster nodding wildly confirmed,

-It would, Az. I owe this entirely to you. Come and join the family hug. You are completely part of this reuniting.

A truly moved Azryel did not wait for another invitation as he joined the group hug, as shyly as the teenage It did before him, and replied as all started shivering under his arms,

-It would be an honour to perform your ceremony. From the bottom of my heart, I wish you both lots of happiness. You all deserve it. You can be sure I will look after the little cushion bearer with those rings, Caro. I know what they mean to you and Walt. Now if you seek my advice about colour theme, I would go brash pink and glittery. Pink glasses transform your days to better days. Let's make all the guests wear them at Workmaster's wedding. That would be a utter treat to witness.

-I am not wearing a pink suit! Hell no, Death, leave the choice of colour to the living.

Breaking the embrace the man carried on,

-What's wrong with blue and white?

A mocking Death Angel teased,

-It's not abrasive enough for the likes of you. As you are barely a quiet man, only loud colours will suit your personality. Your suit could be all glittery silver, a pink tie and the cool pink glasses.

Joining in the argument Caroline agreed,

-I like that! I think Azryel has taste, more than you have Blondie Bear. Besides I'd rather have a brash-y wedding than a dull one. Pretty please, can we have the pink theme?

Walter Workmaster looked to the ceiling in desperation as he gave up,

-Okay, we will go pink crazy, just for you my Caro.

Kissing her future husband again, smiling like an happy child, Caroline jumped up and down. Seeing the kiss the Death Angel took the hand of It-666 and told,

-Time for It and I to split before someone learns to do proper kisses by watching you two lovebirds. Wrath must be pining for us right now.

Verse 31. Meeting.

The Death Angel appeared with It in the loophole room where they saw that Wrath had already started the war meeting with the Angelic soldiers. Beside him in the middle of the circle, the Archangel Gabriel was kneeling humbly, yet his head lifted up as soon as Death and the young Beast arrived. His eyes lighting up as he considered It from head to toe, he could not help welcoming them,

-At long last Azryel, Wrath has been uttering his favourite sentence every five minutes. What took you so long?

Giving him his wicked smirk, Death stepping forward with It, splitting the circle of soldier without care to access the middle and his place by Wrath, replied,

-Let me guess! That would be the death sentence of everyone's ears: where is Az when I need him? Well, I have been sorting out issues with my Soul Takers. There's a few matters that need my attention and investigation. I am afraid Raphael you will always see me disappear every now and then. However if it can make up for my wait I have excellent news to convey, if you care to hear them during a meeting?

A deeply annoyed and impatient Wrath, looking at It and Azryel, told sternly,

-I can see it from my own eyes, the young It had a makeover from Caroline and she looks simply stunning. If you had to push your way in the Angelic circle, my soldiers made way for her. Now as I want everyone to think on their feet in that meeting I recommend you two to take your Being's shape at once.

Both obeyed immediately and knelt by him and Gab, yet the black winged Death teased the Archangel,

-Let's get on with the meeting, my news can wait. Assumptions have been plaguing my day all the way through. So much so that I am very willing to let them carry on without addressing every single one of them.

This had Raphael coming by him at once, lifting the chin of his Angel, scolding,

-Right, don't you dare slack in front of me, Az. News does not improve with time, spill the beans.

Widely smiling, Death announced,

-Your niece is to be married again. Our human Workmaster finally found the courage to ask her for the second time. She was overjoyed. Caroline wishes her wedding to take place on her birthday, hence in two days time, for the best present she could have in her life is Blondie Bear.

Immediately Az had his shoulder grabbed by a teary Archangel Gabriel,

-How did it happen? Wreck-man still has big confidence issues since his breakdown.

Shrugging his shoulders proudly, the Death Angel confessed,

-I played a part. I am to be his best man and I will perform the wedding for them. All I did was talk to the man the way I do.

A very pleased Wrath tapping the shoulder of his nephew commented,

-Death has a specific way to solve humans, also Angels and Beings. Don't ask him. You will end up with a software of ready solutions that had an eternity to be foolproof. Azryel, that little nugget of news makes my day. Well done. I will go lavish on that wedding regardless of the short notice. Let's get Asha to take our betrothed on a big shopping trip tomorrow. For Us, we will have to head back to Boston's sewers. Let's resume the meeting. Gab, dry your tears and proceed by briefing Az and It where we are so far.

The Archangel standing up, obeyed, apologising,

-I am sorry to be emotional, Workmaster means so much to me. Knowing what he went through, that man deserves true happiness. Finally he will get it back. We will certainly have to help him make his big day with my sister Caro very special.

Interrupting him, Azryel could not resist to say, winking to Asha doing so,

-Of course we will make sure of it. My entire Army will be present, in pink suits and pink glasses. Caroline is set on a big brash pink and glittery silver wedding theme.

A falsely revolted Wrath stated with an amused growing smile,

-Ghastly! My niece never had great taste, it started with her teenage self wearing boyish dungarees up until she went to university followed by the worst choice in men. If I grew to be fond of Workmaster after all our bickering, I am not convinced I will rave about wearing a 'Barbie' pink suit. However seeing the soldiers wearing one might make me giggle all afternoon.

-You have a common point with our man Walter, he didn't fancy the thought of it, Wrath, yet he gave in to Caro's wishes and settled for the glittery silver suit with a pink tie option. The pink glasses, however are compulsory.

-Right, I think I will settle with that option as well, for all the soldiers, we will go for the pink suit for we mustn't disappoint my niece on her big day. Asha, I think you will enjoy your day tomorrow, make sure you accommodate all of her wishes to render her wedding the most ridiculous I ever have seen. Use my Amex blindly without restriction, for it will amuse me greatly to see the result.

Grinning wickedly the Death Angel watched in pure glee the

Angelic soldiers becoming livid at the mere thought of the ceremony. He clapped his hands and enjoined,

-Let's get on with more serious matters. Now that we know that we are going to enjoy a pretty in pink Archangel Gabriel, let us hear the brief he has to do.

His Angels responded by laughing heartedly, while Gabriel looking at him in desperation, started,

-Somehow I have a feeling that we owe to Az the pink theme. It would not go past him to treat one day of his eternal morbid dreary life to a pink Angelic Amusement park. More importantly now, Death we went through with the soldiers the results and findings of the hypnosis session of Eremiel. We are respectful that It did not desire to hear what he would say. However, we will now inform her of what she must know in order to proceed with our mission as a soldier. We will keep away the parts which could give her concern. The delivery will be a filtered version, which all Angels have been warned about and would keep it this way with their questions and interjections. Wrath had the worry that you may not be ready for the version we have prepared for your young Being, and if it was the case that you should remain with your family while the Angelic Army will carry on the fight until you are ready to cope to what is thrown at Us. You would be given a leave, well earned especially for your last mission in the Boston sewers. The new mission involves the same location, and we all know it was very tough for you down there as you almost lost your life. Therefore, we voted a motion, which passed, giving you the choice between having a childhood or remaining and growing as a soldier during it. Let's hear you, come to the fore. If your answer is the first choice, you will be sent back to Walter Workmaster and his family and you will enjoy the rest of your childhood protected by Us. While the other choice will mean you will stay in this meeting and fight the upcoming war with Us. What would it be, It?

The Devil looking like teenage Beast stood up, a little nervous by all the eyes scrutinising her, bowing her head respectfully, as she replied,

-I thank you all and Wrath in particular to give me the choice. I am sorry to have raised your concern, Raphael. Knowing that your next mission involves me all the way through, I will not bow out from it for you. With all my powers I will support you and help you. From my last mission, I learnt that Azryel and you would not leave a soldier behind, that you would try everything to save my life. My life is devoted to Us, you, Az and Gab but also humanity. I vowed to myself not to be what I was meant to be when I met the arms of Walter Workmaster freeing me from my fate. That man taught me about being free to make your own choices, to listen to your own heart, and my heart tells me to help humanity, and my choice is to fight to protect it in your Army, Wrath. I want to grow as your soldier and protect my human family and their kind. I am ready to hear filtered or unfiltered version of Eremiel's revelation.

When she knelt back by the side of Azryel, he put his hand upon her shoulder and pressed it strongly. She remembered what it meant. Blood tears coming to her eyes, she simply whispered,

-Thank you so so much, Master.

Death had just made it clear to her and the Army that he was embracing her fully. He would lay down his life for hers. Coming by her side, the Archangel Raphael seized her other shoulder silently. All the Angelic soldiers acknowledged that It was fully endorsed by two extremely powerful Angels. They also recognised that she had just given up the rest of her childhood to protect humanity and fight with them. She was a Being to be respected.

Welcoming her decision, Gabriel stated,

-Well, we can then proceed with our meeting. It, make sure you honour your full embracement as there is no backing down possible from now. However you have three pairs of shoulders ready to support you whenever you need it, young soldier. Mine are joint to Wrath and Death. You can call upon me and count on me to respond. The mission we are proposing is involving you fully as you know. Raphael wishes to put a decoy snake looking like Eremiel's black mamba in the sewers of Boston to keep the witch and P occupied for a while but he also would like the decoy lethal. First and last, the operation requires you to transform genetically that water cobra into it's nasty family counterpart, then we need snaky to have mojo added on which can pass for your father's ones. Let's say bloody walls when it is in a room, talking with strange sentences which will drive our evil two up the wall, and why not poltergeisting the witch's place so she is losing most of her working gear. For the lethal stuff, when they intend to sacrifice a human, a powerful incurable bite to a demon and cambion could teach them a deadly lesson of don't do it again. I worked on the real black mamba's poison and demonic blood, I may have found something you can improve on. What I have created induces an immediate coma in demons. It will only take a bite or sting directly in their blood stream to disable them for a few days. Now the handling of the decoy snake can only be left to you who talks to animals and orders them about. Can you control that animal from afar? Can you see as they see?

The teenager wrapped in her demonic wings, yet still standing answered,

-I can see through the eyes of any animal upon Earth. I can control the decoy snake from afar easily. Handling the snake and transforming it poses no problem for me. Making it do things my father or I can do, is child's play. I will make it a point for that snake to destroy the witch's paraphernalia. For the poison I have to work upon it. You have to show me your creation, Archangel Gabriel to see if I can reproduce it and improve it. Usually I induce comas by touch and depending on the creature it takes me different timing. On the battle field in P's wood and in Hell, I tried it. On the beasties in the wood, they took three minutes before collapsing, enough time to injure someone in the meantime. On a patrol soldier in Hell, it took five minutes before I saw him fall before me. He gave me a nasty one with his battle axe in the mean time upon my ribs. Couple of fractures, nothing Az could not deal with. Gosh, Walt confessed to me he loved seeing Azryel whenever he was in trouble. For he knew he would be sorted, harshly maybe, but sorted. When I saw Death in Hell, I knew we were going to get out of there. Are we going to get out of the sewers okay this time around?

Reassuring her at once Wrath replied,

-It should be just a depositing the snake for the Witch and P to find. We will get out as soon as and not linger on. We can also make it clean sewers as we walk in and dirty as we walk back out.

The few soldiers who were on the previous Boston's sewers mission smiled widely, commenting,

-Then you can count Us in Wrath. Death, care to join the trip or Ash getting Us pink suits?

Azryel pressing the shoulder of It strongly, answered,

-I will go where that kid goes and make sure she comes back. I will join the sewers party.

A welcoming Wrath smiled widely as he announced,

-Same party as last time then. Angels, I don't want any of you dreading it as much as you did. Anyhow we have Az with Us not to mention It. It, I need you to spend a few hours after this meeting performing the snake genetic change and then to learn with Gabriel his demonic poison, and whatever he sees fit for you to know. Azryel, if you have any business to do, do it now for we are moving tomorrow morning at 6 am.

Coming and kneeling by Wrath, the Death Angel held his hand before disappearing,

-I have. Two souls, one involving better days for humanity, one involving a simple woman with no confidence at all, unable to look after her own self. I will also do a trip to Paradise, for there is a soul I need to talk to for our matters at hand. I will be back on time Master.

When Az left the room, Wrath called it a day,

-From now on do not be caught unaware soldiers. The Apocalypse is upon our doors. Be prepared at all times. It, follow Gabriel and I.

Verse 32. S-Ample.

Sitting quietly upon the lab chair, her left arm attached and given to Gabriel for experiment, It was watching him tinkering with his test tubes, needles and glass bottles. She had no idea what he was doing precisely but if it was to help Wrath and his mission then she was a willing lab rat. Raphael and him, had ordered her to remain in her bestial appearance. She felt like a freak being studied and analysed under a magnifying glass. Her nose diving and her sad demonic black eyes closing she tried to push away the feeling, but before she knew it, the walls of the lab started bleeding.

Stopping immediately what he was doing, a concerned Gabriel enquired taking her hand,

-Hey, Bambi, what's up?

While Raphael standing by the teenage Beast demanded,

-Did Gab hurt you with his needles? You need to be more gentle with her.

Shaking her head negatively the young Being opened her eyes and realised the cause of their concerns,

-I am sorry. It's not Gab, it's just me, Wrath. I just had a low.

Making the blood disappear, she smiled sheepishly to the Archangels, who asked her,

-A low what?

-Feeling.

Detaching her arm from the chair, Wrath announced,

-Off that chair, little one. No more experiments for you. Hope you got what you needed, Gab. What is that low feeling about, kiddo?

-I am a freaking freak.

Embracing her at once, the Archangel scolded her,

-You are a Being, a supernatural one. Remember that, that is your own adopted father's qualification for you. It is adopted and respected by all Angels. One of them, Azryel would even slap any across the face if they would mention the word freak about you. He, who knows you most of all, sees you for who you are, a Being with extreme powers and a kindness to match. Death, who is a judge of all souls, knows best how to qualify you and you are a very good Being in his own eyes. Beside he has made his mind up about you, and he will fetch your little arse wherever it gets stuck. All of my Angels would dream about his shoulder's accolade. Yet, only Gab had it beforehand. You are a very special Being, It. Do not feel low, feel proud of how strong you are dealing with your issues. You never had an easy life and to remain as good as you are, is an amazing feat. Death knows it and appreciates it, so do I and Gab does just as well.

The girl closed her eyes upon his chest as he tapped her shoulders gently before he seized her chin and lifted it to make her face his amazing Archangelic gaze,

-Trust me, we only accept the best of the crop in this Army by Death's will. My general has always picked the best Beings and hearts. Any failing his standards does not qualify as a sound heart and soul and therefore does not qualify as a good Being, is discarded within hours or a couple of days. You are his keep, you are sound and as far away from being a freak as one can be. Don't let your appearance or powers fool you. You are a good supernatural Being. Understood, Soldier?

A positively nodding teenager, tried to voice a strong answer,

-Understood.

She fell silent and stayed nestled upon his chest as Wrath asked his nephew,

-Have you got all you need from my young soldier?

-I think I did, Uncle. To do all I can, I need samples from Eremiel. But in her state I think it would be asking too much of her. It may be better to let her rest for the night bearing in mind she is going on a mission with you at 6 am tomorrow morning.

Wrath shook his head negatively, stating,

-War is on. Rest will be scarce and time precious. Let's get the samples from Eremiel while we all can. It, soldier, I need you sharp. There's a big task I need you to perform. This will help Us all. I need you to help Gabriel in analysing Eremiel.

As soon as her father's name was spelt out, Raphael felt a shiver shaking the teenager all over. Yet her demonic eyes closed themselves in a resigned agreement, as she agreed,

-I will do anything to help out. What is my task?

Gabriel answered sternly,

-I need to get samples from Eremiel, in his snake form, in the shape Wrath saw him behind the mirror at P's house, and in its purest Archangelic form if you can retrieve it from his deformed self. He will be comatosed all the way, so they should not be any worry. We will not wake him up just test his body. Are you up for it?

-I am. Wrath, may I hold your hand throughout?

-You may, and are welcome to, Soldier. I will stand by you, during the whole feat, making sure you are alright. I also require you to feel Eremiel like I and Gabriel will do. He has been victim of Cato who he named as a Swallower. A Swallower is a kind unknown to Us, yet Cato is building an Army of them. They swallow the supernatural powers of their victims which they keep imprisoned in a diminished state. We have a list of numerous Swallowers to tackle and their preys that we need to free. Analysing Eremiel may allow us to find how a Swallower proceeds and Gabriel will then work upon a possible solution for it not to happen to any of Us, especially you It, but we could also see if the damages are reversible or not. However we will certainly not reverse them upon your father. This is a crucial task as Cato and her Army of Swallowers cannot be underestimated. Is the task clear, soldier? After it we will head back here and help Gab as much as we can.

Nodding positively her head, the teenager answered,

-The task is clear. I can perform it, Wrath.

Teletransporting to the prison chamber, the two Archangels and the Beast came by the box. Gabriel warned, considering the young It, before he lifted the lid,

-Do not get a case of bad nerves once the lid is off, Bambi. If you do, warn us at once by pulling the hand of Wrath beside you. Then I will replace the lid upon him. Remember he is comatose and only you can wake him up. Now, be ready. I am planning our visit to be very short indeed.

Withholding her breath the Beast gave a short nod reassuring,

-Trust me, Gab, I won't cock this one up. He is one that will stay knocked unconscious for eternity. I am going to keep us three safe throughout. You can do all your samplings.

Raphael staying by It smirked wickedly, ordered his nephew then confided to her,

-Good, Gab get cracking. Eremiel thinks that you are dead my little soldier, he believes you did not make it. We know better, and we didn't correct his assumptions, Az, Gab and myself. Because we are keeping you with Us, Being. We care for you, for you have found in Us and the Workmasters your family, and I can tell you it is a loving one.

The elder Archangel took her hand and held it strongly, while they watched Gab who had been listening, smiling as he scrapped scales off the snake's skin, asking her,

-Tell me, Bambi, will you play a part in the wedding? Az did manage to be best man and will perform the ceremony as well. I am a tad envious. I would have loved to get the best man part at the very least. But I may have swung my bat on my human's shoulder one too many times. I must say I was very scared to lose Workmaster to suicide a few times six years ago. I was very strict upon him. Sometimes it is the way I show I care.

Getting involved Wrath could not help correcting him,

-Not just sometimes, this is the only way you show you care. I do not blame the man to forget to give you a role in his wedding when you sent him to your clinic with a broken shoulder. I must confess that I have the same problem and nearly only know to give tough love. Caroline coming to mine with Bud a few weeks ago now put me to shame. She proposed friendship to my Az. You can imagine the maelstrom it caused to my Death Angel. She could not understand why the Angels, his own Army and I never thought of befriending him, him who laid his life for Us day in and out. She stirred his heart so much he could not conceive without unforgivingness why a human was the first to present him with that offer of friendship when working for an eternity with Angels no one ever did. I was moved, and yes a little heartbroken that I did let that one go past me for so long, thinking of my general as the Grim Reaper and not like an Angel with a caring and devoted soul. When I proposed finally my friendship to him, do you know what happened? My request was to be considered. Asha's one was the first to be accepted then Caro's one then Walt then I. I was truly humbled by it. For I remember Az protecting me, fighting above me as I lay wounded with an astonishing loyalty turning the situation around me to a sound victory. We Angels do care, but we do not show it as well as humans. We do lack that 'Je ne sais quoi' of human touch. I am glad to have my Angels in the same compound as Workmaster and Caroline for they truly can teach Us a thing or two. I can speak to Az and Walt for you and see if they could consider you as Best Man on this occasion. So It, were you given a role for their ceremony?

Seeing Gabriel pouring carefully the poison from the black mamba into a test tube, after having taken a flesh sample and filled a needle with strange fluids coming from the snake's body, the teenager answered thoughtfully,

-I am to be bridesmaid. Caroline asked me. I have no clue at all about what that involves, but also I don't know anything about weddings. I understood it is about two souls and hearts saying publicly they are with each other. Micky will carry the cushion with their former wedding rings to them. When Azryel stepped into the room, when he realised that Walter's proposal had been accepted by Caro, he was all smiles and satisfaction. He would have accepted to fetch the moon if my parents required it at that moment. I think talking to Az and Walt about the best man position is possible. The moment was a blur of happy decisions made like the brash pink theme, which Az promoted. Walter understands your tough love Gab, and appreciates it. He respects you very much and it was far from his thoughts at that moment to discriminate you because of a past glitch. Ask him and he will consider you straight away. Ask Az and he will let you play that role.

Putting all his samples in a special case by his side, the Archangel muttered with a growing smile,

-I knew Azryel would have been behind the pink affair. I will ask him and Walt if I can be a best man. To be honest It, I only went to one wedding in my entire eternal life, their first one. It was a very small affair as Wrath disapproved of their union back then. I was there as best man then and witness. Azryel came and stood in the back ground all the while quietly, he watch it all, never spoke a word and left after the reception in a small downtown bar. The other witness was Wendy and she stood as a bridesmaid too. Only my then new receptionist, Wendy's back up and helper, Liz came. She thought that because Walt was white and Caro was coloured they had faced prejudice upon their wedding and made a point to come.

I could not possibly advise you on human weddings. Uncle, are you more versed upon the subject? Now, It transform Eremiel in the state he was behind the mirrors as Wrath witnessed him at P's.

The girl did so with no further ado. The box extended itself to receive the new shape. The full length of the room was occupied by Eremiel. A sleeping Devil lay before them and took their breath away for a few long minutes before Wrath scolded,

-Gab, shut your gapping gob and get on with it, will you. We have the worst of him before us. Get cracking and no small talk this time around. It, the wedding will be a walk in the park, not a walk in Boston's sewers. Being there is the most important thing. I regret not being at Caro's first wedding.

Taking a glimpse at Eremiel the teenager's eyes filled with tears, and sorrowfully asked,

-Do I look like him in my Being's state?

Raphael embracing the teenage girl at once, holding her tight within his arms, replied,

-You do, in a teenage state and a female one of the creature you see before you.

Burying her head within his shoulder, It cried. Comforting her, the Archangel cradled her Being slightly,

-Ssshhhh, ssshhh, and your look does not match your good heart for one bit, little Sweet Heart. His shape was imposed upon him, it's a punishment. The punishment would have affected all his children. Eremiel is very proud. He wanted a child to avenge him, the best one he could ever create. He created you and no one else. He wanted you to be his destroyer of humanity. Yet your heart is good and sound while your shell and powers could make you a devil. Remember this, your choice is substance over physical matter. You fight for good and that is all that matters to Us, me, Az and Gab. Come, come, Soldier.

Having taken all his samples, Gabriel enjoined,

-Let's check him out fully, now, Wrath. Bambi, get over your
appearance. As Wrath said he was punished and his blood line
would carry the Evil look. It does not mean that you can't earn your
angelic wings and gain for your own self an Angelic appearance.
Following Death's tuition, and knowing your self sacrificing heart
all too well, I have no doubt that you will achieve the feat at some
point. Azryel is set to make you earn your wings big time, he set a
motion through, and the all Army agreed to help you do so, little
Soldier. Now, let's check Eremiel. This is him as we fear him. This is
the form when he was drained of his powers by Cato the witch.
Both of you try to feel where she attacked him, and try to guess the
date of her attack.

All their hands reached for the body of Eremiel. Wrath was the first
to raise the attention of the others, holding the demonic wrist
tightly,

-I think I have the point where she did her damage. The whole wrist
is still dysfunctioning badly. It is pretty recent in Being's longevity's
terms. I would say it was done eleven to ten years ago.

Giving the wrist to his nephew to check, the Archangel held it
slightly backwards, eager to listen to the findings of Gab,

-Definitely the point of drainage, Wrath. She used it over and over
again throughout those eleven years. I can feel his full strength prior
to that. Cato leaked him of his power little by little so he would not
notice. I can feel her impact as pervasive as mould or a fungi upon
his Being, lasting and doing it's slow damage long after the initial
contact. The beauty of it is that she left her sucking bugging
compound in. Wrath, we have something to work on against any
Swallowers. Bambi, get your feeling hands in here and tell us more
if you can.

The anxious teenager came by him and held the wrist at first then
moved on to other parts of Eremiel's body. She commented

throughout,

-The point of the attack is definitely his left wrist. The suck bug is definitely there, Gab. Be careful sampling it, do not ever touch it, ever. It does work like an infection which she increases over time, the more powerful she gets. She is extremely powerful right now. A Swallower does not need to attack, she talked to my father eleven years ago, he was boasting about the death of Father Williamson and she just praised him holding his left wrist. The contact only lasted a few seconds, less than a minute. The damages of a Swallower are reversible. You just need to remove their swallowing bug from the victim, and if possible inject their powers back. Please do not do that to Eremiel. Cato was at the state of her art when she did him. I believe she has been building her Army for more than eleven years. The bug is not lethal but damaging. It is like a symbiosis going solely one way, and keeping the host alive for it to survive and thrive, hence Eremiel ended behind the mirrors at P's house. I feel him depleted, so much so that he relished being in snake form swallowing rats.

Having taken the Swallower's bug sample Gabriel demanded,

-Well we will get him back to it, after we have him in his initial form. Hold my hand and Wrath's one, we will perform the feat together. For to bring back an Archangel you need Archangelic powers.

Holding their hands the teenager saw the Devil creature before her being restored to an Angel. The four golden winged Angel was extremely beautiful, his blond curls flowing upon his shoulders like a mane enclosing a surreal face neither masculine nor feminine. His vacant beautiful aquamarine eyes stared fixedly upon the ceiling of the room. She turned to Wrath and asked, her voice failing her before she could finish her sentence,

-I saw my incarnated face in the mirror today for the first time. I am identic...

Nodding positively Raphael stated,

-Your human form looks like his Angelic one. He was one of the most beautiful Angels that ever existed. When we saw the colour of your eyes little It, we knew we had Eremiel's child before Us for sure. You had no hair, your head having being shaved to make sure you would not get any identity, like a tortured prisoner you were for so long. Now that your hair is growing back, you can look forward to the blond curly mane. You can expect to be one of the most beautiful incarnated Beings walking upon Earth beside being the Beast. Now, let's get cracking, Soldier. Let's help Gab further shall we?

The teenager beside Wrath felt through her fingers all over the body of Eremiel, when she stood by Gab, she announced,

-The Swallower's bug is reacting differently in his Angelic body, it is like it's fighting off something. It's still potent but it is struggling. Gab, do you want to check?

Beside her the Archangel took the left wrist giving It-666 a winning smile,

-Absolutely fabulous, do you want a job at my Angelic clinic as a doctor instead of being a soldier It? Well spotted, when his demonic shape has no response to fight off the infection, his Archangelic body has. The result is a tiny miracle of nature called antibodies. Eremiel's antibodies may be the clue to finding a cure to the Swallowers' bug. I reckon his antibodies are not doing a bad job either at neutralising the bug. They make it difficult for it to spread. Uncle, tell me if I am right or wrong?

Checking the wrist out, Wrath told him straight,

-Don't you ever try to take that soldier from me. She is a brilliant fighter of a quality I hardly ever get to see. Beside my battlefields will be her breathing space. But on the other hand I think you are right about those blood proteins, they are fairly effective. Shame we can't take his whole hand and wrist and put it in a test glass tube to observe longer. Blood supply wise, the experiment could not be done, the hand would be a dead limb.

Looking at him with a very wicked smirk Gabriel advanced,

-That would not be a problem for me, Uncle. Azryel was not joking when he said I kept living parts of demons in my lab. I have a little saw among my instruments. At the end of the day it would be for the good of everyone.

The pungent smell of a smoking cigar reaching Wrath and Gab's nostrils made them jump and turn at once. They saw the sarcastically grinning Death Angel peering over their shoulders. Raphael scolded,

-I told you Az, to warn me of your presence. My blood just freaking turned. Do you realise who we have in front of us?

Coolly and calmly puffing a perfect ring of smoke to his face, Azryel replied unfazed,

-I just did warn you of my presence, Wrath. Stop being so jumpy old soldier, I will tell you when your death is about to come. At present, I am watching your backs. There is no mutilation of Eremiel to be done. No shortcuts to be thought of upon that Being for if he ever wakes up in the future without a limb, your Archangelic arses are so so gone and dusted. And yes, I do realise who we have in the room more than you two seem to do.

A downhearted Gabriel asked almost begging,

-No cutting? Think of it like taking a cutting from a nice strong plant and letting it grow somewhere else...

His lips drawing into a firm line, yet with the edges rising Death replied strongly,

-Yes, no cutting of that damned Archangel. Tut Tut for thinking we want him to grow somewhere else too. I have apocalyptic alarm toll bells ringing in my head just thinking about it, Gab. Just sample his antibodies and a bit of the reacting bug, and that will do for tonight. Minimal mess, Gab, minimal mess with that one. Seeing your little suitcase of filled test tubes, I would say you have enough to keep you occupied for a while, at least a good couple of days if not a week, don't you Doctor Frankenstein? Now, my teenage soldier needs her rest for tomorrow's mission. Get cracking for it is well past her bed time, and I will be on both of your backs until she gets her rest. No grizzly cutting daddy up scene for you little one tonight, it just went Azryel's PG motioned.

The youngster smiled with relief. She did not know how long the night would last and the arrival of no non-sense Death promised to make it shorter and sweeter. She saw Gabriel taking all his last samples in a hurry, and finally close his special lab case with a confident smile,

-I think I am done, Azryel.

A satisfied Death enjoined Wrath,

-With me, Raphael, let's put the lid upon it's imperial 'Nastiness'. Word of warning to you both, do not play or mess up with his body, for I am called Death and not the Resurrector. Capish?

Winking back at Death, Wrath helped him put the lid back upon the box, covering the comatose Eremiel, acknowledged,

-Thank you for stepping in, Azryel. I must admit the thought of Wiz Kid Gab with a piece of Eremiel did sound attractive for a minute. It, you can snake the big Bad up now, we have finished with him.

Without further ado It did so, only too happy to have Eremiel contained in a manageable form, which she knew all too well was still extremely dangerous. The Death Angel ordered,

-Back in the lab, now.

All left the jail and teletransported back to the lab. Death pulling two hospital linen camp beds enjoined,

-Right, Wrath, you have done enough looking after for today, your wits are flying out of you, time to regain them before tomorrow's mission. Bed. It, sleep time. You will decoy that snake in the morning. By then hopefully Wacky Gab would have worked out something out of his samples. Both of you can rest I am going to keep an eye on him from now.

Raphael did not wait for another word and fell asleep almost immediately. A little baffled, the teenager apologised, as she lay on her linen bed,

-I am sorry Az, it will take me longer to close my eyes. I do not mean to be awkward.

Death giving her his hand, explained,

-I know. I am a Watcher. Wrath feels at peace when I am here, that is when he can let go and sleep properly. In time, with trust you may do too. I taught Raphael to let go for a while by holding my hand. It is cold enough to be recognised as mine at all times. No Being bestows icy cold hands. You can close your eyes, and know I am by you by my single touch. Just get a feel.

As the teenager did, she whispered,

-And I can rest because you are here.

-That's right, now close your eyes before Madcap Gab needs to do more experiments upon you.

Holding her hand until she was fully asleep, Death stayed by her bed quietly.

A few hours later, a jubilant Gabriel came by Azryel who was watching over the bunk beds like a guard dog. Tapping his shoulder, he exhibited a blue liquid in a glass jar with his brightest smile. In desperation, Az asked,

-It's too early in the morning Gab, to make me guess and jump about. What is it?

-Our little It can not be swallowed! Her powers, I mean. She just needs to drink that and she will be safe from any Swallower in town, well in the all universe.

A smiling Death looked upon him with glee, and scolded,

-About time, you had only two hours until the wake up call. Stop dangling about the precious bottle like a lunatic and put it somewhere safely where I can see it. By the way, Gab, you earned a favour from me for this magic potion. If you think of one ask away at anytime.

Putting the bottle safely upon the desk, the Archangel came to kneel by Death and simply said,

-I would love to be Walter Workmaster's best man if he would have me again, and if you would not mind.

Putting his hand upon the Archangelic's shoulders strongly, the Angel of Death confided,

-Pray, Gab, the man would have asked you if you were there. Like I do, he rates you greatly. Leave it to me, Angel. As I am performing the ceremony, I do not mind one bit you being his best man.

Verse 33. TLC potion.

Although Gabriel was cramped, he also felt extremely peaceful and rested. Someone kept stroking his head, gently and the sensation was so very soothing that he was very reluctant to open his eyes. Yet his mind was hearing a soft internal voice which was calling him to do so. As he opened his eyes, he realised he had slept, kneeling by Death, his head resting upon his lap. He saw Wrath watching him with a smirk upon his lips, while in her camp bed the young It was still sleeping all wrapped up in her demonic wings. His Uncle welcomed him,

-Finally awake, Gab. With only two hours to sleep, Death decided to give you a proper peaceful rest. According to him you are so hyperactive that you hardly get any sleep at any point in time. Always fiddling, messing about with experiments, and finding genial things which almost keep you awake day and night. Lack of sleep may be an underlying cause of your almost constant irritability. If you can't find enough hours in a day to allow yourself a rest, my general has the solution for you, a very efficient and tested one which we have implemented in my Army for a very very long time. How do you feel?

Standing up the Archangel felt his cramped legs at once but Az's long fingers touching the tip of his own ones resolved the issue with his blue healing energy going straight where it was needed. Gabriel didn't know what to say at first, and looked at the teenage Beast sleeping peacefully wondering if she had the same treatment. He finally told strongly,

-I am very unsettled about it however I must admit that I had the best rest I have had in a very long while. Thank you Azryel, but what the hell was going on with the gentle stroking of my hair? Did Bambi get the same RIP rest? As far as I know I am not irritable, far from it, I am just more reasonable than the norm.

Laughing out loud Raphael replied to his nephew,

-Care to disagree, you are an irritable sod, Gab, you always have been but with time and your lonesome way of life, it just got worse without you ever noticing. As for more reasonable than the norm, it could be argued, with all the living bits of demons in your very lab, like that brain that pulsates in that glass tank over there, with the two eyes linked to it that watch everything and follow the moves about the room. Talking about unsettling, how dare you? As for It, she had the same treatment as you did, due to her nature she can hardly sleep, just like Azryel. Unlike himself, however he can provide a true night of recuperative sleep for restless soldiers prior to a battle or a mission. What is to argue about that? As for the stroking, Az was simply dreaming about the Great Dane puppies I promised him, that's all, nothing more, nothing less.

Starting to smile and choking with a retained laugh, Gabriel commented,

-A freakin' puppy prop! Great. I feel much much better now. When are you going to get him the real McCoy? ASAP I hope.

-Well I did not want to overcrowd your tree house too much so I was putting Az on a patient scheme.

-My freakin' home is a f'in Noah's Ark at the moment, Wrath. I can deal with eight more puppies, more than Az imagining I am one for a single second. I need an exact date for those puppies or something more concrete than your mere promise of getting him some.

The Death Angel ignoring totally the discussion yet liking very much the way it was going, went to the camp bed of It and touching her wrist with his cool hands woke her up. When she opened her black demonic eyes, blinking at the sight of Az, she uttered in a mumble,

-Hi, Az, I slept.

Smiling back to her, the Death Angel answered,

-I know Soldier, I made you, for you deserved a nice sleeping break for once. How do you feel?

Giving him a bear hug the teenager answered,

-I feel buzzing and refreshed.

-Good, first we need you to drink a potion. It's freaking blue but don't ask as it's Gab's creation.

Getting up, and spreading her bat wings and arms in a big waking up yawn extending her body up, the Beast asked, in good spirit,

-I can drink the blue thingy stuff, after all I ate rodents for eight years, so it can't be worse. When can I be allowed to get back to my incarnated self?

The Death Angel getting the glass flask containing the potion upon the desk grinned wickedly as he answered,

-Can't be worse? Coming from Gab and bright cobalt blue, I would still be worried myself. But as my hands read him for the last two hours, I think we do have a true winner of an Anti-swallowing-swallowers potion here that works. His processes and methods if a little unusual are very effective. It truly might be humanity saving and preserving your full Being strength at all times. Hence you should drink it all.

As Az handed the fizzy and smelly blue potion to It, Gabriel apologised and cautioned,

-I am sorry, Bambi that will taste rank, I don't do the sweetened stuff of witches. Keep your demonic shape for a good hour after ingestion for it to work at it's best. More if you can. The anti-virus will last for about six months before needing another ingestion. The recipe is well nailed for you and your genetic make up. I need to change it just a little for the other soldiers of the Angelic Army and I will have you all safe from the Swallowers's bug.

The teenager started drinking the potion, tapping her clawed feet doing so to encourage and force herself to swallow. The more she swallowed, her wings started to flap with extreme force against one another. When she had finished it all, she threw the bottle and grabbed the edge of the desk nearby her, her claws digging in the wood by a good inch and fire came straight from her mouth. The intensely hot flames reaching the glass tank with the demonic brain, dissolved it to liquid glass while the brain vanished within seconds in a little pile of ashes.

Realising the damage, the Beast put her hands in front of her mouth sealing it, to prevent any more bursting flames, yet coughing upon them and burning her own self.

Stunned from the scene the first Angel to gather his wits about him was Raphael. Going to the teenager Wrath ordered, while he held her,

-She needs help, she is choking on her flames. She is going to have bad internal damage if she doesn't let those out. I am taking her outside, bring me water, lots of it, Az. Gab, needless to say, sweetening the stuff in the future is strongly advised.

Teletransporting It-666 to the yard, Wrath removed her hands from her mouth and maintained them behind her back strongly as he told,

-Let it all out Soldier, you are outside, aim for the sky if you can control that bout of fire. You are going to be alright, just let it go out of you. I am here and Az is going to be there in a minute to help you.

She obeyed, as her flames came out from her mouth powerfully, aiming for the cloudy grey winter sky. When the Death Angel appeared, her flow of flames was finally slowly running out, she coughed a few more fire balls, then it stopped. Shivering, her sheepish and apologising demonic eyes tearful, she tried to talk but could not, so she used telepathy instead sending her message to the three Angels,

-I am so sorry. I never expected to react so violently to the potion. When I realised I could not help the fire coming out, I tried to contain it from damaging Gab's lab by swallowing it back.

Removing his strong hold from her, Wrath acknowledged with a sarcastic smile,

-Well, if I would certainly not miss that freaky demonic brain watching us in Gab's lab, I would miss you very much, Soldier, if you had burnt yourself all away to make sure his damn tree house didn't burn down. Let's cool you down a little, for you did reach a few Fahrenheits far above safety level, Being. Azryel, assess her damages, internal and external. Her hands started blistering badly and need immediate cooling to not carry on consuming away. We can't have her soldiering without her skillful mitts. I will administrate the water. It will hurt a bit as you drink but your tongue needs that extinguishing effect right now. Stay still and you will avoid choking again. Az, bet on Gab's reaction on that one? Understanding or missing his brainy demon's sample? I think it could be a close call for once, I made him feel shit about his powerful potion. He needs to correct the taste of it, I can't have my soldiers burning inside out drinking it. It is only just lucky that he had the most willing lab rat and the strongest one at hand to try his stuff without question.

Concentrating upon salvaging the hands of It-666, Azryel stated,

-He definitely needs to correct that potion. It is far too powerful. He aimed to protect for the longer term, the dosage is too high for one to cope with. Maybe he should go for three months or less? What do you think would be suitable for our Angels, Soldier? Your mitts are getting there by the way, all is under control. As for the bet, I will go for the compassionate and understanding Gab. For Christ's sake, he has to see that she preferred burning herself big time to protect his lab.

It answered him by telepathy sending the same message to Wrath's mind,

-No more than a month for Angels and three for Archangels and myself. The taste is disgusting but the major issue of the anti virus is its strength, so much so an intravenous injection might be preferable if it can be considered. Yet I will have to try it first and see how I would react to that to be able to recommend it over the other method of absorption.

As both Angels were mending her back to health, the Archangel Gabriel appeared in the yard, his lab coat blackened in areas. He asked worryingly via telepathy,

-How is Bambi? I put the flames out in the lab, no extensive damage done, just superficial, really. I tasted what she drank. It's not only vile, it's bombastic. I am ever so sorry. I would make it palatable next time around, I promise.

Turning to him Wrath asked him sternly out loud raising his eyebrows,

-Pray, what do you mean by bombastic, Gab?

His sheepish nephew answered in their Angelic minds before pulling his tongue to him,

-I mean that. It almost blew my tongue off with a single drop.

Looking at the star shaped hole in his tongue, Wrath and Azryel burst out laughing.

The Death Angel wiping a tear from his jubilant eyes from his strong laugh, could not resist teasing and scolding the Archangel,

-Someone French kisses are going to be exceedingly fun from now on. I definitely think that you just learnt a lesson. Your guinea pigs, Gab are proper humans, Beings or Angels which need to have a little consideration. Trying your stuff on yourself first, rather than when it is too late could be an excellent idea. It would prevent you from blowing the guts of my soldiers but also might blow your crazy professor's head off to a sensible level of sanity.

Having her throat and own tongue now fully fixed, a sorted It-666 intervened, going to stand by Gabriel,

-That would be a terrible idea. He would get badly damaged and would not be able to run the Angelic clinic being a casualty himself. I have no problems with carrying on being the lab rat, I would be able to tell him when it is safe for others or unsafe. I could help him correct and fine tune his discoveries. I sincerely believe that we need to encourage and support his investigating mind, not treat it as insane. Although his ideas carry potential risk, I am ready to take that risk upon my shoulders, for they also have a potential to solve and help in our futures battles.

The Archangel Gabriel gave her an impulsive tender hug silently. He closed his eyes, with the realisation that he wanted that Being as his eternal partner. He was truly touched by her defending stance especially after what just happened. He broke his embrace and looked at Wrath and Azryel with embarrassment and resignation. There was no hiding place for him under their combined scrutiny. He confessed in both their minds,

-I can't deny it as compassion anymore, I am deeply in love with her Being. Her great kindness touches my heart, and I would have to be blind and deaf to escape loving her. I want to devote myself to her as much as she does for me by her constant self sacrifices.

Coming to him, Wrath patted his nephew's shoulder reassuringly, talking to him by telepathy while Azryel enjoined It to follow him as they needed to make a move very soon for their mission, allowing the two Archangels their private necessary talk.

-The way she stood up for you was very moving. Like her adopted father, she certainly knows how to put a plea forward. There was no mistake to be made that it was her loving you and not wanting you to get hurt at any point in time. She is a very caring Being and a true Sweet Heart. I was touched myself by her plea for I very well know how hurt she was in trying to contain herself to not burn your tree house down just now. For you to try to understand her reactions to your potion after seeing how appalling they were did take some courage. To tackle the leftover flames, ignore the few damages in the lab as inconsequential was your own empathy at work. I more than welcome your devotion to her Gabriel. Make your devotion not a self sacrificing one, make yours one that will bring her back to health again and again and again, each time my soldier decides to use her good heart for others, getting thoroughly hurt doing so. Be there for her at the Angelic clinic to welcome her after any battles. Be there for her at your tree-house in which you kindly accepted her into, and in which she feels home. You are the original Master of the Beast which means she will lay at your feet humbly each time she comes back home from her fights. It will be comparable to Az and I Being's bonds yet yours will be strengthened by a powerful love. As a Master you have to nurture that bond. Hugging, listening very carefully and understanding where one comes from are essential. We mended It, Az and I this time around, we expect you to take ownership the next time she comes to you wounded. Be prepared. Let me repair your blown up tongue, but don't talk to me just think of what I just said, for I need to go now with my soldiers on our mission for today. It should be easy so expect Us for dawn. If not worry and call upon Demeter. Find out if her spell upon Boston was still working for I didn't give her the authorisation to lift it yet. Which means my all crew should be coming back to you safely tonight. Do me the favour of the safe check as the sun goes down below the horizon, not before.

Kneeling by Wrath, Archangel Gabriel bowed his head in total allegiance. He felt the hand of Raphael giving him back his power of speech and repairing his tongue. His thanks were sent by telepathy as he kissed the hand of the elder Archangel respectfully who teletransported elsewhere.

Reappearing in the tree house's kitchen, Wrath saw his Angelic soldiers finishing their breakfast, and Az and It starting theirs. Workmaster welcomed him,

-What will it be for you Archangel?

Declining the offer, Wrath answered,

-Nothing for we should be departing now.

Pointing to a corner of the kitchen where a black mamba was moving in a vivarium, which had its four internal panels bleeding, the human demanded,

-Wrath, my girl did her mojo on that damn decoy snake of yours and she deserves to eat something before she goes on your dangerous mission, and properly seated that is, and so do Az and so do you. What is it going to be for you if you do not want the burning oil from my frying pan on your lap?

Taking a seat the Archangel agreed smirking at the daring threat of Walter,

-Well, I guess we can spare fifteen minutes. I will have scrambled eggs with your sauteed woodland mushrooms if you still have them, with toasted bread. Your girl does indeed deserve a seat by any table and to eat properly.

Noticing Caroline eating at the table, he added with a bright smile,

-Our bride to be is already up. Eager to go shopping with Asha to get all you need for tomorrow, Caro?

His niece giving him back his smile, replied,

-Yes very eager, Uncle, however we are going shopping this afternoon. I am up early because I am going to the clinic. Asha will give his angelic tuition to Micky this morning and my Blondie Bear will be fight training with the rest of your soldiers. Since his trip to Hell, he keeps saying that the training Az gave him has been priceless. He praised Azryel to me as the ultimate warrior, who should open a 'Bruce Lee' type of school for all.

Her Uncle, a little incredulous upon the last part, asked,

-Is that so? I thought you were a born pacifist Walter. I am surprised to hear you are keen to learn how to fight properly. Never too late, I guess.

Putting his breakfast in front of him, the man replied unfazed,

-Very much so. I am still a pacifist yet from my trip to Hell I gathered it was very handy to have some fighting skill, and I am keen to learn more. I am also a man of opinion, and if you slapped me you will never see me turn to present you my other cheek for I would more than likely have responded by punching your nose. Now, tonight make sure you bring my girl back in one piece and before sunset, otherwise there will be some nose punching and slapping.

A deeply amused Azryel intervened,

-Stop threatening an Archangel, especially one that doesn't stand fools too well, human. His patience has limits and if he decides to kick your arse, I will have to pick you up with a little spoon. You can reassure yourself that he has the best interest of your daughter at heart, that him and I will protect her, and that it is our plan to be back by sunset.

The teenager added feeling strongly about it,

-I am a soldier, Pa. You need to come to terms that I will get scratches and bruises in battles, but I will tell you what: I will always come back from them because of those two, Wrath and Az. I also know that they always fix me right up, in a Being's way which maybe hard to understand for humans. Knowing that I will be picked up and looked after when wounded, makes me dare more to ensure the protection of others. I want to help and participate in any fights, battles and missions of Wrath. This is my calling, Pa, and I am conscious there are risks, but I am more than willing to take them. Please, do not take it upon my Army's leader Wrath and its general Azryel, if I ever come back injured from any battles. Please accept that being a soldier is very much my choice, it gives my life, a purpose, all my supernatural skills and powers a beneficial use.

An emotional Walter came to her, putting his hand upon the clawed hand of the Beast which was resting on the table, held it in a reassuring fashion, tapping it gently, before stating,

-I am very proud of you. You are one brave and courageous Being. I approve of your choice of being a soldier with all my heart. Yet, my It, I will always lookout for your every return with sheer anxiety and I know that Gab does too. We saw you in Hell and we know the type of fight that you face. At the last Boston trip, we were upon that platform worried sick for you, non smoking Gab was chain smoking all night and I was turning around him helplessly like a tiger in its cage until we saw you arrive and in a bad state. I do understand the Being ways of recovery as I witnessed it that night being by poor Az as he helped you out. I have also been mended by him a fair few times now. This does give me a reassurance, yes, but not as much as seeing you safe and well in the first place. I care for you, Being, as soon as I opened my arms to remove you from the cage you were held in, my heart was ready to give you TLC. You have to bear that in mind, in your battlefields, my young soldier, that we love you and want you back in one piece. For my sake and Gab's one, take calculated risks, where I can behold my daughter alive at the end. Because I have a dream, the one to hold that very hand above mine one day, and give her a way at her very own wedding. As you deserved to be very much loved I will not give you away lightly, and it will have to be the very best of man, Angel or Being and they will have to ask me your hand in the purest tradition. Pray, why couldn't you have been the zoo keeper at Gab's tree house, your Solomon's skill would have been right at home?

Standing up, It gave a massive hug to her adopted father. She loved that human to bits, his good and caring heart, his wit and last but not least his humour. When she sat back she replied,

-Well, I do not think Gab intends to have a zoo at his tree house any time soon. Yet, since my chipmunk stunt, he allowed Bud to be here, then the two hamsters which he had the idea of, and then he accepted for Az to get eight Great Dane puppies in the very near future, that's without mentioning the Evil black mamba and the Water Cobra. Soldiering, it is a calling most of all, Pa. Gab tried to tempt me to be a doctor like him, but I do not want to receive and deal with the wounded, I want to prevent them. I need to be on the field and protect them as much as I can with my whole strength and powers. However, I will bear in mind what you said, because I want your very hand to give me a way too, one day, very much so. You always make me dream of the unthinkable, Pa and somehow the unthinkable does happen. I was an experienced pessimistic before you arrived and stood by my cage and turned my whole conception of the World upside down. I thought I never had a place in it, and I learnt otherwise from you, Gab, Az and Wrath. I know now I can make a world of difference and earn my wings and I intend to do so. There's a few human words and things I still need to know about for comprehending everything. You and Gab use TLC an awful lot when talking to me, what's that? What is kissing the French? Why would it be more fun than kissing anyone else? Does Gab love kissing the French?

A nose diving Azryel sarcastically smirked at her last questions and attempted to finish his breakfast without being noticed. Yet he could feel the darkly disapproving grey-green gaze of Wrath upon him, as Workmaster scratched his goatee inquisitively, yet showing clear signs of anxiety by fiddling with the last button of his white, black and red tartan hunter's shirt, opened upon a black Rolling Stones T-shirt. The Death Angel was waiting expectantly to what the man would have to say and hoped it would be pure enjoyment when finally Walter tried to answer his adopted daughter,

-TLC are three little letters which means a great deal to all of us around the World. For they stand for Tender Love and Care. When anyone uses their heart that is what you could expect in a better World. At the very moment, humans are indulging in SBR, aka Shoot or Blow your Religious counterparts, which is far from their religious teachings and doesn't show or display one ounce of tenderness, love or care. They are simply heartless humans. Without TLC you will end up in a concentration camp because an ideology was promoted and implemented. With TLC someone is there to hide you and save you until the madness passes. Without TLC someone will ask you to recite his own prayers without a fault in the middle of a shopping centre in front of your kids and shoot you if you can't, heartlessly, even if you were a decent human and a very good father. Simple factor is your religion doesn't match his, he is into religious totalitarianism, he cleaned you away without any more questions. The scariest thing on Earth is the nonsense of beliefs, cults, ideologies, which drive humans to become inhuman, to forget their own hearts and humanity and kill each other heartlessly without remorse. With TLC you have nations catering for every souls, being cosmopolitan, and fully democratic. With TLC, everyone Tend the Laws to Care for every human being. As for Gab kissing French people, he kissed the Au-Pair, Cecile, hello on her cheek like it is done in France, yet he never multiplied those cheek kisses as much as it could be done over there, in the Gallic hexagon. Sometimes it reaches a super flux of four pecks per cheek depending on the fashion. I never kissed a French bird to tell you it was more fun than anyone else, I would never be racist either, I would give everyone a fair chance to impress me.

Caroline interrupted him right off,

-You can forget about giving anyone a fair chance, I am the only one claiming it.

Going to her, Walter kissed her mouth in an appeasing fashion. Azryel smiling thoroughly could not help to get involved,

-That was a peck on her lips and no French kiss, Workmaster.

Getting the hint, Walt looked upon Azryel with desperation, becoming livid, making the math of the previous questions of It-666, repeated in a muted voice, which grew stronger the more he spoke,

-Gabriel and French kisses... They do not go well together. I remember him banning them from his properties. In his clinic, there is a notice saying 'no kissing allowed, keep your germs to yourself'. Gabriel is definitely not the kissing type. No swirling tongues for him, heaven forbid, he would sanitise his mouth with bleach, if no one stops him. As for you, my It, the family rule is no French kisses until at least 18 years old, and engaged. Those can lead to other things and are not to try until then.

Giggling endlessly, Caroline teased him,

-Come, come, Walt, are you exaggerating and over-protecting? 18 for French kisses, I had my first one at 17. It didn't lead me into more as it was an appalling saliva thing then. It works like trial and error. I could not be messed about, and I am sure our 'Blondie' will not be messed about either. I trust her own will and judgement and so should you. You can influence It but not dictate her. Caro is on the parental guidance board now.

The Archangel Raphael smiling thoroughly agreed,

-Thank heavens for that, for Caro is a breath of fresh air. Come Workmaster, you are being an arse just as I was when my niece started dating. I could not come to terms with the fact she was, yet when my spies came back to me each time she had a date, I laughed my heart out. A couple were taken to the emergencies, saliva guy was one of them. The only one of her dates, she decided to present to me was you. She was 19 and blown away by your French kisses done to perfection, but also that you were an anti-war student leading demonstrations in Washington and major towns. I was very worried and gave you the coldest reception you could ever get. Yet, watching you ever so closely, and having hawk eyes Gab on your case, I warmed to you everyday that passed. In a sentence Walt, do not be over ruling for you might be missing the real love between two hearts, and it always goes beyond boundaries because it is pure love. Cast, colour, religion, wealth, nationalities has nothing to do with it. Love rules, always. By the way, Breakfast was delicious, human. Thank you for feeding my incarnated Angels this morning. Talk to Caro about how I raised her and learn upon it not to repeat my mistakes. I will make sure your daughter comes back safe and well from Boston.

Standing up Wrath ordered, and once his Army left the room he carried on talking to the man,

-All of you to your duties, now. Boston's mission crew in the van. It, you are in charge of that snake from now on. Az, carry the vivarium for her to the van. Legna you are in charge of the Army training session today. Yffub, you had the incarnated chance to enjoy the teachings of Bruce Lee, treat our man Walt to them this morning. I am sure he will enjoy to have his human arse kicked that way, as much as I am convinced that he will stroke it better with lots of Bruce Lee vocal noises. Workmaster, make the most of this morning's lesson, and have a lovely afternoon shopping with Caro and Micky. I know you have concerns about money but I want you to forget them all for the sake of Caro and your wedding, therefore ignore I will be paying for it. You will never be in my debt either. I want you two to have the best day of your lives tomorrow for yesterday you made mine Workmaster, by proposing to my niece again. I was deeply saddened when she decided to leave you six years ago thinking Micky was unsafe and I was also deeply worried about you. Our estrangement since my non-approval of your very first wedding prevented me to get involved. I can confess to you that this was one of my biggest remorses in my eternal life, to let loved ones slip away from my tender love and care. For when I finally heard what happened to you and her, I wished I would have been there to help you two throughout. The Archangelic net of Gab was enough to catch you back and put you back on track thankfully. I consider you as family Walter Workmaster. I hope you will consider me as such and forgive me in time. When I say sorry, and I hardly say so, I mean it, Walt. I only hope your forgiveness will make you respect me once more if I ever deserve it to your eyes. Think about what I said and please, don't you ever reproduce my mistakes.

Taking the Archangelic hand within his human hands, Walter Workmaster responded,

-Wrath, you are an Angel, correction, Archangel, with definitely a different edge to you. It may be grand time I pay respect to you. Like you said I have been an arse especially with you. I never expected good from you only dread. I must say like me you listen when someone talks, pay attention and correct yourself. My girl It has always spoke of you very highly. I know she rates you as much as laying her own life for you. Since you came and dealt with her with Azryel, I do rate you guys, myself more than I can express. I saw her grow from a suicidal little thing to someone with a purpose. You made her achieve a massive step which I could not have done on my own. Wrath, please accept my sincere apologies for my years of disrespect.

Embracing the man, smiling widely, Wrath answered,

-Please accept mine for the same reasons. Whatever happens in my Army I will make sure we bring your girl back. It is an Archangelic promise, human. We will never give up on her, like I will never give up on you. See you tonight.

Verse 34. Of Godzi-Rats and Angels...

In the van going to Boston, wrapped in her demonic bat wings, the Beast was sitting very quietly and anxiously, yet she did not know exactly why as the worst she could have ever met there was Eremiel and he was captured and boxed away. She kept tapping her clawed fingers with great rapidity and irregularity upon her thighs, each time denting her thick leathery skin a little more, until pearls of her blood appeared. Lost in her own dreary thoughts, she didn't notice the incarnated Angelic soldiers, blocking their nostrils one after another. Until one of them dared to touch the tip of her wing trying to recall her,

-Pray, It, do not think of the sewers that intensely. The only two windows in this van are at the front and we have to stay at the back for the long drive. This mission will be easier than last, much easier for you. Try to reassure yourself a little.

Azryel siting by her sides looked upon her, tried to assess her nervous state as he demanded,

-Soldier, open your wings, I can smell your blood from here, and as it is full of that gloriously scented potion of Gabriel, it isn't smelling like flowery meadows right now.

Shyly, she obeyed, standing up cramped in order to do so and folded her wings neatly upon her back. She stood before Death, who knew exactly within seconds of looking at her what had happened under her wings. He teased,

-Right, let's seal all those puncture points before we are all gasified alive. I could get you little stress balls to squeeze with your claws before any mission if you wish to, Soldier, that would be much better than doing a piercing spree on your thighs. Besides after all the trouble you went into swallowing that dreaded Anti Virus, every drop counts, so your blood needs to stay in. With the smell, it will have to for six months, the motion is passed with our Angelic noses, that it is a 'in' with your blood at all times.

The teenager managed to smile back at her general as he placed his healing hands upon her thighs, and apologised readily,

-I am ever so sorry, I was lost in my thoughts and just anxious. I didn't mean to stink like hell doing so.

One soldier replied straight away, and exhibited to her the handle of his own dagger,

-You are forgiven, your case of nerves is understandable since what happened in Boston last time. I do not attack myself with my nails anymore although I did so in the past, upon my forearms. Azryel got me this special dagger. It absorbs my fears and anxieties. Do you see the nail digging marks in the handle? Just look at the intricately patterned blade now, it represents the fear of my opponents facing me and terraced by me. When I started my Angelic journey, the blade was a shiny silver. Then it became silver and black, now the black pattern dominates the silver, as demons fear me more than I do fear them. When that blade becomes entirely black, I will know all my fears have absolutely disappeared.

Death ordered,

-On that bench, It, you are sorted. I wish it was that easy each time I have to mend you. As I mentioned every soldier does face anxiety, fear and nerves. I will always be here for any of my crew when it happens. You can just hold my hand and I will read you through Soldier, and know how to deal with you.

Before he finished his sentence, the Beast taking her place by him gave him her clawed hand to hold. Azryel smiled at her eagerness, asking,

-Still not afraid of me, Soldier?

She replied pressing his hand,

-Always very afraid Az, especially when I have done something stupid I could not control. Yet I need your readings to reassure me that I am still a safe Being. They are my spot checks. The day I shun them I would have turned for the worse. I expect and respect your hands strongly to get rid of me then, as fast as you can. The day they would fail your expectations I expect just the same.

Reading her Being, the Death Angel could not help admire the deep honesty she displayed day in and out since he had met her and prior to that when she had sought the Angels out to deal with her. All he could read was a brave teenage soul full of anxieties, but also full of love and respect for others. Her devotion to the Angelic Army and her human family was so strong that he felt her powerful will to protect them at any point in time. Maybe he had an anxious soldier, but she was the soundest one he ever met since the advent of Asha. Smiling to the teenage girl, the Death Angel squeezed her hand back,

-You are still very safe Soldier, so much so that I can vouch for you, right now. So, your new mum hinted on the name Walt and her agreed on for you. What do you think of Blondie, better or worse than It?

The teenager looked at him, her heart feeling more at peace and secure. She confided,

-Any name would be better than It. I have no clue where it came from yet I like it. It does not give me an Evil number which I am very grateful about. I would love to know its meaning for Walt and Caro.

Thoughtfully smiling for a few seconds the Death Angel answered her,

-I need to introduce you to human culture for it is very deep, rich and has a beautiful history most of the time. Knowing their cultures will make you understand them better but also acknowledge how cherished they can be at their individual best. For Blondie's choice, I can give you all the info. Workmaster's favourite movie of all time is

Sergio Leone's 'The Good, the Bad and the Ugly'. The part of the Good, played by famed actor Clint Eastwood has no name apart for the one of Blondie, which is based simply on his hair colour. The character of the Good is very much liked, feared yet controversial and lethal when needed. If we are back on time tonight, we could watch that film all together with Walt. It's a must see and the music by Ennio Morricone carries the film to the sublime. It is just a little nugget of spaghetti western culture worth the 'Ecstasy of Gold': awesome. As for Caro, her culture trips are Joss Whedon'ian, she called Walt 'Blondie Bear' because of 'Spike' the platinum blond vampire was called so by one of his ex' in a TV program called 'Buffy'. She loved the character 'Spike' who sacrificed himself for others at the end of the whole series. Although, he does comes back in the spin off series of 'Angel'. Walt owns the whole collection of both and I know that Gab has been watching a fair few episodes since we arrived at the tree house. He is hooked upon the Buffy's and Angel's. So you are Blondie for your adoptive parents if you want and agree with their cultures. Your choice, your call, your freedom, your own name stays with you for life, you have a right to change it if it displeases you, or just does not suit you. Your own choice at age of conscience is always primordial and prevailing. The cultures of your parents may not agree with your own heart, and being imposed upon by a filial something is less than love but some sort of disrespect of your freedom of choice which could be hard to deal with. To the extreme that disrespect can be perceived as hatred of your own being and go far, to take an example, Eremiel, your birth father which tried to kill you when he knew you would never follow his hate of humanity path, he wanted you to. Around the World many children who have not turned the way they were intended by their parents, have been bullied by them, humiliated, demeaned, ignored, ostracised and at its worst murdered. As for the Workmasters, this will never happen with them, as your name choice was very much a common brainstorming, which also involved Micky, Gab and my advice was asked upon the result. The final say is all yours because they are all ready to go back to the drawing board if you do not like it.

Nodding full of understanding, she enquired full of curiosity,

-What did 'Blondie' mean for Michael, Gabriel and you?

Azryel knew he had succeeded in diverting the mind of his young
soldier from all her anxieties towards something altogether more
cheerful, the fact that she had been adopted and given a chance to
live happily within a loving human family. By the sheer glow of her
eyes, he also knew that she was very interested to know what Gab
thought of the name choice. Without further ado he indulged her,

-Micky has heard his dad being called Blondie Bear by his mum all
his life. For him, because you are adopted, his father is stamping you
with his own favourite pet name making you family. Like we have a
plethora of John and John Junior, in his young mind we have
Blondie Bear senior and Blondie Beast junior. For me, his
interpretation worked like a little treat to my ears and heart. I just
loved it, as much as I did the reasons for the choice of your name
by Walt and Caro. I think it is a cool name to bestow. A famous
eighties female singer icon has it and her most famous hit was
'Atomic'.

Grinning ever so widely Az carried on,

-No pun intended, it was a very good hit. As a general, I like to see
my soldiers not missing their targets... As for Gab, well, like his
sister he is getting hooked on Joss Whedon's 'Buffy' and all the
characters. You can blame Walt for demanding a TV to not be
bored in the tree-house for that one. Now Gab associates you as a
twisted mix of Buffy and Spike. I will brush up on your human
cultural education when we have time. We will start by 'The three
musketeers' of Dumas, the favourite book of Wrath and I. Our
Angelic Army motto is directly inspired by it. So is it going to be
'Blondie'?

The teenager smiled peacefully, as she replied,

-I will watch their cultural references and make my decision. From
what you are telling me it is a strong contender in my mind already.
In the cabin in the Black Forest, we had only very few books, about
a dozen, one was the bible and the rest was about the lives of

Saints. I did find the latter interesting and inspiring. It made me think of the human world very much and I could not understand why I had to live apart from all humans apart for Tess. Later my Tutor explained it to me. Yet I was stupid enough to give into the temptation one day as I ran to meet the school children.

She fell silent took a breath and added,

-Being found by Workmaster was the best moment in my life.

Suddenly Wrath turned the volume of the radio up with a big fat winning grin upon his face, and demanded,

-No more chatting in the back just listen.

A formal lady's voice presented,

'It has been confirmed to us that the result of investigations at Paul Peterson's burnt down house in Boston and at a wood which he has the propriety of, is the warrant for the arrest of the politician. It comes as a bombshell as Paul Peterson always seemed to be a strong contender for the presidency. His fans and followers are chocked and horrified at the news. Our journalist going to the headquarters of the politician was refused entry but has confirmed that Paul Peterson is on the run. He has not been seen for the last 24 hours. The gruesome discovery in the wood, of human remains upon every single tree by a team of geological experts who went there to investigate the apparition of a giant sinkhole a few days ago, has left everyone stupefied by the barbaric horror that was carried out for over a decade. We were unable to interview the leader of the geologists Raphael Wrath who had warned the FBI of the grizzly findings. The forensic team of the FBI is still working day and night to associate all the victims with missing persons and has so far released a list of 21 individuals identified. The relatives of some have been asked to come forward while others have been informed. The FBI is now investigating if the practice of ritualistic human sacrifice is widespread in the political world and by the few names whispered in their corridors, by the rich and famous. More to come on this terrifying story later.'

A proud Wrath commented as he turned down the radio,

-This is what I call a 'Demon-Buster'. This one will not be able to show his face in the human world anymore nor gain the presidency he was aiming for. Well done crew, we nicely undermined that bugger of a Demon. High five!

All went to high five the Archangel in turn then each other with satisfied smile upon their faces. Azryel asked out loud as he sat back,

-I wonder where the bastard is hiding his demonic arse?

By him the young Beast's eyes turned from her demonic black to ruby red and her head turned slowly in a 360 degree spin. The Angels looked at her worryingly and all ever so slightly shitting bricks, apart for Azryel who demanded with a deadly smirk drawing upon his lips, teasing them in the meantime,

-Party trick turned useful, I like that, very neat. I definitely should show you more horror movies. What's the score, Soldier? Did you scan him out on Earth's surface?

She answered in an eerie voice,

-Below ground, general, he is at the very place we are going, in the Boston's sewers and the witch Cato is still with him. Demeter's shield is still very much in place and Cato is wondering if she has lost all her own powers. While bad arse P is thinking he lost his glorious luck with the runaway Eremiel. He is desperate to get his hands on an Evil snake. Both took a blow but do not underestimate them. She has an Army of Swallowers although not by her at this very minute, but we don't know how she can call them out. If it is magical, there is no worry to be had, if it is physical we can shit ourselves and leg it as fast as we can. As for P, he has not lost the part of his followers involved in his crimes, and some of them are powerful demons.

Seeing all the faces of his soldiers deeply sinking into worry, the Death Angel commented cheerfully, tapping the clawed hand of It-666 doing so,

-Don't you just love her! We just acquired the most powerful radar on the planet. It makes the difference between being prepared and unprepared. Plan of action, Wrath, deploying decoy snake is not going to be a piece of cake anymore. Have you got any bright ideas to make your former bright idea painless?

Unfazed Wrath replied immediately,

-Those two and Swallowers can not cross Archangelic fire without killing themselves ultimately. For the Swallowers it all depends on how many they are and how disposable in the eye of Cato. The feat could teach Us that crucial info.

Narrowing his eyes in a displeased fashion, Azryel barked,

-Not good enough Raphael. I am not ready to lose a single of those soldiers to put a fake snake in P's hands so that he could rattle it in peace if it works like intended. And I am certainly not ready to lose one of them for you to gather info on the enemy we are dealing with. For your information, my Angelic soldiers are not, underlined and bold letters, 'disposable' individuals. Soldiers, does any one have a better idea? So we will have a ring of Archangelic fire surrounding P and the witch, but we need more than that, just in case the worst case scenario occurs. Fire away, I am waiting and thinking myself.

One soldier hazarded,

-Isn't Boston a teletransport free zone at the moment? If so Cato's Army could not respond to her call.

Wrath answered him,

-It is a secluded zone at the moment for teletransportation but what if they use other means, we do not know enough about Swallowers until we grab one alive or dead and bring it to Gabriel for thorough investigation. This could be one of our chances to do so but at this early stage, a very risky one.

It proposed with confidence,

-I can deal with bringing a sample of the Swallowers home if we ever meet one, Wrath. Got a f'in twisted potion within me that should protect me from their swallowing touch, and it needs to have a real trial. We just need to find a way to keep the Army safe. I could use my army of rats, since I cleaned their sewers they just love me.

Smiling wickedly, Raphael stated,

-That's my Eager Beaver. I started liking rodents very much. Which size of rat soldiers are we talking about this time around, It?

-Well, because, I am slightly crapping myself, I was thinking two metres long gigantic rats, with teeth that could sink into a Swallower's shoulder injecting my special kind of rabies for them...

-I like that, I like that very much, indeed, this kiddo is phenomenal.

Moving his index upright in the air in a small circular fashion, Az could not resist teasing,

-We kind of gathered that one out, with the head spinning and all, Wrath. Also we were a bit unsettled by the thousands of rats we saw last time around, especially when they bumped up in size reaching the ground. Now we are talking of Godzilla rats, double the size of the first round, with the addition of rabies, will they recognise my Angels from Demons and Swallowers? That is all I need to know to pass the motion.

It-666 nodded with a wicked smile, winking at him,

-Trust me, the Godzi-rats will know the difference and attack the right kind. We could do with no filthy water to wade in and out. For ease of movement when we get out of there running but also, no water would render my rats much more efficient at their tasks.

One of the Angels grinning, deeply amused by the use of rats of the Beast, asked her,

-General 'Ratissimo', pray, enlighten Us upon the private tasks of the rat soldiers? And is it at all possible to add one specific order to eight of them, like assigning a Godzi-rat bodyguard to each of Us?

Unfazed by the mockery she replied,

-If it can make you not chicken out of Wrath's mission, I can ratify that with my rat soldiers. If needed I could supper-dupper sized your personal Godzi-rat to three metres, but I can only do that for the most terrified of Us as we will be then in danger of rat blocking the Boston's sewers. Their tasks is kept simple, overwhelming the assailants and preventing them to touch any of you guys with the added bonus of biting the Swallowers to give them rabies.

Laughing his heart out, Azryel putting his arm around the shoulders of It-666, patting them, stated,

-I must admit that I do enjoy working at your side Being, there's never a dull moment. I have no clue of how your brain works those weird ideas out but they are superbly twisted and clever. You are showing remarkable capabilities to think outside the box not unlike Archangel Gabriel. It makes you a resourceful soldier and a definite plus in this Army and with that Solomon skill of yours, the cherry on top of the ice cream. I am in favour of the Godzi rats, one hundred per cent. Now tell me, why inoculating the Swallowers with rabies? As for you guys, which one of you want a super-duper Godzi rat?

When all the Angelic hands lifted themselves up, Death shook his head in half desperation, and barked,

-Wrath, did you molly cuddle my guys in my absence? They are all shitting bricks again.

Uncle Raphael looking at his Angels with disappointment ruled,

-I won't be accused of molly cuddling, Az. Let's teach them a good lesson, no supper-dupper Godzi rats for anyone, and if I hear a whisper of complaint there will not be any rodent bodyguard at all. For Christ sake when will you ever learn to curb that fear. You are all extremely good fighters not little school girls with pony tails and lollipops to fight the enemy with. It, on your account I totally agree with Azryel, you are one soldier I am very proud to bestow in my Army. What you said at breakfast this morning, touched me and showed you as a strong, dutiful and committed Being. I appreciated your stand and the deep respect emanating from you for someone so young, and I wish my Angels could take you as an example. You do have your bouts of nerves at times however it never stopped you from thinking on your own two feet but more importantly on the field and missions, you were always very brave. Besides, it took some sheer guts to go to Hell almost alone to prevent one of Us, Gab to go there regularly and find what he was after. As for protecting and preventing, I take my hat of to you Soldier, for I witnessed you doing so many times now. Those soldiers sitting around you, should thank you to have worked out a way to protect their Angelic arses in those sewers. Now, like Az I am interested to know the reason behind the rabies given to the Swallowers. For that is a clear addition to my initial plan which was easy come, easy go, however we acknowledged it is probably not going to be the case.

As Wrath saw his soldiers going to shake the clawed hand of the Beast one by one, It's demeanour was one of great shyness, and if she had been in her incarnated human shell he had no doubt that she would have been blushing thoroughly too. Sending a message via telepathy to Azryel only, he recommended,

-That soldier is getting there faster than I expected, yet her confidence about her own self is still lagging far behind. I know years of tortures are going to be hard to erase but she needs to understand that she is fully backed up, endorsed and embraced. Whoever she is, we will always be there to help her control her powers. How do we raise her confidence up, Az? Is it a good idea to raise it at this moment in time, as you did a spot check read on her just now? Do you think she will respond to praises or something else? I am dying to know what the rabies deal is all about, pure evilness or else?

His general replied to him the same way, as he considered her very shy gestures and how she tried to squeeze her bat wings to a very uncomfortable position, so as to not take much space in the van,

-I do not think she will ever accept her bestial and evil appearance, Wrath. Her conscience of it undermines her and reminds her every second, of her links with hell and demons. She has a very teenage mind and craves acceptance by every means. This Army is the best place for her Being to blossom. Every single word she said at Breakfast is valid and true. We can attempt to raise her confidence for from the spot check, you have a very devoted soldier in her, Wrath. Praises do not make her proud but uncomfortable. You will not be able to make her respond to you either by buying stuff of value to her, for she is not materialistic whatsoever. I think she is a Being that could respond with quality time spent with her, not using her as a soldier, but pure one to one or even as a group, with moments of bounding friendship. Simply letting her know that her company can be and is sought.

As he finished his message, he enjoined the young Beast,

-Soldier, the rabies explanation, now overdue by sixty seconds.

Joining her clawed hands together and twisting them about, she tried to explain,

-I thought and I can be very wrong doing so, that if we could set our hands upon a Swallower without rabies, and one with the disease, it would be two very valuable samples of Swallowers to bring back to Gab. Rabies is a well known disease which is fully documented upon, and bestows a vaccine in case we have a Swallower on the loose. So it would give an easy one for Gab to solve on how Swallowers respond to disease, by analysing their immune systems responses to it. It could help him create the disease, lethal or not that could render them harmless and protect Earth from them. Well this is as far as the big idea behind it works.

Oh, and if we catch one more inoculated Swallower at a later stage it would be even better for Gab, for his live sample would have probably died within his hands by then...

Taking a cigarillo out of his jacket, the Death Angel quizzed her further as he lit it, a growing wicked smile upon his lips,

-Very interesting, Soldier, yet did you think of the logistics of it, like how are we bringing the samples safely home to Gab and how is he supposed to keep them, for we are not talking about pet hamsters here? And pray if the disease is well studied, how do you know Gabriel knows everything about it? Is it just because he is Doctor Purallee?

The straight answer of It-666 was said with an almost secure tone,

-Safest part, I will knock the samples down to a deep coma before we take them in the van and they will remain so until Gab asked me to do otherwise for his experiments. Gab did his thesis upon rabies. He misdiagnosed a child when he was learning medicine, one bitten by a bat. His teacher at the time saved the child's life in extremis. Gab made a point to learn everything about it then, and do his thesis upon the subject. So yes, it is just because of Doctor Purallee and his peculiar past that I chose that disease over all the others my own body can generate from scratch. Az, to calm my nerves down when I am in Gab's lab being an experimental Guinea Pig, I read all his books and studies held in there, one by one. I do not have to physically hold the book to read its content. I can just look at its binding and read. Rabies is such a pet subject of Gab, he inoculated some of his live demonic samples with it. Plenty for him to know the difference between demonic reactions to the disease compared to the Swallowers' ones.

Taking a long hard puff, Azryel put the motion forward,

-Right, soldiers, we have a 'Pasteur and Roux' partnership here working out how to defeat the Swallowers and they need two samples of them now and one later. As it will protect all of your arses ultimately, I think the trouble is worth it. Your call, soldiers.

All the hands rose at once confidently.

Wrath called out,

-We are in Boston, guys. It, you clocked your two hours in beastly form you can now revert, Gab's potion should now be fully working within you. Let's try it out my little lab rat, you are staying by me and Az at all times on this one.

They pulled in the exact same spot as before. They all jumped out apart from the driver who advised,

-Retrieval by the trees, Wrath. All for one, one for all. I expect the complete crew before heading back home, no one missing, and no one hurt. It, Workmaster wants you back in one piece tonight, understood Soldier? Don't make it a habit of being revived in my van. Protect your little arse as much as ours. You have lot of people on the look out for you that care, at the tree house and around you. Myself, I won't depart from Boston without your arse in my van even if you make it fly on the way back.

Reverting herself to her incarnated self before stepping out of the van, she stood carrying the vivarium and the decoy snake within it with a big bright smile by Death, and replied to the driver,

-I will bring it back, Met', safe and well. I will make sure all of Us don't stink your van up like last time too. Clean sweep, Met, clean sweep with two dirty buggers if we are successful.

Saluting her goodbye the Angel left with a secured nod, driving away. She turned to Azryel who enjoined,

-Let me carry that box, Soldier. I will keep my eyes on you. Now lets start emptying the water from the sewers, and if you tell Wrath the exact location of P and the Witch, he will have them secure within a perimeter with his Archangelic fire. Then it's Ratzilla time, which I am very much looking forward to. Do super-duper Godzi-rat ones for Tibs and Bob, normal double size ones for the others, I managed to get a telepathic authorisation for them from Wrath. I want you to stay close by me and Wrath at all times, Soldier.

Nodding and giving the vivarium to him, she followed him to the entrance of Boston's sewers. She stood there for a good long minute her demonic eyes turning from black to red assessing the sewers then feeding back her results via telepathy for all soldiers, Wrath and Azryel,

-P is actually hiding down there still in search for Eremiel. He has no intention of coming back to light. The witch thinks she has lost her powers and that P is doomed. Their relationship is strained to breaking point. They are two kilometres away from here Wrath so you can put your fire a kilometre from them safely. I will leave some water around them to make them unaware of our presence.

Touching the water of the large concrete drain, the Beast made the water disappear. Then the Angels heard a stampede coming towards them, as the girl stood up. Thousands of little beady eyes seamed to watch them from the darkness of the sewers. Wrath encouraged as he stepped in,

-The Welcoming Rat soldiers committee is here. Come, let's meet the bodyguard crew. My barrier of fire is up. Let's make a move.

When a three metre Ratzilla nudged his head gently within his thigh he turned to It, stating,

-I did not ask for a giant rodent bodyguard following me, Soldier. If I did it would have been a call for a giant rabbit named 'Harvey'. But then your human culture needs to be developed.

Grabbing his hand at once, the Beast transformed his rat into a giant rabbit, and told,

-Here is 'Harvey', Wrath. James Stewart sounds nice. I wanna watch the movie with you when we come out of that shitty sewer. Deal?

Giving her a high five, watching his giant white three metre high rabbit, the Archangel agreed with a huge ear to ear smile,

-Deal!

As he moved forward with her, followed by his Angels and more closely by the Death Angel, the Archangel felt safe. Until they reached the Archangelic barrier of flames. Az released the black mamba from the box, discarding the container in the flames. The burst of flames was enough to cause the awareness of P and Cato who came running to witness what was going on. P recognised the Beast through the flames and stood still, warning the witch through silent gestures. Raising his voice he addressed her at once,

-Long time no see. If it is not my dear deceptive It-666. I thought you were in Australia, one of my men has reported you down there.

Warning via telepathy all angels, Az and Wrath,

-I am going to lie through my teeth. Send him on a wild goose chase, his witch and him if I can.

The teenager shrugging her shoulders announced strongly,

-This is because my father fooled you. We were three to be born on the 6th of June 1996. One of my sisters Cherry is in Australia. There are three sixes not just one, Paul... Overwhelming, it is going to be so and you will feel the full grunt of It-666. You tortured me for eight years and I will drag you back to Hell, alive or not.

Spitting by her, a little sink hole formed with a puff of sulphuric fumes as she transformed herself into her demonic form spreading her bat wings. Azryel transformed himself by her and the whole crew of soldiers behind her followed suit. When Wrath spread his four golden wings, the Witch and P knew they could not cross the fire surrounding them. The Demon took his rightful shape while the Cambion knelt, drew her own blood with her extremely long nails and started to sing in a weird language. Drawing strange figures upon the ground with her blood, she glowed strangely.

The Beast warned all the Angels within their minds,

-Cato is calling her Swallowers. She is using her blood on the ground, they will appear from it. Watch your feet, I would say fly right now above it. My rats will give them a good reception. Do not go close to any walls either, stay safe.

Wrath ordered via telepathy,

-Do as she says, now. We need two samples, only, with minimal risk taken.

Then looking at P from head to toe, he stated,

-Gosh, you are freaking ugly, aren't you? Mother nature wasn't very kind to you. Is it why you hate everybody? You can't even show your pretty face above ground anymore. You've blown it big time. I guess you've got Wrath on your case and you know where it will end...

The fiercely looking Demon barked, yet stepped backwards well away from the Archangelic fire, going by the witch,

-I knew you sussed me out, Wrath. I will be back and destroy you. As for you It-666, I will have your sisters fighting you.

With those last words the Demon disappeared within the ground in a burst of flames.

Turning to his Angels, cocking his eyebrows, the Archangel mocked within their minds,

-That was short and sweet of him. He split back to Hell leaving the witch with all the trouble. Let's see what she can come up with if it is any better than words. She seams very busy, I wish we could break her concentration.

As the ground trembled, It told him wildly by telepathy,

-Off that ground Wrath, stay safe, the Swallowers are on their way. It will be a dozen of them, she thinks them sufficient for her safety. Touch the black mamba so it could cross your fire, it will impress her that she beholds Eremiel. She will lose her concentration and she will get a nice bite that will make her sleep for a while.

Wrath looking at the girl a little worried, met her self assured gaze and did as he was advised. The black mamba was raised as if it was waiting for his touch, its head subdued and bowed. His snake decoy was fully under the control of the young Beast. Putting his Archangelic touch upon the reptile, he saw it glide away across his Archangelic fire and sure enough, the feat impressed the witch which had her head bowed down onto her schemes all the way through. She stopped what she was doing to coax the snake to her, thinking she had Eremiel coming to do her bidding. However when the black mamba arrived by her, the bite it delivered to her presented hand was not the one she knew of, the one which rejuvenated her, it sent her to a deep comatosed sleep.

When her head slammed upon the ground, a jubilant Wrath announced to his soldiers,

-Only Swallowers to deal with. Just keep away from their reach.

When they crawled out from the sewers ground, their monumental size sent shivers to the Angels. It shouted,

-Out of the sewers, all of you, Wrath close the path behind the soldiers. I am staying behind.

Azryel standing by her stated,

-I am going to help her get those Swallowers samples for Gabriel. I am staying behind as well.

Landing by them, holding their shoulders, sealing the way out behind his exiting soldiers with his Archangelic fire, Wrath announced,

-All for one, one for all. My Soldiers are safe now let's make sure the three of Us get out of here with two samples.

Swinging his silver scythe around beheading three Swallowers at once Death called out,

-It's slaughter time.

The Army of rats attacking the Swallowers did their overwhelming job, to the point that they were on top of them preventing them to move freely. All but one Swallower was bitten by the Godzi-rats, which was stunned to a comatose state by It. All Swallowers were killed within minutes by Wrath and Death, but three were left alive, two held by them strongly upon the ground. The young Beast came to stun their catch. She marked one with a special scent with the order,

-We will let this one survive. I got rid of his short term memory. He will never know what bit him nor the witch. He has rabies and we will let him develop it until I will hunt him back down. We are taking the other one back home however with my one. The witch will wake up in 72 hours from now. With the decoy snake by her, she will be weakened a bite at a time exactly like she did to Eremiel. We will see how she likes it.

Around them the giant rats had started eating the dead Swallowers. Wrath brought his Archangelic fire down and ordered,

-Let's get to the van before Met' gets worried for Us. Will your Godzi rats not chew upon this Swallower we have to catch later?

-No, he has a safe Beast stamp upon him.

Putting their Swallowers across their shoulders, Wrath and Az ordered,

-Good job, Soldier, let's clear it.

When they reached the van and laid the two comatose Swallowers beasties by the feet of the soldiers, Wrath, Death and It gave each other a silent high five. Raphael took his place by Met' the driver and asked to head home, commenting,

-Back to Gab's. I need a proper meal. My 'Harvey' was so useful, I am considering giving up rabbit in my diet. What about you and rats, It? Those soldiers were a helpful treat. I am honestly considering one for each of my soldiers as constant bodyguard.

Sitting by Az, her heart racing through the roof, holding the Death Angel's hand tightly, It confided,

-The witch makes her Swallowers appear with her own blood. If they have the same power that is scary shit we are dealing with. However big they are, they can get overwhelmed easily and are not the brightest of creatures. We've got two. Let's hope, good Gab makes sense of them. Like my blood at the moment, they do not smell of flowery meadows though. Can we do something Angelic about it Az?

Nodding positively Death told,

-Met', open both freakin' windows and drive as fast as you can to the tree house.

Drawing his Jean Paul Gaultier perfume, the Death Angel sprayed the Swallowers, followed by all of his soldiers by their personal perfumes.

Met' opened both of his windows faster than he expected, swearing,

-Holly shit, Bros, Az! Hell on fuckin' Earth! Do you want to perfume me to death?

Smiling wickedly Azryel replied,

-Not at all. Just giving you a sense of timing. With winter days, sunset is earlier... Workmaster is waiting for his girl to be back before dawn. Push it safely.

Verse 35. Cup of Tease.

As their van pulled in the yard of the tree house, Wrath noticed a car beside the ones of Gabriel and Caroline. He announced,

-Gabriel has a visitor. Yet trust him and Walt to be on the lookout for Us upon the platform. Well we did make it on time. Fifteen minutes to sunset, well done Met'. We are in pretty good shape to, considering who we faced for the first time. I wonder who is visiting that aloof of an Archangel, I hope it is not someone undesirable.

It-666, her eyes turning red, scanned quickly the whole wood from within the van. She reassured him,

-The human is a guest. It's Liz the receptionist at Gab's and Caro's clinic. She has a good soul about her, but an atypical mind. Caroline has invited her for the wedding and she will stay overnight. Liz Arczy has been Caro's confident for ages. Therefore she knows more than she should about everything but she is safe.

The Death Angel cocking his eyebrows questioned,

-How do you know that human is safe from here? I do not like the sound of a human knowing too much. If revelations of a certain kind have been made to her, she may have to be quarantined in the tree house. I will have to assess her.

The teenager added undaunted,

-She is one of the odd humans Gab likes the company of. He protects her as an Angel without her knowing, as like Walt she is Atheist. This is partly why I think she is safe. I read her many times during my clinic stay and just now, she is a damaged human hanging by a string, yet one I would choose to befriend for her soul sings life to others despite it all.

Looking at her, and grabbing her hand enjoining the Beast to come out of the van, Death asked,

-Clear this one for me, is she deemed safe because she is an Atheist or because Gab protects her?

As she jumped on the ground by him, It told bluntly,

-It could be a bit of both to be true, Az, yet, that human gets my faith and respect because she thinks and care for others more than her own self. Liz is a fairly lost soul if no one catches her. I sympathise very deeply with her soul being there, and done just that.

When she saw Walter Workmaster running to meet them with Gab in the background, she ran to him. Giving him a silent bear hug. The man looked at Death and asked,

-How did it go? My girl is running this time around so I am crossing my fingers.

Walking to the man yet keeping an eye on Wrath dragging the two Swallowers out of the van who refused that any Angels touched them, Az replied,

-You should be proud of your girl, Workmaster. You have a true soldier in your arms, a very much valued one. Let us take her to Gab's lab to make sure we are all safe for we met the Swallowers for the first time. Unknown nasty beasties, we have two for Gabriel to assess though. Little It, Wrath and I dealt with them, we do not know if we are infected by them yet. Your girl was given something which should have protected her strongly. I only hope it did for all of us.

Walter went to embrace him silently for a good long minute before saying,

-Were you protected too, Az? What about Wrath? Thank you for bringing my girl back, walking.

The touched Death Angel hugging the man replied, smiling,

-We had Godzilla rats to protect us, discretion of your daughter, a very intriguing creation that worked particularly well at keeping away from us the beasties attacking us.

When he broke the embrace, Azryel realised that It went to hug Gabriel. Walter turning to look at what captured the attention of Death but also his irresistible smirk saw the deeply silent hug of the Archangel and It. He could only acknowledge the deep emotion between them. Somehow he did not find in his own heart to split them apart. Death by him tapped his shoulder knowingly, which reminded the man that he was standing by a mind reading Angel.

Wrath pulling the Swallowers by them, did not show the same consideration as Az and Walt and ordered,

-When you lovebirds have finished your welcome home hug party, we will be able to do some work. Azryel, it's with me in the lab with It and Gab. Your assessment of Miss Arczy is to be done later on this evening. Walter work with Caro and Asha about how you want your wedding organised tomorrow. As for my crew take a break.

Workmaster surprised the elder Archangel by embracing him warmly,

-Come and get your big hug, uncle Raphael. Today, you made my Caro an extremely happy woman. The big shopping spree reminded her when she was a teen when you lavished upon her. I want to thank you very much for your generosity. I am in your debt.

Tapping the man's shoulders, Raphael replied,

-You are not in my debt, Walter. You and Caro are family. Therefore you are back in my care. You will have to accept me lavishing upon you from now on for it is my way of showing that I care for you both. I am hardly a very demonstrative huggy type of Archangel, however I do feel affection for my humans and my Angels.

Interrupting the teenage Beast asked somewhat shyly but eagerly,

-Does it include someone strange and awkward like me?

Smiling irresistibly to her, Wrath reassured,

-Oh, yes it does. You are my pet project of a soldier, Being, and I am very fond of your weird ways of doing things. Now, let's work out those Swallowers with Gab. You, Az and me need to be checked thoroughly for having dealt with them. See you at dinner, Walt.

The man saw the Archangel lifting a Beastie like if it was a bag of potatoes, with Azryel doing the same with the other one, then vanishing along with Gabriel and It.

Within the lab, they reappeared and deposited their Swallowers by Gab's feet. The younger Archangel stated,

-It looks like a successful mission from the result that lay before me. I expected only one sample, yet I see two, all the better. Gosh, they are truly ugly, like gigantic, squashed head toads.

-Wait until the little one explain to you why you have two, my Gab. We will also get you another one at a later stage. It's quite ingenious. Are you fond of rabies?

Worried by his last question, his nephew enquired,

-Not really, pretty nasty stuff, why?

Grinning sarcastically Azryel lit up a cigarillo, teased the Archangel,

-Shame, one of the Swallowers we brought back is infected by rabies. Little present for you courtesy of the Beast in case you would not be afraid enough of them in their awake state.

Crossing his arms upon his broad chest, a very stern look upon his face, Gabriel rose his voice,

-Pray, It, do you mind bringing to my enlightenment your explanations. For if I have to deal with a foaming and enraged beastie roaming in my tree house biting all that moves, I will not be extremely pleased to say the least.

Wrath intervened vigorously,

-Calm down, Gab, you are being shamelessly wound up by Az. Anyway I do not want those Swallowers awake at any point in your lab or home. For your safety and the one of all, I want your two new lab rats in their comatose state at all times. Come, Soldier, explain to Gab your correct intentions. Don't worry I won't let that Archangel bite you because he can be easily teased to death by Death and he always falls for it.

The teenager regaining a little courage tried to express herself,

-I was thinking that it would be useful for you to have two samples of Swallowers, with one infected by a disease which you knew all about in order for you to find out how they would react to a lethal virus. I hoped it could help you find or create a virus that could disable the army of Swallowers of the witch Cato. I didn't mean to cause you any hindrance, on the contrary.

Taking a long puff of his cigar, the Death Angel asked the Archangel seriously,

-Now, the question is, Gab, do you know all about rabies or not?

Turning around the Swallowers considering their massive sizes and batrachian appearance Gabriel responded,

-I did my thesis upon rabies, subsequently wrote different papers upon it in medical reviews. I still study the virus therefore have some demonic live samples infested with it. I must admit it is one of the diseases which I am well versed in. In per say, I am not fond of rabies, I decided to know all there was to know about that virus for myself in one of my many guilt trips. In that sense, it is not a bad choice at all, indeed it is a very good one, how did you know that, It?

The girl smiled shyly and blushed thoroughly under his scrutiny. Smirking while considering her, the Death Angel came to her rescue, teasingly stating,

-That would be because we have our own little Swallower... of a different kind, she swallows pain. Remember Gab, that you have a very special Being in your home, a cross between an observing Sherlock Holmes and a big hearted Hound of the Baskerville. With a sprinkle of love added to the mix, you end up with a big sample of a Swallower infected with rabies at your feet my dear Archangel. A loyal dog would have brought you back his stick, an affectionate cat would have given you a dead mouse or a bird. It is definitely more bespoke for she knew about the misdiagnosis you did on that child when you were studying medicine and how it influenced you to be a geek on rabies.

Biting his lips with slight concern, realising that once more the Beast's actions were intended to please and help him, the Archangel Gabriel enjoined all of them,

-Let check you all out. Wrath talk to me about how everything went in your eyes, then I want the same from you two. What one may have spotted, one might have missed, it will give us a well rounded view of what went on.

Two hours went by in the lab until a loud shout from Az woke up a dozing It, her head resting on Wrath's shoulder. The elder Archangel opening his eyes at once, stood up and barked,

-Oï, what are you doing to my Death Angel to have him screaming?

A scalpel in hand, and a very sheepish look upon his face Gabriel tried to explain,

-I told him all upon anaesthetic but he wouldn't have any 'human shit for scared-y-cat' that knocks you right down. Of course without it, he doesn't keep still making it difficult to be precise. I am deadly scared to take away more than I should.

Looking at him with a fierce look, Death warned,

-And you should, Archangel. You can shit in your pants right now, if you mess me about by one single blood cell. Wrath, he pricks like a prick. Gosh, help me! Why did you have to take the poncey human stuff that makes you sleep for ages?

Raphael coming to Azryel smiling with irony answered,

-Because when it comes to my nephew, I prefer not to see or feel what he is doing to me and just trust the order of things and that they will get it right somehow.

Pestering Death commented,

-Great, I have a mad Archangel who is removing bits of my body haphazardly and a very wise one that is playing Russian roulette with himself and others. I am doomed to have a crater in my wrist for eternity.

The teenage Beast came by his side, knelt and proposed kindly,

-I can make it easier for you and Gab with my powers. It would be very localised to the area he is dealing with. You will be able to keep an eye on his every move, yet the part of wrist dealt with would be still, enough for him to not mess it up, however your arm would still be able to remove it from him if you decide. It works like localised human anaesthesia yet will not give any chemical in your body and respect its integrity. All it requires to make it possible is a little bit of trust from your part to my own abilities. General, what do you say?

Widely smiling a self secured Azryel replied,

-Give me your little hand to assess right now Soldier, and you will know the result.

Nestling her hand straight away within his reading one, It waited for his answer anxiously. Sending a telepathic message to Gabriel and Wrath, the Death Angel mentioned,

-The devotion she has for us three is amazingly strong. Her list is long and includes humanity. Bless her beastly cotton socks.

Azryel took her out of her misery telling,

-Like you do, I will trust you with my life, Being. Just do as you said.

Numbing the area of his arm, It gave the go ahead to Gab to pursue his surgical removal of the Swallower's viral bug. Watching attentively the operation, Death gave a bright smile when it was all over and when It gave him back his full sensation within his arm. He swore,

-Swallowers are definitely nasty buggers to deal with in my book. Gab show me the stuff.

Within a flask, a large greenish moving compound swam in sterilised water which Gab presented to him. Pouting his lips Death asked,

-Is it just my bug or the amount of Wrath, It and I?

-Just your own one. It is less lively than Wrath's one, though. It one's was already attacked by her anti-virus, and looks already pretty dead. I have to be thorough on that one, Az, all of your tests are separated and will benefit of their own research. I want my Anti-Viruses created to be bespoke to all of you. I do not wish to see as strong a reaction to something that should help as I saw this morning with poor good willing It. I want all my Anti-virus potions to be well adapted to each soldier of the Army.

-And all of my own bug is out? Same for Wrath and my pupil?

-Since It made sure you could not move for a little while, yes. Gosh, although you are hard work Azryel, like my uncle always says. In comparison It was ever so compliant and understanding, and Wrath gave me a little benefit of the doubt and a little nugget of trust. Wrath is safe and so is It. If you could double check them for me, it would be much appreciated.

Removing his arm from the Archangel and looking at it full of suspicion, Death strongly commented,

-I gave you my arm to deal with Archangel. In my book no one makes a dent to my body without passing away apart from my Master, Wrath. You just butchered my arm for half an hour with your soul still among the living, if that doesn't show my extreme trust, patience, and respect, I do not know what will. You had a golden bar of my trust right now, Gabriel: you made me scream in pain and you are still very much alive. Now if you would be so good to make my arm look like it has not been dug into, with no visible scars at all, you will be completely forgiven for your lack of sharp and precise surgical moves on that occasion. I offered you pure trust while the others are slightly blinded, one by love and the other by some sort of extremely strong filial love which will anoint you as the next Archangelic leader in the near future.

Gabriel obeyed, sighing somehow, while repairing the wrist of Azryel as the last point of Death had mentioned clearly that Wrath had already thought about his next reincarnation. The elder Archangel at 76 looked so young, so fit, so handsome, and was so strong that Death's hint took somehow Wrath's nephew aback. Gab did not feel ready whatsoever to take any lead of the AA at that very moment in time. He told by telepathy to Azryel only,

-Teach me to be a good Archangelic leader. I am no military Angel since a very long time, since regretting obeying the orders of destruction which happened to be so very false. I am still guilt tripping upon that one, Az. If Wrath is thinking to renew himself, please, prepare me to step into his larger than life wings.

Seizing his hand strongly with his repaired arm, the Death Angel stated out loud,

-I am there for you all the way, Archangel.

Then winking at him with a wicked smile, he added,

-First lesson, Angelic soldiers come first. Pretty much a humble pie to eat yet enjoy it as you will learn most from them. My incarnated Army needs to be fed right now. The way to a man's heart is through his belly, that human expression works just as well with my Angels I found out. Care for all their basic needs, and you will be sought like a father, like Wrath is. You can come back to your test tubes later tonight, after dinner, or even later, after watching a movie with the Workmasters, we intend to show to It to give her some referential human cultural clues upon the choice of her new name. Think about what you wish It to see, 'Buffy' wise afterwards, thinking lateness is no problem, as good Az will make you catch a beauty sleep of a lifetime with only minutes within my hands. Gab, kitchen is your first port of call. It, I want you to go to Caro, she will make sure that your maid of honour dress is perfectly fitted but also tell you what your role is for tomorrow's big wedding. As for you my Wrath, as always you do as you want.

All teletransported elsewhere in different places.

The Death Angel appeared upon the wooden platform seeking some peace to smoke. As soon as he arrived he leaned upon the railing breathing the cold air of the night, took a cigar out of his silver box and lit it. A human voice warned him of her presence upon the same platform,

-That's big boy posh stuff you are smoking, contained in silver box and all. I think I seen you somewhere... a few times. I am a bit tipsy right now so I would not recall anything precisely. You will have to help me a bit if you remember me if not you are a stranger so do not bother.

Turning around to consider the human, Death took a good long hard look at what he saw and a very good long hard puff on his cigar before releasing the smoke and two words,

-Why not?

The scruffy red haired woman smiled to him with a sheepish smile,

-I think I need a glass of water to answer that one. Caro and I, have been celebrating her second wedding, while dress trying, fitting and chatting. Two bottles of 'Veuve Clicquot' disappeared like that in the making. I have tiny bubbles bursting in my brain right now and it still feels like a happy zone.

Snapping his fingers, Azryel made a pint of water full of ice appear within his hand, and brought it to the human, ordering,

-Drink it all. Sip after sip or in one go, does not matter. The same effect will happen slower or faster. Then try to remember me if you can, if you can't then don't bother talking to me.

Blinking her green eyes to him, the woman simply replied,

-That's harsh.

Sarcastically grinning Death commented, as he noticed the short bitten up nails of the human, a tell tale sign of an anxious person, as her hand grabbed the glass,

-Just mirroring what you said to me initially, Miss Arczy. Are your heart and soul not open to new acquaintances and strangers, human?

Shaking her head negatively, giving a look full of despair to him, Liz Arczy took a long puff upon her almost finished cigarette, before swearing,

-Holy shit! You are Azryel Mortimer. I can assure you that I am welcoming strangers all the time, as I am a receptionist.

Enjoying her reactions as the human realised finally that she was facing Death, the Angel carried on with a most wicked smile,

-You cannot hide your being behind a job. Do you welcome others only when duty calls?

Liz looked upon her glass full of water and wished it was full of Pimm's, Port or Whiskey right now. Then she looked at Azryel and saw his scrutinising eyes upon her, realising she had nowhere to hide. She replied, her voice sinking to a sorrowful tone,

-I do welcome others once in a while when I trust, yet I have a big problem with trust, as I hardly do give it. My own mum gave me up to be fostered at four. I never had enough time to love my new carers and when I did they gave me up to someone else regardless of my feelings. I ended up cocooning myself from getting attached to others. I still do so. That is why I am a loner that rarely gives trust.

She drank the glass of water and closed her eyes for a few seconds. She felt her fingers holding her dead cigarette being moved. Her dead bud was chucked away, and replaced by a cigarillo, which Az lit up, stating,

-You are not the only human with trusting problems. It's very much a worldwide situation, I am afraid to say. What did Caro told you about me? I can feel your fear of me from here, Miss Arczy.

Liz considered the given cigar within her hand, a little scared to meet again the intense gaze of the Death Angel upon her. She thought of everything that Caro had said to her about him and could not agree more with her now that she was in his presence. She replied,

-She told me not to cock up my first meeting with you and to watch my words if I did not want to beg for forgiveness for an eternity. She said you were the most overwhelming Being she ever met yet also the most disarmingly honest. Caroline has a lot of respect for you. By the way thank you for the big boy, I never smoked one of those before.

Giving her his most dazzling smile Az went to lean upon the balcony edge yet still considering the woman this time with sheer amusement, greatly tempted to make sport of the human as he told,

-Big boys are awesome. They are great stress relievers. You should try them more often, as from where I stand I can clearly see the nervous wreck of a woman. I have a lot of respect for Caroline too. She is one of the rare humans who bestow my friendship. Now that you met me what do you think of her opinion and advice? How well did you fare so far, miss Arczy? Isn't it grand time for you to hide under that bench?

Finishing her pint of water, trembling like a leaf, Liz answered, and presenting her hand to shake to the Angel,

-I sure feel like going underneath that bench for I know I cocked up beautifully with no safety net below me. Here, you have been duly introduced to Liz Arczy, a total drunken mess at this hour, a messed up and messy woman the rest of the time. I think Caro's advice was wasted upon me, as I always cock things up anyway. As for her opinion, it is shared, you are one overwhelming Angel and surely commending respect everywhere you go.

She stopped and made a clumsy circular gesture in the air with her cigar towards Az before continuing,

-There's a spooky aura thing about you that makes people shit themselves. I know I am one of them.

As he saw the woman standing up from the bench haphazardly, and attempting to walk towards him in order to present her hand closer, Azryel was somehow touched by her simply honest humanity, full of imperfection and admitting them. He sighed deeply as he could also see the lost soul, It-666 had been talking about. Putting his cigar at his lips and coming to Liz, he shook her hand firmly before guiding her back to the bench stating,

-Right, it is nicely refreshing to meet another human that cocks everything up. Do not feel too ashamed I have yet to meet one that is perfect. Now, let's cut the walking short as we don't want you to fall from the platform and add a funeral to the wedding of tomorrow. We don't want to spoil Caro's big day, now do we? Let's sit on the bench and de-drunk you a little. When did you last eat, human?

Snapping his fingers together again, the empty pint filled itself back with water, which he presented to a stunned Liz. As Death sat by her, he encouraged,

-Stop looking at me like you deserve my silver scythe instead of my attention for being a drunken mess, human. Drink this one up and tell me, when did you eat and what was the constitution of your last meal?

Still deeply surprised Liz obeyed as she sipped the water quietly. Having someone paying attention to her last meal was news to her ears. She felt cared for, and she hardly felt like that at any point in her life. She answered,

-A small bag of crisps at lunch time.

Noticing how slim and small the human was, Azryel's concern grew a notch, as he quizzed more,

-What did you have prior to that?

-A fruit juice for breakfast, well a beetroot one that made me piss purple all day long, but it was organic and meant to be good for you. Prior to that I had a takeaway pizza, a sacrilegious Hawaiian with BBQ sauce at dinner and before that a prawn cocktail for lunch and another juice at breakfast, a tomato one, which didn't turn my piss red... Why do you want to know what I ate?

The Death Angel realised how defensive the human turned when showed a slight interest. He just knew her soul was living in a stronghold carefully built since she had been abandoned by her own mother. Liz Arczy would be a tough nut to crack but he was determined more than ever to do so. Looking ahead of him, taking a long slow puff, he replied,

-I am determining how messed up you are right now, human.

Liz cocking her eyebrows laughed out,

-Well you could have asked me that straight. I am fucked up. I do not give my own self five more years.

Presenting his hand to hold, Death sternly proposed,

-Hold my hand, and I can tell you if your predictions are right or wrong to the very hour and second.

Becoming serious Liz took a long puff of her cigar before she went to courageously hold the presented hand. It lasted for a split second as she removed her hand almost as soon as she realised her fate. Tears started pooling at her eyes, and she remained deadly pale and silent until Azryel spoke after a few minutes,

-You can change that fate, human. You reap what you sow. Start from now. Start from your own self. Show your own self a little respect and grow everything from that point on. If you need a friend to confide into and help you through, I can be there for you. However needless to say I am not everyone's cup of tea, totally black, bitter and unsweetened yet steady and strong. Your own call, Liz.

The frail scruffy woman blinked many times, as it sank within her that the Death Angel had proposed to her his own friendship. If she had to improve to escape her fate, she just knew she could not manage it alone. Although it was a very scary friendship to behold, she saw it as a lifeline being given to her. Her trembling human hand went back to hold his Angelic one, as she said,

-Thank you, Azryel for the offer. I am deeply touched and honoured. I love my tea black, strong with a drop of honey in it. Honey has got antibacterial properties. I would love to be accepted as your friend.

Seeing her shy smile, Death closed his firm long fingers upon her hand, if her lost soul needed directions, he would make sure she would recognise her path. He enjoined her,

-You are accepted, Liz Arczy. Now drink up that water and let's give you a proper meal. How dare you, drinking on an empty stomach, human, recipe for disaster! Trust me on that one, I have lots of real matter of life and death examples to give you. Gab must have prepared a lovely meal by now, care to entertain me with your conversation. I want you by my side at the table, telling me all about the benefits of honey, beetroot and tomatoes...

Verse 36. The Love Bug.

It woke up nestled cosily upon the chest of Gabriel, who was wide awake, as he asked kindly,

-Trust that you slept well, Bambi?

She blinked at him, and taking a good look at her surroundings, saw Caroline sleeping in the arms of Walter upon the other sofa, and the human Liz totally asleep, kneeling by Azryel, her head resting on his lap. Wrath was there very much awake cradling a sleeping little Micky within his strong arms with a blissful smile upon his face. She answered blushing as she stood up,

-I did, very well indeed. I am fully rested. Did you?

Gabriel smiled wickedly and nodded pointing to Death who was smoking his cigar silently, replied,

-I did have my RIP sleep courtesy of Azryel. I feel good and fully rested too. He woke Wrath and I up to enjoy the peacefulness of all of you about half an hour ago. Today is the big day. We have a wedding for the Workmasters and you deciding if you want to be named Blondie. What did you think of the human culture trip?

The teenager recalled the whole evening to her mind. She remembered most of all nestling by the Archangel and being welcomed by him rather than rejected. She recalled his strong arms surrounding her like a blanket as she slept. She sat by him again, held his hand and answered,

-I enjoyed it. I loved 'The Good, the Bad and the Ugly'. My favourite character was Tuco. I did feel for him more than I did for 'Blondie'. Seeing Tuco running in that cemetery with the Ecstasy of Gold tune within my ears, I fell in love with that movie. I think Spike is an awesome character, after watching many 'Buffy'. I wanna be called 'Blondie'. Last night was truly 'Atomic'.

Gabriel standing up welcomed,

-Good to know you had a good night, Blondie. Now, go, have a shower, and when you are ready join me in the kitchen to give me a hand with the breakfast.

The teenager disappeared immediately from the room, her voice replying joyfully,

-Yes, Gab.

The Archangel looked at his receptionist by Azryel, and sent a message by telepathy to the Death Angel,

-Be careful on handling that human, Az, don't be too harsh upon her. She is a nice person who never had lots of good in her life nor happiness.

Playing with the red curls of the woman with his long fingers, Azryel replied in the mind of Gabriel,

-That human has only six months to live before her, Gab. She has played the Russian roulette with her life. I will see what I can do. I may be too late. But if I will not be harsh with her I will be firm and make sure she does not let herself down anymore. What happened to the guardian angel supposed to look after her?

-He devoted himself to an ancient Demon and I never saw him around her ever again. He was pretty useless anyway and could not be bothered to do his job. Since she works at my clinic, I kept an eye upon her.

When the woman stirred, the Archangel disappeared from the room, leaving Azryel to deal with her as he realised that Death had decided to take her lost soul on board. Yawning and stretching herself before opening her eyes, Liz discovered herself upon her knees by the Angel and swore,

-Crikey, that's another odd position I ended up waking up to in the morning to add to my collection... Can't remember fuck all of how I got up on my knees. What have I been up to again?

She gazed worryingly at Azryel whose eyes glowed strangely green considering her, while a wicked smirk drew upon his face. Growing more anxious by his silence, Liz looked for clues surrounding her starting by the knees her head had been resting upon, and stated,

-You do not look too messed up, everything is tidy below your belt apart for the drool from my yawn. Did I make a fool of myself? Did I talk bullshit?

Finally surrendering to her questions, with an hilarious grin, Azryel took the woman out of her misery,

-You were surrounded by a happy family enjoying movie time, and you just watched TV with us, however you were tired and sitting by my feet on the floor because there was not enough places on the sofas, you just slumbered upon me. The only mess you made was your freaking drools. They do not only happen when you yawn human, but also when you sleep like a log. You did not behave like a fool last night, I made sure of it by controlling your level of drunkenness, however the bullshits that can come out of your mouth are quite intriguing, constant and astonishing. I am going to walk Walt's dog, and have my early morning smoke, do you fancy tagging along and get a breathe of fresh air? I think it will do you a world of good.

The woman stood up smiling, replying,

-Walkies sound nice. I am sorry for drooling all over your knees all night Angel.

Standing up Az presented his hand to her, as he called out,

-Come on, Bud, my boy, walkies.

The Great Dane stood from where he slept by Walter's feet to come to the Angel. Bud's head went to lodge itself within the palm of the Death Angel, giving it a slight nudge. Holding the hand of the human and stroking Bud, Azryel teletransported them in the forest by the tree house. As soon as his hands left them one went running to a tree to relieve himself while the other went running behind a bush. He could not help his wide grin, pulled a cigar out of his silver box and lit it. Checking his jacket's pockets and finding a pack of Kleenex, he threw it behind the bush by the human, and without a word took the direction of the Indian Waterfall. A few seconds later, Bud was by him again, while he could hear the human getting almost there but also almost lost. Backtracking from a few paces he called out,

-Arczy? Human? Can you follow my voice or do I have to get you?

-I hear you alright, Angel. I didn't do any scouting as a kid though. Keep talking, when I stop bumping into trees I know it could only be you.

This brought Az right by her side, taking her hand and walking her to the Indian Waterfall. He enjoined,

-Wash your face, arms and hands, human. The water is very cold this time of the year yet will wake you up better than anything else.

Doing as she was told Liz stood up from the stream swearing like hell,

-Holy shit! Good, for you, Angel, my human face is f'in frozen for the next thirty minutes at least. Icicles on brows down here. I am awake alright.

-Good, now sit and listen. You can forget about the swearing spree with me, human and give a respectful break to my ears doing so. Your total lack of parents shows in your total lack of manners. How are you feeling this morning? Any hangover?

As she saw the Angel, his face losing his smile, sitting in a lotus position by the waterfall, she sat by him apologising,

-I am sorry Azryel to sound offensive. I do not mean to. I swear a lot, so much so that there was nearly no day without Gab raising his eyebrows at me at the clinic. If I dropped something, I swear, if I hurt myself, I swear, if I spilled something, I swear. I know I should stop swearing and be more ladylike but what is the point? As for hangovers I do not suffer from them anymore, I have been quite immune to them for ages. But I also do know, it is a bad thing and nothing to be proud of. I am a bad nut. You know the kind in the 'Willy Wonka' film which fails to pass the standards mark and gets chucked away in the garbage shoot.

Filling with sadness for her wasted soul and life, Death could only state,

-Self fulfilling prophecy, Liz. Could you not have chosen something a little better for your own sake? But as you said what is the point? The fact is you never saw any point in your being. Throughout you remained blind to realise that there was actually a point in your life and soul. Failing to make something positive out of yourself, you just went on a self aborting way of life. The whole point is you have been so successful at it that you are very close to your final day in which it will pain me to have to pick your soul up. See, you have been successful at your downfall, I wish you had used the same level of energy it took you to undo yourself to make something out of that kind, amusing and clever woman sitting beside me. In a sense shielding yourself from others protected most from witnessing your slow yet fast death. At only thirty three years of age Liz, if you had many friends or a family, they would have been devastated and saddened. As it is the hardship of your untimely loss will only be strongly felt by Caroline, who considers you as her best friend, by Gabriel who cares for you and your wellbeing, by Walter Workmaster who likes your sense of humour and by me who despises having to take a good soul away. Limited damage I guess for you, only four friends, less than the number of fingers on one hand to attend your future funeral. How do you feel about leaving Caroline and us behind too early? Is it sobering enough or do I have to push you human, under that freezing waterfall to give you the cold shower that your soul deserves in order to wake up before it is too late?

Under his scrutiny, Liz bowed her head with deep shame. Her first urge was to run far away, very far away from the home truths delivered by the Death Angel. Yet she could hardly feel her legs, and she doubted she could outrun a flying Angel. She had yet to see wings on an Angel like Caroline told her she saw, and if she remembered right, Azryel was supposed to have raven black wings in his Angelic form. She realised her mind had just run miles away from the subject discussed, and was going to go all 'avoidy' on the serious questions raised. Bitting her cold dry lips until they bled, she finally answered anxiously,

-I do not know what my sake is. What's my worthiness? What can I bring apart from a good laugh once in a while? I admit that I did not take my life seriously. It was so ridiculously hard to live that I decided to try to see the funny side of things and get a strong palliative like alcohol to blur the sharp edges away from them. Double edge sword, it did render me blissfully blind to any point at any point in time. Please do not throw me in the waterfall, Azryel. It is Winter for Christ's sake. That would surely cut my life shorter by a big hypothermia stunt or a nasty cold afterwards. I can assure you that you woke my soul up alright, Angel. I want to run away from my home truth yet I am still here. It is a very sobering morning for me, Azryel. How do I feel about leaving anyone that cares a little for me? I feel very bad, so bad I do not really want to leave, but what are my chances now?

The Death Angel replied sternly, a blood tear slowly running upon his cheek which he wiped off,

-I will not lie to you human. Your chances of turning things around are very slim and rely upon you seeing a point to the mere existence of your own being. If you can not see it for your own self no one will. It is gone that far, I am afraid. I am very far from putting upon you an hypothermia stunt, Liz, for I see a point in you, even if it is only to make people smile and laugh. There is artistry in being able to make everyone smile. To make everyone laugh is not easy, yet just the way you are your honest self, made me, Death, enjoy every single minute in your company. Can you care for yourself just for the very few that care for you? Don't let go of your life for you do count. Trust me. I would not shed a tear for your soul if it was not the case, Liz Arczy.

The woman went to hold one of Az's hand and promised,

-I will care for my own life, from now on.

She hugged the Death Angel silently, before crying gently upon his shoulder, letting go of a hell of a lot. Stroking her back and patting it, Death hugged the human back fully, acknowledging,

-I will be there for you to help you do so, Liz. Do not let yourself down and I will not either. Now, tell me what Caroline told you about us Angels. What do you know?

Sitting back by him, wiping the remaining of her tears with an irresistible smile rising upon her lips, Liz replied,

-Well, she told me the whole lot and at first I sincerely thought she just went bonkers. So much so that when Gab came by my reception I asked him to check on Caro, that she may had suffered from a concussion of some sort or worse, a possible stroke. He quizzed me straight upon what made me think so, extremely worried. When I said that she was seeing Angels and talking to them, he did a shush gesture with his finger and called me to his office. I thought something must be up as I am rarely called to his office, being a good and efficient worker and all. As he sat me down, he asked me what did his sister tell me, and I did so. After seeing Gabriel swearing imprecations, he revealed to me that what Caroline had said was true. I thought he went bonkers too until he held my hand and gave me a vision from my past, that no one knew but me. He added to that the physical apparition of my little notepad where I doodle when I am bored at the reception, when no one is there. I am, was Atheist, well now I don't f'in know for sure, let's say politely that I am confused.com. I have been sworn to the staunchest secrecy by Gab: 'One word about Angels and my receptionist arse will be Archangelically fired at once.' I didn't know what he meant but I do not want to be fired from a job that give me the socialising I need to remain sane as a true loner. Anyway, I would not have talk to no one about it for it is crazy shit. I don't fancy spending the last six months of my life in an asylum. Angels do incarnate and exist, the same applies to demons. Great revelation, I am scared to say the least. I won't share that one and cause all men and women on Earth a panic attack.

Azryel took a long puff out of his cigar, peacefully commenting, with a wide grin,

-Good. Do not ever share that stuff away, human, especially since you gave your word to an Archangel. I burnt my own arse in their fires and they are truly lethally unpleasant. You just lose your life and soul if they do not forgive you or reverse the process. It works like being on a slow burner that is taking you out slowly bit by bit, atrociously painful yet giving you time to do your begging mojo. Begging an Archangel is very difficult, I have been closed to my last breath doing so, although fully dedicated to them. The label is 'Do not try this at home'. Just be sworn to the Angelic secrecy, Liz and stay safe.

Death presented her cigar to her, yet the human declined,

-I decided to stop chain smoking. It may be too late but I wanna do so. For drinking I can cut down with help. I will not try to defy an Archangel. My lips are sealed upon everything from the existence of the Beast to incarnated Angels walking upon Earth.

Impressed he stood up and asked helping her up,

-What do you know about the Beast?

-Everything Caro told me.

Keeping her hands within his, Death read the woman's mind thoroughly. He warned her,

-It-666 must be kept hidden from all. She is not to be mentioned at any point. She has been dealt the worst deal anyone could get at birth. She is an extremely and dangerously powerful supernatural Being. Yet she surrendered to Angels, and we are raising her, giving her the chance of her life. It has an excellent heart and a sound sweet soul about her. But at sixteen, she is still a young impressionable Being and we must protect her from ever falling into the wrong hands. If she does, they will have the power to start the Apocalypse. This is why keeping her existence secret is paramount. Do you understand, Liz? Not to mention, if you ever spill the beans, you will have Wrath, Gab and I, falling like a ton of bricks upon you.

Nodding with understanding and slight fear, the woman swore,

-I promise to you Azryel that I will keep the secret with me till my grave. I will be silent about It. I remember seeing her so pale and weak at the clinic, when Gab pretended she was a meningitis case. He never let anyone look after her despite his lack of sleep, he stayed by her bedside in the quarantine room. Meeting her properly yesterday, she struck me as being very kind, shy and with that sweet disposition of wanting to please everyone, especially Gab. She looks far better, healthier and is very pretty. I am happy that she found the secure home of Gabriel and a loving family to adopt her, I would never want to ruin that. Will she ever turn bad? Can she really?

Azryel looking ahead of him at the giant tree house of Gabriel a few miles from their walking path, stayed silent thinking before answering strongly,

-It can turn at any time and be the Beast that everyone fears. She can bring disasters and chaos. Yet since I met her, the willpower of that Being has been to do good and good only. That willpower was tested during her unhappy childhood when she was tortured for eight years. If that is not a steadfast and extremely good heart, I do not know what will. She'd rather be dead and dusted than do Evil. We met her as a very lonely, distressed, and suicidal Being. Her big goal in life then was to get rid of herself to protect humanity from what she could be. We talked her out of that one. Since I have seen her putting her powers to help and protect the Angelic Army, the Angels and her human family. She has adopted a self sacrificing stance as a soldier. I am trying to talk her out of that one too for it is better to stay alive and be able to consistently defend humanity and simply be its staunchest protecting soldier. I am her confident. From knowledge, observation of the young Beast, the loyalty and devotion, she has developed for Gabriel, Wrath and I will grow stronger rather than fade away to nothingness. From gut feelings, I would vouch for her.

The woman walking by his side could not help stating, seeing a blood tear pooling at the corner of his eyes,

-You do feel very strongly about her.

The Death Angel replied at once starchily,

-Everyone in this house feels strongly about her. For me, she is my best and soundest soldier, I ever saw in an eternity. I desire to fight by her sides for a long while yet I have the strong fear that she will self sacrifice herself before I know it and can do something about it. For Gabriel, he just fell in love with her. Just being by her sweet self, her good character and her eager to please manners, his love is growing deeper by the day. As for Wrath, he saw the girl literally protect him and giving her life to do so. As an Archangel, he managed to get her back, putting a plea to the above for her soul to remain with us all. It-666 has an Archangelic Godfather in him, one who cares for her happiness as a Being. That is without mentioning Walter Workmaster, who has pleaded her Beastly case from the start to us, Angels. The human gave It the sanctuary of his good heart and arms ever since he met her. He found her tortured self in a cage where she could not stand nor lay, in her own mess, in a bad state, below a pentagram made of human blood. The Beast is a very compelling Being, Liz. In different ways, we are all getting attached to her and becoming very protective of her. It can be frightening for the lay human yet, Gab and I have the duty but also It's own wish to take her life away if she ever turns. We are her guardians which also means Earth's guardians. Tough call, hence blood tears.

Taking the hand of Death, Liz kissed it, humbly,

-The lay human just says thank you for doing your guardian's duty, Death Angel. Until your faith is strong and alive for It-666, mine will too.

Smiling kindly to the red haired woman, Azryel winked at her,

-Like me, are you growing some kind of unbeknown trust, Liz Arczy?

The woman blushed thoroughly under his gaze, and nodded silently yet positively. The Death Angel kept smiling thoroughly although he swore out loud,

-Hell on Earth. Falling for someone six months before being RIP is not a good idea, human. Even if it is never too late to finally allow yourself to love, I am the worst Being to fall in love with. They should teach you that at school. Yet your attendance then was appalling and you just dropped out. Keep it steady and think very much about it. I am not a joy to be with, and I wish you better for your last remaining months. There are plenty of human good hearted sods about that would dote upon you endlessly. I can help you find one.

Ashamed of herself, Liz shrugged her shoulders and replied sternly,

-Please don't help me find anyone. At six months left, I would grieve someone. I didn't think about that. I don't want a poor sod heartbroken. I will keep steady until I pass away. I simply just missed the love call all my life. That's my own bad for never being able to trust anyone. I dealt with that for so long that I can carry on another six months. Do not worry about it Az, I will be fine. I will be strong.

The Angel saw the woman pick a branch in her path and throw it far away to an excited Bud who went running to get it back to her feet with his tail wagging endlessly. Witnessing the sad smile raising upon her face as she threw the stick once more, he confided,

-By not offering you love Liz, I am protecting my own self from the heartbreak that you will definitely give me. I have enough on my plate. I kept love at bay for my own sake and sanity for an eternity, human.

Pressing his cold hand strongly, Liz acknowledged,

-I understand you, Angel. Where you come from and all, I am far from blaming you, I am agreeing. Somehow I did the very same. You can't miss what you do not know. It kept me strong and will until my death.

A hail storm broke out from the deeply grey sky. Pushing the woman within his strong arms, Azryel called the Great Dane who came running by his sides at once. When the dog's head nudged itself against his thigh, the Angel teletransported them in the kitchen.

There he saw his soldiers with pink suits on peacefully eating their breakfast. A wicked grin grew upon his lips, as he praised,

-Pretty in pink! Love you guys for doing it for Caro and me. Liz, can you be kind enough to sit by me again at this table?

Put on the spot, Liz went to sit by her best friend Caro and apologised,

-I promised to Caro to be her 'Ear-bin-been' all day.

At the head of the table Wrath asked intrigued raising his Archangelic eyebrows,

-Pray, human, what is a 'Ear-bin-been'?

Liz answered with a good willing smile,

-The Gossip Garbage friend that was there at a special occasion and understand when one comes from having witnessed it all or partly.

Sitting by Wrath, Death could not help looking downcast. When Walt was by him to ask for his breakfast order, he was faced by a total silence. When Az's leg was kicked strongly under the table by Wrath, the Angel paid attention and replied,

-Your nice woodland mushroom scrambled eggs if there is still some to have, otherwise just plain.

Getting a wink by Wrath and a short telepathic message from him, Workmaster stood still,

-Az is not is normal self, just find out for me what is bugging him if you get a chance, human.

Walt winked back, then demanded out loud,

-My Hell Princess, one Workmaster's house special scrambled eggs breakfast for a downcast Angel that looks like he has been a little caught out in a hailstorm. Thanks for walking my Bud this morning Azryel, much appreciated. I got to snog Caro a little longer. Besides it's getting colder by the day. I give it two weeks before our first freezing nuts on the trees spell of snow. What do you think?

Blinking in a sort of haze, Azryel found it hard to concentrate and just being present within the cheerful room, yet watching It by the stoves under the watchful eyes of Gab learning how to make breakfast the human way, with a joyous grin upon her face, he found his smile back and replied to the man,

-I tend to not do weather forecast, Walt. Like the unpredictable weather I would always get caught out in the rain if I ever did. I am happy you enjoyed more minutes within the warm human arms of Caro because of me walking Bud. Now, tell me what is your special this morning? Is my soldier a good cook?

Workmaster going by It, held her shoulders shortly before replying,

-She is awesome, precise to a T. Your soldier learnt to control that fire in two shakes. My special is eggs done your way which is scrambled with a splash of truffle oil, and truffle slices in, with little fried cubes of pancetta, toasted hazelnuts and walnuts on a bed of cavalo nero, plus two buttered toasts on the side to dig into. Prepared with love and care, I hope you will enjoy it, Angel. I also hope it will put your wicked smile back upon your face for it truly does make my day.

Death smiled irresistibly back to the human,

-It sounds really good. Please care to feed the same to Miss Arczy, she is on a healthy diet and I am sure she will love it. Will you, Liz?

The woman found the Angelic green gaze and answered,

-I like my eggs fried and runny. I have a nut allergy but if you can recall me from the dead it will be fine.

Smiling widely Az, ordered,

-I guess you got that Walt. Don't tempt me to send her to hell with nuts on her plate, please.

Walter giggled while replying,

-A fried egg breakfast on its way, no nuts.

Wrath asked his Death Angel by telepathy,

-Is the human safe and secure to our secret?

Replying without further ado, Az reassured within Wrath's mind,

-The human is safe, Wrath. Gab made sure of it. I just had to reinforce his warnings. Besides she has not much to live. She messed about big time for herself.

-Is it upsetting you that she did?

-It does.

-That would explain your mood then?

-It certainly would.

-Did you befriend the human?

-I did, Wrath. I am sorry, I could not help it.

Sighing deeply, the Archangel replied in his mind,

-I will see what I can do for her. I won't have you, my Az losing your sarcastic grin for the world. Leave it to me and trust.

Smiling when his breakfast was delivered, Death tucked in ever so silently and contented.

Wrath by him was amazed by the deadly silence during the entire breakfast of his normally mouthy Death Angel. He considered Liz Arczy attentively. Despite her untidy red hair, and her scruffy appearance, there was something beguiling about her. He realised that her lively green eyes looked very often in the direction of Azryel, and that each time she did so, she blushed slightly but that his Angel kept his head down and focused solely on his breakfast. The Archangel wished he could read minds of others constantly like Death was able to, for he suspected the human to have fallen for his Angel and that her love was unrequited yet that her love affected him somehow. Smiling to himself, Raphael wiped his mouth with a napkin, thinking that a human throwing herself onto Az's neck could be an interesting thing to witness. He knew for a fact that Azryel was very cynical when it concerned love, and that is only eternal love has been his dedication to the Angelic Army. He doubted that the cold arse of Death would ever fall in love, yet he could only witness that the pale frail woman had some effect upon his Angel. Wrath decided to take Death out of his misery as he stood up, and called,

-I've finished. Az, finished? I have a suit waiting for you in your bedroom. Come, let's get you ready and prepared for the wedding.

Smiling with relief, Azryel stood up and excused himself,

-I will be with you in half an hour. I am heading for the shower.

Death disappeared from the kitchen. Giving a quick look at his Angel's plate, Wrath noticed that it was almost empty and that Az's love of human food was still fully there. He waited five minutes giving orders for the wedding to his Angels before teletransporting himself in the bathroom.

The shower was running and the Death Angel was where he said he would be, under the hot and steaming water. Seeing the steam all across the mirrors, while sitting upon a stool, Wrath announced his presence,

-Gosh, judging by that steam, you like it burning hot.

Azryel could not believe his ears and swore,

-For fuck sake Wrath, can I not have five minutes of privacy?

-You have Az, with all that steam and within the shaded cubicle, I can see fuck all of your deliciously angelic body. What's up with the human?

Death closed his eyes. He could not hide anything from Wrath. He asked,

-What did you suss out, Raphael?

-The woman is blushing every time she looks at you, Azryel and that you avoided her beautiful green eyes all the way through breakfast. How did your befriending go along?

Smiling irresistibly, the Death Angel started to clean himself thoroughly as he replied,

-It went very well, Wrath, thank you for being concerned. Can you wait for me in the bedroom?

-I am afraid I can't. When I see you Angel that affected by a mere human, I will not go away until I get to the bottom of the matter.

Sighing deeply annoyed, Azryel staid silent within the burning hot water.

After five long minutes Wrath stood up from his stool, asking in a sorrowful tone,

-Am I that bad as your Archangelic Master for you to be unable to confide in me? Do you want me to release you from oath, Azryel?

Death walked straight away out of the shower, seizing a towel, covered himself and went to kneel by Wrath. Taking his hand firmly, he whispered with emotion,

-Please, Wrath, do not question yourself on my account. I do not want to be released from my oath to you. I find it difficult to express myself right now. That is all.

The Archangel smiled to him full of kindness, and enjoined,

-Try to put your emotions into words, my Death Angel, just try. I can read you if it is easier.

-Read me, Wrath.

Satisfied that Azryel was still fully trusting him, Raphael read him and could not help grinning wildly afterwards as he commented,

-My poor poor Az, you finally caught the love bug. The human is very likable, I am afraid to admit. You refused her love, but her reply to your refusal made you fall for her. What are you going to do about it? Let her know, and give that doomed human six months of love, or protect yourself from grief, this is the question. Let's make you look the part for this afternoon.

Verse 37. The Wedding.

As Wrath put the last red roses upon an arch by the Indian Waterfall with Azryel, he commented,

-The constant rain has finally stopped. What are your thoughts upon the wedding my Az?

Wearing a silver suit like Wrath, the Death Angel replied with a cynical smile,

-Why do we have to make a big fuss of loving one another? Why don't we love simply and hug each other?

Scolding him Raphael, went to his Angel and put two red roses heads in the pocket of his glittery silver jacket,

-Because everyone loves significant gestures. Give a red rose to your human if you want to be true to your own heart, Azryel. Love hurts as much as it warms you more than a freaking hot shower. Let yourself feel loved a little.

Coming running with a red velvet cushion, little Micky shouted wildly,

-How is it going? Dad said I had to rehearse my part with the cushion.

Azryel welcomed the child by lifting him from the ground and spinning him in the air. When he put the little Archangel on the ground, he asked,

-So you are going to be my little helper for the big wedding? Everything is going fine so far. No more rain to be had hopefully. Wrath, looks like a wet dog, as he helped me put all the decoration into place. Your role is easy. I will put two ring on that cushion when the time comes, which you will bring to Mummy and Daddy.

As you stand still, Dad will take the ring that belongs to Mum and put it on her finger. Mum will then do the same. Then you can either stand by me or great Uncle Wrath until the end of the ceremony.

The little boy replied joyfully,

-I am going to be big helper! I will go to stand by Uncle Wrath, Mummy said we owe him shit lots. Where I am supposed to stay during the ceremony?

The Death Angel replied,

-Stay by me and you will be fine, kiddo. I will tell you what to do all the way through.

The little boy nodded and grabbing Death's hand, stood there smiling happily asking away,

-Mum has been crossing her fingers whole morning, Az. Do you know what crossing fingers mean?

Death replied,

-I do. Wrath, go to your niece. It is a superstition thing, Micky, when you just hope for the best to happen.

The Archangel disappeared from the wood and reappeared in his niece's bedroom. Fully ready, in a gorgeous baby pink dress, Caroline was taking a last glance at herself in the mirror, asking away,

-Will my Walt accept me back?

He replied at once,

-Of course he will. Stop checking your beautiful self out and let's give you a walk. You look fantastic. I am so proud to give you a walk my Caro. Walt is a man of his words. The first oath he took with

you has never died within his heart. He is renewing it just for your
sake.

As Raphael checked the bridesmaids, he could not help smiling, and
stated,

-Miss Arczy, that silver number is suiting you to perfection. If my
Az ever does something, it will be to undress you with his eyes.

Considering It-666, in a lovely mini baby pink version of the bride's
dress, the elder Archangel retained his breathe for a few seconds. It
was like having a flashback, and seeing the magnificent Eremiel
before him. But regaining his composure, Raphael saw in his
incarnated daughter an humility and a shyness that her father never
had. Her kind aquamarine eyes blinked at him, as she came to him,
holding his hand at once, and asked concerned,

-Wrath, are you okay? Shall I fetch you a glass of water?

His fingers firming into her hand, the Archangel expressed himself,
making the teenager turn upon herself,

-It will not be necessary, Blondie. I was simply blown away by your
beauty. Atomic moment. Why did you have to incarnate Being when
I am about to finish my own incarnation?

Blushing thoroughly, It whispered,

-I had no desire to be. I just got thrown into the mixture somehow
at random.

Keeping her hand firmly within his one, Raphael assured,

-Not at random, Bambi, you were conceived with an explosive plan
perfectly timed. Salt or pepper, perfect balance or not, you are going
to spice things up during your life that's for sure Being. From no
desire to be, now you have one, my soldier. Just make sure you do
not destroy the dish. Just enhance it for the better. Make sure your
incarnated life and heart count. If I have any valuable advice to give

you it is that one: Always listen to your good heart, fight for it and never give up. I have a dream too, the next wedding is yours and Gab's. Remember Walter is to give you a way, I will do too, and reserve the right to hold your other hand to walk you to my Archangelic nephew.

Throwing her arms around his neck, It kissed Wrath's cheek, with a very happy smile upon her face. She looked back at bride to be Caroline feeling fully accepted and at peace and went to nestle into her arms for a silent minute. Gently scolding, Caro, enjoined,

-Shall we keep everyone fashionably waiting or shall we make a move? Blondie, my baby girl, it's your call. Just remember I wanna throw myself to my Blondie Bear's arms for at least whole afternoon. No pressure...

Wrath presenting his hands to hold, invited,

-Let's teletransport you all, beautiful ladies. The wedding is missing you badly already.

When Caro, It and Liz grabbed his hands, they disappeared to reappear into the woods by the Indian Waterfall.

Everything was stunning and ready. Red, pink and white roses with silver glitter decorated the trees of the whole path to the Waterfall. The incarnated Angels in their pink suits and sunglasses waiting on either side of the path, cheered as they saw the bride. Caroline checked her dress one last time anxiously, under the approving eyes of her Uncle and Liz who gave her the thumbs up, with a confidant,

-Perfecto, Baby, you rock this boat.

Putting her hands to her cheeks in disarray, Caroline gave Raphael a panicked look,

-My 'Bouquet'. I forgot it on the bed.

Giving a desperation look to the dark grey sky, the Archangel smiled widely, commenting,

-Big drama... It will be worst when that hail storm above us decides to knock us down. Let's crack on.

Clapping his hands together, Wrath made the wedding bouquet of red roses appear and gave it to his niece, asking with a reverence,

-May I be so honoured to give you a way, my Caroline? May I be forgiven for my first miss, dear child?

Caroline gave a right hug to her Uncle, for a long minute, before saying,

-Uncle Raphy, stop beating yourself up. You are entirely forgiven. I am the one to be honoured by holding your hand, Archangel.

As they took position in the middle of the alley, as Wrath walked Caroline, followed by the two bridesmaids, an anxious Death in a glittering silver suit stood by an arch of red roses wondering where the husband to be was.

When Caroline arrived a few inches from him, the Great Dane of Workmaster jumped from the nearby bushes, holding a red rose which he deposited at her feet. The dog sat in a stately position, with a proud look in his eyes and Caro could not resist hugging Bud. She asked worryingly,

-Where is your Master, my Bud? Where is my Walt?

Coming by the same path that the dog had come, Walter arrived, slightly dishevelled, wearing his usual clothes, jeans, opened Tartan shirt and a fit T. He held a red rose in his mouth and knelt by Caroline and looked upon her with puppy eyes, flicking his blond long hair away from his face.

Caroline could not help smiling, embracing him while she removed the rose from his mouth, kept it in her hand, as she kissed Walter's lips fully forgetting about the crowd watching them.

A delighted Death Angel clapped his hands, watching the kiss unfolding with great pleasure, stating out loud,

-No words needed, just love. Here you have before you Walter and Caroline Workmaster, for the better and the worst. If any want to disagree with their loving union, say it now and get lost.

As little Micky brought the velvety cushion carrying rings to his parents, he felt the ground moving and pounding. Behind him, It-666 broke her bridesmaid's dress at once and took her fearsome demonic appearance, her eyes braising red and glowing.

Verse 38. The Wedding Crashers.

All the Angels got a telepathic warning from the Beast,

-Be ready, Hell is coming out. We need to get the humans out of here, Wrath. I sense P. He is coming for revenge. Surround the area with Archangelic fire, protect Earth.

Before anyone could react Demons rushed out from the Indian Cave by dozens, P leading them. The Demon headed straight to Workmaster shouting,

-I have a predicament, Walter Workmaster is a dead man.

Leaping in front of her adoptive dad straight away, the Beast confronted the Demon,

-Over my dead body! Walter will be.

She tackled P strongly to everyone's fears. Wrath ordered within all the Angelic minds, once his Archangelic fire secured the all area,

-Gab, take the humans in the loophole room, stay there until I come to get you. Soldiers, all for one and one for all. Take shape and fight.

Protecting the family, Azryel rounded the humans, pushing the dog within the circle by Gabriel, ordering strongly,

-Take them now, Archangel, protect them with your life.

Being given little Micky to carry by an anxious Liz, Gabriel disappeared with all the humans and Bud.

When he turned around Az saw It-666 still in a tough tackle with P, in an ugly fight. She came on top throwing the Demon upon the waterfall's rocks. She gave him a quick wild glance before attacking more demons sending Death a telepathic message,

-We need to protect Wrath. P is angry with him. His hit list today includes Walt and Wrath. Walt is out of the way, not Wrath. Those demons are on a mission Az and we need to stop them.

Her fighting shaft appearing between her hands, she was soon surrounded by a dozen demons trying to prevent her from moving. Azryel spread her concerns for Wrath by telepathy to all his soldiers and made her way to the Archangel as soon as. Wrath was in a similar position as the young Beast with a dozen demons surrounding him. P came back charging, full of hatred, going straight for the elder Archangel, shouting,

-Raphael Wrath, you will learn what wrath is! You destroyed everything. My life on Earth, everything.

Making it to the demons encircling Wrath, P was let in to fight the Archangel as the demons closed their circle again. Death reached the demonic circle trying to break it, decapitating the demons, one after the other, yet he was consistently tackled and hindered doing so. Asha tried to help him, piercing that circle as he realised the engagement between P and Wrath was fiercely violent.

Desperate to intervene to help Wrath, the Beast managed to get away from the demons encircling her, flying her way out. She lounged straight into the circle where Wrath was fighting for his life. Seeing part of an arm and hand on the ground and recognising Raphael's one, she threw herself on P, dragging him away from Wrath by sheer incredible force, the demon did not have time to react when he was pierced through by her fighting shaft. The speed of her moves, left him looking dazed upon her, yet he stood up, she removed her shaft from his body ready to engage with him again. However, the scythe of Azryel beheaded P, sending his head flying at her feet. Checking upon Raphael, she saw him fighting strongly against the other demons of the circle that went charging in, his Archangelic sword causing his usual damages. Attacking his assailants the young Beast realised that they came in an incessant flow. She could see them crowding the waterfall area as they could not pass the Archangelic wall of fire surrounding them. If the demons ever succeeded in killing the elder Archangel, the protective wall would disappear and they would start causing their disastrous chaos, starting by the tree house where her family of humans took their refuge. By telepathy she warned every single Angel of the dilemma and the need to protect the life of Wrath at all costs. To Az only she added upon her thoughts,

-We need to find a solution to close that Hell passage. The harassment by demons will be endless otherwise. They are bleeding out of Hell like a bloody hemorrhage. I am going to go at the door, Master and try to control that evil leak somehow, making sure it's manageable at all times for the Army. We must not lose Wrath, never.

It-666 flew off and landed by the entrance of the Indian cave starting making a carnage of the demons coming out of it as soon as she arrived. Worried about her, Azryel told his Army, via telepathy,

-It is going to control the entrance for a while, let's cull all those demons that managed to leak out. Together, steadfast. Wrath, I know you are still a strong warrior but as your life is on the line and purposefully attacked, I suggest strongly that you teletransport to the loophole room. It will protect your fire walls to not fall and Earth's from those demons. We need you alive Archangel. Motion?

Wrath received all his soldiers' wills within his mind which wanted overwhelmingly for him to stay safe from now on. The message from It touched him deeply,

-Your life means to me, Archangel. I want you safe and alright. Get mended by Gab, before the hemorrhage from your forearm's loss gets worse. I will look after your Army with my life. We share a dream together, Raphael. Let's make sure it comes to pass. I will stay alive for you and you will for me. We will keep on fighting and well, protecting all doing so.

Bowing to his Army's safe call, Raphael teletransported to the loophole room. When he faced his nephew, cradling all the humans within his arms apart for a worried sick Workmaster who paced the room to and fro, Wrath explained his state with a short,

-Quite fierce down there, everyone of you stay put, it's safe in here. I am the target of the demons hence my state. They want my guts and yours Walt. However It and my Az took P out of the game. That is one mastermind less to deal with. He is the one that ripped my arm apart. Gab, I need you to look at it. Bambi was worried about it. She is still fighting fit and gosh she is strong. Walter, I have faith in your girl making it through. You and I gave her a dream. She wants that dream to come to pass.

Gabriel coming to the Archangel looked at his damaged arm, a blood tear rising at the corner of his eyes asked,

-What is my fighting Bambi dreaming of? Do you have to go back to battle Wrath? I'd rather you sit this one out.

Taking a seat on the presented stool, Wrath wiped the blood tear of his nephew with his thumb gently, and confided,

-I have been ordered to sit this one out, by motion. If my guts are dead, my Archangelic containing fire dies with me as there is Hell on the loose, the Apocalypse will truly starts. Little did I know when I ordered for you, my Gab to be the doctor for my soldiers and to get your Angelic healing skills up to scratch that I would be one of the first casualty to stand before you. Our little Beast is dreaming of being given a way to her own wedding by me and Walt. Like the human, I used the suggestion of a possible happy future for her to unsure my soldier stops self sacrificing and stays alive battle after battle.

Workmaster came to the wounded Archangel and hugged him silently, before stating,

-I sincerely hope her future wedding will be less apocalyptic than mine. Did you keep her mind opened on a potential bow or did you play on her present love?

Wickedly smiling back to the man, Wrath replied,

-I am an old dog, my Walt, I used whatever was more powerful to unsure her desire for survival. The concrete vision of somewhat a very strong and handsome Archangel seals the trick better than any vague idea of someone. Wouldn't you agree, human, take a good look at my Gabriel, he has got to inspire a will to survive.

Looking after his arm, Gabriel shook his head in desperation, commenting,

-A little consultation to her adopted dad and I before suggesting anything would have been appreciated. Saying that I sincerely hope your old trick works. However, what is not a trick Workmaster is that I do love your daughter and that I intend to ask for her hand, to you and her in the future. By the way where are your wedding bands, human?

The man nodded in part resignation and part agreement silently before saying,

-Our rings are probably lost in the commotion. We did not have time to exchange them.

Little Micky ran to his father, pulling out the two wedding rings from his pocket and presenting them to him,

-They are not lost, dad, I looked after them with eagle eyes like Azryel said.

A proud and smiling Walter, patted the shoulder of his Archangelic son, as he called out,

-That's my boy! Now why don't you finish the union of mummy and daddy? Just put the rings where they belong. Mrs Caroline Workmaster, our little ring bearer has a surprise for you.

Caro came to her husband at once. Micky put the ring first on his mother then on his father, clapping his hands and wishing,

-I wish Blondie was here and safe, witnessing that moment. She was so brave tackling that big demon to protect you Pa.

By the Indian cave the Beast was fighting the steady flow of demons, by her was Azryel and Asha. The Army of Angels had suffered some casualties yet there were more bodies of demons on the ground than Angels. Looking at the situation, Azryel sent a telepathic message to It and Ash,

-We have to close that entrance yet we can't bring Gabriel forward to do so. We have to think of something fast before we lose any more soldiers.

Within their minds Ash replied,

-If we manage to close this one what are the chances for them to leak out from the other Hell gates?

It-666 stepping forward told them wildly by telepathy,

-I have got a solution. I am going to close Hell entirely. There will never be an Apocalypse as long as I am alive. Demons will be able to go back to Hell but will never be capable of coming out. I will have to go down there to accomplish the feat, Azryel. That means as I am part demon I won't be able to come out. But I mustn't die down there. I am going to give you the formula that I am going to use for the feat, Gabriel will have to work out a solution to get me out of there. I will wait for you Master Azryel impatiently to fetch me back. I will keep you updated via telepathy and you will know if I fell prisoner to the enemy. One for all, all for one.

Cutting her palm with the fitting shaft, she held the hand of the Death Angel, who replicate her gesture knowing how important it was for the young Beast,

-I will get you out of here, Soldier as fast as I can. Don't you dare make me fetch you in any other way than alive. Wrath, Gab and I will work on your solution, so don't you ever give up, Soldier, be strong, for I will never give up on you. One for all, all for one.

When he released her hand, he nodded with Asha as they fought their way to help her reach the leaking secret path to Hell. As soon as the Beast stepped in the entrance, they felt a powerful earthquake below their feet, the demons surrounding them in the cave burst into flames, combusting within seconds. A green light sealed momentarily the Hell path while a deafening thunder resonated from outside the cave. Azryel watched as the path closed into a solid rock surface with an elaborate marking upon it made of blood. It looked like an algebraic formula mixed with magical signs throughout. Death could not help stating to a bewildered Asha,

-Courtesy of the Beast, from her own blood, that's the formula to shut Hell from the World. No Apocalypse now. Got to love that soldier. Fancy deciphering that, gosh Gab is going to have a fair few nightmares. Do you have a photographic memory, Ash? We have to wipe it all off and not let it be seen.

Putting his Angelic hands slightly above the formula, the soldier nodded positively,

-It's safe for me for you to erase. What about you Az?

Pointing at his head, Death replied,

-Embedded in there, because it's the only way we can rescue her. She is putting herself through Hell to prevent an Apocalypse. I am going to make sure her arse come back safe and hopefully well.

Asha asked concerned,

-What if she is killed? What if she becomes a bad arse down there?

Erasing the formula from the wall, Azryel stated sternly,

-Then we have just raised an Antichrist. But I firmly believe in It to stay true to her own good heart.

When the two Angels came out of the Indian cave, they witnessed the Angelic Army fully standing up, under a hail storm. One Angel came to Death and knelt by him,

-Something happened, something not short of a miracle. All the demons combusted at once and our five dead soldiers woke up, alive and well. They are properly there, general, as we checked for their souls.

Death turned back to his incarnated self at once and took a cigar out, lit it and swore, addressing his Army,

-Fucking damn courtesy of the Beast again. That's the deal, she closed Hell for Us, the United Souls, yet she put her arse on the line, big time. We have got to get her good little beastly arse back before it turns bad. Race against the clock, guys. Up for It?

His soldiers's unanimous response came as a loud shout, as he saw them all join their hands in solidarity with a wickedly satisfied smile,

-Up for It, general, let's get her beastly arse back.

The End.

It-666's Saga

From the moment she is born on the 06/06/1996 to the one she is raised by Angels, passing by the one where Walter Workmaster finds her caged below a pentagram and saves her, It-666 can only boast to an abnormal life as the Beast.

Feared, tortured, yet alive we discover It-666 when ex human right lawyer Workmaster pulls her out of her cage and raises her to broad day light. The Atheist that he is treats her as a Supernatural Being and not as an Antichrist. The man adopts the lost teenager, becoming her staunch advocate, and a father that can show her what it means to love and care tenderly the human way.

Embraced within the dysfunctional family of Walter, the Beast meets his next of kin, a lot of them are Angels and Archangels, unbeknown to the human. When an incarnated Archangel Gabriel encounters a very damaged It-666 in his clinic, he knows how to spell out BEAST but also HEART. Like Walter Workmaster, he decides to give the teenage Being a chance, a fair chance.

When the heavy cavalry of his Archangelic Uncle Raphael Wrath descends to investigate the advent of the Beast, the decision is taken to extend her chance. Offered to be raised up among Beings, within the Angelic Army, by its general, Azryel Mortimer, the Death Angel, It-666 accepts.

Under his wings and fierce training, she becomes a soldier at heart, an Angelic one. Blossoming within Workmaster's family, the Beast learns loves and devotion to one another. Soon she is strong enough to lay her life to protect them all...

Love is her guide, where will it lead her?

Death?

Life?

?

Enjoy the Saga so far

Book 1:

Finding It-666: The Beast.

Book 2:

Raising It-666: The Teenage Beast.

Book 3:

Saving It-666: The Archangelic Beast.

By the same author:

Hair Rising, Heir Raising, Erasing

A vibrant beyond the grave tale which will chill your bones while warming your heart. When the deadly serious is delightfully hilarious, you will know you have just been acquainted with Abraham Wilton-Cough. His skeletal hand will drag you from grave to grave, under the moonlight of the night where many dead are rising... Could it be the apocalypse?

Cordelia Malthere's
Compendium of Characters

Take a guided tour in the IT-666's saga and the Author's fantastic stories' world. Switch gears from Earth to Hell to the unknown... Meet the characters, their pasts, their presents, and maybe their futures... This Codex is the ultimate companion to Cordelia Malthere's universes.

Finding It-666:
The Beast

Book One of It-666's Saga

Born on the 06/06/1996 in London, the young It is a sweet sixteen supernatural Being of a special kind, one meant to bring the end of the human world: the Beast incarnated, the Antichrist.

Fall 2012, the Beast was found. From the deep darkness of her hole, she is raised up to the light. From her closed cage below a pentagram made of blood, she is freed. The human who found her, Walter Workmaster, is a firm atheist, a private investigator and former human rights lawyer who becomes her staunch advocate. Adopting the lost It, the man released her to his world to make her face humanity and unknowingly much more... The advent of the Beast has started. Step one, she is found.

Coming Soon:

A Ghost Spell:
A W-C's Haunting Return

Abraham Wilton-Cough is back! The proud Banker wakes up in his coffin once more for our terrifying enjoyment in this spooky tale of Tender Love and Care beyond the grave. The troubled heart of Wilton-Cough cannot rest in peace until the Curse affecting Wilton Town is broken. Knowing that one of his sons will be afflicted by it in the future and will become a flesh and marrow devouring Ghoul because of it, the father returns as a Ghost, one with a mission, one on a crusade to save the children of Wilton Town.

From communicating with the living to haunting the Priest of the town to make him fight the terrible spell with cross, bible and all in the middle of a Ghouls infested cemetery, passing by playing Poltergeist in the church of Father Odell, the desperate spirit of Wilton-Cough will try everything to save his son's soul. His ghostly self is helped on his journey beyond the grave by his tiny big mistake, the Angelic Abigail, his spiritual guardian. Their partnership pushes a fair few to free Wilton Town of its terrible curse. A Ghost Spell is a gospel of love after death, where laughs and tears are shared.

Saving It-666:
The Archangelic Beast

Book Three of It-666's Saga

The young It-666 is a determined Being who will do everything to prevent an Apocalypse in order to protect the ones she loves. Raised by the Workmasters, taught by Angels in the magical tree house of Archangel Gabriel, the Beast dedicates herself to them with a loving devotion. They are the ones who gave her a chance, a hand and a welcome that touched her heart.

To protect them, the courageous soldier that she has become goes on a mission to close Hell for good. Follow her footsteps in the hellish flames as she fights demons for her survival, hoping that her three Angelic Masters, Raphael, Azryel and Gabriel, will be able to rescue her.

Considering the teenager very much part of their Army, the Angels embark on a huge mission: Saving It-666...

About the Author

Cordelia Malthere is riding the wave of her dreams and nightmares which are translated into tales and stories. Sometimes dark yet always full of humour, her writing words/worlds are an invitation to open one's heart and mind fully to simply love one another.
Escaping prejudice age 5 from a school that saw her as a devil child for being left handed and breaking free from the chair she was attached to, Cordelia ran away back home and from any restraining bonds that made no sense at all to her.
Ever since she fought the tough fight to be her own self and not the person others wanted to impose upon her. She believes in free will bestowed to all humans, and took full advantage of hers. She went on to choose everything that suited her best, from country, religion, sexuality and name.
After studying Literature, Philosophy and Art for her Baccalaureate, she carried on studying Art in the Fine Art school from her home town for a couple of years. Her love for drawing especially caricatures never left her. She uses that skill to draw the characters of her stories, and be fully involved in the creation of her book covers.
She came to London in 1996, age 20, in order to perfect her English, yet fell in love with the cosmopolitan British capital and never left it. After a Bsc in Archaeological and Anthropological sciences, the author started to write her imaginary world down bit by bit, story after story.
The 'Clementine's epic adventures in the After-World' blog and story brought her many fans worldwide. Sadly the loss of her father in 2013, prompted the author to make every day count from then on: 'Carpe Diem'.
'Malthere Publications' was then created in 2014 to carry all the Born to be Free Loving Voices that want to be publish

Cordelia Halthere

<<<<>>>>